George Walter Prothero

A Memoir of Henry Bradshaw

Fellow of King's College, Cambridge, and University Librarian

George Walter Prothero

A Memoir of Henry Bradshaw
Fellow of King's College, Cambridge, and University Librarian

ISBN/EAN: 9783337311926

Printed in Europe, USA, Canada, Australia, Japan

Cover: Foto ©Raphael Reischuk / pixelio.de

More available books at **www.hansebooks.com**

A

, MEMOIR

OF

HENRY BRADSHAW,

FELLOW OF KING'S COLLEGE, CAMBRIDGE,

AND UNIVERSITY LIBRARIAN

BY

G. W. PROTHERO

FELLOW AND TUTOR OF
KING'S COLLEGE,
CAMBRIDGE

LONDON

KEGAN PAUL, TRENCH & CO., 1, PATERNOSTER SQUARE

1888

PREFACE.

THE subject of this memoir was in no sense, except in so far as was inseparable from his official position, a public man. During life he rather courted obscurity, and his name is but little known, except to scholars, beyond the precincts of his own university. He never led a party, he founded no school, he never wrote a book. His life was spent in quiet study and self-denying labour, sweetened not by fame, but by the companionship of friends and the consciousness of many-sided utility. Under such circumstances his influence could not be very widely felt, but within his own circle it was deep and permanent. Over those with whom he came much in contact, over many whose hand he touched but once or twice, his intense individuality, with its strange blending of strength and tenderness, of frankness and sensibility, of human affection and scientific enthusiasm, exercised an irresistible fascination. Nor was his example as a scholar less attractive than his character as a man. The width and exactitude of his knowledge, the thoroughness of his research, his elevation of science above all thought of self, his respect for genuine study in all branches however remote from his own, gave to many students a new ideal and a stimulus all the more potent because it was suggested rather than enforced. It is this rare and admir-

able combination of qualities which it has been my principal object to portray. The life of such a man may, it is
hoped, be interesting, not only to his friends, but to students
of character and lovers of learning to whom he was personally unknown.

Of his literary work I speak with great diffidence. The
quantity and quality of that work are but little known,
partly because of its abstruseness, but chiefly because so
much of it lies half concealed in books which others have
given to the world. The help which he so ungrudgingly
gave is acknowledged in many grateful prefaces and recorded
in many learned notes, but such indications attract little
attention, and the original worker is easily forgotten or
ignored. It is due to Henry Bradshaw's memory that the
abundance of his self-sacrifice in this respect should be
fully recorded. I have not attempted to criticise his conclusions and discoveries, or to estimate his position as a
man of letters and science, for to do so would require a
fund of special knowledge to which I can make no pretence.
I have only endeavoured to give some account of the results
which he attained, of the methods which he employed, and
of the spirit in which he worked.

I cannot but be conscious how imperfectly I have discharged my task. Those who felt the charm of Henry
Bradshaw's personal presence will most easily understand
the difficulty of presenting to those who did not know him
an adequate portrait of his character. Those who are
nearest him in learning will most readily condone my
inability to follow him through the intricacies of the many
subjects which he made his own. To his friends, who have
helped me in the production of this book, I tender my
hearty thanks. Such as it is, it could not have been pro-

duced without their aid. They are too numerous to be
mentioned here by name; they will, I trust, recognise
their own impressions in many of the following pages. I
must, however, acknowledge my special indebtedness to
the Rev. H. R. Luard, D.D., who read over and corrected
the earlier chapters; to the Rev. Christopher Wordsworth,
who did a similar service for Chapter IX; to Professor
Herkomer, for the portrait which forms the frontispiece
to this book; to Mr G. I. F. Tupper, for the facsimile of
a letter; and to Mr Alfred Rogers, assistant in the University Library, who gave me much help in various ways.

I have only to add that I should have incorporated
more of Henry Bradshaw's letters and unpublished work in
this memoir, but for two reasons. In the first place, such
an addition would have enlarged the volume to an excessive
bulk; and, in the second, a collective edition of his published papers will shortly be issued, to which it is hoped
that a volume of his letters on scientific and literary subjects
may subsequently be added.

G. W. PROTHERO.

CAMBRIDGE,
November 1, 1888.

CONTENTS.

ADDENDUM.

SINCE the sheets on which I have given an account of the discovery of the Barbour fragments (pp. 134–139) were printed off, I have learnt, through the kindness of Dr Furnivall, that the poems in question.are no longer regarded by scholars as Barbour's. So late as two years ago, Dr Horstmann, who edited these fragments, appears to have entertained no doubt that they were by the "Father of Scotch poetry." But within the last few months, two German scholars, Dr Emil Köppel ("Englische Studien," x. 373) and Mr P. Buss ("Anglia," ix. 493), have decided, on the ground of internal evidence and language, against the authorship of Barbour. Their conclusions are supported by Professor Skeat in his forthcoming preface to the edition of the "Brus," published by the Early English Text Society. Had Bradshaw studied these poems as minutely as he studied those of Chaucer, it is possible that he might have anticipated these results ; but he does not appear to have gone beyond the initial examination, which pointed to Barbour as the author. A new edition of the "Legends of the Saints" is being prepared for the Scottish Text Society by the Rev. W. W. Metcalfe, and the last word about the authorship of the poems is perhaps not yet said. It need hardly be remarked that, even if the authorship of Barbour be disproved, the discovery of so large a mass of mediæval poetry loses little of its importance.

HENRY BRADSHAW.

CHAPTER I

SOME of Henry Bradshaw's most remarkable qualities may perhaps be traced to his Puritan and Roundhead ancestors, his Quaker connections, and the mixed English and Irish blood which ran in his veins. He belonged to an old Lancashire family, which took its name from Bradshaigh, or Bradshaw, a manor near Bolton-le-Moors. Members of this family represented their county in the Parliaments of Edward II and Edward III, as well as in those of the seventeenth century. The elder branch, which had migrated to Haigh Hall, near Wigan, in the Tudor times, and had taken the king's side in the civil wars, became extinct towards the end of the last century. Haigh Hall passed by marriage to the sixth Earl of Balcarres, in whose family it still remains. Early in the fifteenth century a younger branch of the Bradshaws established itself in Derbyshire, at Bradshaw Hall, near Chapel-le-Frith. A member of this branch, named Henry, settled, in 1606, at Marple, near Chester, and founded a third line, to which the subject of this memoir belonged.

Henry Bradshaw, of Marple, grandson of the before-named Henry, sided with the Parliament in the civil wars, and headed a petition from the county of Cheshire for

B

the establishment of Presbyterianism. He afterwards joined Cromwell, became colonel of a regiment of foot, and fought at Worcester. His younger brother was the John Bradshaw known to history as president of the court which tried and condemned Charles I. These two Round-heads were not, however, the first of their stock who had shown Puritanical tendencies. A generation or so before the civil war, one William Bradshaw, a member of the Cheshire branch, was disinherited by his father for holding heterodox opinions. William's elder son, Richard, was the Protector's minister at the Hague; another son, James, served in Crom-well's army, distinguished himself at Drogheda and else-where, and settled at Milecross, County Down.

James Bradshaw's descendants joined the Society of Friends. His great-grandson, Thomas, married, in 1777, a daughter of Mr Samuel Hoare, banker, of London. Their eldest son, Robert, who lived on his father's estate at Milecross, was regarded in the neighbourhood as a remark-able man. Among other marks of that originality which cropped out elsewhere in the family, it may be mentioned that he used to drive into Belfast on market-days in a closed carriage of his own construction, with a stove inside, the smoke and sparks from which excited in winter time the wonder and admiration of the neighbourhood. A younger son, Joseph Hoare Bradshaw, married, in 1823, Catherine, daughter of Mr Richard Stewart, of Ballintoy, County Antrim. Henry Bradshaw was the third son and fifth child of this marriage. He was born on February 2, 1831, at 2 Artillery Place, Finsbury Square, where his father then resided.

Mr J. H. Bradshaw had been in his early life much devoted to field sports. He was a healthy, robust man, over six feet in height, and possessed of unusual physical strength. His son Henry could recollect standing, as a small child, on the outstretched palm of his father's hand.

While still young, Mr Bradshaw settled in London, and became a member of the firm of Barnett, Hoare and Co., Bankers, Lombard Street, with which his mother was connected. He was a man of scrupulous integrity, outspoken truthfulness, guileless and unworldly, but possessed of considerable practical sense and capacity for business. He was peculiarly quiet in manner, devoted to his wife and children, and a great reader. He had a large library, and made a valuable collection of Irish books. These he bequeathed to his son Henry, who owed to them the foundation of his bibliographical studies. Mr J. H. Bradshaw was no bookworm, but he loved his books, and preferred the best editions. Like his son Henry, who inherited and developed his tastes, he had a horror of a dog's-eared page, or of a book carelessly cut. He had many literary friends, and was fond of conversing on literary and bibliographical subjects.

While keeping up an amicable connection with the community to which he had belonged, he practically ceased, on his marriage, to be a member of the Society of Friends, and his children were brought up members of the Church of England. Mrs Bradshaw was the youngest but one of fifteen brothers and sisters, and not the least handsome of a handsome family. Her sisters-in-law, Miss Sarah and Miss Lucy Bradshaw, used to enjoy describing the excitement which was caused by her first appearance in their quiet Quaker circle. These ladies, who after their father's death lived for the most part in Dublin, devoted themselves to charitable works, and died members of the Society of Friends. Miss Lucy Bradshaw was very fond of Henry, and eventually left him a little property at Lindfield, in Sussex, which she had inherited from the well-known philanthropist, William Allen. Henry Bradshaw himself never lost sight of the Quaker connection, and treated any Friends whom he came across as in some

sort relatives of his own. Of his ancestors he seldom
spoke, though he knew all the details of his pedigree.
He had no objection to acknowledging that he was related
to John Bradshaw, the regicide. One day, while he was
a boy at Eton, some one asked him half in jest if he was
connected with the Bradshaw who tried Charles I. "Yes,"
he replied ; "but my mother was a Stewart."

Soon after Henry Bradshaw's birth, the family moved
to Hornsey, and here he passed the first eight years of his
life. In the thirties of this century, Hornsey was still a
country village, with fields and shady lanes, where the
boy may well have learnt that love of natural objects,
especially of flowers, which was so strong a feature in his
character. The traditions of childhood are not always
trustworthy or important, but one or two traits may be
mentioned as indicating tendencies which were clearly
innate. An old friend of the family tells me that she
remembers Henry, then a child three or four years old,
lying at full length on the drawing-room floor, absorbed
in the study of a genealogical map of the kings of England, with their portraits and the dates of their reigns.
In a short time he committed this map to memory, and
could repeat it word for word in imperfect baby-speech.
The floor seems to have been his favourite place of study,
for another friend frequently observed him lying under
the table with a sheet of the *Times* open before him, by
the aid of which he was learning to read. He was a quiet
grave child, happy enough so long as he could follow his
own devices, but with no superabundance of animal spirits.
When people asked him what he was going to be, his
invariable reply was, "A scholar."

When he was about eight years old he went to school
at Temple Grove, East Sheen. This school, afterwards
presided over by Mr Waterfield, one of Henry Bradshaw's
oldest friends, was then kept by a Mr Thompson, whose

wife, the daughter of an old Waterloo officer, was a first cousin of Mrs Bradshaw. The house is a fine eighteenth-century building, on the site of one inhabited by Sir William Temple—hence the name—with large grounds adorned by those noble cedars which it was so much the fashion to plant a hundred and fifty years ago. Here Henry got his schooling for about four years. Not long after his arrival, Mr Thompson wrote to his mother as follows :—" Harry gains the first prize of the lower school, and with truth I never examined a little fellow with a sounder head or better memory. He is a boy of the greatest promise, so zealous and steady, and *unswerving* from his point, that I will back him against any that have yet gone through my hands. He has made deep inroads upon his Latin grammar, and has done in one quarter what costs the toil of four or five to most children."

In 1843 Henry left Temple Grove for Eton. The school was then hardly two-thirds as numerous as it is now. The number of masters was insufficient, and the school divisions were unmanageably large. Dr Hawtrey was head master, and Dr Okes, the present Provost of King's, was lower master. Dr Goodford, late Provost of Eton, and Bishop Abraham were among the assistants. Bradshaw entered the school as an oppidan, and boarded at Angelo's, whose house was a tall, red-brick building, standing in its own grounds, some way down the lane which now leads to the gas-works, on the right-hand side. His tutor was the Rev. W. G. Cookesley, a man of considerable reading and literary taste, not very learned, but interested in learning, quick-witted and sympathetic.

One of Bradshaw's contemporaries, well qualified to judge, writes of Cookesley as follows :—" He was no accurate scholar ; he was erratic, and a bad disciplinarian. But he was altogether a stimulating teacher, and, at the time I was at Eton, almost the only man of the whole lot of masters, except Goodford, who knew what literature meant. On him first of any at Eton dawned the idea that there was a science of philology, and though his excursions into that field were wild and wonderful, he excited in us the liveliest interest and curiosity. He generally came into school at least a quarter of an hour late, but his short lesson was of really inestimable value. Altogether he remains on my mind as the chief intellectual element among the masters of his day."

Such a man may well have encouraged his pupil in his multifarious reading, and fostered his nascent love of literature. Bradshaw seldom spoke of him in later years. When he did so it was with affection, though not with reverence. When Cookesley took a living and left Eton, some of his old pupils got up a subscription towards furnishing their tutor's parsonage. This was mentioned to Bradshaw in the Combination Room at King's, where-upon he silently passed a five-pound note behind another man's back to the collector of the subscription. He was anything but well off at the time.

When Bradshaw had been two years at Eton, a great change in his fortunes took place. In the summer of 1845 his father suddenly died. Mrs Bradshaw was left a widow, with three sons under twenty-one. The eldest, Thomas, was at Oxford, and was intended for the bar. He after-wards became a county court judge at Durham, and died in 1884. The second, Richard, had just entered the navy, in which profession he afterwards rose to be an admiral, and earned distinction during the Zulu war as commander of the *Shah*. Though Mr J. H. Bradshaw had been in receipt of a good income, he was prevented, by the failure of investments supposed to be perfectly secure, from making any large provision for his family. Henry could no longer afford to remain an oppidan, and accordingly passed for college at Election, 1845.

When he went into college, the barbarous system of earlier days was giving way to a more civilized régime. Hitherto almost all the foundation scholars had been packed into Long Chamber, an enormous room, where they were left to do pretty much as they pleased. From lock-up to early school, a period of twelve or fourteen hours in winter-time, not a soul came near them. At rare intervals they were disturbed, perhaps in the midst of an unlicensed supper, by the vision of Dr Hawtrey, preceded by an aged domestic with a lantern, emerging from a door at the end of the room. Everybody was in bed in a twinkling, and the doctor, having gone through the form of calling absence, retired. Other supervision there was none. Strange stories are told of the orgies that went on, of the quantities of beer surreptitiously introduced in the capacious pockets of the heavy cloth gowns, of the animals kept on the leads above, of fagging and bullying unknown in these milder days. Porson used to say that his only pleasant recollections of Eton were the rat-hunts in Long Chamber. The floor of that apartment was occasionally polished by a method probably unique, which went by the name of "rug-riding." The process was as follows. Several "orders" of tallow candles, the only light of those dim days, were first smeared along the floor. A small boy, generally an oppidan, if he could be caught, was then tied up in a rug, and hauled rapidly up and down the room by three or four others until the boards were in a satisfactory condition. The diet was wholesome, but monotonous—mutton almost every day, with the addition now and then of tough suet dumplings. Baths were unknown. The bigger boys could escape during day-time from the pandemonium of Long Chamber to studies "up town," but the mass of collegers had no other home but their dormitory.

Such was the state of things when Bradshaw went to

Eton, but when he entered college it was undergoing a rapid change. The "New Buildings" had just been erected, and he was one of the first occupants. Every boy, except a few of the youngest, now enjoyed the luxury of a separate room. A still more important change was the appointment of a "Master in College." Mr Abraham, afterwards Bishop Selwyn's right hand in New Zealand, gave up his house to take the new and responsible post. Bishop Abraham tells me that Bradshaw was one of the first with whom he made friends in college. "In his room," says the bishop, "I always found a welcome, and he was always ready to talk. He was of a gregarious temperament, and I could be sure of finding a levée of boys in his room, ready to talk on books, politics, etc.; and so he smoothed the way for me more than any other person or thing could do."

This gregariousness was, however, a comparatively late development. At first Bradshaw was but little known. His quiet, bookish ways and his distaste for games were enough to account for this. He was not bullied; his physical strength and a certain dignity, which was already apparent, and which boys are quick to recognize, prevented this; but he was regarded as rather a "muff," and quietly ignored. In dress he was scrupulously neat, but carefully avoided anything like show. He read much, but in a desultory way, and was apt to neglect his school-work. His tutor complained of his "want of energy." He got "pœnas" for not knowing his lessons, and, with that mingled dilatoriness and perversity which amused and sometimes irritated his friends, he often failed to show up his punishments in time, and once at least had to undergo the extreme severity of the law. Naturally, he was at this time not on the best of terms with the masters. It is said that Dr Hawtrey, who used sometimes in his allocutions to the school at the end of the half to mention

names for praise or blame, on one occasion held up Bradshaw to universal reprobation as an idle boy, from whom
it was impossible to extract a "pœna." The invective was
heard by one who knew that the reproof was hardly
merited, and who, in sympathy for the reprobate, established a friendship with him which lasted for life. This
was comparatively early in his school-life. Dr Hawtrey
afterwards came to know him better, and admitted him
to great intimacy. He had begun to learn Italian, and
in 1846 got the second Prince Consort's prize for that
language. He also touched on Spanish. This taste for
modern languages was enough in itself to attract Dr
Hawtrey.

Bradshaw was already a lover of books, and possessed
an extensive library. He had carried off a considerable
number of his late father's books, and had had a book-
plate struck for them. In several of the books which
were still on his shelves at the time of his death was to .
be found a book-plate with " E libris Henrici Bradshaw
Reg : Coll : Eton : Alumn. MDCCCXLVI. " inscribed on it.
Among the books which belonged to him at this time are
many not often found in a boy's library. One of them is
an " Officium Beatæ Mariæ," printed at Antwerp in 1564 ;
another is a Bede, printed at Cologne in 1501. In a copy
of Bond's edition of Horace's "Odes," printed at Amster-
dam in 1686, is an inscription in his neat, boyish hand :
"From the library of the late William Allen, Esq., at
Stoke Newington. John Bond was a celebrated commen-
tator and grammarian, born in Somersetshire in 1550 ;
died at Taunton in 1612. N.B.—This is the best edition."
He had already begun to feel his way about libraries.
Some forty years later, in 1883, he says in a letter to
a friend about Bishop Cosin's library at Durham, " I so
well remember going over from Darlington, as a boy of
fourteen, and being locked in there all day, working at

Strabo or any books I could find bearing on the geography of the Crimea, which happened to be a pet subject with another Eton boy and myself at that time." Not many boys of fourteen indicate their future pursuits so clearly.

In 1847, when he was sixteen, Bradshaw suddenly emerged from his chrysalis state into comparative notoriety. Collegers were in those days superannuated in their twentieth year; that is, if they had not "got King's" on the election Saturday (the last Saturday in July) next after their nineteenth birthday, they had to leave the school. During their last three years they could sit for a scholarship at King's, but in election trials their places were seldom changed. In their seventeenth year they entered for an examination called "Intermediates," by which their places in their year, and therefore their chances of getting a scholarship, were practically determined. In this examination Bradshaw, who, having entered the school late, had hitherto been at the bottom of his year, suddenly leapt to the top, to the surprise, not unmixed with indignation, of his contemporaries. He wrote at once to inform his mother.

"Eton College, July 23, 1847. Friday afternoon.

" MY DEAR MAMMA,

"I'm captain of my year in trials!!!!! Did you ever hear anything like that? I hadn't the most remote notion of anything of the kind. Instead of being simply put up into my year, which I hardly expected to do, I have taken thirteen places. . . . I can hardly now believe it. . . . Pickering told me this morning that if I had done my exercises some of them rather better, I should have been sent up; but he was glad to see me taking such pains in schoolwork. Good-bye, and believe me,

"Ever your affectionate son,

" HENRY BRADSHAW."

It was certainly a surprising promotion, but it did not
the least throw him off his balance. He wore his laurels
with so conciliating a mien, that his competitors could not
but submit with a good grace. Stacey, hitherto captain
of the year, a boy made for popularity, frank, generous,
athletic, and a fair scholar, shook hands with him cordially,
and bore him no grudge. Bradshaw never forgot the
kindness, often spoke of it in later years, and remained
Stacey's friend as long as he lived. Stacey followed him
to King's, and not long before his death, in 1885, saw the
wish of his heart accomplished in the gift of the stained
glass which now fills the great west window of the chapel.
One of the last things in which Bradshaw was engaged
was the drawing up of an inscription for a tablet to be
placed in the chapel in memory of his old friend.

Once in his proper place, at the head of his year, Bradshaw began to be known, and to make friends whom he
never lost. Not that he made very many, for he was
fastidious and not easy of access. When on the defensive
he could make cutting remarks, but he never attacked
any one wantonly. His comrades began to perceive that
the shy, unobtrusive lad had something unusual about
him. One of his contemporaries writes, " There was always
a thoughtfulness and a gentleness that attracted me to
him, not unmixed with a slight vein of sarcasm or raillery
that made me a little afraid of him at times. I was struck
by the appearance of indolence, and yet I always felt that
under it lay a reserve of power." Another says of him,
" He was often extremely odd, often humorous and
ironical, and rather fond of paradoxical propositions. He
showed the same delicate perception and discrimination
of externals, the same penetration, the same rapid recognition of realities, logical acuteness, and immoveable fairness and charity which his friends found in him as a man.
His refinement, good breeding and delicacy gave him an

air of distinction which was by no means common, and which was directly due to his home education."

It was to his character entirely that he owed what influence he possessed, for he was not distinguished at this time for scholarship, and, though healthy, well-made, and strong enough, he was no athlete. Nor, until he was captain of the school, when he felt it his duty to exert influence, did he ever try to put himself forward. He abstained from games, except football now and then by way of exercise. He learnt to swim, but never rowed, though he was fond of being rowed about by a companion. His friend Waterfield used to take him up the backwaters of the Thames on botanical expeditions, and they explored the rich meadows on its banks for water-plants and flowers. His old friend Mr Allen had left him a collection of dried specimens, gathered towards the close of the last century in the course of morning walks before office hours into the country from Lombard Street. This collection was the foundation of Bradshaw's botanical knowledge, and at this time it was as great a joy to him to find a rare plant as in later days to discover a new Caxton.

He not unfrequently fought little battles with the masters, in which he never lost his head, and sometimes came off victorious. On one occasion he was caught wearing a straw hat in Weston's Yard, tall hats being in those days the only recognised headgear. He was observed by one of the masters, who made him give up his hat, saying he might have it back at the end of the half. Bradshaw did not forget the promise. On the last day of the half he lay in wait for Mr X., and, meeting him as he passed through the school-yard, asked him if he might have his hat. Mr X. had forgotten all about it. Bradshaw reminded him of the circumstance and of his promise. The master thought the hat could not have been

taken to his house. "That can hardly be, sir," rejoined
Bradshaw, with perfect politeness and gravity, "for it was
only yesterday that I saw your foot-boy wearing it."
These little skirmishes did not, however, hinder him from
being, during the latter part of his Eton career, on excellent terms with those in authority, especially with Dr
Hawtrey and his relatives, John and Stephen, two of the
assistant-masters, and with Mr Abraham.

The boys' library, often called Hawtrey's Library, one
of the most delightful reading-rooms in the world, was
his favourite haunt. There he spent the greater part of
his playtime. Bibliographical questions already interested
him, as well as the history of language : he studied Dibdin
and Ducange. The great dictionary "Mediæ et infimæ
Latinitatis "—" middling or infamous Latin," as he jokingly
translated it—always reminded him, he used to say, of
Cookesley's scholarship. In connection with the library, a
story is told of him which illustrates the power he already
possessed of saying the unexpected. He was one day
carrying off from the library to his room two or three
massive folios, when he was hailed from a window above
with the question, " Hullo, Bradshaw ! whose books have
you got there ? " " Yours," was the terse reply ; for the
books, being library books, belonged to the questioner and
the questioned alike. He thought about philology, and
doubted the then received derivation of *bonheur* and *malheur*
from *bona* and *mala hora*. " I can't believe that is right,"
he said ; "they would never have altered the gender." He
worked at divinity too, filled the margins of his Bible with
careful references, and studied the contents and history
of the Prayer-book. Of the beauties of the latter he used
often to talk to one of his sisters. " He was the first
person," she says, " who taught me to know and love the
Prayer-book, and that while he was a boy at Eton." But
English literature was his chief study. In one year he and

his friend Waterfield read through all the standard poets, including the whole of Spenser—not reading together, but simultaneously, and talking the subject over afterwards. Chaucer already attracted him. He read the moderns too, and delighted in Tennyson, then in the zenith of his powers. Whenever a new volume of Tennyson came out, he would take it home with him for his holidays, and read it aloud to his sisters.

In 1848 he moved into a room in the upper passage of New Buildings, where there was more space for his library. This room was the large one on the right-hand side of the passage, with an iron pillar in it supporting the ceiling. He writes home on Whitsunday, 1848 :

"I have at last got all my books in order, and my room perfectly neat, and in consequence of being a large room it looks dreadfully bare ; but if it had a few things in it, I could make it look perfect. . . . I have, according to request and desire, got a few flowers for my window, which cost me hardly anything ; and, indeed, I can't afford to spend much, as I haven't got the means. . . . Tell Sarah that I have a Cape jasmine which has more than twenty buds, all in different stages, some of which will be out in a day or two, and it will keep on flowering till near the end of July. Won't that be delicious ? " The same love of flowers comes out in another letter, dated May 27, 1849, in which he speaks of giving some flowers to Mrs John Hawtrey, on the occasion of a christening. "I went to Slough and got some cut flowers, about three shillings' worth, and brought them to John Hawtrey's. Certainly they were most exquisite flowers, and even now they scent the house whenever I go in there, which is very often. . . . I presume there was no harm in making an offering of that kind. When you see Sarah, would you give her the enclosed firstfruits (so to speak) of my lilies of the valley, which she asked for, and which I am only too glad to give ?" He always kept flowers in his rooms, if possible ; and when his friend Stacey went down to play in a cricket-match, Bradshaw always had a flower ready for him to put in his button-hole.

During all this time he was making progress in scholarship, in his own way. But it was not a way likely to lead to much immediate result in the winning of prizes and school distinctions. He liked to prepare his lessons in the library, where there were dictionaries and commentaries in plenty. If a passage of Homer were to be "got up," he would seize on some unusual form or word, and pursue it and all its relatives up and down the lexicon, into byways and recesses unknown to any but the most curious scholars. "Dear me!" he would say, "this is very odd. I *must* look it out;" and the exploration would open up half a dozen others. A single line would occupy all the time during which he should have been preparing sixty or seventy, and then he would go into school and contentedly get punished for not knowing his lesson. He was not what is called an accomplished scholar, but knew what he knew thoroughly, and never made blunders. He was in the select for the Newcastle Scholarship in 1849, and might have distinguished himself still more next year, had he not left before the examination. Composition was not his strong point; he always composed with difficulty. He was nevertheless "sent up for good" three or four times before he got into the head master's division, and there is a story told of him which sounds apocryphal, but which shows that he had the reputation of being able to do good verses. Being in for election trials in 1849, he showed up only three Greek iambics. When the examiners were looking over the exercises, Dr Hawtrey produced a copy which he had himself written, to serve as a standard. Rowland Williams, one of the "Posers," glanced at the copy, and, holding up Bradshaw's verses, remarked curtly,

" Excuse me, Dr Hawtrey, but these three lines are worth
the whole lot."

During the Easter holidays, 1849, he went as private
tutor to the family of Mr Wicksted, at Shakenhurst, in
Worcestershire. He appears to have been happy there,
though he did not repeat the experience. He used to talk
of it as "the time when I wore plush." At Shakenhurst
he met Mrs Severne, sister of Mrs Wicksted, and of Mrs
Clive, the authoress of " Paul Ferroll." Mrs Severne was
a charming and accomplished person, and took a great
fancy to Bradshaw. She divined in him what most people
failed to perceive, and probably, as my informant writes,
" rescued him for a time from the cloud of listless diffidence
which a lad of lymphatic constitution carries about him
while living among lads of high spirit, by whom he is more
or less misunderstood."

That he was already becoming known as a bibliophile
is shown by the following story, which I give on the
authority of Mr Kershaw, librarian at Lambeth. One
day Bradshaw entered Pickering's shop in Piccadilly. The
Earl of Lincoln was in the shop, and an assistant named
Craven was serving the customers. When Bradshaw left
the shop, Craven said, " Do you know that young Etonian ?
He is a great book-hunter even at his age." To which
Lord Lincoln replied, " I wanted to see him, but he's
gone." *

Some little time before Election, 1849, Bradshaw became
captain of the school. In this position he displayed
to the full the moral courage which distinguished him
through life. He had little or nothing to do with the
general discipline of the school, but the position of captain
of college was at that time a very responsible one. Quite
as much, probably, depended on him as on the master in

* The story was told to Mr Kershaw in 1866, and related by him in a
letter to Mr Bradshaw himself.

college. For petty breaches of discipline, the captain could inflict punishments in the shape of lines or "epigrams;" more serious offences entailed a thrashing or "working-off" at sixth-form table. Bradshaw's discipline was severe; he put down card-playing and smoking to the best of his ability, and remonstrated with those who were guilty of worse things in a way in which not one boy in a hundred has courage to speak to another. Towards the end of 1849, he writes to his mother as follows :—" This school-time has passed away like a dream. I feel changed, and, indeed, I know not how; I hope, however, for the better. My captaincy is fast departing, and it is a comfort to think that I have done some good in college; indeed, I hope it will be lasting. Dr Hawtrey has always looked to us (my year) to do some good, and I hope it will be realized. I have seen more of him, and been drawn nearer to him, than ever this school-time; and, indeed, I hardly know what I shall do without Hawtrey, Abraham, and Procter when I go to King's."

Soon after leaving Eton, he writes to tell his mother that the fruits of his work were already visible. "Notwithstanding the severity, as you thought it, of my discipline at Eton, it has, I am thankful to say, made me some of the best friends I have, who at the time were most violent against it, and yet now write and send me beautiful books, thanking me for having opened their eyes, and saying how beneficial my captaincy has been to college. It is enough to make one proud. I only trust it may not."

What was thought of him at Eton may be gathered from a letter of introduction to Professor Sedgwick, written by one of his Eton friends, Charles Evans, a boy of his own age, in January, 1850. "I should not have troubled you at present, but for this reason. A very dear friend of mine, Henry Bradshaw by name, is going up to King's from hence in a few days. He knows hardly any one in the

C

university out of that college. . . . Bradshaw has been captain of the school for the last three months, and stands very high in the opinion of the masters and every one else. We look to him to do something towards a reformation at King's, which I dare say you know is a good deal needed. He is a boy of very high abilities and attainments, and I think you will like him."

Towards the end of the year 1849, the news arrived at Eton of an impending vacancy* at King's. At that time vacancies were filled up as soon as they occurred, the head boy at Eton going at once to King's, where, after three years of probation, he became, without further trouble, a Fellow for life. It was Bradshaw's turn, as head of the school, to go, and he quitted the microcosm of Eton for the larger world of Cambridge early in the year 1850.

* The vacancy was caused by the marriage of Mr (now Bishop) Abraham.

CHAPTER II.

ON February 1, 1850, Henry Bradshaw became a member of King's College, Cambridge. In a letter to his mother, dated on that day, he writes—

" I have just this instant come from the Vice-Provost, having been admitted a scholar of King's College. . . . You see by the date that I am admitted at the age of eighteen, and I shall enter upon college life on my nineteenth birthday (February 2), and on Founder's Day, being the Feast of the Purification of the blessed Virgin Mary. Altogether I could not enter King's College under happier auspices, and I look forward to it as the commencement of a new life, and trust and pray that I may gain possession of that energy of mind which I have for so many years totally disregarded. I feel it to be such a blessing to begin every day with chapel service, at half-after seven in the winter, and seven in the summer ; to think that one is strengthened for the work of the day, by beginning every day with prayer. Little as the work at King's seems to be, it is, nevertheless, much harder than at Eton, and there is much more to be done, odd as it may seem."

He goes on to draw an elaborate comparison between the school-hours, or half-hours, at Eton, and the lectures at King's, which gives a somewhat unexpected result. The hours of work at Eton amounted to eight and a half in the week, those at King's to eleven. This is, of course, exclusive of time devoted to preparation, and—at Eton—

of "private" work, or "construing," done with the tutor. "Then it is to be remembered," he continues, "that there are two services in the chapel every day, and that the work altogether is much harder stuff than at Eton. Now, all this gives me a far better idea of King's than I before entertained, and I trust that I shall not fall into the habit of doing things in a slovenly manner."

At the time when Bradshaw entered the college, it was not in all respects what might have been desired. It was a great disadvantage that it was confined to those who had been on the foundation of Eton College, and that its members were excluded from competition for university honours. Bishop Abraham, writing to Bradshaw in 1851, says, "No man can doubt that it was a bad thing for us being excluded from the university society and honours. It narrowed and dwarfed our moral and intellectual growth; we became exclusive and bumptious about nothing but our supposed privileges, which were really evils." Good scholars and excellent men there were, of course, but the college contained more than the usual proportion of black sheep. It was, generally speaking, idle, and had been at times disreputable. The following epigram by one of the society on his fellows is perhaps a little severe, but is probably not far from the truth, as it was during the second quarter of the present century:—

> Πάντων πλὴν ἵππων ἀδαήμονές ἐστε κυνῶν τε,
> Καίτοι γ' οὔθ' ἵππων εἰδότες οὔτε κυνῶν.

It was englished thus by another Fellow—

> "To be knowing in horses and dogs
>   Is all we pretend in our college,
> And even in dogs and in horses
>   We are only pretenders to knowledge."

There had for some time been a party among the fellows anxious for reform, but Provost Thackeray opposed it, and during his life nothing could be done. On his death in 1850, the present Provost, Dr Okes, was elected. His first step was to throw all his influence on the side of those who were anxious to give up the obnoxious privileges, and to place the college on a healthy level with the rest of the university. The result was a resolution passed by the governing body of the college in May, 1851, which gave up "the present practice of claiming for the undergraduates of the college the degree of B.A. without passing the examinations required by the university." This was the beginning of an era of reform, with which Bradshaw was in hearty sympathy.

But though the party of reform was victorious, it was only natural that the results should take time to display themselves, and much of the exclusiveness which had characterised Kingsmen in earlier days was still apparent. Bradshaw was by no means inclined to give way to this. He had naturally many friends in King's, but from the first he sought acquaintances elsewhere, and many, perhaps most, of those who knew him intimately in his undergraduate days were members of other colleges. One of these, Arthur Gordon,* gives the following account of their first acquaintance. He had been asked by some common friends to call on Bradshaw on his arrival at King's. "I did as I was asked," he says, "and, calling one raw February evening, I found Bradshaw alone and engaged in preparing the tea, which, in those days of early dining,† we were accustomed to drink before setting to work for the evening. He invited me to remain with him, and I did so. On the table lay a book, handsomely bound, and lettered on the front with the strange motto, "Morituro mortuus." My new acquaintance told me its history. It was the gift of an old Etonian and a great friend, a son of Vice-Chan-

---

* Now the Hon. Sir Arthur Gordon, Governor of Ceylon.
† The hour of hall at King's was five o'clock, which was then thought very late. Other colleges dined at three or four.

cellor Shadwell, who, having himself quitted Eton, intended the book as a present to Bradshaw, when he too, in his turn, was on the eve of leaving Eton for King's. It was to this cessation of Eton life, and to this only, that Shadwell had intended the motto to refer. But before the binding was completed he was really dead—drowned in a ditch running out of the Thames. The incident naturally made a deep impression on Bradshaw's mind, and the peculiar way, full of simplicity and feeling, in which he told the story to me, a stranger, gave me a strong interest in him, and made me soon seek him out again."

The attraction was mutual. Writing home shortly after this, Bradshaw says, "I am delighted with Gordon, . . . and, to tell you the truth, I could hardly have found a man more thoroughly to my mind. . . . His friend M. said of him, 'If you go to tea with Gordon, you will have plenty of intellectual and good conversation, but not very much to eat and drink.'" This defect does not appear to have hindered the speedy formation of a close friendship, which lasted unbroken to the end of Bradshaw's life. The introduction to Trinity which his intimacy with Gordon gave him was of the greatest advantage, and principally by its means he was launched into the wider world of university life, with which many Kingsmen of his day were almost entirely unacquainted. A little later he writes home, " I am most comfortable and happy here. I should like you just to see me. All the out-college men that I know as yet are Trinity men—they amount to five or six ; but they are remarkably nice men, and, what is better, none of them Eton men except one, who has just taken his degree."

An attractive peculiarity of which his friends will need no reminder had already been remarked—I mean his intimate and unexpected acquaintance with the relationships of those with whom he came in contact. When he had been about a month at Cambridge, he wrote to one of his sisters, "I am accused of knowing everybody, and never meeting any one without knowing something of him. It was always a subject of great amusement at Eton, and it has not stopped here. You have heard me speak of George Williams. I was at breakfast ·there a short time ago, and there happened to be a clergyman there, stopping at Cambridge, on his way from Ely to London. Of course, Williams did not think it necessary to introduce me to him, or mention his name to me. However, he was evidently an Irishman and from the North. The conversation turned, of course, upon Ireland and upon the state of the Church there, and it came out accidentally that the name of his parish was Holywood, in the County Down.* You may imagine how I was amused! . . . It amused George Williams highly; he said he had often heard of my peculiarity of that kind, but had never witnessed it before."

His letters about this time are full of good resolutions, and show a strong conviction that desultoriness and indolence were likely to be his besetting sins. Few who knew him only in his later years, when he was busy almost every minute of the day, had a chance of seeing any trace of the natural indolence which lay deep down in his character, and which nothing but a high sense of duty and the intense interest which he took in his favourite studies enabled him to overcome. As at Eton, so at the university, he read eagerly but discursively, poetry, novels, anything that came in his way, without apparent method. His friend Hort, now Lady Margaret Professor, introduced him to Kingsley's works. He read "Alton Locke," "Yeast," and "Two Years Ago" with enthusiasm. He revelled in Tennyson. He studied Chaucer and read him aloud to one of his friends, showing as he did so that he had found out already *how* to read him and how to pronounce his rhyme-endings.

* Close to Milecross, the birthplace of Bradshaw's father.

Meanwhile, he did not altogether neglect his classics. Tacitus had a special attraction for him. He read Plato, too, and Homer, and other classical writers, widely but without much persistence.

His friends thought he was wasting his time, and losing his chance of distinction. Had he applied himself to classical scholarship, there can be little doubt that he would have taken a high degree; but he had no ambition that way, or indeed any way. He read, or dreamed, or talked, as the humour was on him, and his desultory general reading was perhaps, after all, the best preparation he could have had for the work he was to do. His memory was like a vice, and never relaxed its hold of what it had once fastened on. But he always maintained that it was not to be forced; he could remember nothing that did not interest him. To read the books that every well-educated person is supposed to have read, to read a book in order to be able to talk of it, or because people in general are talking of it—these were ideas and motives entirely foreign to his character. Consequently he was, to the end of his life, ignorant of some things which most ordinary people know, while he knew many things with which few or none were acquainted. A friend, somewhat his senior, whose own reading was wide as well as orthodox, writes of him at this time, "I well remember Bradshaw saying to me, with a sigh, that he felt he had never read any useful, instructive books, meaning Ranke, Macaulay, Adam Smith, and the like, the sort of things he heard other people refer to. Of course, I used to feel the refreshing originality of the man who had no taste for such things." It was not so much that Bradshaw had no taste for such reading, for he read many such books when he came across them, but he adopted no system of reading or self-cultivation. If he read a classic, it was because he liked it, not *because* it was a classic.

He brought up with him from Eton a library which both in size and character was unusual for a young man of his age. Among his papers I have found a complete catalogue of it, written out carefully in his neat, small hand. It numbered nearly five hundred volumes. About one-fifth of these were Latin and Greek books, or books connected with classical history and literature. Divinity, ecclesiastical history, and devotional works made up another fifth. The greater portion of the library consisted of English literature. All the best poets were in his collection, and a good many of the historians. Forty or fifty Irish books appear in the list, a selection apparently from his father's legacy. Natural science was not unrepresented. The books are catalogued as they stood on the shelves, the shelves being marked by the letters of the alphabet, and the sizes of the books, folio, octavo, etc., are noted throughout. Books being the only possessions that he cared about, it was natural that he should keep a record of borrowers, and what they borrowed; and, as he had probably already acquired the habit of keeping books belonging to other people for an unconscionable time, he also noted down his own borrowings. But this system was too methodical for him, and was soon dropped.

Philosophy and philosophical discussion had no little charm for him. Ridler, a member of his own college and an excellent scholar, who died too soon for fame, said one day in a large company, that he believed there were only two people in the room, Bradshaw and Waterfield, who really knew what was meant by induction and deduction. He and a friend read Miss Martineau's translation of Comte together. For Positivism he always felt and showed a certain liking, not as a religion or rule of life, but because there was something in Comte's view of knowledge akin to his own mental habit. In his own researches nothing but the most vigorous scientific proof would satisfy

him, and he would trust no authority but the evidence of
his own senses. Many years later, an undergraduate, who
once ventured to say in his presence that Comte's system
ought perhaps rather to be called Negativism than Positivism, was promptly told that he had better hold his
tongue till he knew more of the subject. In his early days
his friends often debated, in undergraduate fashion, the
standing problems of philosophy. He was fond of listening to such discussions, but seldom took a very active part
in them. Every now and then he would throw in an acute
remark, showing that he fully grasped what was going on,
and he took especial pleasure in making mischievous
allusions which he knew would set his friends by the ears.

More or less connected with these interests was an
inquiry into supernatural or, as people now prefer to call
them, psychical phenomena, which was made about the
year 1851. A paper, inviting the communication of any
experiences of this nature, was drawn up by a sort of
committee, including among its members a good many
friends of Bradshaw's, now well known in the university
and in the world at large. Bradshaw had nothing to do
with the starting of this inquiry, but he was sufficiently
in sympathy with its objects to undertake the distribution
of the papers and the collection of information. The
paper contained a preamble explaining and justifying
the inquiry, followed by an elaborate classification of
supernatural phenomena, under the heads of appearances
of angels, spectral appearances, dreams, feelings, and
so forth. This curious anticipation of the "Psychical
Society" of our own day called itself the "Ghostly
Guild;" scoffers nicknamed it the "Cock and Bull
Club." It does not seem to have obtained very satisfactory results ; at all events, its originators did not go
beyond the preliminary inquiry. Sir Arthur Gordon
informs me that they came to a conclusion very similar

to that which the modern Psychical Society has arrived at—namely, that, while for the ordinary run of ghost-stories there is nothing in the nature of trustworthy evidence, an exception must be made in favour of phantasms of the living, or appearances of persons at the point of death.

The religious turn of mind which was characteristic of Bradshaw was very evident to the friends of his under-graduate days. He never had a taste for dogmatic theo-logy, and even at this time avoided formulating his beliefs, or reducing them to a rigorous system. "His religious views," says Sir Arthur Gordon, "were at that time those of what would then have been called a moderate High Churchman. He had no doubts or misgivings, and fully intended to take orders." He believed in the Church, and nourished a warm love and admiration for the institution itself, its history, and its external manifestations. He had no liking for ceremonies in general, but he considered the fasts and festivals of the Church as indispensable aids to faith, and as encouraging a devotional and reverential habit of mind. He was not a Ritualist, though he numbered among his friends men who set great store by ritual. His own interest in ritual was, it may be inferred, mainly of an historical kind. He occupied himself already in tracing the origin and development of liturgies, and laid the foundation of his vast liturgical knowledge. He was also much interested in ecclesiastical architecture, made draw-ings of window-mouldings and tracery, and belonged to an architectural society. He regularly attended the university sermons, without regard to the question who was preaching. In later days I have heard him strongly reprehend the practice of going only when a popular preacher was to be heard. He was much influenced by the preaching of Frederick Denison Maurice. On one occasion, when Maurice had taken for his text the Lord's Prayer, he remarked to a friend, on leaving the church, "It never struck me before that all Maurice's teaching is contained in it." Another preacher of whom he speaks with great approval was Mr Elliott, of Brighton. He used generally to go to his own parish church of St Edward's in the evening, where he much enjoyed the practical preaching of Mr Harvey Goodwin, now Bishop of Carlisle. For some time he also went regularly to the weekly communion, then a rare institution, at St Giles'. Mr George Williams, a Fellow of King's College, a man considerably his senior, and of marked High Church tendencies, rapidly acquired much influence with him—as much, that is, as it was possible for any one to exercise over an independent and original mind. Still more influence was exercised over him, Sir Arthur Gordon tells me, by the preaching of Dr Mill, who was then often resident in Cambridge. "His strong personality, his unfaltering dogmatic teaching, his vast stores of learning, and the modesty and simplicity with which he made use of them, exercised over some minds a strong fascination. Bradshaw was one of those who were thus attracted."

From the time when he was a freshman, he belonged to a little coterie of earnest Churchmen, differing considerably in university standing and in age, who used to meet in each other's rooms by turns and spend the Sunday evening together. George Williams; C. T. Procter, Vicar of Richmond ; G. M. Gorham, Vicar of Masham ; A. T. Lee, afterwards secretary of the Church Defence Institution, and editor of the *National Church;* A. H. Gordon; A. D. Coleridge, and several others, were members of this society. Bradshaw was the youngest member of it. He and his friends generally attended certain services together. The evening gatherings were of an informal, social nature. The society had no propaganda, and undertook no action beyond its own limits. It displayed no spirit of religious partisanship, and had no very serious object or stringent organization. It was known by contemporaries as the "clique," and furnished a butt for some of the wits of the college, but such light shafts as were aimed at it fell harmless. "We used," writes one of its members, "to enjoy our quiet fun as we made merry (not, I hope, ill-naturedly) at the expense of the frothy declaimers of our day; the sophists, philosophers, and politicians of the Union; the 'Apostles,' *et hoc genus omne.*"

There were other clubs of more or less similar nature in the university at the time; the "Church Reading Society,"* for instance, nicknamed "The Chrysostoms," of which several of Bradshaw's friends were members. It may be doubted, perhaps, if there was much more religious feeling among the undergraduates of that day than there is at present, but there was unquestionably a more open expression of it. "Men," writes a contemporary, "conversed freely, as a matter of course, on purely theological topics, from the discussion of which they would now usually shrink. The famous Gorham judgment was pronounced during Bradshaw's first term at Cambridge. It was not the less hotly discussed by undergraduates for being but imperfectly understood by them, and contentions as to 'prevenient grace' were to be heard in hall, at wine-parties, on the river, and elsewhere, mingled most incongruously, as we should now think, with secular topics." Such was the atmosphere in which Bradshaw passed much of the time in which a man is most susceptible to impressions, his first years at the university.

Meanwhile, in these conversations and meetings and saunterings by the banks of the Cam, he was learning the art which he carried to such unique perfection—the art of making and keeping friends. He was doubtless regarded by many as unsociable, for he cared nothing for company

---

* This club was afterwards reconstituted on a wider basis, as the "Theological Society."

in which he had no choice. The society of his own college was very limited in those days, the number of undergraduates being seldom more than twelve or fifteen. It was the custom for the resident graduates to drink wine together every evening after hall, and the undergraduates followed suit, meeting in each other's rooms by turns. Bradshaw had no taste for these carouses, which wasted time and money, if they did not lead to worse results, and from the first refused to take part in them. Among his friends, besides those I have already mentioned as members of the religious society to which he belonged, were E. W. Benson, now Archbishop of Canterbury; J. B. Lightfoot, now Bishop of Durham; H. M. Butler, now Master of Trinity; F. J. A. Hort; B. F. Westcott; H. R. Luard, and other well-known names. Over many of his contemporaries he exercised the same strange fascination, and with the same absence of apparent effort, as over his friends of later days. With several he exchanged favourite books, the "Imitation," or the "Lyra Apostolica," or the "Christian Year;" for others he would write out favourite pieces of poetry, which have been carefully preserved.

The recollections of a generation ago are naturally dim, and one peculiarity of Bradshaw's friendship was that, however strong an impression it left, it was extremely difficult to analyze or to put it into words. One friend remembers nothing but quiet walks and intimate conversation. Another writes of him, "His quiet humour and gentle winning ways were highly appreciated, and, hardly less so, sundry quaint characteristics which almost amounted to eccentricities. He had, among other oddities, a group of door and cupboard keys all welded together and radiating from a common centre. All the stray pamphlets he then possessed were bound into a single volume, the back of which was of portentous width. He would do odd things, too, but, as far as I can remember them, they were

always remarkable for their singular unselfishness ; and
his determination it was impossible to gainsay or resist.
Never shall I forget his sisterly sweetness and attention
in my long illness. . . . There was in all his bearing a
simplicity and unrestrained kindliness which made his
friends as much at ease with him as schoolboys."

Sir Arthur Gordon says of him, "In many respects
Bradshaw was in taste, habits, and character much the
same in 1850 as he was thirty years later. He had at
no time any liking for athletic amusements. His hardest
exercise consisted in long walks, which he took not in-
frequently, and ordinary constitutionals, taken almost every
day. He was usually an early riser, but if by chance he
did not get up at his regular hour, he would sleep on half
the day, and repel all efforts to rouse him. His manner
was then just what it was to the last. There was the same
caressing sweetness, the same irony, which left his interlocutor in doubt whether he was in jest or earnest, the same
delicate suggestion of doubt or negation by a word or
question. The ordinary tenour of his life was monotonous
and uniform, emphatically that of a student, though not
always that of an industrious student. He usually worked
steadily at lectures and in his own rooms till two, but had
occasional fits of singularly torpid indolence. At two he
went out for a walk, always with a companion, returning
at four for chapel. After hall he usually passed some time
in the company of others, either at their rooms or his own.
He was fond of poetry, of which he read a good deal.
Shelley and Tennyson were his favourites among modern
poets. But he had a special affection for the quaint
conceits of the seventeenth-century religious poets, and
was thoroughly familiar with George Herbert, Quarles,
Crashaw, and their fellows. He had a fondness for the
lives of obscure people, and especially for obscure religious
lives. Of such books as Maitland's 'Dark Ages,' and

'Essays on the Reformation' he was an eager reader and ardent admirer. But of all the characteristics of Bradshaw's undergraduate days, he will be best remembered, by those who then knew him, for the warmth and number of his friendships."

Towards the beginning of his first Long Vacation he went northwards, and met his friend Gordon at Glenalmond College, where he made a short stay. He was much impressed by the reality of the religious life of the place. He writes in a diary which he kept for a short while about this time, "I ought indeed to be thankful to God for bringing me to such a place as this, where one sees so much devoted energy. There seems to be every temptation to work hard in such a place, though an indolent mind can find food for itself almost anywhere. I hope I may at least make some progress before I leave this. . . . The fasts of the Church are, of course, here observed, and one feels the blessing of being reminded of the days of old. I never before remember having felt the reality of these things—that they are really a commemoration of things, and not an empty ceremony. . . . The beauty of the country grows upon me daily, and everything is so new and different from what I have been most accustomed to in the way of scenery. . . . Really I must not give so much to one day again. I must learn to abridge." Here the diary unfortunately breaks off, and no attempt to continue it on an "abridged" scale seems to have been made for several years.

His first Long Vacation was almost entirely spent in visits to friends. He walked with Arthur Gordon from Glenalmond to Torland, a distance of about a hundred miles. This tour ended with a visit to his friend's home, Haddo House. "The library there," says Sir Arthur Gordon, "contained a good many books of some rarity and interest, which were generally shown to visitors. Bradshaw did not neglect these, but when they had received their due share of attention, he pounced upon and lugged out from its place a by no means specially conspicuous volume, a Spanish edition of 'Sallust,' and on the arrival of my father [the late Lord Aberdeen], questioned him about it. My father was much struck by the bibliographical instinct shown by the selection of this book, and during the remainder of Bradshaw's visit treated him with marked attention." "I can't tell you," he writes to a friend, "how I enjoyed being in Scotland for the first time in my life; everything was so entirely new to me. Our longest walk was from Blair Athol to Braemar, about six and thirty miles. I never saw anything like the view from the top of Lochnagar, and the precipice on one side, going straight down fourteen hundred feet. . . . Good-bye, my dear Gorham, and believe me to remain always, I hope I may say,

"Your most faithful friend,

"HENRY BRADSHAW."

His letters about this time often ended in this cautious way.

From Scotland he went to stay with some Quaker friends at Darlington; thence to Methley, where he passed a few days with Mr George Williams. When the latter departed to resume his charge at St Columba's, Bradshaw spent a day or two in the clergy-house at St Saviour's, Leeds. Here he was again brought in contact with advanced High-Church observances, and was entertained by hosts who were, as it turned out, on the eve of going over to Rome. He writes to a sister about this visit as follows (August 24, 1850):—"I had tea there (at St Saviour's), and spent a most pleasant evening, and, as the vicar was away for his health, I had his room and chair-bed. They live as simply as you could wish, and though

I have no great fancy for Church principles carried to their full extent, yet there one lost sight of the forms in the solid reality of the undertaking. I never saw a place where they seem used so purely as a *means* and not as the end of religion. When one knows the vast amount of good they did there in the cholera time, and sees the earnestness and real life of the whole thing, it is a great comfort."

October found him again at Cambridge. On October 9, 1850, he writes to his mother, "I hope and trust I may be able to be a little more regular in every way now that I have come here. I look upon this, which is the beginning of the academical year, as the beginning of my university career ; so now I have a fair start." These good resolutions were, however, doomed to be disappointed, to some extent at least. The habit of not answering letters, which one of his oldest friends describes as "the only foible he had," was growing upon him. On November 30, 1850, he writes to his mother a very repentant letter. "I am afraid you are too much accustomed to my excessive and painful dilatoriness in writing home to be much astonished at my not having written to you long ago ; and though it is but comparatively little use saying how sorry one must feel for it, I must say I always am stung with a sense of the sinfulness of it—for it is nothing short of that—as soon as ever I am brought to my senses. You will be aware, from the fact of my not writing—for it is a sure clue—that I am not, or rather, I hope I may say, *have* not been going on so well. I have felt as if a sort of spell was over me. . . . Few men that I know have had such ample opportunities of being good and earnest in life as myself, and the natural consequence has followed, that few men have used those opportunities so sparingly. I know how bitterly I have often grieved you, and doubly so by your seeing so many, many good resolutions on paper, and then seeing them so systematically broken. However, I do not yet despair, and I trust that by earnest prayer I may yet be able to seek and keep to the right path. . . . You will not mind my saying all this, for of course I have no one else at home to whom I can open out my heart in a way that one can to a mother." From this time forward for two or three years there is hardly a letter home which does not begin with an apology for dilatoriness in writing or in answering communications, and with fruitless promises of amendment. "If I don't write," he says on another occasion, "I can seldom work much ; and if I don't work much I can't write." Gradually both he and his correspondents seem to have acquiesced in the irresistible. The complaints and apologies ceased, but the habit was unreformed.

When he had been a short while at Cambridge, Bradshaw's ecclesiastical tendencies led him seriously to contemplate taking orders. When the idea first dawned upon him I cannot say. In the spring of 1851 he was much interested in the results of the Tractarian movement. On April 9, 1851, he writes home, "I am very sorry to hear of Mr. J. It ought to open people's eyes to the fact that when they pretend to attack Tractarianism they really attack the whole Church system. . . . I see Archdeacon Manning has at last gone over. You have seen also, I suppose, the secession of seven of the Leeds clergy, the late and present vicar, and three of the curates who were so kind to me in the summer."

In connection with this phase of feeling, I may mention an anecdote communicated to me by Sir A. Gordon. Towards the end of 1850 great excitement was caused by the so-called "Papal aggression." The pope, influenced by the sporadic conversions to Rome, and considering the time ripe for a great stroke, had set up a new Roman Catholic hierarchy in England, conferring on Cardinal Wiseman the title of Archbishop of Westminster. All England was in arms at once. The University of Cambridge, like other public bodies, addressed the queen on the subject. Some of the hotter heads among the undergraduates, anxious not to be behind their seniors, determined to get up a meeting of those *in statu pupillari* to denounce the pope and the Puseyites. Sir William Harcourt and Mr Llewellyn Davies, then a scholar of Trinity, were the chief promoters of this movement. Some of the unpopular High Church party were not unwilling to face the storm, and to figure as martyrs; but the cooler members, perceiving the mischief and bitterness likely to be engendered by such a meeting as was proposed, resolved to put a stop to it. A deputation accordingly waited on the Vice-Chancellor, Dr Corrie of Jesus, and requested him to forbid the meeting. Bradshaw, along with his friends Hort and Westcott, was among those most active in organizing this opposition, which was successful, and the meeting was stopped.

On May 20, 1851, Bradshaw writes to his mother, "I have been often thinking over what we talked about before I left you, and I see more than ever the absolute necessity of turning one's mind to some definite purpose and aim of life—not to let the time all pass away, though it is very difficult to know what to do. I suppose it must be that my mind has been turned *only* to Orders, from the very nature and circumstances of one's life and position here. I cannot say my whole thoughts have been turned that way, but only, if you can understand, they have seen that view without ever definitely making an aim at any line. I have never thought of anything else latterly; and then comes the question, *if I think of this*, it must be soon and definitely, and [I must] make it have more influence on my life. . . ."

A fortnight later: "I can assure you I have thought very much over our last conversation, and it brings before me the utter state of thoughtlessness I have been living in; by which I mean, not perhaps what you would *call* thoughtlessness, but an utter absence of thinking what is to become of me, and what I am to do when set at liberty in a year and a half or two years from this time. One thing, of course, is plain—if I have any idea of remaining a Fellow of King's, I must take Orders, as I have pledged myself to do; and then comes the thought, How am I fit? How am I prepared for such a life? and how am I living as if such were to be my destined course of life? I very much fear I can give but a very unsatisfactory answer to every one of these questions; and I find a weight, an accumulated weight, of listlessness in the action of mind, heart, and body. . . . I have now completed exactly half of the appointed time of my scholarship here, and I cannot but feel, and I say it to my shame, that though I hope I have gone on in some things, yet that in many things I seem, if anything, to have gone backwards."

Bradshaw's life as an undergraduate was uneventful. His last two years seem to have passed much in the same way as the first two, but unfortunately there are hardly any letters to illustrate it. In the Michaelmas Term, 1851, he attended Professor Blunt's lectures on the Liturgy. In the Lent Term, 1852, he attended the lectures of Professor Jeremie. He was clearly preparing in earnest for the Church.

The religious tone of his mind, as well as his charitable instincts, may be illustrated by a trifle. During the academical year 1851-2, he kept an account-book in which every item is carefully noted down. This account-book is arranged in three divisions. At the head of the first division, that for receipts, is written the text, "Take no thought, saying, What shall we eat, or what shall we drink," etc. (Matt. vi. 25). The second division is in two parts, the one for ordinary expenditure, the other for "the Lord's rent," that is, charity. At the head of the first section is

the text, "Owe no man anything, but to love one another,"
etc. (Rom. xiii. 8); at the head of the second, the texts,
"He that hath pity upon the poor lendeth unto the Lord"
(Prov. xix. 17), and "The poor shall never cease out of
the land" (Deut. xv. 11). That this division was no mere
form is shown by the fact that out of his total expenses
for the year, amounting to about £115, he spent over £11
in charity. The proportion, it will be observed, is almost
exactly a tithe.

During the whole of his undergraduate career, Bradshaw read much in the University Library, and in the
libraries of his own and other colleges. That he was
already engaged in making a personal acquaintance with
their antiquarian contents is clear, but the subjects of his
researches can only be guessed at. A contemporary note-
book contains hints of this occupation—extracts from
Panzer's Annals, and notes on manuscripts and on Irish
books in various libraries. It is probable, from several
indications, that Irish literature was, during this part of
his life, his chief subject of study.

In the autumn of 1852 he spent a fortnight with his
friend Booth among the English lakes. He fell in love
with the country, and it was ever afterwards his favourite
haunt for a summer ramble. The pocket-book in which
he noted a few facts of this tour, and between the leaves
of which he dried flowers picked in his favourite spots,
contains also, characteristically enough, an elaborate
bibliographical note on the various editions of Camden's
works. The following scrap from a letter dated October 12,
1852, to Arthur Gordon, is of interest:—"Gorham is down
at Brighton now, reading; from him I heard the delightful
news of Hort's Fellowship. . . . You will be glad to hear
that I had a very pleasant walk with Waterfield and Hort
yesterday; as also that, after all, Benson did go in for a
Fellowship this year, and beat everybody but Lightfoot in

classics, and, had he been in the second year, would
certainly have got a Fellowship this time. This is comfortable intelligence."

The following fragment of a diary, kept assiduously
for just one week, gives a glimpse of his daily life towards
the end of his second year :—

"*Advent Sunday, November* 28, 1852.—After sitting up
late, or rather lying awake very late to finish the first
volume of 'Alton Locke,' I was up only just in time for
chapel. I made a determination, on Matthias' example,
and I suppose somewhat stirred up by some expressions
of the young tailor-poet, to set about reading 'Paradise
Lost,' at any rate, as Sunday reading, and was charmed
with the first two books and part of the third, which were
all quite new to me, except the merest scraps of quotations
of a few lines here and there. A pleasant evening with
Witts, to meet Gorham, Arthur [Gordon], and Wayte.
The conversation was very desultory, on the Crystal
Palace, the duke's funeral, and such topics. Boudier came
in at the last, and was less Etonian than usual. By the
way, I must try and remember Arthur's practical resolution of not discussing any book with me until three months
after I have read it. There is too much cause for it, I
suppose, resulting from my having read really so very little,
and having no fundamental ideas to start with. I must
see what more cultivation in the way of reading will do.

"*Monday, November* 29.—I finished the third book of
'Paradise Lost' before going to bed last night. . . . . I sat
down to my Plato between eleven and twelve, and
enjoyed the Phaedrus until it was time for me to walk with
Wayte. It was bitterly cold, and we had a profitless, argu-
mentative talk on Kingsley in 'Alton Locke,' and theories
of the creation. I read more of 'Alton Locke' after
dinner, and then went to Booth's, intending to stay a short
time ; but Waterfield came in, and we discussed Lewes and

absolute truth and metaphysics and religion until after
tea, when I again sat down to my Plato, until ——
appeared, and I had an unpleasant argumentation on
definitions of time and possible conceptions, which ended
about one.

"*St. Andrew, Tuesday, November* 30.—I made some
progress in the Phaedrus, every now and then feeling
inclined to lay it down for a short time, when some fresh
beauty gave me a fresh stimulus. The want of my walk
made me dull and uncomfortable in the evening, when
Arthur appeared. He took me to the Union, to hear
Vernon-Harcourt speak on the present ministry. He did
not, however, appear. . . . On coming back to my rooms,
I read a little more of 'Alton Locke,' which grows more
and more intensely interesting, though I don't know what
to make of the principles. Sandy Mackaye is certainly a
glorious character.

" *Wednesday, December* 1.—Not much read in the way of
classics. I finished 'Alton Locke,' much to my satisfaction, and enjoyed a walk to Hauxton with Rolleston, who
is revelling in Kingsley, and seems to believe in him fully,
more so, possibly, than Kingsley intends any one to believe.
. . . I borrowed 'Yeast' from Hort, and began it before
I went to bed.

" *Thursday, December* 2.—Read 'Yeast' until nine,
and between the lectures, and I fear my Phaedrus did not
proceed much in consequence of the absorbing influence of
Kingsley. . . . After chapel I read 'Yeast' until it was
time to go to Trinity, and at half-past six I went to a
Fellowship dinner with Hort, and spent a very pleasant
evening. We met in his rooms, and dined in Freshfield's,
used Scott's as a drawing-room, and Clark's (those who
wished) as a smoking-room. There was hardly a face
that I did not know, and, fortunately, I was quite on
speaking terms with many. Howard of Sidney was the

only extra-Trinity man except myself; the Scotts, Brim-
ley, Clark, Vansittart, Rowe, Yool, Watson, Schreiber,
Williams, Lightfoot, Gorham, Butler, Pottar, Freshfield,
Hawkins. I had a discussion with E. A. Scott and
Hawkins on the merits of Arnold, and the meaning of the
'Strayed Reveller,' and I am glad to see that, whatever it
does mean, it is something more than a mere picture,
which is what Hort was inclined to think. The 'Em-
pedocles' seemed liked, from what I could gather. ——
seems to have a pious horror of Kingsley, and seemed
shocked at my wasting my time over his books. I am
afraid, however, his advice was to no purpose, for I have
sat up till three to finish 'Yeast,' and am delighted with
it. I cannot yet see where the fallacies are, but I am
quite convinced of the main truths, and that the truth in
him compensates for the bad. The chief fault of his I
have been able to extract from people, seems to be the
rejection of asceticism, and his 'God's-Earth' *versus*
'World-and-Devil-and-human-corruption' theories, as well
as the bad effect upon 'the masses' who will carry out his
principles further than he intended. . . . But the 'godli-
ness' of the books is the most striking feature to me. . . .

"*Saturday, December* 4.—I managed to read a little
more of the Phaedrus, though not to my satisfaction. . . .
After hall . . . I went to see Hort, and made him tell me
something about Kingsley and his political and theological
tendencies. Then we went on to Maurice, and he [*i.e.*
Hort] read me some parts of Maurice's sermon on the
Temptation, and made me bring away the book; and
then he took down his 'Kingdom of Christ,' and went
through the Analytical Index with me, and made me long
to read it. The immense fund of thought, and materials
for thinking upon in every page, are wonderful. Maurice,
it seems, first taught Dr Hook that a man could do good
without belonging to a 'party.' After leaving him, I came

home and went up to see Moody, and had some discussion
with him and Ridler, and came down and read some of
Charles Tennyson's sonnets, which I like more and more.
—— came in, and we had an unpleasant discussion on
Scott, etc., till nearly three."

Twenty years after this, writing to thank a friend for a
birthday present of the collected edition of Kingsley's
poems, he wrote, " I am indeed pleased, more than pleased,
to have from you a volume of such things, 'a box where
sweets compacted lie,' and, above everything, to find at the
beginning a comfortable edition of my pet 'Saint's
Tragedy,' which I devoured during all my undergraduate
Mays with fresh pleasure each time."

On February 1, 1853, Henry Bradshaw, having satisfactorily passed through his three years of probation,
which was all that was necessary for obtaining a Fellowship at King's in those days, was elected a Fellow of the
college. In the summer of the same year he began
seriously to prepare for his degree. At that time Kingsmen still possessed the privilege of obtaining the B.A.
degree without examination. They were allowed to enter
for a Tripos if they wished to do so, but it was not till
1856 that an examination became compulsory. Bradshaw
declined to avail himself of the so-called privilege. He
was not the first, but one of the first to do so. With the
object of showing his approval of the new system, rather
than with the expectation of gaining distinction by taking
a high place, which he must have known was at least
doubtful, he resolved to enter for the Classical Tripos.
As a preliminary to this, it was necessary either to take
honours in the Mathematical Tripos, or else to obtain a
first class in the examination for an ordinary degree. He
chose the latter alternative. During the Michaelmas Term,
1853, he read with Barnard Smith, the leading "poll-
coach" of the day. In January, 1854, his name appeared

in the first class of ὂι πολλόι, as being qualified for the
ordinary degree.

For the Tripos he read, during the Long Vacation, 1853,
with H. J. Roby, of St John's College, the well-known
author of the Latin Grammar. Opinions in King's were
divided as to the probability of his success. He does not
appear to have distinguished himself in the examinations
for the University Scholarships, for which he entered at
least once. In his own college he obtained prizes for
Divinity and Classics, but from such data little could be
deduced. His contemporary Ridler, who, with one other
Kingsman, Charles Evans, entered for the same Tripos,
remarked to a friend just before the examination, "What a
dark horse Bradshaw is! I wonder what he will do?"
Mr Roby thought well of his chances. He wrote to him,
apparently during the examination, "I am sorry to find
you are so despondent about your place. I thought, and
still think, that you will get a first class, though your
slowness, as I think you told me, in composition may
possibly put you in the second." Ill-health had prevented
Bradshaw from getting as much help as he might have
obtained from Mr Roby during the time when he was
reading with him, and want of funds made a continuance
of "coaching" impossible. What money he had to spend
he spent upon books, and a year or two later he told his
mother that he had spent a great deal in this way. It was
the only extravagance which he allowed himself. His
friends more than once asked him to go abroad with them,
but, fond as he was of travelling, he was obliged to
decline. From other allusions in his letters, it is clear
that, though he managed to pay his way, he had no money
to spare for a luxury like private tuition. It was, however, a luxury which in those days hardly any one who
aimed at distinction in the Tripos could forego.

When the list came out, his name appeared bracketed

tenth in the second class. What his own feelings on the subject were does not appear. Mr Roby writes to him (March 29, 1854) as follows :—" I was sorry to find you had been endowed with a gift of prescience as to your own fate, . . . but I think even now that your failure is to be attributed rather to lack of reading than of scholarship. I certainly thought you had more notion of this latter qualification than many others." Almost immediately after taking his degree he went as assistant-master to St Columba's College, near Dublin, to serve under his friend the Rev. George Williams.

CHAPTER III.

ST COLUMBA'S COLLEGE, near Dublin, was the outcome of
the High-Church movement combined with Irish patriotism.
It was founded in 1843, by the efforts of the primate, Lord
J. G. Beresford ; the Earl of Dunraven ; Viscount Adare ;
the well-known antiquary Dr Todd; the Rev. William
Sewell, Professor of Moral Philosophy at Oxford, afterwards founder of Radley, and other gentlemen. Their
scheme was originally a wide one, and embraced a college
and a school. In the college, a body of clergy were to
be educated in divinity, and trained to speak and preach
in the Irish tongue, with the object of winning to the
Church the great masses of the Irish-speaking population.
The school was to be on the same system as the great
English public schools, and to provide the children of the
upper classes in Ireland with a place of education which
should obviate the necessity of going over to England for
the purpose. It was natural and appropriate to call the
institution after the name of St Columba, the great
missionary-saint of the early Irish Church. The scheme
began well, but after about five years' trial want of funds
compelled the governors to modify their plan. The first
part of the original programme was allowed to drop, and
the school alone was maintained. After a temporary
residence at Stackallan, on the Boyne, the governors
bought a site on the spur of the hills near Howth, over-
looking Dublin Bay, and in this beautiful spot the college

took up its permanent abode. Under the statutes given it by the primate in 1852, it was governed by a warden and fifteen honorary Fellows. When Bradshaw joined it there were five assistant masters, appointed by the warden, and some thirty-five boys.

In the spring of 1854, Mr George Williams had been in charge of St Columba's for three or four years. His health was failing from the pressure of school work and anxiety, for the financial position of the school was then far from satisfactory, and about the middle of March he asked Bradshaw to come to his assistance. A few days later Bradshaw arrived at St Columba's, and at once got into harness. To a man of his somewhat desultory and irregular habits, the discipline and responsibility of the teacher's life must have been a great change, and a wholesome if not always agreeable tonic.

Mr Tuckwell, one of his colleagues, now Rector of Stockton, says of him, " I well remember Bradshaw's first appearance, and how he startled our Oxford primness by shaking hands with us all round. We were slow to appreciate him at first." His manner seemed repellent ; he seemed to have no enthusiasm. But he soon made his way ; boys and masters alike grew fond of him. Mr Tuckwell was doing more than his share of work, "but no one found it out," he says, "till Bradshaw came one day to remonstrate, and succeeded in carrying off a pile of exercises, and in arranging to relieve me periodically in future."

Ten days after his arrival he writes to his mother, " I felt that I was only going for a short time to relieve Williams and to make the best of it, though I fancied it would be uncongenial work. And I confess I had some prejudices against the place. However, once here, I feel differently. The place is as different as day from night from what I expected to find it. . . . My respect and admiration for Williams have increased tenfold. I was half afraid of a system of confession and absolution, or some approach to it; but I find there is not a shadow of anything of the kind. Nor, indeed, does there seem any room for it; for I never saw a place where things were so practical and so utterly devoid of any morbid tendency. The boys are the freshest and most honest set I ever knew. I must say this—that Williams seem to have eradicated the propensity (which in English schools is the *rule*) of lying to a master and thinking it no harm; and if it is in any way the bane of the Irish as a nation, as is so often said, I am convinced that when once eradicated, the superiority of the character comes out. It amuses me immensely to see the way they scorn to give a shuffling excuse."

"I have had no time for theorising," he continues, "and I find no one here who is inclined that way. My hands are full from morning to night with either positive school work or verses to look over, or helping the boys to do their exercises, etc.; but with this, indeed on account of this, I make a point of always getting my regular exercise, and yesterday I had a regular good three hours' run over the mountains. . . . It seems a direct call to me to active work, and I have every reason to be most thankful for it. And as far as I can see, it may influence my future course considerably, and I may continue here for some time."

He seems to have been really happy for some time. He threw himself into his duties with good will and even enthusiasm. His intercourse with the boys was by no means confined to school-hours, but was almost continuous throughout the day. "At dinner," he writes, "we all sit at the head and foot of the several tables—I, at least, at the warden's left hand, carving for him. You will be amused to hear that, after avoiding the office of carver

regularly at Eton and at home, as well as at King's, I
have fallen into a place where I have to practise my hand
regularly every day. There are no symptoms of fasting—
to be seen of men."

When the summer half came to an end, he had
made up his mind to go back in the autumn. In July,
1854, he writes to his friend Edwin Freshfield, "When
I had been a few weeks there (at St Columba's), I was
doubly glad I had gone. I found it a plain, ordinary
school, somewhat better managed than most schools ; . . .
no ecclesiastical nonsense of any description, and, what
relieved me most—thanks to Tuckwell of New College—
no ecclesiastical small talk among the tutors, at the breakfast-table and elsewhere. I soon fell into it, and took to
the work kindly enough ; and, contrary to all my views
when I went there, I shall probably go back in the
second week in August, and very likely stay working
there till I am ordained, which will not be very far hence.
Of course, one great attraction to me is having so many
old friends, besides perpetual aunts and cousins (whom I
do like), in or near Dublin and in the north of Ireland."

August found him again at St Columba's. But his
letters begin to show signs that the work was not so congenial as it had seemed. The experience of this term
seems to have driven him to the conclusion that schoolmastering was not to be his trade, though he was fated
to continue it for more than a year longer. In January,
1855, he writes to a sister, "I have not, for fourteen
years or more, had such an utterly miserable leaving home
as I have had this time. It is, of course, the last time
I shall ever leave under the circumstances of going back
to school, and it seems as if all the happiness there had
been in former times in going back to school had given
way to this feeling of going back now." When he was
once at work again, his spirits partially revived, but mean-

while the chief motive for remaining at St Cólumba's was removed by the departure of its head. Towards the end of 1854, Mr George Williams had been elected Vice-Provost of King's, a post which involved his almost continuous presence at Cambridge. This was a serious loss to Bradshaw, and eventually determined him to leave the place.

It will be remembered that in the summer of 1854 he was looking forward to being ordained in a short time. But he had grave doubts as to whether he could conscientiously enter the service of the Church. On February 7, 1855, he writes to his mother, his constant and sympathetic counsellor, as follows :—" Thanks very much for your letter ; thanks for every part of it. I hope I shall not soon or easily forget what you say. With reference to want of energy making me shrink from taking Orders, I cannot allow myself to make this any ground ; for my conscience tells me very plainly that, once conscious of a want of energy, you are bound to shake it off, as a Christian and a man, in any position whatever, and all I wish is to be honest with myself. My real fault has been—my tendency has been, certainly—not to too much fine-drawn speculation on the matter, and troublesome argument with myself, but rather to an absence of sufficient thought upon the matter at all, an unwillingness to give my thoughts to it. And this was curiously corroborated at Cambridge the other day, by a fact which may amuse you, if you are fond of drawing inferences—as I am—from such things. I was looking over all my divinity books. Some were from the Hyde Park Street library [left him by his father]. A great number —eighty or a hundred, maybe more—were presents from people who were supposed to know my tastes ; whereas of what I bought at Cambridge (and here I must say that I have spent a considerable sum on books in the last five years—much more than I ought) of these, I say, not one

E

in forty or fifty was theological, and, with the exception
of a few of those books of Mr Maurice which you have at
Brighton, they did not amount to more than half a dozen—
certainly not a dozen. It is a curious fact, as I said, and
one that I was not at all aware of. I have continually
made men show me on their shelves what books they have
bought at the university, with a view to judging somewhat
of their character and tastes, but never dreamt of applying
this test to myself."

It is remarkable that, in the list of the books which he
took to Ireland, hardly any theological works are to be
found. Those which his friends gave him were for the
most part, as far as could be judged from the volumes on
his shelves at the time of his death, not, strictly speaking,
theological. They consisted, for the most part, of devotional
works, religious poetry, ecclesiastical history, and biography.
It seems that, though he was on the one hand deeply
religious, and on the other warmly interested in ecclesiastical history and antiquities, as well as in the problems
of Church government, dogmatic theology seldom formed
a subject of his thought or conversation. Whether this
consideration had much effect or not, is impossible to say.
It is more probable that he gradually relinquished the idea
of taking Orders, from a conviction that for the ordinary
duties of a clergyman he had no special inclination, and
that the ecclesiastical studies in which he delighted might
be at least as profitably pursued if his connection with the
Church remained that of a devout layman.

The line which he would have taken, at any rate at
first, may be gathered from much that has been said already.
It may be illustrated by the following extracts from a letter
which he received in the autumn of 1855 from one of his
most intimate friends, who happened to be staying at
Oxford at the time:—"All Oxford is ringing with two
sermons from Dr Pusey, just preached before the univer-

sity. They consisted in an onslaught on the infidelity of
the day, crashing down upon Jowett, Maurice, Frank New-
man, and a host of writers, whose degrees of aberration are
—as you will guess from these instances—very remote.
The sermons were wonderfully eloquent, stocked with
exquisite illustrations, and sparkling with patristic anti-
thesis. Men came away, from the last especially, as the
Hipponese might have come away from hearing St
Augustine. . . . I was shocked to see this morning that
there is a rule granted for a *mandamus* to compel the
Archbishop of Canterbury to proceed in the Denison case.
What can come of it, humanly speaking, but misery and
mischief? . . . It is a comfort that at this juncture the
Bishop of Oxford has just enunciated the doctrine of the
Real Presence very distinctly from the university pulpit."
It need not, of course, be supposed that Bradshaw was
ready to endorse all the opinions implied in this letter, but
it could not have been written for a totally unsympathetic
eye.

His interest in English literature was as vivid as ever
during this period. He often wrote to his sisters to send
him books. He read "Westward Ho," then just published,
with avidity. His love of giving and receiving appropriate
presents of books was observed by Mr Tuckwell. Bradshaw writes to him early in 1856, "I don't know anything
so pleasant as presents that are *really* acceptable, and how
rarely they are so ! The 'Excursion,' which came on
Friday last, and your letter of this day week, have both
been treasures to me during the last few days. I ought to
have *acknowledged* it by return of post, but that would have
been thanks (1) for your thoughtfulness in choosing wholesome food for me, and (2) for the beauty of the binding, but
no thanks for the book, which I had never read. But I
have been reading it now, and have read three books, parts
of them over and over again, and am charmed with them

beyond what I can tell you. I have often wondered when the time would come for me to read and love Wordsworth, and, as I said about Dr Pusey to you before, I am delighted to think that you have been the first person in both cases to make me read them. I am longing to get on to the fourth and following books, and by the next time I write I shall probably have finished the poem, and be more prepared to dive deeper into it by reading a great deal over and over again. The charm to me about all his things is so much more that of familiarity than of novelty, just as with good music. . . . Was ever anything like ' The Brothers' ? "

The severe "Crimean" winter of 1854–5 caused him much discomfort, and inflicted on him a variety of ailments. On February 9, 1855, he writes to Mr Hort, " I am enjoying my second day of influenza, and wondering what will come next. The plagues have been sweeping clean through me, as regular as the clock : a week's inflammation, a week's face-ache, a week's incessant headache morning and night, and a week's sore throat, which has now made way for a combination of almost all. I hope this may be final, for it is a bar to work, and I can get no regular exercise." All his energies were taxed in amusing the boys, who soon grew tired of snowballing, and, like explorers in an Arctic winter, became discontented and troublesome. The sub-warden, Mr Walford, was absent, and Bradshaw for a time had triple work on his hands. Nevertheless, or perhaps on this very account, he found time to write many letters home. " I feel it is such a blessing," he says to one of his sisters, " being able to write more, for it was so dismal—dismal enough for me so seldom hearing from any one, and ten times worse for you never hearing at all." And again, " If letters make you half as happy as they make me, whether writing or receiving them, you ought to be happy enough."

It is, perhaps, a little surprising that his letters during this period allude so seldom to the great events then taking place in the East. Some remarks, however, on the death of the Emperor Nicolas, in a letter to his youngest sister (March 29, 1855), deserve quotation. "I must say I agree with mamma that I cannot see the slightest cause for exultation at his death, any more than in any other person's, particularly as it seems very uncertain that the result is likely to be a peace. If it results in a peace, there is every reason to be thankful; but it is precisely the fact of his sudden death being the cause that prevents the great exultation there would otherwise be. The natural thing to exult in is the man's pride being well taken down, and this his sudden death prevented, so that you should be rather disappointed than not. But I don't want to give you a sermon, especially as there are much more shocking things which might bring one on."

His short Easter holidays this year were spent in an excursion through County Wicklow. The following letter was written to a sister just after his return :—

"April 17, 1855.

"What a heavenly day! This and yesterday have been our first spring days. I have just been up to the top of one of our ranges of hills, sitting among the ruins of a great Danish fort, about fifteen or sixteen hundred feet above the sea, reading your and mamma's letters. . . . We had such a happy week last week, from Monday to Thursday, fifteen of us: to Bray the first day ; then on to Arklow, the southernmost part of Wicklow, through the vale of Avoca. The rock scenery was very grand. Of course, the vale is only at its beauty in summer, but as we came back and went through the Devil's Glen and the Seven Churches in Glendalough, it was worth anything. . . . Altogether I have great reason to be ten times happier this year than last, so do not, dearest K., think me unhappy."

Part of his summer holidays were spent in a tour through the north of France with his friend Gordon. He visited Paris, Rouen, Rheims, and other places, and wrote an enthusiastic letter to one of his sisters about the beauties of Soissons by moonlight, and the view from the terraced ramparts of Laon.

The October term at St Columba's found him sustaining, with very insufficient aid, the greater part of the business of the school. The warden was again absent at Cambridge, and one of the most energetic of his assistants took a post at Eton. "His going away so suddenly," writes Bradshaw on October 9, 1855, "has thrown a good deal of extra work on my hands, and, as the warden went on Monday, I have all the college accounts to keep, calves to sell, and pigs to buy, potatoes to see brought in, and oats carted, etc., besides servants' wages to pay." This seems to have been the last straw, and in the autumn he resolved to resign.

He spent the Christmas vacation, lonely and depressed, in the empty house at St Columba's, his solitude interrupted only now and then by visits to his friends Dr Todd or Dr Lee in Dublin, and somewhat solaced, we may hope, by reading Wordsworth. Early in 1856 he was preparing to leave the school. On January 3 he writes to one of his brothers, "We are all here in the midst of confusion, caused by giving up house and home, packing books, etc.; we all leave this to-morrow morning." However, as the warden had been compelled finally to give up his connection with the college, Bradshaw consented to fill his place—as, indeed, he had been practically doing for some time past—till another warden could be appointed. For some months he had the whole charge of the school on his hands, and only one assistant to help him. The work was heavy, and the responsibility, to a man of his temperament, very trying. The details of management, in addition to the tedious routine of school work, were almost more than he could bear. At length he was able to shake off the load, and on April 5, 1856, he wrote, "The matter is now not settling, but settled, and I leave the place on Tuesday afternoon, with feelings of nothing but the most unmitigated disgust."

So ended an episode in Henry Bradshaw's life, on which he never looked back with much satisfaction. The discipline through which he had passed was doubtless beneficial. He learnt, among other things, what he was *not* fit for, but it may be regretted that two valuable years were spent in making this discovery. It was no natural attraction, but a chivalrous devotion to a friend, which led him originally to take up the work, and so long hindered him from laying it down. It is difficult to gather how far he was successful as a schoolmaster. He did what he had to do energetically and conscientiously, but it is clear that he was not in his element.

Whenever he could, he escaped into the library of the college. It was a good library, and during his residence he made a catalogue of the books which it contained. A colleague, Mr Beck, now Rector of Rotherhithe, tells me that "it was his happiness to spend what few hours he had of leisure time in the library. Irish antiquities were a special study with him at that time, and I remember with what pleasure and enthusiasm he would talk with the learned and genial Dr Todd on these topics." But it was not much time that he could spend in his favourite pursuit, especially during the latter part of his time at the school. When Dr Gwynne accepted the post of warden, early in 1855, he found Bradshaw utterly worn out. I cannot do better than quote Dr Gwynne's remarks on his position during the autumn of 1855 and the beginning of 1856. "The work was uncongenial to him, and teaching was a mere trial of his patience. But so long as George Williams was present to direct it, I have no doubt that Bradshaw was fairly happy. Then came the change. Williams was absent; other tutors one by one dropped off; their places were filled by strangers, temporarily engaged; the school was dwindling rapidly. Nothing could be more dreary than the position, or more unpromising than the prospect. Up to the close of 1855 he had at least the satisfaction of feeling that he was working for his friend, but after Williams' resignation his steadfastness was still the same; so long as the school held together, he was ready to stand by it. It may have been partly a feeling that the work which George Williams had carried on for five years must not be let drop, partly a desire to help Dr Todd to save the school from final collapse; but I believe it was mainly a strong sense of duty that held him to his post—a feeling of loyal obligation, binding him to hold on till he should be relieved of his charge by some one who would undertake the office of warden."

His temper suffered. He left on Dr Gwynne " the impression that he was a man of gloomy, almost morbid temperament. He was pale and meagre, with the worn look of a man who neither ate nor slept enough, as if the anxieties of his life fretted him all day and kept him awake half the night, and left their lines upon his face." " One of the most lively images," says Dr Gwynne, " which I retain of him is as I found him sitting over a handful of sixth-form verses—the sixth being at a low ebb in numbers and in scholarship alike. The passage he had set them to translate began with the line—

" ' Yes, Earth shall lead destruction ; she shall end.'

I well remember the unhappy first line of the copy sent up by the captain of the school, the despair and disgust with which Bradshaw showed it to me :

" ' Dux erit exitii tellus : immo illa finibit.'

I can recall no more ; this sample will suffice.

" Then there were the accounts. How he worried his soul over them ! Day after day I found him labouring at them. But at last, before he left, he handed them all over to me—school accounts, house accounts, farm accounts— all made out with perfect neatness and clearness, and calculated literally to the last farthing. And so with everything that had been committed to his keeping. He had labelled every key, arranged the contents of every drawer and pigeon-hole, and classified all letters and papers, before he gave them into my hands.

" But what I think impressed me most was his solici- tude about what I may call the minor morals of the school, the maintenance of all the observances and proprieties which George Williams, who was a punctilious man, had laid down as rules. Any laxity about the regulations as to dress, any disregard of the boundaries which divided the region where caps might be worn from the region where caps must be taken off, distressed him sorely. I hardly think this strictness in regard to petty rules was of his own nature ; I suspect that it was rather part of his desire to keep everything as George Williams had left it."

Even his liking and admiration for the boys seem to have given way to very different feelings. " To individual boys," says Dr Gwynne, " he was strongly attached, but boys as a class had no special interest for him. Except a few, he spoke of them with distrust—I may say, disgust, for I well remember the word he very often used in sum- ming up his ill opinion of some boy whom he disliked— 'loathsome boy'!" The disappointments of which every schoolmaster's life is full must have soured him for the time, and it is evident that during these latter days at St Columba's he was not himself.

Nevertheless, Mr Walford tells me that "his influence with the boys was great, and exerted in a gentle way. He could insinuate good advice or reproof by the simplest words, combined with a manner which told of a truly loving heart." Many boys thought him odd ; some found him "shy and dreamy ;" but he was certainly attracted by others, and attracted them in turn. In his discipline he was severe, as he had been while captain at Eton. Letters have been preserved in which he refused, courteously but firmly, in spite of reiterated requests from parents or friends, to allow pupils to stay away a minute longer than the rules of the college permitted. He says himself, in a letter to a near relative, "I have put a ban entirely on my boys saying 'I had no time to do it.' There are few greater mistakes than to allow yourself to suppose that you have not time for anything you really want to do." Still, a former pupil says of him, "He was, I think, fairly popular ; always kind and just ; not severe in his punishments, but always down upon anything which was not honest and straightforward." Another pupil writes, "My happiest recollections of school-life are associated with Mr Bradshaw, whom I learnt to regard more as a friend than a master. His love of books, even at that time, impressed me much ; and to this day I never see an uncut book without its reminding me of him and his instruction how it should be cut and its back ' broken,' so as to open flat without starting the leaves."

That he continued to take interest in the school is evident from the numerous letters which he received for some time after he left, from Dr Todd, Dr Gwynne, and others. He preserved till his death a large number of these, many of them covering eight or ten pages, and full of minute details about the school, which could not have been communicated to any one unable to reciprocate the vivid interest and sympathy which they evince. But his direct connection with St Columba's, once broken off, was never renewed. He was now to be transferred to a more congenial sphere of action. Shortly after leaving St Columba's, he settled down in the University Library at Cambridge.

CHAPTER IV.

WHEN Henry Bradshaw first accepted a post in the University Library, that institution was in a comparatively backward condition. The Library Syndicate, in its remodelled form, had only been in existence some three years. Its labours were far from being so arduous as they are now. Its principal business appears to have been to decide what books should be bought for the library. The amount of time at its disposal may be guessed from the fact that each book to be bought was discussed by the whole Syndicate and voted on separately. The Syndics were not always conversant with the books on whose merits they debated. A story is told that on one occasion, when some works on Romance literature were under discussion, the chairman objected to their purchase on the ground that there were "novels enough in the library already." There was little communication between the executive and the governing body, for the librarian was not present at the meetings of the Syndicate. The attendance of the librarian did not, in fact, become customary till Bradshaw himself held the office. There was not too much supervision, and the rules for admission and for taking out books were frequently violated. Bradshaw himself, in the early days of his appointment as library assistant, once came upon two ladies busy in exploring the treasures of the novel-room. When asked if they had any tickets of admission, they replied, " No, but papa has ; " and upon further inquiry it turned out that for a long time past they had acted on the assumption that the paternal rights were transferable.

To manage so large an institution as the University Library under the conditions of free admission, which make it unique among the great libraries of the world, must always be difficult ; to do so with the staff then at the service of the librarian was well-nigh impossible. The staff consisted of one principal assistant and four assistants. The first of these offices had only been created in 1853, with a salary of £120, and was held by a foreigner, Mr Heun, who had previously been secretary to the librarian. There were no assistant-librarians, and Mr Heun was not a member of the university. The librarian's salary was £210 a year. It was hardly to be wondered at if his attention was not exclusively devoted to the library. The catalogue of books was entirely in manuscript, and the system of writing the titles on slips and pasting them in was not yet in use. Not that the University Library was behind other libraries in this respect : on the contrary, it was the first to adopt (in 1861) the system of printing the slips. The present catalogue of manuscripts had just been begun, and the first volume, containing many errors, was published in 1856 ; but for the greater part of the manuscripts there was as yet only the defective list made by Nasmith in 1796. Little care had been taken to secure the contents of the library from loss or damage. Precious books frequently disappeared, or came back mutilated, docked of engravings or other matter which gave them peculiar interest or value. Priceless volumes were stowed away in inaccessible places, a prey to dust or damp, while others were left where the hand of every passer-by could touch them. Others, again, had been altogether lost sight of; no one knew where they were, or even that they had ever been in the library.

The illness and consequent resignation of Mr Heun, in October, 1856, gave Bradshaw an opening for which, during the greater part of his life, he had been unconsciously preparing. His previous studies—those, at least, which he had pursued with interest—pointed to a library as his natural home. He had been conversant with books from childhood. At Eton, at Cambridge, at St Columba's, his friends had observed his propensities and recognized his learning. But there is nothing to show that he had haunted libraries and passed his time among books with a view to professional employment as a librarian. Indeed, as we have seen, he had quite other notions of a profession. He simply studied books because they interested him more than anything else.

A great part of his undergraduate leisure had been spent in the University Library, and many of its most valuable contents were already familiar to him. While at St Columba's, he wrote to Mr Heun for an account of certain early printed books. His letter, written in 1854, concludes with the words, " I forget, by-the-by, whether you know my name. At any rate, you will easily recollect me as the B.A. of King's College who gave you so much trouble about the Irish books in the library." Another letter to Mr Heun shows that he was already well acquainted with the scene of his future labours, and that this acquaintance had been gained, apparently, in the pursuit of Irish books, at this time his chief subject of research. " It would be a charity," he says, " to rescue from the dust in which it lies buried a copy of Wynkyn de Worde's ' Nova Legenda Anglie.' Fol. Lond.: 1516. It by rights belongs to K*. 10. 38 ; but it is lying (or was when I left) on the top of the bookcase next the staircase leading up to your room, so that, when I wanted it, I could not find it for some time. . . . I have been looking carefully right through the first two volumes of Mr Grenville's catalogue for Irish books, but I am disappointed, for the two volumes only contain half a dozen, certainly not a dozen, books which I did not know of before, on that subject. Of those which I know well the account given is so very bad *generally* that I have no faith in the way in which those are entered which I have not had a sight of; but it is specially disappointing, because that is always held out as the finest private collection, and that catalogue as a model of what such books should be. I see there is nothing for it but to examine every single book with my own eyes and hands, and to take nothing second-hand."

Mr Heun resigned his post towards the end of October, 1856, and Bradshaw at once made application for the place. It had not been held previously by a member of the university. He was appointed early in November, 1856. It had been his wish that the title of the post should be altered from "principal assistant" to "assistant-librarian." This may appear a trivial matter, but Bradshaw probably felt that the change in title would confer some increase of authority, and would also make it easier in future for a member of the university to accept the post. It was, however, thought better on this occasion not to make the change. Some time later his wish was carried into effect.

Almost the only record of the two next years which I have been able to find, consists of a few notes on a journey to France in the summer of 1857. This fragment of a diary possesses no particular interest, but it contains one little incident which illustrates the writer's practical sagacity. I will let him tell it in his own words. "July 27, 1857.—Left Cambridge by mail; reached Shoreditch [then the terminus of the Great Eastern Railway] at 4.30 a.m., and walked over to London Bridge. Having intimated to S. the possibility of our starting from Brighton this morning, and not having told Waterfield the contrary, I was most anxious to see him, for fear he should start for Newhaven, and then not find us. So, by an Edgar Poe process of analysis, I inquired at Burrell's [hotel], and, not finding the name, I was reduced to inquiring how many had arrived the previous night, and of these how many were to be called very early, by which the number was reduced to three ; and an inspection of the *boots* led me to the right room. Without much delay, Waterfield was up, and we had breakfasted and were off by the six train to Brighton." In the course of the short expedition that followed, he revisited some of the spots in Normandy— Rouen, for instance, which had delighted him as an Eton boy, when staying there with his sisters ten years before. But the diary records hardly any impressions ; and at Grenoble, where he thought " the fountains perhaps the prettiest things in the place," it abruptly breaks off.

Bradshaw held the post of principal assistant for somewhat more than two years. The reasons which induced him to resign the post do not appear, but may, perhaps, be surmised. His object in entering the library was not simply to obtain employment among books, but to get an opportunity for research under favourable conditions. He doubtless found that his occupations were such as to leave him too little leisure for study. He was engaged for seven hours of the day in routine work, and was practically responsible for the general management of the library. The vacations which others enjoyed were not for him. He wrote home in April, 1857, regretting that he had been unable to visit his mother that Easter, though he had "long looked forward to it as his first real holiday." These things told upon his health. He grew depressed and discontented with his position. In the early part of the year 1858, his friend, George Williams, remonstrated with him on his "continued absence" from the library,

and Bradshaw replied that he intended to resign. Mr
Williams endeavoured to dissuade him from a step
which he regarded as suicidal, but in vain. In June,
1858, Bradshaw sent in his resignation. "I have wished,"
he says, "to give notice thus early, in order that the
Syndics and the library generally may not be put to any
inconvenience from difficulty in finding a member of the
university to fill the place. I cannot forget the honour
which the Syndics paid me in first making the appointment,
much less the uniform kindness which I have received from
every member of that body during my term of office." In
a subsequent letter he informed the vice-chancellor that
the state of his health would not allow him to retain the
post. His resignation was accepted in October, 1858. At
the request of the Syndicate, he continued to act as principal
assistant till the end of the Michaelmas Term, when he was
finally released from what had clearly become an intolerable
burden. So ended the first phase of his connection with
the library.

It must have been in the interval between his first and
second appointments that, as Professor Mayor informs me,
he made inquiries about a post in the British Museum.
The limit of age had, however, been fixed only a year
before at twenty-five, and his application was therefore
unsuccessful. Meanwhile he was able to work unencum-
bered in the University Library. In exploring its hidden
recesses, and making himself acquainted with every
valuable book which it contained, Bradshaw was doing a
work equally beneficial to the library and to himself. His
friends were anxious that an office should be created in
which he could prosecute his researches without risk of
interruption, and with the sanction of the university. All
that he wanted was the permission to work, and the opportunity of showing that he could work to some purpose.

. Accordingly Dr Luard, who was then engaged with

F

others in drawing up the catalogue of manuscripts, addressed a letter to the Library Syndicate, which was laid before that body by Mr George Williams, and eventually led to Bradshaw's appointment. Some passages in this letter deserve quotation, as showing the state of the manuscripts before Mr Bradshaw took them in hand. "The manuscripts," says Dr Luard, "have in all probability not been dusted for centuries, certainly not since George I gave them to the university. In many instances the dust has got into the leaves and seriously injured them. The bindings of the greater portion of the manuscripts are in a most disgraceful condition. . . . Many leaves are often misplaced by the carelessness of the binder, and parts of the same treatise are sometimes bound in two separate volumes, and placed on separate shelves. As to lettering, a volume might be written on the absurd mistakes in this respect. A well-known manuscript of Chaucer's 'Canterbury Tales' is lettered 'Piers Plowman.' A fine York Manual is lettered 'Ritule (sic) vetustum.' Our well-known Winchester Pontifical has 'Missalia' on the back." Dr Luard recommended, among other things, that a careful and thorough examination of the manuscripts should at once be made, and that all such as required binding should be bound under proper supervision.

Acting on these suggestions, the Syndicate, of which Dr Lightfoot, Dr Philpot, Dr Guest, and Professor Mayor were members, reported to the Senate that, in their opinion, the department of manuscripts and early printed books stood in need of a thorough overhauling ; that the bindings of the manuscripts should be properly repaired and re-lettered, and the manuscripts themselves rearranged They proposed "that authority be given to Mr Bradshaw, of King's College, to carry into effect the above-mentioned suggestions, under the direction of the Library Syndicate, and to perform similar duties in regard to rare and early

printed books ; and also that the Syndicate be authorized
to pay to Mr Bradshaw, from the Library Subscription
Fund, the sum of twenty pounds a year so long as he
continues to be engaged in the discharge of these duties."
The report was confirmed in June, 1859, and Bradshaw at
once entered on his duties. His appointment, in the first
instance, was for two years.

The nine years that followed were, in some respects,
the happiest period of his life. He was engaged on work
of which every detail was a pleasure. He was constantly
adding to his store of information ; he was exploring
untrodden ground, unravelling secrets of which no one else
held the clue, bringing to light new facts, establishing new
conclusions, rebuilding and illuminating the past. His
reputation as a scholar was constantly increasing, but on
this he never appeared to set great value. It was a truer
satisfaction to him to feel that his services were more and
more appreciated in the university, to whose interests he
was so assiduously devoting himself.

The task which he had undertaken was no light one.
He had, in the first place, to teach himself to read manuscripts of all dates and countries, and this he did apparently
without any extraneous assistance. But this was only the
first step. To understand, describe, and classify them
correctly required intellectual powers and moral qualities
of a high order. The work of dating and arranging the
early printed books, devoid as they often are of any direct
indication of time or place of publication, was equally
difficult. In both departments, especially perhaps in the
latter, Bradshaw had to find his own way, to make his own
rules, and create his science as he went.

The mere physical labour involved was considerable.
He would stand at the top of a long ladder for hours
together, taking down one book after another from the
shelves. To determine the date or authorship of a manu-

script, to settle the question whether an early printed book
was perfect or not, whether it was a unique copy or a
specimen of some well-known edition, were problems the
solution of which might entail hours or even days of labour.
For the purpose of his researches he frequently visited
Oxford, Dublin, and many other places both in England
and on the Continent. He thought little of making a long
journey to see a single book or settle one knotty point.
For instance, in January, 1866, after jotting down in his
note-book the results of a day's work in the British
Museum, spent mostly on a famous early edition of
Tibullus and other poets, he concludes, " What does the
Paris copy want? On to Paris by the 8.30 train." And
to Paris he went. Once there, he spent several days in
the National Library, and visited Canterbury for the sake
of seeing some other books on his way back.

The sum which he received from the university was at
first merely nominal. It was hardly sufficient to pay his
postage, much less to cover the expenses of the journeys
he made in the fulfilment of his task. But it must be
remembered that the general scale of payments to university officials was far smaller then than now, that the
appointment was confessedly experimental, and that before
long the stipend, if such it may be called, was raised to
a respectable figure. Bradshaw himself was wont to speak
of the assistance which he received from the university at
this time as a genuine instance of the endowment of
research. To some this may seem ironical, but it was not
so intended. In later years he always looked back on
this period of his life with gratitude and pleasure. " My
happy time," he told Dr Furnivall long afterwards, "was
when I was looking through the manuscripts, free to come
and go, and to cut up books as much as I pleased, for
twenty pounds a year."

During this period Henry Bradshaw's labours were,

of course, mainly confined to examining, restoring, and arranging books and manuscripts already known. But at intervals he brought to light hidden treasures, both in Cambridge and elsewhere, the discovery of which deserves special mention. While acting as principal assistant, he had already made himself remarkable in this way. Some time before March, 1857, he unearthed a valuable manuscript which had once belonged to Trinity College, Dublin. This was a copy of the Apocrypha in Irish. It had been deposited in the Trinity College library, says Dr Todd in a letter to Bradshaw, by Archbishop Marsh. Before the archbishop was dead, it had disappeared. Dr Todd thought that it was probably brought to England by Provost Huntington, when he fled from his own country in the disturbed times of James II. It was in the course of his researches in Irish literature that Bradshaw came upon this manuscript. The same researches led shortly afterwards to a more important discovery.

In the autumn of 1857, he found in the University Library the manuscript containing a copy of the Gospels, with Gaelic charters inscribed, known as the "Book of Deer." It will be well to put together here all that need be said about the discovery and publication of this remarkable manuscript. "Books on Irish affairs," writes Bradshaw in May, 1858, "in the widest acceptation of the term, are my speciality, having inherited from my father almost the most considerable private library of the kind in the United Kingdom, and having since nearly doubled its value by my own exertions. It was this circumstance that led Mr Hardwick to draw my attention to the volume, as containing the Gospels in 'handwriting Anglo-Saxon not later than the tenth century,' with some notes apparently in the old Irish language. This was last autumn, and I at once set to work and was happy enough from these 'notes' to discover the real nature of the book." Bradshaw at once communicated the fact to the well-known Scotch antiquary, Mr John Stuart. He describes the manuscript himself as follows :—" It is an unfinished manuscript of the Vulgate version of the four Gospels, with the Apostles' Creed, written by a scribe whose vernacular language was Gaelic, in which the subscription at the close is written. The first three Gospels are unfinished, not mutilated ; St John is complete. The cursive character, the size of the volume, and the portion of the Visitation Office (in a slightly later hand) corresponding almost verbatim with that in the Book of Dimma, lead one to believe that its original use was to be carried about the person, not used in the choir ; while the transcripts of documents and lists of possessions inserted in the blank spaces at the beginning, etc., as in the Book of Kells, show that it was venerated as a relic and so used, as a depository for these documents, and as the book, apparently, on which they swore in claiming their lands." It is in these insertions that the principal value of the manuscript consists. Mr Stuart writes to Bradshaw on May 6, 1858, " The discovery of the Deer manuscript is to me most interesting, and I think its importance to our early history and philology will prove to be great. Already from your transcript I get glimpses into old Celtic times and offices, regarding which we have hitherto nothing but vague tradition. . . . I must congratulate you on having brought to light this curious and to us most interesting volume."

Mr Stuart proposed that the Spalding Club should print the book, and suggested an editor. Bradshaw, however, at first intended to edit it himself. He had, as he says, gone far towards collecting the materials necessary for its illustration, but a few points remained on which he desired further information. He transcribed the Gaelic charters, which constitute the chief value of the book, and also other portions of it, and had facsimiles made of the illuminations.

Unfortunately, as in so many cases, other subjects of interest attracted his attention, the doubtful points were not cleared up, and the book remained unpublished. In 1860, three years after its discovery, Mr John Stuart was again negotiating with him for its publication. His friends urged him to do the work by instalments if he could not bring it all out at once. " The discerning antiquaries of Scotland," writes Dr Reeves, " are looking out most earnestly for the book, not so much in its Biblical character, as in its accidental qualities of a revealer of ecclesiastical secrets, and the oldest specimen of their native language." Thus stimulated, Bradshaw took up again the thread of his researches in connection with the manuscript, and early in 1861 was on the point of printing his results. His intention, apparently, was to publish a portion of the manuscript separately at first, and to make this publication one of a series. The title was to run as follows : " Cambridge literary remains. Miscellaneous pieces, published from the originals now remaining at Cambridge, with brief notices by Henry Bradshaw." Something, however, again interfered, and in 1863 he reluctantly came to the conclusion that it was better to hand over the work to some one with more leisure than he possessed. Mr Joseph Robertson undertook the task, on behalf of the Spalding Club, but died before it was completed. Mr John Stuart then took it up, and gave it to the world in 1869.

I have mentioned these details in connection with the editing of the Book of Deer because they are only too good an example of the procrastination which was, unfortunately, characteristic of Henry Bradshaw. The delay in this case, as in others, was due to his reluctance to publish anything so long as any point, however minute, remained to be explained, and to the difficulty which he always laboured under of concentrating himself on one subject for any length of time. The learned world was, no doubt, put to inconvenience by the delay, but after all Bradshaw himself was the chief sufferer, for he had to see others enjoying the pleasure and credit of publishing what he had brought to light. It is certain that all his unselfishness did not prevent him from feeling a good deal of annoyance and disappointment on these occasions. It may be of some interest to add that this same Book of Deer was produced in the Mar Peerage case before the House of Lords in 1870. The charters in it, "the only Gaelic charters in existence," as Bradshaw calls them, were in some cases witnessed by the "Marmaor of Mar," and therefore contained the earliest documentary evidence on the question at issue. Bradshaw was called upon to attend at the trial, and related the history of the book, and the way in which it had come into the possession of the university.

Another discovery made about the same time as that of the Book of Deer, and also contributing new materials for the study of Celtic languages, was that of the Irish glosses and poems in the manuscript of Juvencus, in the University Library. Bradshaw was already acting as a sort of "purveyor" of materials to Mr Whitley Stokes, the well-known Celtic scholar, to whom he at once communicated his find. These Juvencus glosses appear to have been the first of a long series of similar discoveries, by means of which many difficulties of Celtic philology were cleared up, and the distinctions between early Breton, Welsh, and other branches of the Celtic family placed upon a firmer basis.

It is not surprising that these and other successes attracted considerable attention among antiquaries and bibliographers. In a letter dated December 24, 1859, Mr Winter Jones, of the British Museum, writes to Bradshaw, "Skill, knowledge, and opportunity do wonders, and I have no doubt that you will yet make many interesting discoveries." The prophecy was amply fulfilled.

Irish literature and antiquities probably occupied at this time the first place in Bradshaw's mind. Dr Reeves, now Bishop of Down and Connor, writing in April, 1861, to thank him for copies of some documents concerning the district which twenty-five years later was to be his diocese, concludes his letter with the words, "I am glad to be able to regard you as a semi-Hibernian by blood, having long since known of you as Hibernicissimus in sympathies and studies." But he by no means confined himself to Ireland. Other departments of study already engrossed much of his attention, and gradually usurped the first place, though to the end of his life he never ceased to keep the subject of Irish antiquities before him. His range of interests corresponded with that of the books and manuscripts committed to his charge. There are many indications, in his correspondence and elsewhere, that he was pursuing simultaneously several independent lines of research.

Perhaps the chief of these was early typography, especially that of Caxton and his successors in England. He communicated many of his results to Mr Blades, who was at this time engaged upon the first edition of his " Life of Caxton," and Mr Blades repaid him in the same coin. Bradshaw's correspondence with Mr Blades extends over a period of twenty-five years. The earliest letters I have found are dated 1857, when Bradshaw was only twenty-six years old. He was already deep in the minutiæ of Caxton typography. The correspondence was particularly active during the autumn of 1860 and the spring of 1861. In September of the former year Mr Blades paid a visit to Cambridge, taking with him the first two sheets of his book in type, and the rest in manuscript. It was a fine, warm afternoon, and after dinner—they dined earlier in those days than now—they went down, as Bradshaw was fond of doing, into the college garden. A bottle of wine was ordered out, and there and then, without moving from the place, Mr Blades read the whole of the historical portion of the book to his willing listener, who frequently interposed criticisms and suggestions of the most useful kind.

For several months after this visit Bradshaw's letters to Mr Blades were very frequent. He was busy with the early printed books in the University Library, and was making fresh discoveries from day to day. His letters are full of new typographical facts, of minute observation and ingenious suggestion, all of which he placed with open-handed generosity at Mr Blades' service. Writing in August, 1860, he says, " I fear a lucid style is what I must cultivate more, but I trust you will be able to unravel what I have written. . . . You must remember that all my inferences are drawn from the incomplete collection in our own library, and therefore are liable to be corrected by the inferences you draw from having such much fuller collections to go to. My grand object is to render our collection just so complete that a person may be able to see at one glance all the early varieties of our English type."

It was by no means the case, however, as might be inferred from the above extract, that Bradshaw confined his attention to the University Library. His letters themselves show that he was already well acquainted with the college libraries in Cambridge, with the British Museum, the Bodleian, and many others. He was not satisfied till he had searched with his own hands and eyes for everything that could aid him in classifying and describing the books in the Cambridge collection. He visited many private libraries too. "Why did you not tell me," he writes to Mr Blades in June, 1861, " of the magnificent copy of the 'Propositio Johannis Russell' in the library at Holkham? It is the only Caxton they have, certainly, but then, it was so unexpected and so large, etc., that it quite took my

breath away." "I did not mention the Holkham Propositio," replied Mr Blades, "simply because I had never even
dreamed of such a treasure being there. It would have
'riled' the old Earl Spencer dreadfully to have heard that
his copy was not unique." This great example of Caxton's
press was known at Holkham, the Rev. Alexander Napier
has informed me, some time before this, but it was not
known to the world at large. Mr Blades congratulated
Bradshaw on his "discovery," for such it practically was,
as far as Mr Blades himself and Caxtonians in general
were concerned. Bradshaw, however, with characteristic
modesty, disclaimed any credit. "You may say you are
indebted to me for a notice of it, but it is not my discovery,
as it is in a modern binding by itself, and was shown to me
by the librarian as one of the greatest curiosities at Holkham." Shortly afterwards Bradshaw writes, in September,
1861, "I had the satisfaction of discovering at the Museum
on Thursday, that their unique copy of the first English
Psalter (1530 : 16mo) is the copy which was stolen from our
library some years ago."

The first volume of Mr Blades' work on Caxton was
published in 1861. Writing to Bradshaw in May, 1861, Mr
Blades says, "Your acceptance of the accompanying volume
will give me sincere pleasure, and afford me another opportunity of thanking you for the very great assistance you
have afforded me in my researches. That assistance has,
I believe, been more immediately connected with the
bibliographical and typographical aspect of Caxton's art
than with the personal history of the printer, and as such
I hope freely to acknowledge it in vol. ii. In the mean time,
I look forward to your strictures upon the contents of
vol. i., and hope to profit by them should a reprint ever be
undertaken by me." When the second volume was going
through the press, Bradshaw undertook, at Mr Blades'
request, to revise the proof-sheets, and actually revised the

first two or three. "Do not scruple," he writes in December, 1861, "to be as importunate as you can. I sometimes need stirring up, but you will, at any rate, see that I have not been idle on your behalf. You must remember that my remarks are only my criticisms freely enough given *before* printing, that you may have the means of judging for yourself; otherwise I should not have the face to send the proofs back with such a mess of ink on them. If you like me to correct the sheet again, I will do it in no time, as there will then be nothing to investigate." That his criticisms were of great use is clear from Mr Blades' letters. Unfortunately, this assistance was only given for a few of the sheets. Circumstances and habit proved too strong for Bradshaw. "He kept the proofs so long," says Mr Blades, "that I was compelled to go to press without waiting for him, a proceeding in which he quite agreed." No doubt, his habitual dilatoriness was chiefly to blame for this; but his notions of accuracy and responsibility were such that correcting a sheet cost him nearly as much trouble as writing it. To send back a proof with his *imprimatur* on it without having verified so far as possible every statement in it, was more than he could accustom himself to do. Accordingly, after several failures to get anything more in the way of answer or correction out of him, Mr Blades was obliged for a time to drop the correspondence.

With all this devotion to learning and research, Bradshaw never forgot his duties to the college. During his whole life at Cambridge he took an active part and exercised an important influence in college politics, but this influence was perhaps never more important than in the critical period of transition which followed his return from St Columba's. He was elected dean in 1857, and retained the office till 1865. As dean he was necessarily a member of the Educational Council, which, in the interval between the statutes of 1861 and those of 1882, managed the educa-

tional affairs of the college. In 1863 he was appointed
prælector, or "father," of the college, in which capacity it
was his duty to present candidates for degrees, and generally to superintend the relations of the junior members
with the university. He held this office till 1868. There
was at this time no tutor at King's. The first of many
letters from Dean Blakesley which I have found among
Bradshaw's papers begins with the words, "My son informs
me that you fill at King's the position which is occupied at
other colleges by the tutor." According to a paper in
Bradshaw's handwriting, "the duties of a tutor, as they
exist at other colleges, are here at King's performed by the
following persons :—the provost, the vice-provost, the bursar,
the prælector, the butler, and the cook." This may have
been the formal state of things, but what are generally
understood to be tutorial duties were certainly discharged
by Bradshaw. He was for a considerable time almost the
only link between the authorities of the college and its
younger members. A long series of letters shows that he
was consulted on all sorts of topics, and that for many
years hardly any matter of educational importance was
settled in which he did not have a hand.

His official relations with the undergraduates were very
amicable. There were not many rules to be kept, though
in some respects discipline was more exacting than it is
now. Attendance at chapel both morning and evening
was the rule when Bradshaw himself entered the college.
By the time when he became dean, one chapel a day was
considered sufficient. The fact that the college had till
lately consisted of "a provost and seventy scholars," that
all came from the same school, and that the youngest
resident looked forward with certainty to becoming in three
years a Fellow of the college, had at all events one good
result. It prevented the formation of a gulf between dons
and undergraduates, and produced a community of feeling

which is still and, it may be hoped, will long remain a
distinctive feature of the place.   The existence of this
feeling made Bradshaw's task less onerous than it would
otherwise have been.   One who was an undergraduate at
the time writes to me as follows :—" His duties towards us
were mainly confined to the receipt of the formal excuses
for absence from morning chapel, which ran thus:
'Matutinis precibus non interfui, vespertinis interfuturus.'
He treated us almost, if not quite, as if we were on his own
level.   In some respects this was successful, as it engendered
an unwillingness to do anything that would hurt his feelings ; on the other hand, he could not pull us up sharply, on
the few occasions that required it, after letting the reins
hang loose so long.   I remember once his catching a man
coming in about 5 a.m.'; the only result was that he shut
himself up in his room for two or three days, inaccessible
to all.   Once only he was downright savage : it was when
some one 'unsported' him [that is, opened his outer door]
with a dinner-knife."

He had already begun to form those lifelong attachments to junior members of the community which followed
one another in an unbroken series for thirty years.   The
discussions respecting the new statutes, which became law
in 1861, displayed and strengthened his influence with his
contemporaries and seniors.   The rules under which the
college had existed for more than four centuries were at this
time undergoing radical changes at the hand of the university commissioners.   The college meetings summoned
to discuss these changes were frequent and prolonged, and
the private debates were at least equally lengthy.   In all that
went on Bradshaw took an active part.   He was strongly in
favour of a liberal policy with regard to scholarships and
fellowships.   I have been informed by a contemporary that
he displayed much courage in asserting his opinions, though
by no means always pleasing to the majority, and that his

efforts, though he was one of the juniors, produced much effect. The tendency to pay excessive regard to "vested interests," naturally powerful in a collegiate body, was one to which he was all his life opposed. The details of college history are not likely to be interesting to many readers, but one point may be mentioned. It was a difficult question how best to effect the transition from the old system, under which every one who entered King's became a Fellow as a matter of course, to the new scheme, under which the Fellowships were to be reduced from seventy to forty-six, and to be obtained by competition. It was held by many members of the college that an injustice would be done to the existing scholars if the competitive system were introduced at once. Bradshaw, if he did not actually originate, had at least the chief share in devising and formulating a compromise by which the difficulty was satisfactorily overcome.

Bradshaw's attitude in these discussions was characteristic. In regard to the affairs of the university or of any institution with which he was connected, he was neither optimist nor pessimist, but—to use a word which has the sanction of George Eliot—a meliorist. He always refused to disbelieve in the possibility of making things better. His reverence for the past and his consideration for others made him averse from needless alterations and from petty tinkering, but he had no instinctive fear or dislike of change. If he saw a possible improvement, and felt convinced that it was for the general good, he would push it without pausing to consider its effect upon his own interests, or even those of his most intimate friends. That this was so on this occasion is proved by his letters to several undergraduate friends whose chances of promotion were gravely endangered by the impending reforms. In these letters he explained quite clearly the effect which would be produced on the position of his correspondents by the changes for which he intended to vote, never fearing for an instant that

he would forfeit their friendship by voting for what he considered best.   But, reformer as he was, he was at once politic
and generous.   He endeavoured to arouse as few antipathies
as possible, and to allow to existing interests their legitimate, though not more than their legitimate, weight.   A
contemporary writes of his conduct at this time, "I remember being struck by the way in which he always tried
to get at the element of right, however small, which he
held must exist in every man's mind, no matter how
extortionate his claim.   He would say, ' The way so-and-
so looks at it is this,' and then, putting himself into the
other man's place, do full justice to his views."   It was this
combination of fairness, unselfishness, and judgment that
gave him such weight in the counsels of his college, and, on
the few occasions when he interfered in them, in those of
the university.

In June, 1861, the term of Bradshaw's appointment in
the library came to an end.   The Library Syndicate were
naturally anxious to secure a continuance of his services.
In their report to the Senate they state that " the work in
which Mr Bradshaw has been engaged, under the direction
of the Syndicate, has been carried on in a highly satisfactory
manner," and " as much work of a similar nature remains to
be done, they recommend that Mr Bradshaw be re-engaged
for a period of two years, at a salary of one hundred and
fifty pounds per annum."   The experiment which had been
tried in 1859 had proved completely successful, and the
merely nominal recognition of his services was now turned
into a more respectable though still inadequate compensation.

Nevertheless, he was about this time much in want of
money.   The emoluments of a Fellowship at King's had not
then passed beyond the narrow limit to which they have
unfortunately since that time returned.   Bradshaw had, as
we see from letters already quoted, made great additions

to his Irish library. Mr Quaritch tells me he bought largely from him during this period. Sometimes his superior knowledge enabled him in these cases to make a good bargain. He once bought from Mr Quaritch for a few shillings a copy of the first edition of the New Testament in Irish printed in Ireland. This transaction gave him much pleasure, and he used to quiz his friend the bookseller about his mistake for twenty years afterwards. In other cases he was undoubtedly extravagant, as when, in 1861, he bought one of the only two copies on vellum of Mr Quaritch's reprint of Carve's " Itinerary." He had also large dealings with Mr Boone, Mr Stewart, Mr Ellis, and other "antiquarian" booksellers. With most of these his relations were by no means only those of business ; he was on terms of intimacy and friendship with them, for common interests brought them together. His bibliographical knowledge not unfrequently enabled him to render them services, which they repaid by giving him the first chance of rare books, or in other ways. In later times he used to lament that the old race of booksellers, the men who knew and loved their books, like Mr C. J. Stewart, was all but extinct. But these pleasant acquaintances were, no doubt, conducive to considerable expenditure, and however parsimoniously he lived in other respects, he clearly bought more books than he could afford. His frequent journeys must also have carried away no small part of his income.

The result was that he was forced to take a step which was very painful to him at the time, and which he never ceased to regret. Not long before this date he had announced to Dr Todd his intention of handing over his library to a public body. "Your noble proposal," writes Dr Todd in March, 1857, "of ultimately depositing your collection of Irish books in the academy, will, be assured, prove most acceptable, and will cause your name to be honoured here as a benefactor to Ireland." Eventually the

G

greater part of these books, as we shall see, found another
home, but he was now compelled to bring a number of
them to the hammer.   He at first intended to part with
only a few, but eventually he determined, no doubt after
a painful struggle, to get rid of a great part of his library.
Writing to his brother-in-law, Mr Daniell, on January 9,
1862, he says, "K. will have told you what I told her
when I last saw her in October, about my determination to
get rid of my books, at least a portion of those which I
have been weak enough to buy during the past eight years,
and I have to-day sent off to Mr Boone the last of twenty
large cases containing rather more than two thousand
volumes, which will, I hope, be sold at Sotheby's as soon as
possible.   It is a great wrench, as you will readily believe ;
but the incubus has been so great that it is a relief to have
sent them off.   I have not sent off a stick of what my
father left me, but only the best and choicest of those I
have bought myself. ; . . For the last two years I have
been paying and paying, and have never had anything in
my purse. . . . My two years and a half at the library
without any pay were anything but encouraging, and I
almost wonder how I managed ; but now that I have begun
to receive my £150 a year from that, I am already feeling
lighter. . . . The books cannot well bring less than £200,
and they ought to bring much more."   They were sold at
Sotheby's in July, 1862, "as the property of a gentleman,"
and realized a nett receipt of £136—a ridiculous price.
Carve's "Itinerary" fetched only £5 15s. 5d., and his "Lyra"
only £3 5s. ; other rarities went for equally absurd sums.
Well might Mr Boone express his astonishment that the
University Library should have made no effort to prevent
such books from leaving Cambridge.   Bradshaw was so disgusted with the result of the sale that he formed a resolution never again to part with any books by auction, and
adhered to it.   More than twenty years later, when some

one recommended him to part with some of his treasures, he wrote, "As for realising money, I have had enough of selling books. I never did it but once, and I got just six-pence a volume for every pound that I gave, sometimes less. This was a sufficient dose."

Soon after the renewal of his appointment at the University Library he was requested by Dr Smith, who was then proposing a scheme for a new Biographia Britannica, to write some lives for the intended work. This was the first, I believe, of several similar proposals made to him from time to time ; but he never did much in this way, and it was perhaps well that he did not attempt it. He was too conscientious in his own work, and too sceptical about the accuracy of others, to publish anything of the truth of which he had not convinced himself by original investiga-tion. The amount of labour which he would therefore have gone through in order to write a short article for a publication of this kind would have been hardly commen-surate with the result. He was, in fact, too busy with his researches in the library, and too much occupied in going over new ground, to be able to spend time on work of this kind. He contributed much to the catalogue of manuscripts then in progress. Dr Luard, writing to him in October, 1861, says, "I am sure if all the assistance you have rendered to me and others in the course of the publication [of the catalogue] were paid for, no share in the amount paid by the Library Syndicate would compare with what you would have earned."

During the early months of 1862 he was actively engaged on the Oriental manuscripts. He mastered the elements of Sanscrit, Arabic, and other Eastern languages, so far as was necessary for the purpose of cataloguing. He writes to Mr Blades in February, 1862, "Except a few minutes given to you, I have been collating Sanscrit and Arabic books all day. We have just got a large parcel

from Calcutta, and I am almost tired of the sight of them."
Such was the multifarious character of his work.

In the spring of 1862 Bradshaw made one of the
most interesting and important of his many discoveries,
that of the long-lost Vaudois manuscripts. These manuscripts had been brought to England and deposited in
the University Library by Samuel Morland, Cromwell's
envoy to the Duke of Savoy. The persecution of the
Vaudois Protestants will be remembered as having occasioned one of Milton's most famous sonnets. Cromwell
sent Morland to the duke in the year 1655, in order
to induce him to put a stop to the persecution. It is
matter of history that the mission failed, but that Cromwell
succeeded in extorting from the duke by means of French
intervention what he was unable to obtain by a direct
appeal. Morland's journey was not, however, altogether
fruitless. On his return to England he brought with him
a number of books and documents which, at Archbishop
Ussher's suggestion, he had collected while in Savoy·
These records formed the basis of his " History of the
Evangelical Churches of the Valleys of Piedmont," and
of much that has since been written on the subject. Some
of them are in the Ussher collection in the library of
Trinity College, Dublin ; but the larger and more valuable
portion was, according to Morland's own statement, presented in 1648 " to the Public Library of the famous
University of Cambridge," where the books have remained
ever since.

The manuscripts so deposited were marked by the
letters of the alphabet from A to W. The first six of them
possessed special interest. They contained translations
of portions of the Bible, religious treatises, and poems,
the earliest remains of the Waldensian language and
literature. The manuscripts themselves were said by
Morland to date from the thirteenth century ; the originals

he supposed to be much older. One poem, entitled " La Nobla Leyçon," or " The Noble Lesson," contained, according to Morland, the following couplet :—

> " Ben ha mil e cent an compli entierament
> Que fo scripta lora, car son al derier temp ; "

that is, " There are already a thousand and one hundred years fully accomplished since it was written thus, for we are in the last time." These lines appeared to fix the date of the original poem at the beginning of the twelfth century. Two other copies of the poem, preserved in manuscript at Dublin and Geneva, gave the same reading. These manuscripts were, indeed, declared by experts to be not earlier than the fifteenth century, but there was no reason why they should not have been copied from twelfth-century originals. The lines in question were the more important, since, according to Mr Algernon Herbert,* "the only date really exhibited in the text and body of any Waldensian document whatsoever is that in ' The Noble Lesson.' " Other evidence for the high antiquity of these records was entirely external. A great point was made of this date by those who wished to show that in the southern valleys of the Alps there existed a Protestantism of the Genevan type four hundred years before Calvin. The whole history of the Vaudois was influenced by this belief, and was brought into confused connection with the Albigensian movement in the south of France. On the other hand, Dr Todd and Mr Algernon Herbert distinguished the Vaudois movement from that of Peter Waldo, which was declared heretical in 1183, and maintained that the " Pauperes de Lugduno," as Waldo's followers called themselves, had little or nothing in common with the Vaudois Protestants. In the discussion of this question the date of " The Noble

---

* British Magazine, vols. xviii., xix. : cf. Dr. Todd's " Books of the Vaudois " (1865), p. 93 (note).

Lesson" was a matter of primary importance. No one suspected that it was incorrect. Those who doubted the antiquity of the poem only sought to show from internal evidence that it could not be so old as was supposed, or attempted to make the line containing the date mean something quite different from its obvious signification. Evidently a great deal depended on the genuineness of the reading in the manuscripts which Morland had brought from Savoy.

Unfortunately, these precious little books had disappeared. It was not even certain, in spite of Morland's assertion, that they had ever been deposited in the University Library : at all events, no one knew where they were. Dr Gilly, in his "Waldensian Researches," 1838, speaks of them as having "been removed nobody knows how or where." The catalogue of manuscripts, of which the first volume was published in 1856, described the rest of the Morland collection (Dd. iii. 25–38) as "Waldensian manuscripts, presented together with other and more ancient but *now missing* documents," to the University of Cambridge. Various theories were invented to account for their disappearance. Some maintained that these invaluable testimonies to the antiquity of Protestantism had been spirited away by the Romanists in the days of James II. Others believed that the Puritans, fearing for their safety after the Restoration, had secretly conveyed them away to some safe hiding-place, where they probably lay forgotten. A third theory, strongly supported by Mr Algernon Herbert, was that they had been destroyed by Morland himself or his confederates, on discovering that they could not pass muster as manuscripts of the age ascribed to them. "A deep and ugly suspicion," says Mr Herbert, "hangs over all the dealings of these people with the books." Fortunately, all these ingenious hypotheses were superfluous. In the printed catalogue of 1856 six little volumes (Dd. iii. 29–34) are described, but the authors of the catalogue, following in this respect Nasmith's earlier list, classed them as Spanish. No one thought anything about them ; they were, as a later volume of the catalogue says, " considered to be of no interest or value." Yet these uninteresting little Spanish books turned out to be the missing Vaudois manuscripts.

Bradshaw, when he came to examine the older catalogues, found that the books were in the library as late as 1689. It was possible that, after all, they might be there still. He set to work to look for them, and he was successful. Whether he was guided in his search by a suspicion that the catalogue was incorrect, or whether he was simply following his usual plan of taking down every volume from the shelves and turning over every page, I do not know. At all events, he found the books.

" It will be readily believed," he says in March, 1862, in a paper read before the Cambridge Antiquarian Society, "that it was with some pleasure and some surprise that I laid my hand upon the whole of these volumes a few weeks ago. In the same binding as the rest of the documents—three of them with Morland's and the donors' names and the date on the first page, all six with the reference-letters A, B, C, D, E, F clearly written inside the cover, and all standing on the shelves as near to the ' documents ' [the rest of the collection] as the difference of size would allow—the only wonder is how they could ever have been lost sight of."

His work did not, however, end here. A few minutes' examination of the books disclosed the fact that they were by no means of so early a date as was supposed. In the passage from " The Noble Lesson " already quoted, which was thought to establish the early date beyond dispute, Bradshaw found an erasure before the word " cent," and by the aid of a glass detected the remains of an

Arabic 4. More than this, in another manuscript of the same collection, hitherto entirely unknown, was a fragment of the same poem, in which the line was written in a slightly different form, thus :

"Ben ha mil e. cccc. anz compli entierament."

It was thus placed beyond doubt that the date of the poem was the fifteenth instead of the twelfth century. A similar fate befel another manuscript, supposed to have been written in 1230, which Bradshaw showed to contain an allusion to Wyclif, and to be not earlier than the beginning of the fifteenth century. Under these blows the foundation, on which the supposed antiquity of Waldensian Calvinism had so largely rested, crumbled away. The philological importance of the change of date need hardly be pointed out.*

These discoveries naturally provoked some resentment on the part of supporters of the theories which they overthrew, and doubts were thrown on Bradshaw's conclusions. But the best authorities accepted them. Dr Maitland, the well-known author of "The Dark Ages," in a very characteristic letter to Bradshaw, dated March 18, 1862, says, "The matter is most wonderful, and most particularly interesting to me, and not the least wonderful part of the business is that the librarian should not, by some accident, have fallen in with the volumes. You will suppose naturally that I have a fellow-feeling for librarians, and I really write without ever knowing who might be to blame, or assuming any right to judge them ; but really, as between themselves, fellow-feeling is quite used up in forbearance, and charity almost choked with holding its tongue. . . . I hope you have told my

* The above account is partly taken from the paper read by Bradshaw before the Cambridge Antiquarian Society, on March 10, 1862, and printed in its Communications, vol. ii. p. 203, partly from Dr Todd's "Books of the Vaudois," 1865, and elsewhere.

old friend Dr Todd. If not too late, may I take the liberty to suggest that it should be communicated to him with great care and consideration, lest it should throw him into fits ? But, seriously, I hope you will make known the discovery to the public, or at least to such part of the public as can be brought to care about historic truth." A year latter, Sir George Cornewall Lewis, in thanking Bradshaw for sending him a copy of the paper which he read before the Cambridge Antiquarian Society, says, " The discovery is an important one. . . . The date of the ' Nobla Leyçon ' seems to be fixed, on unquestionable evidence, to a year subsequent to 1400 A.D."

During the early summer of 1862 Bradshaw spent some time at Oxford, and worked hard in the Bodleian. He writes from Christchurch to an undergraduate friend, " Oxford is extremely pleasant just now. . . . This is the first time I have seen anything like full term here ; though you will say that working in the Bodleian from nine till four is not the way to see much of Oxford life." The greater part of the Long Vacation he spent in a long ramble on the Continent with his friend S. R. Crotch of St John's. Crotch was an enthusiastic naturalist, and possessed perhaps the finest collection of Coleoptera in the kingdom, a collection which he had for the most part made himself, not only in this country, but in Spain, Madeira, and elsewhere. He was in many respects a very original and striking character, with a great turn for philosophy and abstract speculation, but at the same time a strong grasp of facts and details however minute. His eyesight and observation were so acute, and his memory for nomenclature so retentive, that I have seen him name and describe without hesitation a great number of insects placed at random in a box, and at a distance at which ordinary eyes could hardly distinguish any characteristics at all. This kind of power had great attraction for Bradshaw, who himself possessed the

same qualities, except that of long sight, to a remarkable
extent. Crotch was eccentric in his habits, utterly careless
of conventionalities, affectionate, and lavishly generous.
His only accomplishment, in the ordinary sense of the
term, was that of being a remarkable gymnast. He was
a great friend of the late Professor Clifford, and they used
to practise gymnastics together. In 1866 he received a
temporary appointment in the University Library, and in
October, 1867, when a second assistant librarianship was
created, he obtained the post. He resigned in 1871, and
some time afterwards went to America in company with
Professor Clifford. He travelled widely in the United
States for some time, hunting beetles in California and elsewhere, with an ardour and recklessness which ruined his
health. On one of his expeditions he exposed himself to
such privations that he fell into a consumption, and died
on June 16, 1874.

The enthusiasm and thoroughness which Crotch displayed in his scientific pursuits first filled Bradshaw with
that respect for natural science, its votaries, and its
methods which he cherished to the end of his life. He told
more than one of his friends that he learnt from Crotch's
way of dealing with his insects much that was useful to him
in his own bibliographical and typographical studies, and
that under his influence he assimilated his own methods
more closely to those of natural science.

With this friend he travelled over a great part of
Europe in the summer of 1862. He passed through
Germany into Austria, doing a good deal of work in the
libraries of Vienna and Prague. Thence he went on to
Denmark and Sweden. He was abroad for two months,
but one of his anti-epistolary fits was on him ; at all events,
the only letter from him during this period which I have
been able to discover is one written to Mr Blades from
Lund, in Sweden, from which I give some extracts.

"Being in Sweden, I wish immensely I çould afford to go on to 'Stockholm and Upsala,' and see the second copy of the 'Laurentius de Saona,' but I cannot do it now. However, I hope to be again in Sweden before very long. I have never been anywhere except the country parts of France before this summer, and I have not had once more than a fortnight's holiday from Cambridge since I went up to reside there in the spring of 1856, so that it was getting absolutely necessary for me to have a run somewhere. So I have been through Leipzig and Dresden to Prague and Vienna. Here [at Vienna] I amused myself for nearly a fortnight. It is the most delightful place I ever was in, but for me the library is a particularly inconvenient one to use, as they will not on any account allow you access to the catalogues, which for my purposes renders the place next to useless. However, I saw the Caxtons, as far as they knew they had any. . . . They are all in the condition which I most dislike, or very nearly all—patched copies in gorgeous bindings. From Vienna I came back to Prague; from that to Berlin, where, however, I did not see the library ; and thence to Hamburg, where I had a great treat. The library is most conveniently arranged, and the early printed books are all put in order of place and date. No English or Bruges books, however, appear to be there. From that we came on to Copenhagen, and, having been there for nearly a week, we finally settled here. . . . I like the royal library at Copenhagen immensely ; there too everything is nationally arranged, and they allow you free use of the catalogues. I shall go there again when I return, but, as far as I could learn, they have but one Caxton there, the 'Mirror of the World.' I am learning Swedish like anything here. No one here, except a few of the students, who are now away, speaks anything but his own language, though, as might be expected, English is commonly taught as a part of education. This, however, is literary English, and, as every one knows, you may be able to read a language freely, and yet not have a word to say when a person talks to you. The intense nationality of these northern countries is astonishing. Except the mild form of it which tries to exist in Ireland, I have never met with anything of the kind. Their libraries are all arranged on the same principle, Swedish and non-Swedish, Danish and non-Danish. It is very convenient, of course, in many respects."

In the above letter, Bradshaw speaks of learning Swedish. When he and his friend arrived at Lund, they could neither of them speak a word of that language, and they had not the advantage of knowing German. The first thing they did was to buy a dictionary and a grammar and several newspapers. With these they shut themselves up at the hotel, and worked hard for a day and a half, at the end of which Bradshaw was able to make himself tolerably well understood. He afterwards took lessons in Swedish, and learnt enough to be able to read it for his own purposes.

In the early part of 1863, Bradshaw, who abstained from public discussions in general, took some part in a controversy about the authenticity of the Codex Sinaiticus, which made considerable stir in the learned world at that time. This precious document, now generally recognized as the most ancient manuscript of the Bible, was discovered by Dr Tischendorf in 1859, in the monastery of St Catharine on Mount Sinai. The controversy about it, now well-nigh forgotten, is sufficiently amusing to make it worth while to recall its more important passages. One Simonides, a *Græculus esuriens*, who had some time before been convicted by Dr Tischendorf of endeavouring to palm off forged manuscripts, gave out, apparently in order to revenge himself, that the Codex Sinaiticus was itself a forgery. He declared that he had written it with his own hands when a young man. This "whimsical story," as Dr Hort calls it

obtained a certain amount of credence. During the autumn
of 1862 and the early part of 1863 a correspondence was
carried on in the *Guardian* on the subject. In the
number of that paper for September 3, 1862, is a long letter
from Simonides, purporting to give an account of how he
came to write the manuscript and how it passed into the
possession of the monks of Sinai. "Any person learned in
palæography," he remarks, "ought to be able to tell at once
that it is a manuscript of the present age," and he concludes, with an amusing air of injured innocence, "You
must permit me to express my sincere regret that, whilst
the many valuable remains of antiquity in my possession
are frequently attributed to my own hands, the one poor
work of my youth is set down by a gentleman who enjoys
a great reputation for learning, as the earliest copy of the
Sacred Scriptures." The story of Simonides was ingenious
and full of circumstantial details, but it contained statements which, when carefully examined, carried with them
their own refutation. Its absurdities were exposed by Mr
Aldis Wright, in a letter published in the *Guardian* for
November 5, 1862. A month later, a letter appeared in
the *Guardian*, purporting to be written by one Kallinikos
Hieromonachos, who wrote in defence of Simonides. His
letter was in Greek, and a translation was appended by the
editor, who made no concealment of his suspicions. "I
have read," says the unknown writer, "what the wise Greek
Simonides has published respecting the pseudo-Sinaitic
Codex by means of your excellent weekly publication, and
I too myself declare to all men by this letter that the
Codex . . . which was abstracted by Dr Tischendorf from
the Greek monastery of Mount Sinai, is a work of the hands
of the unwearied Simonides himself, inasmuch as I myself
saw him in 1840, in the month of February, writing it in
Athos." In the next number Simonides writes to back up
his friend. "I must inform you," he says, "that the above-

mentioned Kallinikos is a perfectly upright and honourable man, well known for truth and probity, so that his simplest word may be relied on."

Mr Aldis Wright had little difficulty in disposing of his advocacy, and involving Simonides in a tissue of inconsistencies and improbabilities. "What does the evidence amount to?" he asks. "Kallinikos says, 'Simonides wrote the Codex, for I saw him.' 'Believe Kallinikos,' says Simonides, 'for he saw me write it.' We know Simonides, but who is Kallinikos?" Unfortunately, no proof of his existence, much less of his probity, was forthcoming. "His story," says Mr Haddan, in a letter to Bradshaw, "reminds me of an Irish lad from Connemara, who sent his regards to a man who had been fishing there, with the said lad to help, and begged him to tell the Londoners 'any number or weight of fish he liked,' as having been caught by him, and he would be ready and delighted to swear to it." The British chaplain at Alexandria knew nothing of Kallinikos, "the Greek monk who takes in the *Guardian* and the *Literary Churchman.*" In vain did Simonides attempt to strengthen his case by publishing several more letters from Kallinikos. Strange to say, one correspondent of the *Guardian*, at least, appears to have thought that a repetition of unsupported assertions constituted a proof, but the majority were less easily convinced. Mr Haddan urged Bradshaw to interfere. In a letter dated November 19, 1862, he says, "You could really do a service to truth if you would put upon paper the results of your examination of the Codex, and let it be published, with or without your name. . . . The question is really important, and *you* could throw light upon it." To this Bradshaw replied that he thought the time was not yet ripe for discussing the palæographical part of the question.

However, Simonides returned to the charge, and in a

long letter to the *Guardian* (January 21, 1863) stated, among other facts tending to prove his capacity for writing the Codex, that he had written a letter in uncial characters to Mr Bradshaw a few months before, when he was staying at Cambridge during the meeting of the British Association. This produced the following letter from Bradshaw, published in the *Guardian* for January 28, 1863 :—

"SIR,

"As Dr Simonides has cited a letter which he wrote to me in uncial characters in October last, while he was at Cambridge, and as I have with my own eyes seen and examined the Codex Sinaiticus within the last few months, perhaps you will allow me to say a few words.

"The note which Dr Simonides wrote to me was to convince me and my friends that it was quite possible for him to have written the volume in question, and to confirm his assertion that the uncial character of the manuscript was as familiar and easy to him to write as the common cursive hand of the present day.

"He had invited some of us to Christ's College to examine his papyri and to discuss matters fairly. He could speak and understand English pretty well, but his friend was with him to interpret and explain. They first taxed us with believing in the antiquity of manuscripts solely on the authority of one man like Tischendorf, and they really seemed to believe that all people in the West were as ignorant of Greek as the Greeks are of Latin. But the great question was, 'How do you satisfy yourselves of the genuineness of any manuscript?' I first replied that it was really difficult to define; that it seemed to be more a kind of instinct than anything else. Dr Simonides and his friend readily caught at this as too much like vague assertion, and they naturally

ridiculed any such idea. But I further said that I had
lived for six years past in the constant, almost daily,
habit of examining manuscripts—not merely the text
of the works contained in the volumes, but the volumes
themselves as such ; the writing, the paper or parchment,
the arrangement or numbering of the sheets, the distinction between the original volume and any additional
matter by later hands, etc. ; and that, with experience
of this kind, though it might be difficult to assign the
special ground of my confidence, yet I hardly ever found
myself deceived even by a very well-executed facsimile.
All this Dr Simonides allowed and confirmed.   He
gave the instance of the Jews in the East, who could
in an instant tell the exact proportion of foreign matter
in a bottle of otto of roses, where the most careful chemical
analysis might fail to detect the same.   Indeed, any
tradesman acquires the same sort of experience with
regard to the quality of the particular goods which are
daily passing through his hands ; and this is all that
I claimed for myself.   Dr Simonides afterwards told
me himself that this was the only safe method of judging,
that there was no gainsaying such evidence, and that
he only fought against persons who made strong and
vague assertions without either proof or experience. Yet
when I told him that I had seen the Codex Sinaiticus,
he spoke as if bound in honour not to allow in this
case the value of that very criterion which he had before
confessed to be the surest ; and he wrote me the letter
to which he refers, in the hope of convincing me.   I
told him as politely as I could that I was not to be
convinced against the evidence of my senses.

"On the 18th of July last I was at Leipzig with a
friend, and we called on Professor Tischendorf.   Though
I had no introduction but my occupation at Cambridge,
nothing could exceed his kindness ; we were with him

for more than two hours, and I had the satisfaction of examining the manuscript after my own fashion. I had been anxious to know whether it was written in even continuous quaternions throughout, like the Codex Bezæ, or in a series of fasciculi each ending with a quire of varying size, as the Codex Alexandrinus, and I found the latter to be the case. This, by-the-by, is of itself sufficient to prove that it cannot be the volume which Dr Simonides speaks of having written at Mount Athos.

"Now, it must be remembered that Dr Simonides always maintained two points—first, that the Mount Athos Bible written in 1840 for the Emperor of Russia was not meant to deceive any one, but was only a beautiful specimen of writing in the old style, in the character used by the writer in his letter to me; secondly, that it was Professor Tischendorf's ignorance and inexperience which rendered him so easily deceived where no deception was intended. For the second assertion, no words of mine are needed to accredit an editor of such long standing as Professor Tischendorf. For the first, though a carefully made facsimile of a few leaves inserted among several genuine ones might for a time deceive even a well-practised eye, yet it is utterly impossible that a book merely written in the antique style, and without any intent to deceive, should mislead a person of moderate experience. For myself, I have no hesitation in saying that I am as absolutely certain of the genuineness and antiquity of the Codex Sinaiticus as I am of my own existence. Indeed, I cannot hear of any one who has seen the book who thinks otherwise. Let any one go to St Petersburg and satisfy himself. Let Dr Simonides go there and examine it. He can never have seen it himself, or I am sure that, with his knowledge of manuscripts, he would be the first to agree with me. The Mount Athos Bible must be a totally different book;

and I only regret, for the sake of himself and his many friends in England, that he has been led on, from knowing that his opponents here have seen no more of the original book than he has himself, to make such rash and contradictory assertions, that sober people are almost driven to think that the Greek is playing with our matter-of-fact habits of mind, and that, as soon as he has tired out his opponents, he will come forward and ask his admirers for a testimonial to his cleverness.

" HENRY BRADSHAW.

"Cambridge, January 26, 1863."

It will be observed that Bradshaw had his own reasons for concluding that Simonides had not written the Codex which was in Dr Tischendorf's possession. No one else, apparently, had as yet called attention to the peculiar construction of the book itself. But he confines himself carefully to the particular point at issue. He does not trouble himself about the truth of the story told by Simonides ; he only declares that, assuming Simonides to have written such a book as he pretends, this book cannot be identical with the Codex Sinaiticus. This, after all, was the only question of real importance.

The controversy was continued for some time longer, but no fresh facts concerning the manuscript were elucidated, though several were published of a character damaging to Simonides. It eventually appeared that there *was* such a person as Kallinikos Hieromonachos, and that he lived in the monastery on Mount Sinai. But when requested to state whether he had written the letters which Simonides attributed to him, he at once replied that he had never written the letters, and that Simonides had never been at the monastery. Simonides rejoined that his friend was Kallinikos of Athos, and that he had nothing to do with Kallinikos of Sinai. Some time later he produced another letter from *his* Kallinikos, dated from Rhodes, which simply reiterated the previous statements. In the same number of the *Guardian* (November 11, 1863) in which this letter appeared, there appeared also a series of answers obtained by Mr Aldis Wright, through the medium of the British Consul at Salonica, from the Archimandrite Dionysius of the monastery of Xeropotami, on Mount Athos. These answers proved that Simonides in his original story had told a pack of lies. Benedict, whom he called his uncle and declared to have been the head of the convent, never held that position, and was not in any way related to him. Simonides himself had been twice at the convent, but on the last occasion so annoyed the monks with his random talk and disorderly behaviour that they sent him about his business. These damaging disclosures were soon afterwards confirmed, and other things equally discreditable brought to light, by Amphilochus, Bishop of Pelusium. With this the matter closed, and Simonides, who died hard and to the very end was supported by a few dupes of his ingenious mendacity, finally disappeared from view.

In the spring of 1863 Bradshaw's correspondence with Mr Blades entered on another phase of activity. Early in that year the second volume of Mr Blades' "Life of Caxton" appeared. On March 9 he sent Bradshaw one of the early copies, and wrote, "I feel that I owe you very much indeed, and only regret that distance prevented my having the assistance of your critical eye while *every* sheet was passing through the press. Please make a note of the errors which you are sure to discover, and allow me, when next I have the pleasure of a chat with you, to benefit by them." Bradshaw readily acceded to this request. On April 13 he writes, "I was passing through London the other day, and went into the Museum to look after some stolen goods [*i.e.* books which had once belonged to the Public Library at Cambridge*], and I took the opportunity of looking at one or two other things;" and then he scribbles off a letter of five closely packed sheets, full of minute descriptions and observations. On April 16 Mr Blades writes, "Your first lot of criticism has afforded me plenty of mental food. I value it very much, and almost agree in every deduction. . . . Upon my return I found your second remittance, which I must digest before answering." After going through his criticism in detail, he concludes, "And now for a time adieu, and believe me that no review in the *Athenæum* or *Saturday* will give me half the inward satisfaction that I feel when you tell me that my book has enabled or assisted you to write such a body of sound critical notes as now lies before me." In answer to this letter, Bradshaw writes, "Do not be grieved or disappointed about any mistakes. It is only, as I said before, by having such a book before me constantly, and working from that to the particular copies, that any mistakes can be got rid of. You have done far more than all the others put together have succeeded in doing." And again, "The fact is that it is only by having your book constantly before me that I am able to work out any of the many things which are now becoming daily clearer to me. Every day shows the untold advantage of free access to a really large collection [*i.e.* that of the University Library] of entirely undoctored books—at any rate, books which have not been doctored or bound for one hundred and fifty years. Of course, the collections in the Museum and at Althorp are fuller; but there is hardly a volume in either which is perfectly trustworthy evidence in matters of collation, many having been *made* perfect from other copies, and most having been bound so tightly and washed so clean that it is

* Cf. above, p. 75.

difficult to use them." In March, 1864, he writes to M. Holtrop, " Could you see my copy of Mr Blades' book, you would find every article almost crowded with additions and corrections ; and I always tell Mr Blades that there is no such good evidence of the value of his book."

Several quotations from his letters have already shown that he took a peculiar interest in hunting up books which had once belonged to the University Library, but had disappeared, being lost, stolen, or merely forgotten by the custodians and those who had taken them out. The number of valuable books which were unaccountably missing was very large. Of the three hundred and thirty books mentioned in the catalogue of 1473, Bradshaw was able to find in the library in 1862 only nineteen. This year (1863) he discovered one of his lost treasures in a somewhat remarkable manner. It was a book of great value, a Sarum Breviary, on vellum, in one volume, printed at Venice in 1483. The Cambridge copy was the only one known. This book disappeared from the University Library towards the close of the last century. About the year 1825, the National Library at Paris bought from a Mr Macarthy a Sarum Breviary of 1483. This book Bradshaw believed to be the lost Cambridge copy. In May, 1863, Mr George Williams happened to be visiting Paris, and Bradshaw asked him to look at the book and see if it answered to the description of the lost volume, or possessed the class-mark of the University Library on the first page. Mr Williams wrote back, " I was at the Imperial Library yesterday, and saw the Sarum Breviary. . . . It is a lovely book, quite perfect, in two volumes, bound in French binding of about the beginning of last century. No trace of an erasure on the first page, which is blank, the quire being quite perfect." The book, therefore, he concluded, could not be the Cambridge copy.

Bradshaw, however, was not so easily satisfied. He armed himself with a magnifying-glass, noted the class-mark of the lost book on a slip of paper, and set out for Paris.   When the book was brought to him, he first examined the outside, as was his custom, and his knowledge of bindings told him it was not an early eighteenth-century binding, but a modern imitation.   Then he looked at the beginnings and ends of the volumes. "This book was originally in one volume," he said, "for the beginning of the first volume and the end of the second are soiled and show the impress of the original boards, but the end of the first volume and the beginning of the second are clean."   Then, knowing that the ink used for marking the books in the University Library in the last century was of a peculiar kind, which could not be wholly got rid of without destroying the paper, he looked at the first page with his glass, and found a mark which looked like what he was searching for.   Handing the book and the glass to the assistant, he asked him whether he could see the faint remains of a class-mark there.   "Yes," said the assistant, " I can."   " Is this it ? " said Bradshaw, taking the slip of paper out of his pocket.   And, sure enough, the Cambridge mark appeared dimly on the page. Mr Alexander Macmillan met him immediately on his return, and heard the story from his own lips.   He told it, rubbing his hands with glee, almost as well pleased by finding out what had become of the book as if he had brought it back in his pocket.   In his note-book is the entry, referring to this book, "Sarum Breviary, Venice, 1483.   Leaf 2a has C. 14. remaining of our mark. . . . Early in the sixteenth century some one has written on the last page of text—

> ' Væ tibi qui rapida librum furabere palma,
>   Nam videt antitonans cuncta futura deus.'

So much for Dr Combe's conscience."

In the summer of 1863 the term of Bradshaw's re-appointment in 1861 was coming to an end. The Library Syndicate invited him to make a statement of the work done during the four preceding years, and thereupon made a report to the Senate, which, as an official account of his labours, may be quoted verbatim. The Syndicate says—

"That since Mr Bradshaw's appointment by the Senate in 1861, he has been chiefly occupied with the manuscripts and early printed books, of which the university possesses a large and valuable collection, the extent of which has heretofore been very imperfectly known.

"The manuscript department, especially the valuable collection of Oriental manuscripts collected by Burckhardt in the East, which was reduced to a state of great disorder in the process of their removal from the old library to the new buildings, has been carefully rearranged by Mr Bradshaw, so as to be rendered easily accessible to any one who wishes to consult it. Many volumes have been rebound, and very many more have been subjected to a thorough and systematic bibliographical collation, which has led to the discovery of some curious and valuable literary treasures, the existence of which was before unknown. The same may be said of the early printed books, among which Mr. Bradshaw has found many of very great historical and bibliographical interest, as well as of considerable intrinsic value.

"All the manuscripts are now brought together, of which a large number have remained uncatalogued since the beginning of the last century. All the late Professor Dobree's books have been brought up into the manuscript class and catalogue ; as also those with the manuscript notes of various scholars bought at Hermann's sale, which form an entire class of books in themselves, and are catalogued under the head of Adversaria. A variety of miscellaneous matter, discovered in different parts of the library, has been brought together, arranged, bound, and catalogued.

"The collection of the 'old library' books, temporarily arranged on the upper shelves of the west and north rooms, has been brought into a much more satisfactory state ; and as it was found that a large number of choice and rare books had been lost from the general library, in times past, the remaining specimens of early English literature have been selected from the other books, and placed under safer custody.

"Much, however, still remains to be done, as the process of collation, to be thorough and complete, must necessarily be slow and tedious ; and the crowded condition of the library has hitherto prevented any attempt being made to reclass the manuscripts, or to form a regular collection of the Incunabula and literary curiosities of the University Library ; both which objects, it is hoped, may be carried out in the proposed new buildings.

"We cannot pass over unnoticed the very important assistance which Mr Bradshaw has offered, not only to members of the university, but also to strangers from a distance, who wish to make use of the manuscripts or of the older part of the library of printed books for literary purposes. We believe that the presence in the library of an officer deeply versed in so important a department of bibliography, not commonly studied, reflects credit on the university.

"As we should feel it to be a serious misfortune that the University Library should be deprived of the advantage of Mr Bradshaw's knowledge and experience, we recommend that his services be engaged for a further term of five years, and that his salary be increased to £200 per annum."

The grace giving effect to the above recommendation was passed on June 4, 1863. The Syndicate had proposed as high a stipend as it was in their power to suggest, for the librarian at that time only received two hundred guineas a year. Bradshaw's position could now be regarded as established. He had no formal status or title, and a letter which I shall presently quote shows that he felt the want of this, though he was the last person in the world to regard it as a grievance. But he had made himself indispensable to the library, he had established his reputation in the learned world, and he might fairly expect that whatever his profession had to offer would one day be within his reach.

CHAPTER V

In the year 1863 Bradshaw began to fill the long series of note-books which contain a record of his researches from that time down to within a few days of his death. There are thirty-two of these books, uniform in shape and size, not too large to go into one of his capacious breast-pockets. He never went anywhere without one, and in them he wrote down, without any order or arrangement, whatever he thought worth noting. To most persons this mass of *disjecta membra* would be a hopeless labyrinth, but Bradshaw himself never seemed to find the least difficulty in referring to anything he wanted. His memory was so tenacious that he never forgot the place and date at which anything had occurred. All he had to do, therefore, was to turn to the note-book for such and such a year or month, and he found it at once.

The contents of these note-books are for the most part records of facts and observations only : collections of books and manuscripts ; lists of documents or service-books ; notes on public libraries or private collections, on Dutch, Flemish, and other presses, on the order of the "Canterbury Tales" or Chaucer's rhyme-endings, on cathedral statutes or college history—on everything, in fact, which came in his way. Now and then, but very seldom, he wrote down his conclusions or inferences, if made at the moment ; but generally he was too busy at the time to do anything but note what was before him. His deductions were worked out afterwards on large sheets of ruled foolscap, the note-books supplying the materials, with infinite expenditure of ink and manual labour, for writing things out over and over again was the only way, he used to say, to get them clear. One is astonished at the apparent want of connection, at the multifarious nature of these researches simultaneously carried on. His mind was busy on so many subjects at once that he seldom looked for any particular thing without finding half a dozen other matters of interest, each of which was noted down, to form, perhaps years afterwards, a link in a long chain of argument. Here and there he would jot down something personal, some record of his own doings and impressions, if it were of special interest to him. Thus, in the middle of his bibliographical or typographical notes, the most unexpected entries occur, showing how little of a Dryasdust he was, how in the thick of his intellectual labours his heart remained as active as his head. Here it is a pedigree of some friends—for he was never content without knowing all about his friends—crammed in between the collation of a breviary and the Tibetan alphabet ; there, some characteristic remark by an acquaintance, preceded by a list of Caxton's presses, and followed by a bill at the Panier d'Or at Bruges. Sometimes, again, one comes on scraps of conversation, carried on with a foreigner who could read English, but could not understand the spoken word ; or with his old friend Mr Boone, the bookseller, who bought for him at many important sales, but was so deaf that conversation with him in a crowded room was inconvenient. The note-books are thus not only a treasure-house of information, but they are also to some extent a journal of his life, and contain not a few illustrations of his character.

The renewal of Bradshaw's appointment in the library made no difference in his manner of life. That he was happy in his work, the following extract from a letter to a friend, dated November 7, 1863, will show :—" I really

must disagree with you entirely in your theory that work
that is paid for *must* be uncongenial.   I grant that in very
many cases the work which, by circumstances, a man is
doomed to spend his life upon and make his bread of, is
not such as he would have chosen if his inclinations and
tastes had been exclusively .consulted.   But for myself, I
have earned money by very uncongenial work before now,
and at present the university pays me liberally for that
which is of all others the thing which gives me greatest
pleasure."   His duty to the college kept him at Cambridge
this winter.   He had generally spent Christmas with his
mother or his sister, Mrs Daniell, whose house was a second
home to him.   But he was now senior dean, and felt bound
to remain at his post.   He writes to his sister on December
23, 1863, "Dearest K., I wish so much I could come and
spend my Christmas with you, but I cannot manage it
this time.   It is generally such an utterly dreary place at
this time of year, but I have persuaded the Provost to have
service in the chapel on these days about Christmas and
the New Year, and the children at the Lodge have been
hard at work for a week past, with any help they can get
in college, at some decorations for the chapel.   There has
never been anything of the kind before, and it is the only
place in Cambridge where there has been nothing, so on all
accounts I am willing to try and make the place a little
more reasonable.   It is, of course, an experiment, but it will
be a great satisfaction to have tried, even if it fails in the
end."   The experiment was a success, and, though the
decorations have been discontinued, the chapel services
have been kept up ever since.

It was about this time that he began to be well known·
to students of English literature for his acquaintance with
Chaucer, though as yet he had written nothing on the subject.   Mr Alexander Macmillan, one of Bradshaw's oldest
friends, asked him in January, 1864, to join Mr Earle and

Mr Aldis Wright in editing a library edition of Chaucer's works. This project was unfortunately never carried out. Bradshaw had it in his mind, in one form or another, for fifteen years, and made large preparations, but time and opportunity seemed always wanting. It is clear, however, that about this time Chaucer engaged much of his attention. His correspondence with Dr Furnivall had already begun, before they had made acquaintance in person. Dr Furnivall preserves a clear recollection of his appearance the first time he saw him. He was at work in his rooms, in a very airy summer dress, wearing only a grey flannel shirt and trousers, with nothing at all on his feet. In this garb —which at the time was habitual with him—he received his visitor and gave him the heartiest welcome, and a friendship was at once formed which lasted for more than twenty years.

In February, 1864, the office of librarian became vacant through the resignation of Dr Power, afterwards Master of Pembroke. Bradshaw was pressed by several friends to stand for the post, but declined. The Rev. J. E. B. Mayor, now professor of latin, was elected without opposition. It may be mentioned that an important addition was made to the staff of the library about the same time by the appointment of an under-librarian, at a stipend of one hundred and fifty pounds a year, in the place of the principal assistant. This change, it may be remembered, or something very like it, had been advocated by Bradshaw when he became principal assistant eight years before.

In the autumn of 1863, and subsequently, Bradshaw contributed several short articles to a publication entitled *Le Bibliophile*, edited by M. J. P. Berjeau, in which he was interested.* Among these notes is one on Bunyan's " Pilgrim's Progress," and its possible connection with the

---

* These two papers are not signed, but letters from M. Berjeau show them to be Bradshaw's.

"Pélérinage" of Guillaume de Deguilleville. He says, "There is a book called 'The Pilgrim,' which is supposed to be an English translation of the 'Pilgrimage of Man,' printed by Pynson, in quarto, of which the only known copy is in the library of Queen's College, Oxford." He then proceeds to describe the few existing copies of the "Pélérinage," two of which he says "are modern versions of the story, made in the time of Charles I, and transcribed between 1630 and 1660." He concludes by pointing out that Bunyan might have seen and read these copies—a point which he thinks ought to be examined by future editors of his works. His contributions to the *Bibliophile* were by no means only literary. In January, 1864, M. Berjeau writes to thank him for a donation of ten pounds. But the magazine seems to have been in difficulties from the first, and although a year later the editor again acknowledged "the sacrifices which Mr Bradshaw had made for this unfortunate publication," it soon afterwards expired.

At Easter, 1864, Bradshaw paid the first of many visits to Belgium. His studies in the early history of printing in England had naturally led him on to the study of early printing elsewhere, and especially in Flanders. Above all he was drawn to Bruges, where, under the tuition of Colard Mansion, Caxton learnt his art. M. Holtrop, the librarian of the Hague, had published a year before his great collection of facsimiles, the "Monuments Typographiques." This book gave Bradshaw the keenest pleasure. He bought two copies, one of which he kept intact; the other he cut to pieces, rearranging the plates according to a system of his own. In November, 1863, he wrote to Mr G. I. F. Tupper: "I have been revelling for the last fortnight in Holtrop's 'Monuments Typographiques du Pays-Bas'—lithographic facsimiles of all the Dutch and Belgian fifteenth-century printers." In January, 1864, he began a correspondence with M. Holtrop, which only came to an end with the latter's death in 1870. It was continued with M. Holtrop's brother-in-law and successor, M. Campbell. Like most of the correspondence with Mr Blades, these letters are generally too technical for quotation in a memoir of this kind, but I cannot help giving some passages.

In his first letter to M. Holtrop, dated January, 1864, Bradshaw says, "Your catalogue of the Royal Library [published in 1856] has been with me a constant book of reference ever since it came out, and your 'Monuments Typographiques' have given me more pleasure and information than anything of the kind for a long time, but I am most anxious to see it completed." Two months later he writes, "Your letter did reach me, and most welcome it was; for real bibliographers are very scarce in this country, and the study of Incunabula is never carried out in a satisfactory way." Then follows a closely written letter of four sheets, giving a full list of the types (with examples) used by Gérard Leeu, who printed at Gouda and Antwerp in the last quarter of the fifteenth century. This list was to serve as a specimen of the system of classification which he wished to see generally adopted. The list of types is followed by a descriptive catalogue of all the books printed by Leeu of which specimens existed in the University Library. Nothing could show the eager helpfulness of the man better than a letter of this kind. All this information is given without a thought of self, merely in the cause of science and to help another student in whom he recognized a fellow-worker of the right stamp. The value of the help given may be judged from the fact that eight of the ten Gérard Leeus in the University Library were not in the catalogue of the Royal Library at the Hague, and five of them were wholly undescribed. Letters of this kind abound in the correspondence with M. Holtrop.

On the other side, M. Holtrop was equally ready with his pen, and there ensued a mutual interchange of good offices between these two enthusiasts which is charming to witness.   In his second letter Bradshaw had said, " I only wish you could write down a list of Veldener's types with references to the books, as I have attempted to do for Gérard Leeu."   Accordingly M. Holtrop, after sending him, on March 10, 1864, a list of books by Leeu at the Hague, arranged after Bradshaw's system, writes on March 12, "Mon cher monsieur, Pour faire la liste des différénts types de G. Leeu, j'avais dû me transporter dans la salle où se trouvent nos incunables.   Après l'avoir fini et lorsque j'avais eu le plaisir de vous l'envoyer, je me disais : Te voilà en train ; pourquoi pas profiter de l'occasion et essayer de faire une liste des types de Veldener, qui ferait plaisir à Mr Bradshaw ? "   And then follows a list of the Hague books by Veldener, who printed at Louvain, Utrecht, and Culembourg between 1473 and 1484, drawn out as fully as Bradshaw could have desired.   He answers on March 21, " Your extremely interesting letters really make me quite ashamed when I think of the immense amount of trouble it has entailed upon you to make out these valuable tables.   My only consolation is that they are themselves of such really great value in the elucidation of the history and work of your own printers.   What I feel very strongly is that unless you and your colleague, Mr Campbell, do this, no one for a long time will be able to do it."

Under these circumstances, it is easy to imagine with what delight he went to Flanders at Easter, 1864, and saw for the first time the cities where the early printers had lived and worked.   He travelled with two friends, F. T. Cobbold and J. A. Willis, junior Fellows of his own college.   They visited Antwerp, Ghent, and Bruges.   At the latter place they put up at a humble inn opposite

the belfry, the Panier d'Or, which was from that time
forward his favourite resort whenever he visited Bruges.
On this occasion he wished to see a particular book at
the library. The librarian was very polite, but declared
that the book had been removed by the French at the
beginning of the century. Bradshaw insisted that it
must be there, but the librarian stuck to his assertion.
Thereupon Bradshaw blurted out the letter, shelf, and
number under which the book would be found—and there
it was. He had no note of this on paper; the class-mark
was in his memory, along with all other particulars about
the book. From Bruges they went on to Ghent, and
thence returned home. It was but a short tour, but
Bradshaw acquired an affection for these ancient cities,
more especially for Bruges, which led to several other
and lengthier visits.

In the midst of these bibliographical studies, which
to so many persons seem incompatible with the existence
of any human affections, it is not unpleasant to turn to
a correspondence which shows another side of Bradshaw's
character. He had shortly before this time made the
acquaintance of an undergraduate of St John's, who relates
the beginning of their friendship as follows :—" My earliest
recollection of Henry Bradshaw is of an active, bright-
looking man, hurrying along in a college cap, but without
a gown, through the catalogue-room of the University
Library. Though he was evidently in haste over some
papers which he was carrying tenderly in his left hand,
he looked so pleasantly good-natured that I dared to
ask him the whereabouts of a shelf from which I wanted
a book. He stopped at once and directed me, and when,
a short time after, I was still searching for a book suitable
to my purpose, I heard a voice behind me inquiring,
' Still looking for a good little book for our good little
Sunday school boys?' And there he was, smiling

I

quizzically at my embarrassment. He put me at my
ease, however, directly, and pointed out one of Dr Neale's
little volumes of stories of Christian Heroines which he
liked. We had a talk about Neale's liturgical work. That
I took an interest in a special study of his own seemed
to draw us together. I often found myself wandering
into the library with no definite purpose beyond that
of seeing 'Mr Bradshaw,' and having a chat with him.
Sometimes I sought him out in one of the little rooms
where Miss Shields was copying the Vaudois manuscripts
for him ; sometimes he would come hurrying past as
I stood at a shelf, snap his fingers to call my attention,
and hold out his hand behind, as if inviting me to follow
him, but without pausing a moment to let me overtake
him. So it came about that I often saw him, until at
last it became one of my daily necessities. . . . The two
years in which I got to know him so well had their special
seasons, and one was the Long of 1864. What a time
of happiness that was ! Those little dinners in his rooms
—for he seldom went into hall then—those strolls in the
Fellows' garden, where we watched as well as heard
the nightingales ; those readings aloud of Dickens—by
him, for I always listened. Then he would very often
walk with me through the backs to my rooms, see me
get to work, and either stay and read, or more generally
go home to his own labours."

Soon afterwards his young friend was a candidate
for the Mathematical Tripos. The result was a grievous
disappointment to him. I will let him tell in his words
what Bradshaw's sympathy was worth at the time. "We
walked together to the Senate-house on that cold January
morning, when the list was to be published ; we listened
for, but did not hear my name among the Wranglers,
caught a copy of the lists as they were scattered from
the gallery, and went away. Neither of us spoke. He

took my arm and led me to my rooms. . . . He did not leave me for days. He sent off the telegrams that I had promised ; helped me with my letters, or wrote them himself; insisted on my living in his rooms, except merely to sleep ; and, as soon as he could arrange to get away, took me off to Paris. A trip to Paris would do *him* good, was his way of putting it. We stayed in Paris a week. He knew the place well, and gave himself up to amusing me, showing me everything that was to be seen. He greatly enjoyed my astonishment at a scene in the Church of La Madeleine. Passing one day, we saw the exterior hung with black, and, hearing the organ, we entered. In the centre of the church, before the high altar, was a grand catafalque, with hundreds of wax tapers burning round the coffin. A very large congregation was present, and a requiem was being sung. In the middle of it all, the Suisse, in gorgeous black, came down and opened a passage among the worshippers, through which a bride and bridegroom with their party passed to a side altar. The wedding took place, mass was said, the bridal party left the church, and all the while the funeral music never ceased. Bradshaw remarked, as we left the church, ' Nothing reminds you so much as a sight like this, that you are in a Roman Catholic country.' "

From Paris Bradshaw took his friend to Bournemouth, to stay a few days with his mother and youngest sister at their house, Fernside, where they all combined, he says, to " spoil " him. No better solace for a mind diseased could well be imagined. " When our holiday ended, we lived on the same life in correspondence. For weeks we wrote to each other nearly every day." Some quotations from Bradshaw's letters to this friend will illustrate his life at this time. " Dearest Charlie," he writes, on February 28, 1865, in the middle of a college meeting, " I am desperatel afraid of writing you too many letters. I must, however, send you a letter which came from —— this morning. It did my heart good, to see how thoroughly you are appreciated wherever you go. . . . Oh, these people ! they are discussing daily service ; they *do* make me so sick." Next day he cut his right hand so badly as to be unable to use it, but he wrote a long letter with his left. "I hope you have not got two letters from me any day. I have been at considerable pains to avoid it, and, I fear, without success. However, in a week or so, no doubt, I shall have sobered down, and shall find it difficult to write one letter in three weeks. . . . Enter here a letter from the Master of Caius [Dr Guest], to say that Dr Tischendorf (do you know the name ?) is coming here on Saturday, and will I come and meet him at dinner on Monday ? Will I not indeed ? "

On March 4, his friend's birthday, he writes, " You will begin to revive again to-day, I trust, and never allow yourself more than five minutes in any one day for the luxury of dumpishness, in which your last letter shows that you are indulging to too great an extent. Bodily presence is absolutely needed for one to sit upon a person, or I should sit upon you now effectually, which I cannot possibly do by letter." On March 9 he says, " Tischendorf was in here a good part of yesterday, and we had a good deal of talk about the books. He looks much younger than you would think from the amount of work he has gone through. He and I had a long discussion yesterday as to the possible former contents of the Codex Sinaiticus, where we differ slightly, on arguments derived from the actual construction of the volume ; but I shall have to put my views on paper, for it is rather difficult struggling through a mixture of several languages. . . . As soon as I have to *write* you a letter—that is, to stop and think what to write, instead of talking with my fingers as I do at present—I shall leave off altogether, so you know what you must expect in a week or less, perhaps." A little later, "This is the only night no one has been in to tea, and now (9.20) I suppose no one is likely to come in. All the afternoon and evening I have been very busy looking over court-rolls from Henry VI to James I, in search of some particular entries about some rights to timber which the college is supposed to have at Ruislip, in Middlesex, and it is dreary work, though there is to me a certain satisfaction always in getting a minute acquaintance with any kind of legal documents with which I was unacquainted before."

On March 21, "'Dr Lightfoot on the Galatians' is to be out to-day. Will you let me send you a copy? Say no if you had rather not, but the fact is, I have been looking forward for months to getting the book, and on my breakfast-table on Sunday morning there it was, with his kind regards. I could not believe my eyes, but there it is, and all Sunday I feasted on it. . . . Altogether it is a beautiful book, and my expectations are more than realized. I am thick in correspondence with Furnivall just now about his Early English Text Society. He writes (letters) with the most perfect fluency, and gets through an immense amount of work besides (I wish I could). Last night I sent him four closely written sheets, and where it requires some thought, as in this case, such letters take it out of one considerably.* . . . This talk has done me good and quite revived me, so I shall be able to go to my meeting at the Lodge with a much lighter heart."

Here is a sketch of a day's work, all for others (March 30, 1865). "I have been literally overwhelmed with writing work, whether for Shirley or Haddan.† Thanks to an

* This letter is, unfortunately, not to be found.
† The Rev. W. W. Shirley, D.D., Professor of Ecclesiastical History at Oxford, and editor of *Fasciculi Zizaniorum*, Royal Letters, etc., died in 1866. The Rev. A. W. Haddan, B.D., of Trinity College, Oxford, co-editor (with Dr Stubbs) of the "Ecclesiastical Councils, etc.," died in 1873.

excellent device, I got all Haddan's Gildas sent off last night, but it was six hours' work. I got C. to come from ten to eleven, then P. from eleven to twelve, then Miss Shields came into the library most opportunely and read till half-past one ; and then, after a mouthful of bread and butter, P. came again, and we finished the work and the revision just by four o'clock. So that is off my mind. Then for Shirley, I have done about half the fair copy for him, and have sent back all his papers done with, and written him a long letter besides, in which I have given him a bit of my mind ; so I am curious to see what he says. Furnivall has gone to the wall for the present, but I must work him off finally before I leave." And after all this, it is a joy and a relaxation to him to sit down and write a letter of eight sides to his friend. Here is a specimen of an evening in his rooms (April 1). " C. is here thirsting for tea, so I oughtn't to be sitting silent, talking to you ; but M. was here from hall till half-past seven, and P. and H. were here till eight, and then D. was here discussing his prospects till nine, and C. came in at nine, and it is now half-past, so tea ought to be pouring out." There was nothing unusual in this, and what was habitual in 1865 was equally habitual ten years or twenty years later.

The allusions to Dr Shirley in the letters quoted above are explained by a copious correspondence with the professor in which Bradshaw was engaged about this time. How long he had been acquainted with Dr Shirley I do not know, but when the correspondence before me begins, in January, 1865, he evidently knew him well. Dr Shirley was at that time engaged on Wyclif, of whose works he was preparing a catalogue with a view to an edition, which unfortunately he never lived to carry out. He frequently consulted Bradshaw on bibliographical points connected with the manuscripts of Wyclif's works. Writing to him on January 10, 1865, Bradshaw says, " It strikes me very forcibly what an immense boon it would be if you would take Wyclif's greater works and print them first. I don't throw this out as a new idea to you, for it is what you have always impressed upon me ; but I fear it is impossible to move the university to so great an undertaking. Only the more one labours at the subject, the more palpable the waste of time and labour appears to be, when you know that it would be so infinitely easier to edit the minor works (indeed, so impossible to edit them properly otherwise), if you had the 'Summa Theologiæ' and the 'De Sermonibus Domini in Monte,' etc., in print for some time so as to work the subject up." After giving an account of one or two manuscripts, he continues, "I have exhausted Trinity Library by taking every single volume in order from the shelves and examining them all. It is the only way to find anonymous treatises. The 'De Sermone Domini in Monte' in Trinity Library is a very curious book. . . . I wish, in your catalogue, you could treat the 'Summa Theologiæ' with its preliminary treatise, 'De Dominio divino,' as one work. It is most distressing to think how few of the treatises of the Summa are to be found in England—or rather, have been found in England, for I doubt not there are many more than we know of."

In a letter a few days later there is a characteristic bit of scolding, what he would himself have called a "viper," but it illustrates also one of the main principles of his work— the conviction that you must know the history of a manuscript if any sound results are to be got out of it : "I wish you would stir up either your press delegates or the Bodleian people not to send out catalogues of manuscripts in such an extremely unpleasant manner. There is a catalogue of Syriac manuscripts just out without one single word to say where the collections come from. Oxford men perhaps know by instinct, but a very few lines would have been sufficient to say when and where the collections were made, and how they came to the Bodleian. . . . I am afraid, though, that you will say, like every one else, it is not in your department."

The correspondence was interrupted for a short time by the visit to Paris and Bournemouth already mentioned, but was renewed on Bradshaw's return to Cambridge. It is mainly concerned with the arrangement and relations of Wyclif's works, but the points discussed, though of interest to students of Wyclif, are too minute for general readers. In his anxiety to help Dr Shirley, Bradshaw contemplated a visit to Vienna and Prague at Easter, 1865, in order to examine the Wyclif manuscripts preserved at those places, but he did not carry out the project. Meanwhile he was working hard for Mr Haddan. On March 30, 1865, he writes to Dr Shirley, "I have been very much pressed with some other work which I promised Mr Haddan, the full collation of our manuscript of Gildas for the new Oxford edition of Wilkins' 'Concilia,' and this I have got finished to-day, thank goodness. I am sure you have very little notion of the actual amount of time which is required to draw up such a list of sermons as I sent you before. All bibliographical work is very dry and very tedious ; and I never yet met a *literary* man who could in the very least appreciate the difficulties. Literary men find such work an infinite nuisance when they have to do it themselves, while everything but first-class work of the kind is aggravating to the last degree. Take any one of the lists of Wyclif, for instance, and the descriptions are perfectly sure to fail you exactly where you want help. If it is a sermon, and you want the *incipit*, you are sure to find only the *incipit* of the text given, whereas you have two or three sermons on the same text. If it is a treatise, you find the end given—*secula seculorum*, or some such merely formal ending, which conveys no identifying quality at all. . . . As for the arrangement of Wyclif's different Summæ, it has always struck me that it would be as well to look at the arrangements of the similar works of his contemporaries and predecessors in common, however different the mode of treatment might be."

On the eve of his departure for his Easter holiday abroad, he sent to Dr Shirley an account of the Wyclif manuscript in Trinity College Library (B. 16. 2). "I leave this in an hour or two," he writes; "I am thoroughly tired out and glad to get a holiday." On his return, the correspondence was renewed. Dr Shirley submitted to him drafts of his list of Wyclif's works.* In May he was at Lincoln, and sent Dr Shirley the results of his explorations in the chapter library there. "I am afraid," he says on May 29, "that many of the choicest things have disappeared from the library since Tanner's time, and I cannot find any traces of Dan John Gaytrege or the 'Mandatum' of Archbishop Thoresby, though I have taken every single manuscript off the shelves in order, one after another, so that I must have come upon it if it had been there; but this is only my first day, and I have spent eight hours very pleasantly at work there. The library is full of things curious and interesting to me, and with the good-will of the librarian [the Rev. G. F. Apthorp] and the dean's key, I can work just as long as ever I please, which is an immense comfort."

The result of all this work and of the abundant proofs of knowledge which he had given was naturally that Dr Shirley begged him to aid in the edition of Wyclif's works. Writing to Dr Shirley on June 14, 1865, he says, "You say, will I undertake the Postils † instead of the Corpus tracts; but the utmost I ever undertook was to copy or get copied the volume at Corpus.‡ It never entered my

---

* "A Catalogue of the Original Works of John Wiclif." Oxford : 1865. Bradshaw's description of the Trinity manuscript is printed in the preface.

† Commentaries on, or short expositions of, passages of Scripture.

‡ Probably No. ccxcvi. in Nasmith's catalogue, described as a fourteenth-century manuscript containing thirty treatises by Wyclif.

head to edit them. If you are not going to do, or rather would prefer not to do the Postils, so as to set you free to do some other equally pressing works, and you know of no one else to do them, I will undertake them and do my best to carry them through; but remember that I have never edited anything before, and you may not like to trust such things to a new hand. I must begin editing soon, there is no doubt, and there are plenty of things which I can find to do. I only want you to understand that you are not bound to ask me to do the work if you find at Oxford men (as there must be some) able and willing to do the work; all I ask is that you should act freely in the matter, and speak your mind plainly, and I for my part will give you any help I can, and that you think worth having."

But other work intervened; Chaucer proved too attractive, and Wyclif was indefinitely deferred. On January 9, 1866, he writes from Glasgow to Dr Shirley, "I am afraid I am a very hopeless subject to manage. . . . It is very wrong of me never to have written to thank you for the catalogues which I found on my return home in the autumn. I am hard at work at something of the same kind for Chaucer; only it is so fearfully complicated, and the copies are so very much scattered about the country." This did not look much like going on with Wyclif, and Dr Shirley wrote on January 11, "What I meant by asking what you were doing about Wyclif is this. You talked of editing his English Homilies. Are you doing anything at them? Are you likely to be able to work at them soon?" He went on to say that he had just had "the offer of valuable assistance towards editing the English works," and wanted to hear from Bradshaw in order to know what he would be free to propose to his friend. "If you can do the work," he says in a later letter, "nothing so good; but I do not wish to miss a real chance, and then to find I cannot get you either." Unfortunately, Bradshaw felt himself unable to make a definite promise, and wrote on February 2, 1866, to resign his share in the undertaking. "By all means get your nameless friend," he says, "to do all he will do for you, and do not for one second think that I can be annoyed at your doing so. I am more than pleased to find that you have found some one whom you can rely upon to do the work well. I did not undertake the proposed work eagerly, but rather because you were unable to find any one ; and my province is much rather to give help on certain details which most people don't care about, than to undertake the editing of large works, which require a *kind* of research which is rather out of my beat." So ends the episode. On November 20, 1866, as Bradshaw notes in his diary, Dr Shirley died. I have carried on the account of their correspondence thus far, in order to avoid interruption, but must now return.

In January, 1865, he was made an ordinary member of the Deutsche Morgenländische Gesellschaft (German Oriental Society). What caused this honour to be conferred upon him I do not know, but his knowledge of Oriental manuscripts, as of manuscripts in general, was very great, and he had had much to do with the cataloguing of the Oriental manuscripts in the University Library. It is possible that in giving information or assistance to some German scholars, he may have displayed knowledge which proved him to be worthy of admission into the society in question.

The Easter Vacation of 1865 was spent in a journey to Italy with F. W. Cornish and E. C. Austen Leigh, two of the younger Fellows of his college, in the course of which they visited Genoa, Milan, and Venice. His letters home do not often contain anything remarkable, but they show, what no one who was fortunate enough to travel with him could fail to see, that travelling gave him intense and

unfeigned pleasure. His observant eyes and receptive
mind took everything in. His simple but genuine sense of
beauty was delighted with Milan Cathedral and St Mark's,
with the glow of Titian and Veronese in Venetian galleries,
with the distant snows of Monte Rosa, glistening against
the blue, or the wave-like outline of the Euganean Hills
traced on a background of purple sunset; while his
memory, stored with literature and history, threw the
glamour of association over every haunt of fame or
romance. He was not critical; he saw, but did not pause
to compare. It was the open-eyed enjoyment of a child
combined with the intelligent observation of a well-read
man.

While at Milan, he of course visited the Ambrosian
Library. In a letter to Mr Yeld, he relates his first
meeting with M. Ceriani, one of the librarians. "He is
quite a young man, and full of life and vigour, and so
pleasant. I had no difficulty in talking Italian to him to
any extent, and in understanding him. I saw the famous
Plautus, of the fourth century or earlier, and some of the
Irish manuscripts from the old convent at Bobbio, books
I had long wanted to see. What pleased me so immensely
was that, whatever books I asked for, he called a man and
sent him after them, telling the man the number and where
to find them, just as I should do at Cambridge, never
having to look in a catalogue to see where they were,
or whether they had them or not. I wouldn't have missed
him for anything." To his sister he writes that M. Ceriani
displayed "an intelligence I rarely find in large libraries."

Venice was still Austrian in 1865, little guessing that
in another year it was to form part of Italy. Bradshaw
and his friends stayed there more than a week, and his
letters brim over with enjoyment. He found out at once,
what many travellers never find out at all, that it was
possible to *walk* all over Venice, and he preferred this

mode of wandering. On Good Friday, when they had been there two or three days, he writes, "We have not been doing much since we came here, for it takes some time always to domesticate in a strange place, and this, too, such a very strange place; but we have been basking in the freshness of everything without making much effort to *do* a large number of things. . . . Yesterday evening [Maundy Thursday] we went to a service at St Mark's, and it was with some difficulty we made out what the service was. Cornish has an 'Officium Septimanæ Sacræ,' but we were long puzzled, until I noticed that after every *one* thing a candle on the great stand was put out, and by that means was able to calculate that it must be a certain psalm in Mattins for Good Friday, said over-night; and on turning to that part of the office, sure enough there they were. I must try and make out the services, for if there is one thing more uncomfortable to me than another, it is going to a church and being obliged to stand like a dissenter in King's Chapel, wondering and not knowing in the least what is going on."

He visited the Scuola di San Rocco, which he liked "as one of the few places in which you can see a large mass of one man's work. It requires much more drilling than I have ever enjoyed to be able to profit by a miscellaneous collection of pictures. It is a part of a gentleman's education which ought not to be neglected, but it is waste of time trying to pick up scraps of ignorant enjoyment from stray pictures. To my mind it is just like taking up a volume of selections from different national poets, and reading pieces for the beauty of the sound of the verse, without having learnt the language."

"Easter Tuesday.—As it is a strict holiday to-day, I have been amusing myself in St Mark's Library, in the Ducal Palace. Not that the books are accessible to readers, but from a librarian's point of view I have not by any means wasted my time, as it is worth something to me to have mastered the arrangement of the place and the general method of the library; and besides this, the cases are all protected by *very* open wirework, and the books are almost all clearly lettered, so that one can see to a great extent what books they have. . . . You can't think how delightful it is travelling with Cornish and Edward Leigh; they are so utterly different from each other, and none of us, fortunately, are gifted with a disposition to sulk, so I think we all enjoy ourselves thoroughly. Leigh is, fortunately, most punctual and business-like; Cornish is, also fortunately, entirely the reverse; so between the two we manage perfectly. You know what I am."

Next day he paid a visit to the Armenian Convent. "I wouldn't have missed going there for anything. . . . The young man who took us round told me they had but one Greek manuscript in the place, a copy of the Gospels, which I was naturally curious to see; but he said only the librarian had the key. My stupid thought of not boring Leigh would probably have prevented my asking to see the librarian, but Leigh boldly asked him if it would give him very much trouble to fetch the librarian, and off he went at once. When he came I was delighted, for he is a real librarian, and full of his work and his subject; and it ended by our staying nearly an hour and a half at the convent, and I got a great deal of information out of him. . . . I satisfied myself about some things for Light-foot. . . . Altogether my visit there was most interesting and most profitable. I bought a few little books, among them a grammar and an English translation of the Armenian liturgy. I have long wanted to know something of Armenian, so I shall begin at once with this opportunity. We have very few Armenian manuscripts at Cambridge, but I do hate having books under my charge which I am not able even to read so as to see what they are. The alphabet is, however, the very worst I have ever had to deal with—far worse than Russian or Sanscrit. . . . I hope to get something done to-day, both at the Greek establishments and at the library in the Ducal Palace. Fancy a library to which Petrarch left all his books, going on still, containing books written and annotated by his own hand and Boccaccio's, not merely as great curiosities, but part of the staple of the library. It is all things of that sort that make one feel the utter difference between Italy and every other country in the world. The succession of literary life is so extraordinary."

Once back at Cambridge, the almost daily correspondence with his friend Yeld ceased, but occasional letters give us glimpses of his life. "Last week," he says, writing on May 10, 1865, "I did nothing but entertain canons. Philip Freeman was here from Exeter. . . . Then Walter Shirley came from Christchurch ; and on Saturday I had Dr Pusey all to myself for dinner and tea. I must stop ; Dr Bosworth wants me." On May 23, "I shall try and do my best to write to you periodically—at short intervals, if I can. You must not, however, be too sanguine. You know a little of my power of silence." In May, 1865, he went to Lincoln, as I have already said, to do some work for his friend Dr Shirley, timing his visit so as to coincide with the ordination of one of his friends.

From Lincoln he writes to his mother (June 4, 1865): "I had promised Walter Shirley (at Oxford) to send him some information out of the Lincoln library before the end of May, and I saw no way of doing it satisfactorily except by doing it myself ; and I had long wanted to see the cathedral library here, as well as the minster itself. . . . I have been living perfectly in clover, having the full benefit of the minster service, and full liberty to work in the chapter library from morning till night ; and I have used my time well, for I have had eight hours a day on an average, and have been well repaid."

From Lincoln he went to Stamford to see Burghley House. A journey always had the effect of loosening his pen. He writes to Mr Yeld on June 13 "Burghley House is indeed worth a pilgrimage. . . . I spent about four hours there yesterday, and have been there from six to seven hours to-day again. I thought it probable that, as Lord Exeter came from the eldest son of the Lord Treasurer Burghley in Elizabeth's reign, I might find the treasurer's library still there, which would indeed have been curious. A few minutes, however, showed me that there was not a single vestige of his library remaining. The question then arose, whose collection the present library could be, and I soon found traces enough to show that it was made by the fifth earl, who held the title from 1700 to 1721. It is a thoroughly well-formed and well-used library of that date, formed by a man of highly cultivated tastes, who had travelled much and to some purpose, especially in Italy. Thus much the library proved, as also that he was nothing of a book-antiquary whatever. . . . After all, the most interesting thing to me is not so much finding particular books, as tracing the history—the individuality—of great libraries which have come down to the present time."

Although he was clearly in a wandering mood, he does not appear to have gone abroad again, except on the sudden expedition to Paris already mentioned (p. 115), for more than a year. He spent his money in another and a characteristic way. In a letter dated June 18, 1865, he says, "I have just set a Hungarian rabbi [Dr Schiller-Szinessy] at work upon our Hebrew manuscripts, and with his knowledge and my method of cataloguing, I hope it may be a creditable book.* But what with this, and young Palmer [afterwards Professor Palmer] for the Arabic,

---

* The work done by Dr Szinessy was eventually purchased from Mr Bradshaw by the Syndicate for the sum of £300, which he had expended on it, and Dr Szinessy reduced it into the form of a catalogue.

and Miss Shields for the Vaudois manuscripts, all being
paid out of my own pocket, it leaves me but little prospect
of going abroad this summer." In cases of this kind—
and those he mentions are only three out of many—he
always acted on a certain principle. He endeavoured to
give, to those who required and deserved it, such assistance
as would enable them in future to help themselves. If
they were, as he used to say, "worth their salt," that is,
if they only lacked opportunity to do good work, he would
put them in a position to do it. He thus not only did
them the greatest possible service, but did it in the most
delicate way. The recipients of his bounty were intended
to feel under no obligation. They were supposed, in fact,
to be helping him, not to be receiving help from him;
they were merely getting compensation for work which
he wanted to get done. The university had done thus
much for him, he would say; why should he not do it
for others? No one's self-respect could be injured by
receiving a favour tendered with so much consideration.

Meanwhile Bradshaw was taking an active part in
the affairs of his own college, which was passing through
a critical period of its development. The new statutes
came into force in 1861, but various circumstances delayed
their taking effect. It was only by considerable sacrifices
on the part of the governing body that their provisions
could be put into speedy execution, and it was not
without difficulty that an antagonistic minority was induced
to consent. In the contention which arose respecting the
claims of Fellows under the old system, Bradshaw's good
sense and conciliatory bearing gave him considerable
influence. He was nominated on a committee for discussing
the best method of reconciling conflicting claims, and
had the chief hand in drawing up an agreement, known
in the annals of the college as the "Eirenicon," by which
the dispute was brought to a satisfactory termination.

K

In all these proceedings he showed great anxiety that the new statutes should be enabled to take effect without delay. He was so much annoyed at the success of an appeal which deferred their application, that he refused at first to have anything to say to the author of it, and always spoke of him as "the impostor." His wrath, however, soon gave way to kindlier feelings, and the " impostor " became a lifelong friend.

When, a few years later, steps were taken to throw open the college, which had hitherto been confined to those on the foundation at Eton, Bradshaw did all he could to facilitate the change. The chief questions under discussion during the years 1861-1865 were the reduction of the number of Fellowships from seventy to forty-six, of which I have spoken above (p. 79), the creation of exhibitions, the admission of pensioners, and the appointment of a tutor. All these steps were indispensable if the college was to act in the spirit of the new statutes, and to take anything like its proper place in the university. About all of them Bradshaw was actively engaged in correspondence and negotiation with other leading members of the governing body, especially with William Johnson, who will long be remembered as the most brilliant Eton tutor of his day. It is probably not too much to say that to him and to Bradshaw the college owes more than to any others the infusion of a new spirit into its counsels, which enabled it to break loose from the narrow traditions of its previous history. It was Mr Johnson who led the way to the creation of an exhibition fund by the gift of £400 for that purpose—a gift to which he made many later additions. Bradshaw, who himself subscribed largely, was mainly instrumental in collecting the rest of the sum required. Classics and theology had hitherto been the only subjects to which any attention was paid at King's. Mr Johnson was very anxious that the exhibitions should become the means of introducing other studies, especially those of mathematics and natural science, and here again he found an active supporter in Bradshaw.

Many aided in the good work, but it was on Bradshaw that the burden of the struggle chiefly fell. His official position in the college pointed him out as the natural person to urge the wishes of the reformers on the residents, among whom he was then almost alone in his thorough approval of the changes proposed. It was his duty, too, in the absence of a tutor, to carry out the votes respecting the admission of pensioners and the award of exhibitions, to arrange the details of examinations, and to draw up and issue the notices in which the opening of the college was announced to the world. In October, 1865, the first non-Eton men entered King's. The beginnings of a new era in the history of the college were small enough, but a new era had begun. When, a short time afterwards, a tutor was appointed, and the tutorial duties were severed from the disciplinary functions of the dean, Bradshaw felt that the chief attraction which the latter office had possessed for him had disappeared, and he accordingly resigned. But in relinquishing his official position, it need hardly be said that he continued to take an active interest in the development of the system which he had done so much to introduce. The details of college politics will be of little interest to any but those immediately concerned, but it is well to say thus much, in order to show that Bradshaw's favourite pursuits never hindered him from taking a public-spirited share in the affairs of the society to which he belonged.

In January, 1866, he was at Glasgow, working in the Hunterian Museum. From Glasgow he went to Manchester, where he met Mr Crossley, " a wonderful storehouse of information," and saw his collection of tracts and pamphlets of the time of the Great Rebellion, numbering a hundred volumes, which had belonged to his relative, John Bradshaw, the regicide. . "These pamphlets," says Bradshaw, "were bound by the man after whom my father named me, and his familiar signature, ' Henry Bradshaw,' is on the title-page of every volume." Many of his friends will remember a little wooden tobacco-stopper, in the form of a weather-cock, which belonged to the same gentleman.

In June, 1866, Bradshaw was elected a member of the Roxburghe Club, being proposed by Mr W. G. Clark, then public orator at Cambridge, and seconded by Mr Dickinson. He undertook, about the time of his election, in accordance with the rules of the club, to edit the book entitled "The Pilgrimage of the Lyf of the Manhode," a prose version by an unknown writer of the "Pèlerinage de la Vie Humaine" by De Deguilleville. Of this poem he writes in a letter to Dr Furnivall, dated February 22, 1867, "About De Deguilleville's three pilgrimages, please first observe the spelling, which is as I have written it. The three are (1) the ' Pilgrimage of the Life of Man,' (2) the ' Pilgrimage of the Soul after Death,' and (3) the 'Pilgrimage of the Life of Jesus Christ.' . . . Of the first there is a prose translation, which I am editing for the Roxburghe Club ; " and then he goes on to give an account of the various translations of the poem and the different manuscripts in which they are to be found, showing that he had, at all events, taken the preliminary steps for an edition in his exhaustive way. Various causes hindered the execution of this undertaking, and on his election to the post of university librarian in 1867 he handed over the work to Mr W. G. Clark. It was eventually carried out in 1869 by Mr Aldis Wright, who mentions in his preface the "valuable assistance rendered by Mr Bradshaw whenever he had occasion to consult him in the course of the work."

The calls upon his time were indeed too numerous, and he was still too much immersed in his researches in the library and elsewhere to be able to undertake any continuous work. It must be allowed, moreover, that unmethodical ways and dilatoriness in correspondence were growing upon him, or rather had become too habitual to be shaken off. He undertook this summer to correct the sheets of Dean Hook's "Lives of the Archbishops" as they passed through the press, but after correcting two or three he was obliged to give it up. In spite of the delay, which had already caused some inconvenience, the dean set so much value on his services that he tried to persuade him to continue them; but in vain. Bradshaw was fully conscious of his own failings in this respect. Writing to a friend about this time, at the end of a long letter full of valuable information, he says, "I am obliged to write here [in the library] because I know if I were to wait two hours after getting your letter, it would be weighing down my pocket for many weeks."

Early in 1866 Mr Winter Jones, librarian of the British Museum, referring to a discovery which Bradshaw had made at Glasgow,* writes him as follows:—"Pray accept my warm congratulations and the expression of my admiration at your good 'Fortune,' the reward of 'Vertu.' Some time ago, when Elwin was the editor of the *Quarterly*, he asked me to write an article on Bibliography, to be enlivened by anecdotes of remarkable finds and bringing together of *disjecta membra*. I was too much occupied to undertake it, but I think that you have now a sufficient store of materials to make such an article very striking. I used to think Maskell the most fortunate discoverer, but there certainly are now two Richards in the field." A couple of months later Bradshaw added another feat to the many that had already

---

* Bradshaw had discovered, in the Hunterian Museum at Glasgow, a copy of " L'Estrif de fortune et vertu," by Colard Mansion, of which only one copy was previously known.

won Mr Winter Jones' admiration, by discovering two hitherto unknown poems by the early Scotch poet Barbour.

One of these, the "Siege of Troy," consists of two fragments, about 2200 lines in all, tacked on at the beginning and end of a Scotch copy of Lydgate's "Troy Book." In a paper which he read before the Cambridge Antiquarian Society,* Bradshaw says that he had looked into the book merely with the object of seeing "how far Lydgate's southern English had been modified in the progress of transcription by a Scotch scribe." In glancing through the volume, he noticed two lines in larger writing than the rest, one near the beginning—

> " Her endis barbour and begynnys the monk ; "

and another towards the end—

> " Her endis the monk and begynnys barbour. "

Moreover, the verses at the beginning and end of the poem were of a different metre from those in the middle, and the language was not southern English at all.

The poem thus discovered was evidently by Barbour, but no one was hitherto aware that he had written anything about Troy. "After spending some hours," Bradshaw continues, "in searching through the various works on Scottish literary history which were to be found in the library, I wrote to Mr Cosmo Innes to ask for some information about the book, being very slow to believe that it was possible for me to discover anything in such an accessible library as ours, which had escaped the keen and lifelong searches of such antiquaries as Scotland now possesses." It was true, nevertheless. The poem, a translation by Barbour of Guido de Colonna's "Historia Trojana," was quite unknown to Scottish and other antiquaries. "I think it is no mare's nest," writes Mr Cosmo

---

* *Cambridge Antiquarian Society Publications*, vol. iii. p. 111.

Innes, "but a real and valuable discovery—the second * you
have made—for old Scotland. The language is probably
its chief value, but that is no small matter, if the scribe is
nearly contemporary with the translator, and if that translator is our friend the Dean of Aberdeen." Mr Joseph
Robertson writes, "I have just heard from Cosmo Innes
of your very interesting discovery of part or the whole of
a translation of the ' Siege of Troy ' by Archdeacon Barbour.
In so far as I know, there is no trace in Scotland of his
having written such a work, so that you may imagine how
interested we are about it." And again, a little later, "No
doubt we should have been better pleased if Barbour's
whole book had been preserved, but two thousand lines of
the Father of Scotch poetry are a great boon, and to be
received with all gratitude to its discoverer."

But how came these fragments to be combined in so
strange a way with Lydgate's poem, forming a sort of
prefix and conclusion to the latter, in the place of its
own proper beginning and end ? Bradshaw's explanation
is "that the Scotch scribe, wishing to make a copy of
Lydgate's ' Story of the Destruction of Troy,' was only able
to procure for his purpose a copy mutilated at beginning
and end ; and that, in transcribing, he supplemented his
original by taking the missing portions of the story from
the antiquated and in his eyes less refined translation made
by his own countryman in the previous century."

This discovery was sufficiently remarkable, but the
other poem, which Bradshaw identified shortly afterwards
as Barbour's, gave occasion to a still more striking display
of his peculiar powers. It was a volume of "Lives of the
Saints," which Bradshaw "had long known by sight, and
had shown to all his Edinburgh friends in the hope of their
recognizing it as a well-known work, even if not by a known
author." As he found no one to satisfy him on the sub-

* The first was the Book of Deer (see above, p. 69).

ject, he set to work to examine the poem—no light task, for it contains about 40,000 lines, or about twice as many as the Iliad. In mere bulk it was, therefore, a much weightier contribution to Scotch literature than the "Siege of Troy." In the paper * which he read before the Antiquarian Society, Bradshaw explains the grounds on which he arrived at his conclusions about the poem. It may be interesting to quote an extract from his note-book, dated April 24, 1866, in which these conclusions appear as he jotted them down for his own use.

"After four o'clock, I went to get manuscript Gg. 2. 6, the Scotch manuscript of 'Lives of the Saints,' to see if I could make anything of it. It was clearly Scotch, not merely north country; the writing showed that, and the Katherine Grahame on fly-leaf. On looking further, I found a quire with a parchment slip down the middle, containing 'Jacobus dei gracia rex Scottorum omnibus probis hominibus suis salutes.' This was quite enough. The handwriting may not be much before 1500, but the work and its author? In the prologue the author says, as he is too old and feeble to minister in the church, he writes lives of holy men, to eschew idleness. The book divides into two pretty equal divisions. The first contains apostles, evangelists, and ordinary saints, ending with St Maurice and St Macharius. The second contains ordinary saints, among whom St Ninian. Here was clear evidence of the Scottish origin. In the prologue of St Maurice he says he would fain before others say something of the saint as being patron of Aberdeen. So far, then, the author is an ecclesiastic, a very old man, and apparently connected with Aberdeen. But his date? In the story of St Ninian there are many *narrationes* by the compiler. One of a man in his own time personally known to himself, a native of Moray or Elgin. . . . Another story of what

* See above, p. 134, note.

happened in his own time, when David Bruce was king, to a knight, Sir Fergus Macdonel, in Galloway. David II was king 1329-1370, and even from these few facts I think there can be no shadow of a doubt that this is another great poem which, during the past fortnight, it has been my lot to add to the list of the works of John Barbour, the Archdeacon of Aberdeen, the author of the Bruce, and the father of Scottish poetry."

The arguments here briefly stated were developed and supplemented by others, given in the paper, which together appear to make the conclusion incontrovertible. But the "skill and knowledge" which Mr Winter Jones had remarked in him in 1859 enabled him to make discoveries where others had found nothing, while the exhaustiveness of his research constantly corrected the mistakes of more superficial workers. He gave a striking instance of this power a few months after the discoveries which I have just described. In the paper read before the Antiquarian Society he suggested the possibility that other "anonymous copies of Barbour's 'Siege of Troy' might have been preserved, either entire or, as here, combined with Lydgate's work," though none such were then known to exist. In the summer of 1866 he was working in the Bodleian, mainly at printed books; "but, seeing a manuscript of Lydgate's 'Troy Book' in an adjoining case, I was tempted," he says, "to take it down, although I knew that all the Bodleian Lydgates had been recently examined with great care for the committee of the Early English Text Society." The beginning and the end were indeed Lydgate's, but on examination it turned out that in the middle were 1200 lines of Barbour, additional to those found at Cambridge, which previous investigators had either failed altogether to look at, or had observed, but supposed to be Lydgate's work. Thus did one discovery with him lead on to another. The importance of the poems discovered may be appre-

ciated when we recollect that, as he says, "hardly anything
of Scotch literature remains to us earlier than the middle
of the fifteenth century, except the 'Brus' by Barbour, who
died in 1395, Wyntown's Chronicle called the 'Orygynale'
(about 1420), and the poems of King James I, who died
in 1437."

A few words should be said here about the publication
of these poems. No sooner had the discovery been made
known to the world than a member of the Roxburghe
Club requested Bradshaw to allow him to edit them as
his contribution to that society. But the finder of the
manuscripts was naturally unwilling to give them up so
easily. Mr Cosmo Innes suggested that Bradshaw should
edit the poems as part of the series published under the
direction of the Lord Clerk Register, corresponding to the
Rolls series in England. "For every reason," he writes
in July, 1866, "we should wish you to be editor, and to
have the credit of your own *trouvaille.*" Writing a little
later, after Bradshaw had apparently communicated to
him his discovery at Oxford, Mr Innes says, "It is indeed
curious that you should go about, like the loadstone-
fingered hero of the fairy tale, to draw out all the lost
fragments of Barbour;" and he goes on to press him
again for an answer as to the publication of the poems.
As his letter to M. Holtrop shows (below, p. 143), Bradshaw
was seriously contemplating an edition. He made considerable preparations for the work, had a large portion
of the manuscript copied out, and sketched out a title-
page, which remains among his papers. But early printing
occupied almost all his time this autumn, and his promotion
to the post of librarian must have caused further delay.

In the autumn of 1867, Mr Innes, who had meanwhile
visited Bradshaw at Cambridge, writes as follows :—" I
have dreamt of Cambridge ever since I left you. I was
most fortunate in my weather, and shall never again see

anything so glorious as that walk with you through your own garden and through Trinity and St John's. . . . I am to meet [the Lord Clerk Register] to-day, and shall try to have something put in shape about a print of the lately discovered poems of Barbour. It seems to me his lordship points to selections from all, as well the translation of the 'Troy Book,' as the original 'Legends of Saints.' It would evidently form a capital philological and critical opportunity. The contemporary English and Scotch cannot be brought better *en evidence* than in 'the Monk' and 'Barbour.' I fancy the editor must work out the forgotten original of Guido de Colonna. Certainly a scholar familiar with Chaucer would not find his previous study useless. I cannot fancy anything dealing with manuscript and black letter more interesting, more picturesque, than an introduction written by the discoverer of such masses of Barbour's verse at Cambridge and Oxford—one qualified to compare the language of the author and the manuscript of the scribe with the corresponding diction and scripture of English contemporaries." Unfortunately, the proposal came to nothing. Years passed by; one thing after another occupied Bradshaw's attention, and he was never able to set his hand to the work. Eventually, both the "Troy Book" fragments and the "Legends of the Saints" were edited by Dr C. Horstmann.[*]

The history of the Barbour fragments has obliged me somewhat to anticipate. I must now go back a little, in order to take up another thread of Bradshaw's researches. In the autumn of 1866 he made a journey to Belgium, in the course of which he very much enlarged his knowledge of early typography. His researches in the history of Dutch and Flemish printing had been discontinued for some time after the date of the last letter to M. Holtrop

---

[*] Heilbronn, 1881-2 : *cf.* Horstmann's " Altenglische Legenden " (Neue Folge), 1881.

quoted above (p. 112). It was apparently an accident
that led him to resume his correspondence. He writes
to M. Holtrop in August, 1865, "You must think that
I have forgotten you, but I have been drawn away to
so many things which I could not neglect, that I am
afraid my work at the Dutch and Flemish books has
almost gone out of my head. . . . The unexpected discovery of a small quarto volume containing eight pamphlets
printed by (1) John de Westfalia, (2) Gerard Leeu, and (3)
in mortario aureo, has roused me again, more particularly
as several of them are not in your collection. Besides
this, a friend of mine has just sent me three leaves rescued
from a book-cover, part of a book printed by Colard
Mansion in his larger type, and this has again set me
upon investigating his books." A fortnight later, "I am
delighted to get your letter, full, as usual, of most interesting
information. I confess I am very glad to hear you are
forced to extend your 'Monuments' to a 21st livraison. I
could wish it were larger, for without it I can do nothing,
and with it it is hardly too much to say that I can do
almost everything I wish with our Dutch and Flemish
incunabula. I have just identified two little Delf books,
thanks to your Delf livraison. . . . I felt by a sort of
instinct that they were within my beat, and that I ought
to know them. German books for the present I leave.
We have very few, and I must be content to learn one
thing at a time ; and my present object is to take advantage
of your 'Catalogus' and 'Monuments,' so as to make our
little collection of as much service as I can."

On May 10, 1866, in answer to a letter from M. Holtrop,
saying that he has been seriously ill, he writes, "I am
extremely sorry to hear of your illness, and only hope
most sincerely that you are by this time quite recovered.
We cannot afford to lose our master yet ; for I always
look on you and speak of you as the chief of my de-

partment—the *département des incunables*—for, indeed, there
is no one connected with any English library, still less
in Paris, who has the leisure and inclination to study
our subject scientifically ; and a merely dilettante employment upon it is of all things the most pernicious and
contemptible. . . . I find the best way by far is to master
one subject thoroughly before going on to the next. In
this way I have mastered Caxton, and to a good extent
the other English printers during the fifteenth century ;
at any rate, I may safely say (and it is very little to say,
after all) that I know more about the matter than any
one in any of our public libraries, or elsewhere as far
as I know. Next I take Holland and Belgium as the
country from which, until 1491, our English type all came.
Of the mass of undated books before 1473 I know very
little ; we have not one specimen in Cambridge. But
from 1473 to 1500, thanks to your ' Catalogus ' and
' Monuments,' as a basis to start from, I am pretty well
master of the subject. This leads on to the various early
Cologne printers, and this at present is the extent of my
range."

He proposed to send M. Holtrop a fortnightly bulletin
of his work and discoveries, "for I am almost always
finding something concerning your affairs." The first
was to be on Colard Mansion, and was to be sent on
May 15. However, the bulletins never came to the birth.
It was cruel to disappoint M. Holtrop, who writes on
June 4, " Je me permets de vous écrire que ce sera avec
le plus grand plaisir que je reçevrai vos Bulletins : je ne
regrette qu'une chose, c'est que tout l'avantage de cette
correspondence sera de mon côté, puisque je ne saurais
vous aider dans vos recherches sur les imprimeurs anglais,
. . . tandis que vous m'avez donné des observations et des
données si précieuses relatives à mes études sur les éditions
incunables Néerlandaises. J'attends avec impatience votre

premier Bulletin." But the letter-writing fit had gone off, and M. Holtrop had to wait four months and to write several appeals before he could get anything more. In the last of these he begs Bradshaw to let him know if a certain book printed by Thierry Martens is in the University Library. This produced an answer in the shape of a closely written letter of four sheets, dated September 19, 1866. "I send you with this," says Bradshaw, "a description of all the books I can find in our library which are printed by Thierry Martens at Alost. They are very few, but out of the six three are not in your printed catalogue. . . . I should be glad to know if my characteristics are belied by the other books which you have. The descriptions are copied simply from the list which I am making (on slips) of the early printed books in our University Library. It takes some time to make the preliminary investigation, but when that is made, each fresh book falls into its place with ease. My chief wish is to see some simple and exhaustive method of collation introduced, and it is for this reason that I have troubled you with more than you wanted, in order that you may see more clearly what I want. . . . I hope before long to have some kind of trustworthy list of English books to refer to. At present there is none. I have been nearly six hours, I find, at this one letter, and have left neither time nor space for all the apologies which I owe you for not writing for so long. I was all packed up and ready to start for the Hague early in August, when something happened which took me to Oxford instead, and for a month nearly I worked for ten hours a day or more, exploring the whole place in search of fifteenth-century books printed in England, the Netherlands, and the *early* Cologne presses."

His note-books show that for some time past he had been working chiefly at Chaucer, in preparation for his edition, and at early printing. In one of them (No. ix) is a list of fifteenth-century books printed in England and the Netherlands, classified under towns and presses, the fullest and most complete which he had yet made. He was getting all his knowledge on the subject into order, so as to profit as much as possible by the visit to Belgium which he intended to make in the autumn. This time, being intent on work, he went alone. He had intended to be away only a few days, but he remained abroad nearly a month. Early in October he was at Bruges, staying at the Panier d'Or, opposite the belfry. Making Bruges his head-quarters, he wandered about, visiting Ghent, Brussels, Lille, and other towns, and revelling in archives and libraries to his heart's content.

On October 6, 1866, he writes to M. Holtrop:—

"I came here last Monday in consequence of a stupid note in the last edition of the 'Manuel du Libraire,' etc., which speaks of variations in Colard Mansion's 'Boccace,' besides what I had already noticed in the first leaf; and with my very full notes, the result of my work at Paris in January, I thought that two or three days would be amply sufficient to satisfy myself abundantly; and I could not bear to send you my notes, which seemed so incomplete, and possibly inaccurate. . . . I should myself have more leisure for these things were I not at the same time minutely engaged upon collation of manuscripts for a large edition of Chaucer's works, as well as some early unpublished Scotch romances, not to mention that a Jewish rabbi and myself are at work upon a minute and elaborate catalogue of our Hebrew manuscripts, in which everything bibliographical falls to my share. However, the extreme kindness which I meet with wherever I go is most refreshing. Paris is the only place I know where everything in the Département des Imprimés is cold and hard and official, when M. Richard is away. But this is uncharitable as well as uninteresting. Good-bye, my dear sir, and believe me to be always,

"Your devoted disciple and servant,

"HENRY BRADSHAW."

It was, apparently, on this occasion that he made acquaintance with Mr Weale, the well-known authority on the art and literature of the Low Countries in the Middle Ages. Mr Weale tells me that he first met Bradshaw at a book-sale in Bruges. He was bidding for a book. Mr Weale, seeing that he was an Englishman, asked him if he had collated it. Bradshaw replied that he had not. "Well," said Mr Weale, "it is imperfect, and I thought I had better tell you before you bought the book." "It doesn't matter," said Bradshaw, "I don't want the book ; I am only bidding to keep things going ; they are so slow." He then asked if he could see the Archives, which Mr Weale obtained permission for him to do. On hearing from Mr Weale that he had discovered some fragments of early printing in the bindings of churchwardens' registry from the villages near Bruges, he was extremely delighted, and, seizing him warmly by the hand, exclaimed, "Ah, you are just the man for me! If *only* people would find out what treasures there are in the bindings of books!"

On October 13 he writes, still from Bruges, to M. Holtrop, "I went to Ghent yesterday afternoon, and, on the strength of your letter and Mr Weale's promise of an introduction, I boldly called on M. Ferdinand Vanderhaeghen. I need not tell you of his kindness, for you must yourself have experienced that before now. I will only say that I never met anything like it, and I have met with a good deal in my day." From Bruges he went on to Lille, whence he writes to M. Holtrop on October 19, "You will see by the date of this that I find it more difficult to get back to England than I had expected.

What with the books I find, and (perhaps as much) the unequalled kindness I have met with all the time I have been abroad, it will take me long to forget my three weeks' holiday this autumn. I left home for three days, and I have been already three weeks away." From Bruges he wrote to his eldest sister as follows :—

"Bruges, October 21, 1866.

" DEAREST K.,

" I left Cambridge on the first of October for this place, for the purpose of seeing and examining some books, which are here in the library, and also at Lille, which it was necessary to see for my purposes. I fully thought I should be back again in five if not in three days, and accordingly have had no letters of any kind. I hope all is well at home, but I am always haunted with ideas that something dreadful will happen while I am away like this.

" Meantime, to be free for a moment from such thoughts, I must tell you how intensely I have enjoyed myself, both in my work and out of it. If I had been a volunteer,* I could not have been met with greater kindness on all sides, and on Tuesday, when I get back, I shall have been here four weeks without one single unpleasant recollection to carry away with me.

" . . . On Sunday last I made the acquaintance of a young Frenchman [Léon Lefebvre], who was opposite me at the *table d'hôte* that day and the day before. I had been struck with his face, and I can generally judge when a man is worth knowing by his face and manner ; and in the evening we were thrown together, and something led us to talk. I found he lived at Lille ; and it ended by my going to Lille with him on Tuesday last. I had wanted more than anything to go there, because of one book which

---

* A large detachment of English volunteers had recently visited Belgium, in order to take part in the Tir National at Brussels, and had been very hospitably received.

L

exists only there ; but I was afraid, after being here so
long, my funds would compel me to go straight home,
besides which, my shyness would have made me miserable
in a strange place, not having that ordinary *savoir faire*
which helps most people on in the world. . . .

"Léon Lefebvre is in business—a partner in a house
at Menin, in Belgium, and himself lives at Lille and
manages their business there.   Nothing could be kinder
than he has been.   He took me to a hotel, and next morning at nine he came and took me to the public library,
and introduced me to the librarian, and when he had comfortably settled me there, he left me on his own affairs.
At four o'clock, when the library shut, he came to see
what I would like to do.   As soon as my six-o'clock
dinner was over, he came to take me for a walk, and then
to his *société*, the Société des Orphéonistes de Lille, with
his other half, one Jules Lefebvre—the same name, but
no relation—just his own age (twenty-one), and doubles
in friendship from children.

"I cannot express in writing the sensations which this
visit has given me.   To be thrown into the middle of
young French life, and to find it so *utterly* different from
what I had expected.   L. L. is a devoted musician, and
would have devoted himself to music, but that his father
(who is an *ancien professeur*, and a charming old man),
with his large family—three sons and four daughters—
thought it better for him to go into business, and so he
has taken to it keenly, but he still keeps up his love for
music.   I had often heard of the Orphéonistes of Lille,
but I little expected to be thrown among them in this way.
You go there in the evening, and you find a quantity of
people, mostly young men, at different tables, with their
dominoes, or draughts, or cards, or billiards, and their glass
of beer, but what struck me most of all was that it was all
for amusement and for excitement.   At the university it

is rare to find men who will sit down to games, such as
draughts, at all, still less who will play at cards or billiards
for love. They must have some stake, they always say,
however small. Here it is quite different. Then afterwards they go upstairs to their concert-room three or four
nights a week, and have their choruses, all without instru-
ments. I never heard anything equal to the singing.
Then between ten and eleven off they go to bed. It is the
naturalness and simplicity and healthiness of the whole
thing that is so enjoyable to come in contact with (I never
heard an approach to bad language); and. I might have
gone to Lille a hundred times without falling into such
company. . . . Good night, dearest K. I wish these hor-
rible forebodings about some one or other of you being
ill or dying didn't haunt me so. It is enough to make me
break off the habit of never writing letters,

"Your most affectionate brother,

"HENRY BRADSHAW."

The episode related in this letter is a good instance of
Bradshaw's power not only of making friends, but of binding them to him with the ties of a warm and lasting affection. In such cases he simply fell in love with his friends,
and they with him. I have given one example already;
this is another, and many more might be mentioned. The
impression produced was generally immediate, a sort of
love at first sight; but it was indelible. Years might pass,
the friends might hardly ever meet again, but neither he
nor they forgot. At Lille, on this occasion, Bradshaw
spent only a few days, but it was enough. He never saw
Jules Lefebvre again. His friend Léon, having business
in this country, went to England with Bradshaw, who
introduced him to his eldest sister and her husband, and
took him down to their country house at Fairchildes, near
Croydon. It was characteristic of him that he was never

happy till he had made his friends and his family acquainted with each other, and he was also anxious to show the young foreigner the interior of an English country home. Mr Daniell remembers Léon well, as a well-bred young man of pleasant manners and appearance, whose conversation showed considerable intelligence. They were struck by his foretelling the Franco-German war. The battle of Sadowa had recently been fought, and four years later the conflict which he prophesied was raging.

Bradshaw and his young friend never met again. The sequel may have some interest, for few episodes in his life made a deeper impression on Bradshaw's mind, and he used to speak of it years afterwards as one of his happiest recollections. Unfortunately, it was a case in which his incapacity for continued or regular correspondence evidently gave some pain, and can hardly but have been to some extent misunderstood. The letters which Bradshaw received from both his friends for some time after his visit are full of affection. Those of Léon Lefebvre contain frequent allusions to the kindness which Bradshaw showed him while in England. He writes on October 31, 1866, " Mon bon et très cher Monsieur Bradshaw, Je suis arrivé à Lille après avoir passé à Boulogne-sur-Mer ainsi qu'à Calais trois journées bien agréables. . . . Maintenant que vous dirais-je encore si ce n'est : Merci ! Mille fois merci pour tout ce que vous avez fait pour moi à Londres ! Merci pour le livre de calcul que vous m'avez envoyé ! Vous me connaissez maintenant sans doute assez pour savoir que je ne suis pas un ingrat. Sachez seulement, que dans toute occasion où je pourrai vous rendre service, je suis à votre disposition, et que dès à present je vous ai voué une sincère et respectueuse amitié."

M. Léon Lefebvre was known amongst his musical friends of the Société des Orphéonistes by the nickname of " Domisol." " Ce nom de *Do-mi-sol*," M. Jules Lefebvre says

in a letter to me, " il permettait à ses bons amis seulement
de le lui donner. Vous savez que ce surnom lui avait été
donné à cause des ses grands aptitudes musicales, et pour
le distinguer de mon frère, qui se nomme Léon." Writing
to Léon on November 3, 1866, Bradshaw puts another interpretation on the name : ". . . Adieu, Léon ! Vous êtes
veritablement *Domi Sol ;* ce qui est, chez lui, le soleil de
sa famille, et de ceux qui l'àiment comme on doit l'aimer.
Croyez moi de cœur tout à vous, Henry Bradshaw." This
view of Léon Lefebvre is fully borne out by what his
friend and brother-in-law, M. Jules Lefebvre, says of him :
" Domisol était le garçon le plus expansif, le plus dévoué,
le plus courageux et le plus obligeant que l'on puisse voir."

For some little time this mutual correspondence continued. The two friends at Lille showed each other the
letters they received from Bradshaw, complimented him
on his French, or playfully corrected here and there the
slight mistakes they found. The whole family regarded
him as their friend. Léon complained that he wrote too
seldom. He answers on November 13, "Pour moi, c'est
la facilité même de lire qui m'emporte un dégoût presque
incroyable en faisant l'essai d'écrire. Je vois seulement
des pages remplies de fautes de grammaire et d'expression,
que néanmoins je ne sais ni corriger moi-même ni faire
corriger : c'est le dégôut d'un homme qui aime surtout la
langue et la litterature de la France, mais qui n'a pas assez
d'énergie pour se rendre maître des elements les plus
simples de la grammaire." He writes again on November 18, "Ce n'est qu'une petite lettre, mais je suis forcé
de vous écrire quelques mots. Je m'assied tout seul dans
ma chambre, et je ne peux pas faire attention à ce que je
voudrais lire, parceque je me souviens toujours du même
jour (la Dimanche) et de la même heure (cinq à six heures
du soir) du jour auquel, il y'a cinq semaines, je m'asseyais
dans la salle à manger du Panier d'Or, pour prendre du

café. Certes je ne trouve pas à mon côté le bon M. Byron, ni m'attend maintenant la bonne fortune de voir entrer mon jeune ami français pour demander s'il y ait de bonne musique à quelqu'une des églises de Bruges. Mais c'est cela une espèce de bonheur qui ne se présente pas tous les jours, et je dois rester content de m'en rappeler par occasion."

He expected to visit Belgium again early in 1867, but the journey was deferred, and gradually the correspondence dropped. The two friends could not understand it. "Vous aurai-je froissé," writes Léon, "dans ma correspondance par hasard? Alors je vous en demanderai mille pardons. . . . Vous savez, M. Bradshaw, quel attachement j'ai pour vous, aussi je suis malade depuis que je vois arriver la fin du mois de janvier sans voir ni vous ni une lettre de vous." He wrote to tell Léon of his becoming librarian, and received his warm congratulations, but after 1869 he does not appear to have written again. At length, thirteen years afterwards, something caused him to write once more to Léon. The letter was answered by his friend Jules, now professor of mathematics at the University of Lille, for Léon was dead. In the interval Léon had married the daughter of a manufacturer at Lille. He had much improved his business, and was in a fair way to make his fortune, when he was carried off by a sudden illness. His delicate constitution had been undermined by incessant hard work and anxiety, and he died in July, 1882, preserving to the last—so M. Jules Lefebvre informs me — the most affectionate recollection of his English friend.

If this episode shows the geniality and simplicity of Bradshaw's character in the most agreeable light, other qualities are as clearly displayed in a letter which he wrote early in 1867, to a friend, W. M. Young, a junior Fellow of King's, on the occasion of the sudden death of his

brother, also a member of the college. "Long before you
went away, you may remember my telling you how he
won my heart at Eton by coming up to me when I was
there in 1861, and introducing himself to me in the school-
yard as *your* brother. We had a walk together at that
time, and it was the beginning of our friendship. It is
hard to say what made him so much liked by every one
here. That he was so, there is no shadow of a doubt.
Living so much as I do among the undergraduates, and
noticing so much all those little casual expressions of dislike or prejudice which the speakers would be so unwilling
to have brought up against them, I must have seen it. . . .
You may well indeed speak of his example. You may,
perhaps, know the dreadful force which the example of
a younger man has, and how very different it is from that
of one of one's own contemporaries. I cannot tell you
in how many hundred ways he is recalled to me in these
things. He literally *made* me do many things by that
gentle, unspeaking compulsion which it is so hard to
describe and yet so easy to feel." Other passages in the
letter show how deep and real were his religious feelings
and convictions. It was only on occasions like this that
his reluctance to talk of what he felt and thought on such
matters was overcome.

During the winter of 1866–7 Bradshaw was somewhat
disturbed by the prospect of succeeding to the post of
librarian, which Prof. Mayor had resolved on giving up.
He had written to Bradshaw of his intention early in
November, 1866. After expressing his opinion that the
statute requiring the librarian to reside would have to be
modified, lest his successor should be compelled, like him,
to do without a holiday of more than eight days together
for nearly three years, Prof. Mayor continues, "I have left
myself no room to speak both of your generosity in leaving
the field open to me in 1864, and of the ready help which

you have given me all along. Without you, I should have thrown up my post in disgust long ago." Professor Mayor has told me that nothing could exceed Bradshaw's helpfulness during this period, or his readiness to interrupt the researches in which he took so intense an interest, in order to undertake any drudgery which had to be done. On March 4, 1867, Bradshaw wrote to M. Holtrop, "Since my return from Bruges and Lille at the end of October, I have not been able to attend for a single day to my early printed books. The news that Mr Mayor was going to resign his place of librarian unsettled me very much, because it was just possible I might succeed him ; and if not, I should leave Cambridge altogether and go and work for you and myself at Oxford, which is at present an unworked field for true bibliographers. I have accordingly been trying to put into shape and order a good deal of the work upon which I have been employed in a desultory manner for more than eight years past, and this has been no easy task. . . . You are most kind in proposing to dedicate your 'Études bibliographiques' on Thierry Martens to me ; * I know very few things which I should appreciate so much. As for my titles, I have none whatever. In the library I am nothing whatever. I receive a salary on the express stipulation that I tell the world that I have no *status* whatever in the place. It is singular, but true."

Writing to Mr Coxe on February 26, Bradshaw says, "Mr Mayor, I believe, resigns to-day. If I should not succeed him, which is of course easily possible, I shall have to ask you to give me some work for a short time, which I have no doubt you would be willing to do. It will be a great comfort when the matter is fairly settled." On Mr Mayor's resignation, Bradshaw at once sent out the following circular to the members of the Senate :—

* M. Holtrop's pamphlet on Thierry Martens appeared in 1868, with a dedication "à son ami, Henry Bradshaw."

"King's College, February 27, 1867.

" SIR,

" I beg to offer myself as a candidate for the office of Librarian, which has become vacant by the resignation of Mr Mayor.

" My work in the University Library during the last ten years has, I hope, given me some experience of the requirements of the place ; and, if the Senate should so far honour me with their confidence as to entrust me with office of Librarian, I can conscientiously say that it would be my one desire and aim to fulfil the duties of the position to the satisfaction of University and to the utmost of my power.

"I have the honour to be, Sir,

"Your obedient servant,

"HENRY BRADSHAW."

Not a few of his friends had urged Bradshaw to stand for the library in 1864. In 1867, there appeared to be but one feeling in the university. During the past ten years he had gained an intimate acquaintance with the library and its contents. A valuable testimony to this qualification for the librarianship appeared very opportunely just at this time. Shortly before Prof. Mayor's resignation, the fifth and last volume of the catalogue of manuscripts was published. In his report to the Syndicate, the editor, Dr Luard, remarks, " It is believed that now every manuscript in the library, and every book with manuscript notes and *adversaria*, has been examined and catalogued. The editor also hopes that the defects and errors which have been observed in the earlier volumes of the catalogue will be found to be remedied by the *corrigenda*. . . . The editor cannot speak of this part of his work without mentioning to the syndices the very great assistance he has received from Mr Bradshaw, to whom many of the most important *corrigenda* are due, and who has brought together the scattered manuscripts from different parts of the library in such a way as to make the arranging and cataloguing of the additional manuscripts a comparatively easy task." It must also be remembered that he had had valuable experience of the ordinary work of the library during the two years in which he acted as assistant. These and other considerations pointed him out as the fittest man for the post. On March 8, 1867, he was elected librarian without opposition. One among the many letters of congratulation which he received appears to sum up the general conviction of the university. It was from Mr Moody, one of his earliest friends, who says, "You are one of the few pegs I know of that has apparently got into the right hole."

CHAPTER VI.

HENRY BRADSHAW'S appointment to the post of librarian was a turning-point in his life. Hitherto he had been, for the most part, an independent worker in the field of science; henceforward he was to be a public servant, whose time and energies were at the service of others. He never ceased to be a student, but his real student-days were over. The leisure and the opportunities of research which he had enjoyed for the last ten years were no longer his. In the interests of learning, the change may be re-garded as unfortunate, but without it some of the best points in his character would not have fully come to light. He had for some time past been accumulating stores of learning, which he only required time to digest and put into shape; he had struck on rich veins of research, which in a few more years he might have satisfactorily worked out. A scholarly edition of Chaucer, a history of typo-graphy, treatises on Irish literature, mediæval liturgies, and other subjects, might have been expected from him. But for such work time was indispensable, and time was just what was denied him. During the early part of his librarianship, he does not appear to have given up the hope of producing his results; he published more, indeed, after 1867 than before. But his publications were in the main the outcome of previous study, and he was unable to settle down to any task demanding continuous applica-tion. He was, therefore, forced gradually to relinquish all hope of giving to the world the works which at one time he contemplated, and to rest content with directing younger students along the lines which he had marked out for himself.

Nothing in his life brings into clearer relief his strong sense of duty than his behaviour in these altered circumstances. Reluctant as he must have been to give up his favourite pursuits, he never allowed them for a moment to interfere with his duties. In discharging those duties he may not have been uniformly successful; there were times when the condition of things in the library produced some discontent. But no one attributed these defects, if defects there were, to any inclination on the part of the librarian to spare himself trouble, or to any subordination of duty to private study. From the moment when he accepted the post, his studies, dear as they were to him, fell into the second place. For the last nineteen years of his life he devoted himself assiduously to his task. He hardly ever left Cambridge; he was always to be found in the library, always ready to give assistance to any student who required it. It would hardly have been possible for any one to act more fully up to his own maxim, that "the first duty of a librarian is to save the time of others."

One of the first subjects discussed by the Library Syndicate, after Bradshaw became librarian, was an addition to the staff and the increase of the librarian's stipend. At this time there were in the library one under-librarian and four assistants. At the recommendation of the Syndicate, a second under-librarian was appointed, and the librarian's stipend raised from £210 to £400. At this figure it remained till 1883, when it was raised to £500 a year.

Bradshaw's acceptance of the post of librarian almost coincided with the completion of the south-west wing of the library buildings. This addition, the most important

which had been made since the erection of Cockerell's
building in 1842, was originally suggested by his friend,
Mr George Williams. It had been begun in 1864, and
the building was finished early in 1867 ; but the new rooms
were not ready for use till the summer of 1868. One of the
first things, therefore, that occupied Bradshaw's attention
in the library was the transfer of books into the new wing.
A room on the ground floor was allotted to him as librarian, but he never made much use of it, for it was too
inaccessible. For any one much occupied with his own
concerns and anxious to find a retreat where he would be
free from interruption, this room would have formed a
quiet and agreeable haunt ; but Bradshaw preferred to
take up his abode in the large room on the first floor.
Here he was much exposed to interruption, or rather, as he
would have preferred to put it, he was accessible to every
student who demanded his assistance. Here, too, he was
among his favourite books and manuscripts, for he at
once resolved to transfer to this part of the library its
most valuable possessions. The room was shut off from
the rest of the building by fireproof doors, and the treasures which had hitherto been more or less scattered about
and unprotected were brought together into one place of
security.

The new librarian began at once to increase the collection of early printed books, with the view of forming a
sort of museum of typography. An excellent opportunity
of advance towards this end was afforded by the occur-
rence, in December, 1867, of a great book-sale at Haarlem.
This was the sale of the famous Enschedé collection, and
it seems to have been the first chance which Bradshaw
had of ordering books of this kind for the University
Library. The Syndics placed the sum of £100 at his
disposal, and he bought several *incunabula* of importance,
including two books attributed to Ulric Zel, of Cologne,

a printer in whom, as we shall presently see, he took a
special interest.   But a much more valuable accession to
the library was made when, in the spring of 1868, he presented to it his own collection of early printed books.
The donation consisted of no less than fifty-eight books
printed in the fifteenth century, more than half of which
were by Ulric Zel and other Cologne printers, the rest
being mainly Dutch, Flemish, and French books.   Shortly
before this, he had presented to the library twelve folio
volumes of Sanscrit works, printed at Bombay.   For both
of these acts of munificence he received the special thanks
of the Syndicate.   Nothing could more clearly have indicated his intention to identify himself with the institution
committed to his charge than this transference of his most
valued possession to its shelves.

A discussion about the archiepiscopal library at Lambeth Palace, which arose in the autumn of 1867, induced
him to write what was, I believe, the only letter he ever
addressed to the daily papers.   The letter in question
exemplifies his acquaintance with the history of great
libraries, a subject to which he always devoted particular
attention.   It is addressed to the editor of the *Times*.

" SIR,
        " In recent discussions about the Lambeth
Library I find it suggested that the Archbishop might be
relieved altogether from the responsibilities attaching to
its custody, and it has been tacitly assumed in letters
written on the subject that the books would, as a matter
of course, be transferred to the British Museum.   I beg,
however, to suggest that, if for any reason the collection
should be removed from Lambeth, the University of
Cambridge is the body to whose care it should on all
reasonable grounds be trusted.

"Any one who is acquainted with the history of the

library knows that it was established by Archbishop Bancroft by his will in 1610, under the express stipulation that
it should be reserved to his successors if they would enter
into covenants to hand it over intact to their successors ;
or, failing this, that it should go to the King's College at
Chelsea if such college were erected within six years,
which did not come to pass ; and again, failing this, he
bequeathed it to the public library of the University of
Cambridge.

"On the execution of Archbishop Laud and the abolition of episcopacy, the University presented a petition to
Parliament claiming the library on the ground that the
first two conditions of Bancroft's will were no longer
capable of fulfilment. The justice of the claim was readily
allowed, and by order of the Lords and Commons the
whole library, including the additions made by Bancroft's
successors, was removed without delay to its new home.
A large room was set apart for the collection ; various
catalogues (still preserved here) were made, so as to render
it as useful as possible ; and there is ample evidence that
the new acquisition was well cared for and highly prized
by the University. At the restoration the University at
once yielded to the representations of the then Archbishop
of Canterbury, and the library was restored to Lambeth.

"The fact that the original library was contingently
bequeathed to the University, and that, on the contingency
arising, the whole collection was transferred to Cambridge
by the authority of Parliament, affords a strong argument
in favour of a like proceeding now if it should be found
impracticable to fulfil the first condition of the founder's
will. I may further mention that by the rules of our
University the books would be accessible to all real
students, from whatever quarter they come, and capable
of being borrowed under such regulations as form a perfect safeguard for their custody without being a bar to

their free use—a boon fully appreciated by those who have enjoyed the privilege of access while the books have been in their present keeping.

"Your obedient servant,

"HENRY BRADSHAW.

"University Library, Cambridge, October 5 [1867]."

It was about the same time that Bradshaw was requested by Archdeacon Cheetham, then one of the sub-editors of the "Dictionary of Christian Antiquities," to contribute articles on lectionaries and other liturgical subjects with which he was intimately acquainted. He did not like to refuse, but asked leave to defer his decision till he could form a better judgment as to the amount of time at his disposal. He found it impossible to do what he was asked. Archdeacon Cheetham wrote several times, but could get nothing out of him. In connection with this, he wrote to Dr Hort, "I should be very glad indeed to write to Cheetham, if I had anything to say, as I feel very much ashamed of myself for never having answered one of his letters for so many years ;* but nothing but oral communication is of any good with me in these matters, because I really have no ideas in my head, or rather, perhaps, I know a few facts which might be useful, but, from never having talked the matter over with any one and had my facts put into shape, I have no motion what to do either towards writing or helping some one to write an article."

Some time afterwards, in 1869, Dr Westcott was more successful in appealing to him on behalf of the "Dictionary of Christian Biography." By dint of great pressure, in the application of which Dr Lightfoot assisted, Dr Westcott succeeded in obtaining from him four short articles. They were biographies of St Abbanus, St Abel, St Abranus, and St Achea. I can remember his writing them, in great

* This was a slight exaggeration.

haste and with much reluctance, for he detested working under pressure, and the work itself was not of a kind at all suitable to him. After this the editors came to the conclusion that the advantage of his assistance was more than counterbalanced by the trouble which it cost him to give and them to obtain it, and asked him for no more.

But although he could not find time to bring the results of his own research to the birth, he found time, as usual, to help other students. Mr Seebohm was about this period working at the second edition of his "Oxford Reformers." His studies of Dean Colet's writings brought him into connection with Bradshaw. Now and then he would run up from Hitchin for a night, to be hospitably entertained in Bradshaw's college rooms, where all students found a welcome. In the examination of manuscripts, in tracing the history of Colet's portrait in the library, and in many other matters connected with the book, Bradshaw gave him much assistance. Speaking of a transcript of Colet's lectures on the Epistle to the Romans which he was superintending, Bradshaw writes in October, 1868, "It was finished as far as my transcriber could do it last week, and brought to me ; but there are many insertions in that dreadful hand of Colet's, which I can quite forgive him for not having courage to put in, and I am going through it as rapidly as I can. But unless I go to the library before breakfast, which I have given up doing lately, there is but one hour and a half in the day to do any work of the kind. . . . I will make the rest (I have done six chapters already) my Sunday work, and so see if you can't have it by Tuesday at latest." Referring to the portrait of Colet, which he had been trying to get photographed for Mr Seebohm, and on the history of which he writes him a long letter, he says, "I am afraid it will not be possible to trace it out more at present, though I am most anxious to find the pedigree of all our portraits, and I have traced a good many within the last few months."

M

This was in connection with his papers on th history of the library, of which more presently. He rea a paper on these portraits before the Cambridge Antiqr ian Society in 1872.*

At the same time he was aiding   upton, who was editing Colet's works. In writing to   n that he had obtained leave for him to retain a man,   for a longer time than usual, he says, " I hope you wil.   le to use it with satisfaction, and without that sense o   which is destructive of all good work ; " and in thankin.   Lupton for a volume of Colet, " It is very interesting   how your labours and Mr Seebohm's are stirring peo   C take an interest in one who has far too long been ne   ed." A little later he writes to Mr Seebohm, " I am reall   ery much obliged for the copy of Mr Myers's ' Catholic Thoughts' in its complete form, and I have been devouring it in such intervals as I can get from my long day's work. For the last ten days or nearly a fortnight we have been very hard at work moving the manuscripts and all my other belongings down into the new building, and my arms are so tired I can hardly write straight. . . . I hope to get a fortnight, or nearly so, at the English Lakes before the end of this month, to set me up with a stock of fresh air for the rest of the year."

During the Lent Term of 1869 there appeared in the *Cambridge University Gazette*, a publication then lately started, a series of papers on the history of the University Library by the librarian. These papers were afterwards reprinted and published in 1881 as No. 6 of the " Memoranda." " It must be borne in mind," says the author in his preface to the re-issue, " that the papers here reprinted are not the result of any research made at the time or for the purpose, but merely notes embodying a few of the facts picked up in the course of twelve years' work

* *Cambridge Antiquarian Society's Communications*, vol. iii. p. 275.

at the library by one who loved to know something of the personal history of any volume which might come into his hands." Writing to Mr H. B. Wheatley in 1883 about this sketch, he says, "I reprinted [in 1881] everything as it stood, and it is one mass of mistakes. But that matters little, as, though published, it is not likely to be read by many people." However this may be, the papers are not only valuable in themselves as containing the only continuous history of the library yet in existence, but as throwing light on the affection with which Bradshaw regarded the treasures committed to his charge.

In speaking of the fourth side of the eastern quadrangle, built by Archbishop Rotherham about 1475, he laments the "characteristic manner" in which the authorities .of the university afterwards treated the benefaction. A century ago Rotherham's building was pulled down, "and the Gothic front, with the bishop's arms, etc., upon it, was sold off as rubbish, and now forms the entrance to the stables at Madingley Hall. After this it is needless to add that the new building contained no record of its replacing an older one, and all notice of Rotherham is obliterated from the library." The latter half of the sixteenth and the first quarter of the seventeenth century were a very bad time for the library. In Edward VI's reign there was a "general clearance of rubbish, as old books were then considered. . . . The hatred of the old learning seems to have been for a time so intense, that few things having the semblance of antiquity about them were spared. The fact that in the king's own copy of the new edition of the Greek Testament (ed. Steph. Paris: 1550) we find large fragments of an early manuscript of Horace and Persius used for binder's waste, is a fair illustration of the respect in which the different kinds of learning were then held." During the first fifteen years of Elizabeth's reign, the whole amount laid out upon the library was £1 6s. 8d. To the period of

James I may perhaps be attributed "that rebinding of all
the manuscripts which has destroyed every trace of their
former history, even to the names of the donors." Better
times came in the reign of Charles I.   One of the few good
things recorded of the first Duke of Buckingham is that,
when chancellor of the university, he founded the collection
of Oriental manuscripts, and intended to spend seven thousand pounds on rebuilding the library.   A little later many
other benefactions were made, among them the Vaudois
manuscripts presented by Morland.   The ignorance which
prevailed about these books, says Bradshaw, is only "one
example in a thousand of the disregard of such treasures
which the whole history of the library brings to light."

The activity and good management which encouraged
these gifts in the seventeenth century ceased during the
Georgian period.   The most valuable part of Bishop
Moore's library was treated as almost beneath consideration: "Nothing could be more disgraceful than the way
in which the manuscripts were literally shovelled into their
places."   The library was left almost entirely unguarded.
During the thirty-five years that followed the presentation
of Bishop Moore's library to the university by George I in
1715, "the pillage was so unlimited that the only wonder
is that we have any valuable books left."   This culpable
neglect went on throughout the century.   In 1748 over
nine hundred volumes were reported as missing from the old
library alone; at the next inspection, in 1772, many more
rare volumes were found to have disappeared.   And yet
no attempt was made to limit the freedom of access to all
parts of the library.   "The 'Cicero de Officiis,' printed in
1465, on vellum; a Salisbury Breviary printed in 1483, on
vellum (the only known copy of the first edition); the
Salisbury 'Directorium Sacerdotum,' printed by Caxton
(the only known copy), are three instances out of many
scores which might be mentioned as purloined during the

latter half of the eighteenth century, simply from this total disregard of all care for the preservation of the books." One can imagine the pain with which Bradshaw must have recorded these irreparable losses which the library had sustained.

I may mention here that in the year 1869 Bradshaw was made a member of a Syndicate of which Mr W. G. Clark (public orator), Dr Luard, and Professor Mayor were also members, appointed to consider the form of service for the Commemoration of Benefactors. The work of revision was long and laborious. In the addition of names to the list and the correction of errors, Bradshaw's acquaintance with the history of the university was of great service. The form now used on the day of commemoration is the work of this Syndicate.

Meanwhile, in the midst of his official and literary occupations, Bradshaw's social life went on unchecked. The change in his position made no difference in his habits, except that he was more continuously at Cambridge. One of the short absences which he allowed himself was occasioned by the return of his friend, W. M. Young, to India. Bradshaw insisted on "propemping" him, as he called it, on his way. It was in June, 1867. Mr Young tells the story as follows :—" When I left for India, he said he should come and see me off at Charing Cross. To my surprise, when we met there, he said there was a book he wanted to see in Paris, and he was coming so far with me. We spent a day in the Paris Exhibition, and he found out that he had long wanted to see Avignon, and made up his mind to come on. After we had got into the train, I found that he had taken his ticket for Marseilles. He should go to Avignon, he said, on his way back. As he stood on the quay watching the Messageries vessel gliding away, I took off my old silver watch-chain and threw it to him. He wore this as a guard for his keys for years." On his way home from Marseilles, Bradshaw turned aside to Grenoble, where he wished to see a Vaudois manuscript of the New Testament. The librarian was away; in his absence no one could get in. Bradshaw begged for admittance, but the concierge, an old woman, was obdurate. "I only want to see one book," he said, "and I have come all the way from England on purpose." "But if I let you in, you would never find the book." "Oh yes, I should; I know where it is." This persistence, with the aid of a ten-franc piece, which I find noted in his diary, was too much for the old lady, and she fetched the keys. He knew the class-mark of the book, and, once in the library, a moment's glance at the arrangement of the shelves showed him its geography. He went straight to the place, took out the book, made a few notes, and went his way. At Paris he did the work which had been the pretext for his journey, and in six days was back at Cambridge.

Towards the end of the Michaelmas Term, 1868, an incident occurred which illustrates at once the kindness of his heart and the width of his intellectual sympathies. A congress of students was to be held at Ghent, to which delegates from Cambridge were invited. The invitation, being addressed simply "to the students of the University of Cambridge," was handed over, as such postal curiosities generally are, to the librarian. Bradshaw read it aloud one evening for the amusement of some undergraduates who were in his rooms. Two or three congresses, it appeared, had been held already. Their general object seems to have been to promote a *rapprochement* between university students and the working classes, both being the victims of oppression, the former at the hands of the professors, the latter at those of the capitalists. The comic side of the affair was that which struck the larger part of those present most strongly; but one of them, being of a somewhat revolutionary turn, was inclined to take it seriously.

Suddenly Bradshaw, who had been laughing with the rest, turned to the solitary supporter of the scheme and said, "Will you go, and report to me all about it? I will gladly pay your expenses." The proposal was promptly accepted ; a companion was found, and Bradshaw paid the expenses of both, merely exacting from them the condition that he should have a full daily report of their proceedings. The "delegates," B. F. Lock, of King's, and A. C. Cook, of Trinity Hall, went to Ghent, were very well received by the other members of the congress, who were mostly Belgian students, heard and made speeches of an "anti-governmental and anti-professorial" character, drank rather more beer than they liked, but otherwise enjoyed themselves to their hearts' content.

The fortnight's holiday, to which he was looking forward when he wrote to Mr Seebohm, was spent in the Lakes in July of that year (1869), in company with an undergraduate friend. He wanted a holiday badly, for he had hardly been away at all for nearly three years, and during that time had been incessantly at work. A week was passed at Grasmere, and another at Thirlspot. When on these excursions, though he habitually took but little exercise at Cambridge, he was capable of tramping over hill and dale for long distances. During the holiday of which I am speaking, he and his friend walked one day over Armboth Fell to Rosthwaite, in Borrowdale, and thence over Styhead Pass to Wastdale Head. It was very wet, and when they arrived at the little inn, then kept by the well-known Willie Ritson, they were drenched to the skin. Being out for a single night only, they had little baggage ; but Ritson had plenty of dry clothes, and Bradshaw was soon rigged out from top to toe in one of his host's best suits. A sharper contrast could hardly be found than that between the exteriors of the two men, and Bradshaw cut a quaint figure in the tall and meagre north-countryman's clothes, which re-

fused to meet round his waist, and had to be turned up
half-way to his knee. There were other guests too, both
men and women, all equally wet through, but Ritson and
his wife possessed a wardrobe sufficient for all. The
comical appearance of the circle round the fire that evening
was one not to be forgotten. Among the visitors there·
happened to be a member of a Quaker family well known
at Darlington. Bradshaw had never met him before, but
of course knew all about him, and no sooner heard his
name than he began inquiring about his relatives. At
first the young man was a little shy and distant, but Bradshaw's manner was irresistible, and before the conversation
was over he had fairly thawed him out of his reserve.

A month later he was at Liverpool, bidding farewell to
his sister and her husband, Bishop Oxenden, who were
starting for Montreal. He thought nothing of travelling
from one end of the country to the other for a purpose of
this kind, and enjoyed turning up at unexpected hours at
the house of a friend or relative. " I got to London at half-
past four yesterday morning [from Liverpool]," he writes,
"just in time to wash and change and go down to Croydon
by the six-o'clock train ; and then had a seven miles' walk
over to Fairchildes, which I reached just before breakfast."
Shortly afterwards he was with his mother at Bournemouth. Two of his sisters were there too, and this renewal
of the family circle made him very happy.· Writing from
her house there to a friend, whom he had asked down to
stay there with him, he says, " I can't tell you how delightful it is being here in this way. My mother is very
much better than I expected, and altogether I shall not
easily forget the happiness of this visit, short as it is ; and
as I cannot see you, I am at least glad to have the opportunity of talking to you from here, which is the next best
thing to having you." It was the last visit to Bournemouth
which he was to pay under these happy circumstances, for in

the winter of this year, to his intense grief, his mother died. To the same friend, with whose family he had spent a day in town, he writes a little later, "I cannot tell you how glad I am to have seen you all at home, and to have got over that utterly stupid fear of unknown people which somehow I almost always have until I actually see them."

In September, 1869, he was at Longleat, examining the Chaucer manuscripts in the Marquis of Bath's library. It was a member of that family who brought out the *editio princeps* of the poet in 1532. He was delighted with his visit. Writing thence to a friend, he says, "This place is beyond description charming, and I little thought a year ago that my Chaucer studies would be so well rewarded by having a week's enjoyment here, with liberty to explore to my heart's content." Soon afterwards he wrote to his host as follows :—"Dear Lord Bath, I must take the opportunity of the first free hour that I have had after the flood of work which I found waiting for me on my return home, to write and express some little portion of the thanks which I owe for the delights of my visit to Longleat. Your own and Lady Bath's unlooked-for kindness made my stay there so very different from what it might have been that I am not likely soon to forget my week there ; and I can only wish that there was anything that I could do to be of use to you in my own way, in return for the ready confidence with which you threw open all your treasures to me. . . . I look forward very much to two things being carried into effect about which you were speaking. One is that a thorough inventory should be made of all the things in the house, which would be of very great service both now and hereafter ; the other is that, if the Government will really undertake to calendar the papers *within a reasonable time* (this would be a most important stipulation), I am sure you would have no reason to regret allowing it to be done. . . .

I have run on longer, perhaps, than I ought to have done on this subject, but the fact is that the first result of my moving down this summer into a new wing of the University Library, where I have brought together all the manuscripts and early printed books, is that I am now for the first time able to attempt a classification of our collection of manuscripts, which have been classed for more than a hundred years without any regard whatever to subject or even to size. And here my week at Longleat has just had the effect of determining me finally to what had been formerly merely a floating idea, namely, to make two broad divisions into *books* and *papers*, the first containing the *literature*, where manuscripts were succeeded by printed books; and the second, all the letters, papers, accounts, loose charters, and other miscellaneous documents of which there are always so many in any large library, but which it is generally so hopeless to attempt to classify as part of a collection of *books*."

Later in the autumn he made a hasty rush to Belgium, in order to see the Meyer collection, which was to be sold shortly afterwards at Ghent. He took with him the same undergraduate friend who had been with him in the Lake district earlier in the year, and paid all the expenses of the journey. They were away less than four days, starting on a Friday afternoon and coming back the next Tuesday morning, but it was long enough to see Bruges pretty thoroughly. Mr Weale was a kindly and omniscient guide among the churches and pictures of the old Flemish town, and the hospitable Panier d'Or supplied clean beds, fair wine, and an excellent *table d'hôte*. It was Saturday morning and market-day when the friends arrived. The towering belfry looked down from the opposite side of the market-place on the little inn, where the breakfast was served in the sunny *salle à manger;* the great square outside was alive with bustle and colour and spotless Flemish caps ; the whole scene possessed for one of the travellers the ineffable charm of a first day abroad, while the other was no less happy in the pleasure which he conferred. From Bruges they went on to Ghent, where Bradshaw was busy almost the whole day among his books ; but he found time to take his friend to St Bavon, and to show him the great Van Eyck, his favourite among all pictures.

A Christmas present which he received that year was the " Memoir of Jane Austen," written by her nephew, Mr Austen Leigh. Miss Austen's novels were among those which gave him the most unmixed pleasure. As his way was, he liked the book all the better because it was given him by a son of the author. Writing to thank the giver, he says, " I finished it the same evening that it arrived. It was one o'clock before I went to bed, having just finished it and made out a family pedigree, which, with the help of the tabulated information I got from you some time ago, will put me fairly in the way of getting a clear view of the family connections on one side. I am really delighted with the book."

I have already mentioned the gifts of books which Bradshaw made to the library in 1867 and 1868. In both of the two following years he repeated these donations. Among the books which he gave in 1869 was a copy of the first Prayer-book of Edward VI, and early in 1870 he added several more fifteenth-century books to the museum of which he was so fond. But in March of that year he outdid himself by presenting to the library the whole of his Irish collection. It is described in the Library Report as "a collection of books and papers, pamphlets and broadsides, either (1) printed in Ireland, or (2) written by Irish authors, or (3) relating generally to Irish affairs, about 5000 in number." The offer of the collection is contained in the following letter to Dr Atkinson, then vice-chancellor.

" University Library, March 30, 1870.

"MY DEAR SIR,

"There is a matter which has been in my mind for some time past, and which I should be glad if you could bring before the Library Syndicate before they separate for the vacation.

"I have a considerable collection of books, pamphlets, and other printed papers relating to Ireland. The basis of it is the Irish portion of my father's library, that portion of it in which, as coming himself from the North of Ireland, he took most interest, and which, at his death in 1845, he left to me. For several years I did a good deal to increase the collection, especially in the matter of pamphlets and printed papers, though it is still, of course, very far from having any claim to completeness.

"It would give me sincere pleasure if the Syndics would accept this collection as a gift to the library. More than forty years ago, when public libraries were less plentifully supplied than they are now, literary men used to come to my father's house to work at these books when engaged in writing upon Irish affairs, and from the time that I was a child, they have had a particular interest for me. Although I have been able to give but little attention to them for some few years past, yet I have by me a mass of bibliographical notes on the subject, collected during the last twenty years; and if I could feel that these books and papers were deposited in some more permanent resting-place than my own library, I should more readily try to put my notes in order so as to turn them to some practical use.

"There are about 1000 bound volumes; and of the pamphlets and other printed papers there are, speaking roughly, about 2700 in octavo, 700 in quarto, and 500 in folio, including proclamations, broadsides, and fly-sheets.

These, with a number of original signed petitions to the
Houses of Parliament (chiefly ranging from 1809 to 1819,
and relating to the so-called Catholic claims) and a few
other manuscripts, amount in all to about 5000 pieces.
There are necessarily many duplicates in such a collection,
and many also will be already in the University Library;
but, after making all due allowance for these, there must
remain a considerable number which the library does not
possess, and which it would be difficult either to find elsewhere or to bring together again.

"I should not wish to impose any terms whatever
upon the Syndicate, if they should think fit to accept the
books. I have no views about sacredness of duplicates,
or the necessity of keeping such a collection intact. My
whole wish is to enable the University to enrich its library
with a class of books with which, though possessing some
very precious things of the kind, it is on the whole but
poorly provided at present; and I should therefore prefer
that any suggestion which I might be inclined to make
concerning their arrangement, should be made by me as
the librarian to whose charge they would be confided under
the control of the Syndicate, rather than that the gift should
be hampered with conditions such as in many cases serve
to hinder the very object for which the collection was
formed.

" It will not be easy for me to forget the liberal manner
in which the University, at the suggestion of the Library
Syndicate, enabled me for more than seven years to pursue
the studies which I had most at heart, and the confidence
implied in the fact that no report of my work during that
time was ever demanded of me. I hope that the confidence was not wholly misplaced; but I cannot express
strongly enough that the freedom of those seven years of
work, as it has produced results which I could not have

foreseen, so it has given me a sense of debt to the University which nothing can remove.

"Yours most truly,

"HENRY BRADSHAW.

"The Rev. The Vice-Chancellor, Clare Lodge."

The thanks of the Senate to Mr Bradshaw for this munificent gift were expressed in a letter composed by the public orator, Mr R. C. Jebb. The collection was kept together, and was enlarged at Bradshaw's death by the addition of such Irish books as he had acquired since 1870, but had not yet presented to the library.

In the movement for the abolition of tests, which was going on at this time, Henry Bradshaw took much interest. He was strongly in favour of the removal of existing restrictions, but in urging this he took, as usual, a distinct line, and in this case, perhaps, one not generally taken by supporters of the measure. What he objected to in the maintenance of the test was not so much the exclusion which it involved, as the nature of the test itself. While maintaining that on general grounds it was both impolitic and detrimental to the interests of the university that it should be confined to members of any particular denomination, he refused to allow any weight to arguments derived from abstract considerations of justice, equality, and the like. The state, or the university under the state, was justified, he believed, in making whatever limitations it considered expedient. If the state thought fit to admit none but members of the Church of England to university honours, well and good ; he could not deny its legal and moral right to do so. But he insisted that, at all events, the means adopted to distinguish members of the Church of England from members of any other body, or from freethinkers, should be unobjectionable in themselves.

The existing test he considered in the highest degree

objectionable, because it imposed upon young men, at the most critical period of their lives, the burden of making or refusing to make a distinct confession of faith, the full meaning of which the large majority of them could not possibly comprehend. His intimate acquaintance with generation after generation of undergraduates, his knowledge of the searchings of heart which most serious men go through during their sojourn at the university, deepened in him the conviction that the imposition of a religious test was immoral. For the frivolous and thoughtless it degraded a solemn asseveration to a mere form of words.; while many thoughtful men, in the very crisis of a spiritual and intellectual conflict, were placed under an overpowering temptation to swallow their doubts and to tell a lie.

In taking this line, Bradshaw was further influenced, on the one hand, by his natural delicacy of feeling, and on the other, by his general opinions regarding the Church. When asked what test—supposing it to be desirable to maintain the existing restriction—he would substitute for the declaration of faith, he replied that none was required. According to his notions, every English subject was a member of the Church of England, unless and until he was proved to be something else. Those who by birth, or by explicit and voluntary declaration, belonged to any dissenting body, or had cut themselves off from the Church, were obviously excluded from taking degrees, and in their case no test was needed ; all others were admissible, and no question need be asked. If it were objected that dishonest persons, not being members of the Church, would take advantage of such a system to obtain admission to degrees, the answer was clear : against such persons no test would be a barrier. But what weighed with him, perhaps, more than anything else was his dislike of public discussions or statements about religion. It appeared to him, if one may so put it, a sort of profanation to drag a man's doubts or convictions into the light of day. For these reasons he supported the abolition of tests with all his heart, and was opposed to all the reservations, with regard to headships, clerical fellowships, etc., which it was sought, in some cases successfully, to introduce. When Lord Salisbury's committee was sitting, in July, 1870, he was requested by Lord Houghton, as a leading university Liberal, to give evidence before it. Whether he intended to do so or not, I am unable to ascertain ; but the committee came to an end with the session, after examining only four witnesses, of whom he was not one.

In the autumn of 1870 Bradshaw was requested by one of the leading Fellows of the college, in the name of a large portion of that body, to allow himself to be nominated for the office of vice-provost. The office is one which imposes no very onerous duties ; but, as it involves representing the head of the college whenever the latter is absent, as well as a general superintendence of what may be called the social side of the institution, it is one which demands considerable tact, good sense, and social qualities, and is generally held by one of the most prominent members of the resident body. There can be little doubt that, had Bradshaw allowed himself to be nominated, he would have been elected to the post, but he firmly declined. On a subsequent occasion, when a similar proposal was made, he returned the same answer.

It was at the close of this year that he migrated from the rooms which he had occupied since his return to the college in 1856, to those immediately below them on the same staircase. In these rooms, which had formerly belonged to Mr George Williams, he remained for the rest of his life. This change of quarters was the cause of a somewhat amusing incident. For some years past the rooms in question had been held by a non-resident Fellow of the college, now dead. This gentleman showed no intention of living in them ; and, except for two or three pairs of old boots, left as a kind of symbol of occupation, the rooms remained absolutely empty. So unreal a tenancy could only be tolerated so long as there was no demand for the rooms. Accordingly, when Bradshaw applied for them, his application was at once granted, much to the wrath of the quasi-occupant, who protested loudly against his eviction. Finding written remonstrances fruitless, he hurried up to Cambridge to see what he could accomplish by a personal interview. As chance would have it, he met the intruder issuing from the staircase, on his way out for a walk. Posting himself full in Bradshaw's path, with the object of forcing a hearing, he attacked him in a violent manner on the subject of the rooms. To the flood of argument and invective which he poured forth, Bradshaw made no reply, but walked straight on, pushing his assailant backwards as he went. In this way they traversed the court, the one silently and steadily advancing, the other gesticulating and vociferating, but constantly forced to give way. Bradshaw's superior weight and self-control gave him the advantage at all points, moral and physical, in this curious conflict, which, however, was prolonged until the college gates were reached. Then, and not till then, the enemy withdrew baffled from the field, leaving the victor to continue his walk unmolested and triumphant. The scene was observed by several witnesses, who were much amused by the contrast—at once ludicrous and instructive—between his silent but successful resistance and the futile vehemence of his opponent. Had Bradshaw been a Quaker by profession, instead of only by descent, he could not have more pointedly exemplified his creed.

At Whitsuntide, 1871, he enjoyed a short visit to the Lakes, and put up again at the hospitable little inn at Thirlspot. On this occasion he took with him, as a com-

N

panion, one of the younger library assistants. "A more
delightful holiday," writes his friend, "I have never had.
Mr Bradshaw was in the best of moods, and full of playful
banter. I remember his remark that Cumberland was one
of the best places in the world to get cobwebs blown from
one's brain. He made me pass the waterfall at Lodore
without seeing it, in order to prove to him that I did not
want to 'tick it off' as done. He paid all the expenses of
the journey in the kindest and most generous way." This
was the first year in which the library was closed from the
Saturday before Whitsunday to the Tuesday after. For
several years after this he used the short holiday thus
afforded to pay a visit to the Lakes. No season pleased
him so much as this, when the oaks and birches were in
their first and freshest green.

In the autumn of 1871 he made a discovery of considerable importance to Celtic scholars—that of the Welsh
glosses, numbering about 140, in the manuscript of
Martianus Capella, preserved in the library of Corpus
Christi College, Cambridge. He communicated the discovery, as he did all others of a like nature, to Mr Whitley
Stokes, who was then in India. These glosses formed a very
considerable addition to the materials for reconstructing
the grammar and philology of the early Celtic languages.
The existence of the manuscript was, of course, well
known, as it formed part of the famous collection left by
Archbishop Parker to the library of his own college; but
no attention had previously been paid to it from this point
of view. Writing to Mr Stokes in November, 1871,
Bradshaw says, "The handwriting is so beautifully clear
that it is quite impossible to mistake the words, and I
shall therefore print them as accurately as I can, with
a photograph of a glossed page of the manuscript, to give
people an idea of the look of it. This will save you the
labour and risk of copying when time is precious, and will

leave you free to verify and revise my readings at your pleasure. When printed, you must let me place the copies at your disposal, as the least tribute I can give to one to whom I owe so much." After mentioning a number of interesting points, he continues, " As soon as I have done these (I am now going carefully over the whole a second and partly a third time), I must go carefully through the Juvencus again, as I find that the view with which one looks at these things is a good deal firmer (palæographically) than it was some years ago. . . . My delight is that I should have gone to Corpus absolutely with a determination to find *something* to welcome your return with, thinking I might perhaps find a few Irish bits or early glosses, but I little expected to light upon such a treasure as this." Later on he speaks of his intention to print a pamphlet about these glosses, but he never carried out this plan, nor does he appear to have printed even the list. *

The new Lectionary, or Table of Lessons, which is now in general use, came out in 1871. The Syndics of the University Press were anxious to publish Bibles for use in church, showing by some easy system of reference the arrangement of the lessons. It was Bradshaw who devised and carried out the plan of marking the beginnings and ends of the lessons by means of capital letters in the margin, referring to short notes at the foot of the page. This method has the obvious practical advantage of supplying marks which easily catch the eye, and directions which, when once the lesson is found, obviate the necessity of recurring to a table, while the text itself is left untouched. It was adopted by the Syndicate, and has been used in Cambridge Bibles ever since. The chairman of the Press Syndicate, in conveying to Bradshaw the thanks of that body, remarks, " The Syndics are very

---

* See above, pp. 72, 188 ; and Loth, " Vocabulaire Vieux-Breton," pp. ix , 22, etc.

sensible that you have conferred a great benefit upon al church-going people, as well as upon themselves."

In June, 1872, an incident occurred which caused a good deal of feeling in the university, and roused Bradshaw to such a pitch of indignation that he took the (for him) very unusual step of publishing a letter of remonstrance to the Senate on the subject. Mr Kerrich, university librarian at the beginning of the century, had left a large number of pictures, books, etc., to his son, the Rev. R. E. Kerrich, of Christ's College. This collection was bequeathed by the latter to the university in 1868, as "an addition to the Fitzwilliam Collection," together with the sum of £1000. That it contained some things of little or no value is doubtless true. The same may be said of the Fitzwilliam Collection itself, or of almost any collection that was ever made. But the Fitzwilliam Museum Syndicate were of opinion that the valuable part bore but a small proportion to the whole. Accordingly, on the ground that the museum would not contain the whole collection, they recommended that "the bequest, including the legacy of £1000, should be renounced, on the understanding that the representatives of Mr Kerrich should allow the Syndicate to select any portion of the collection which they might think desirable for the university."

The views which Bradshaw held with regard to the treatment of benefactors, and the impolicy—to put it on the lowest ground—of the attitude which the university had too often taken up in such matters, were expressed pretty strongly in his papers on the history of the library.* The proposal of the Syndicate seemed to him only another illustration of the system which he deprecated. To avert what he considered as nothing less than a disaster, he issued the following letter to the Senate :—

* See above, p. 163.

"King's College, June 4, 1872.

" It was only this morning that most of us received the news of Mr Kerrich's generous bequest of his whole collection to the university, 'to form an addition to the Fitzwilliam Collection.' But I am sure that many persons besides myself will have experienced an unpleasant sensation in reading the Grace which was circulated at the same time (though it escaped my notice till this afternoon), by which the bequest is declined on the supposed ground of want of accommodation at the museum. I hope it is not yet too late to urge upon the council of the Senate the need of reconsidering such a decision, and to entreat that the Grace may be withdrawn.

" The extract from Mr Kerrich's will closes thus : '. . . trusting that, in consideration of the acknowledged value of the larger portion of the bequest, the Syndics will pay some respect-to that portion of it which I well know is of little or no value.' Few can have read these touching words without being struck with the characteristic modesty which dictated them. There are many here who knew Mr Kerrich's generous and unselfish character far better than I did ; many who knew the unparalleled devotion which he had for the memory of his father, to whose knowledge and taste the present collection is mainly due, and who for more than thirty years held an office of great responsibility in the university. But it is impossible for those who knew him at all well—and I hope I may consider myself among that number—not to look upon it as a natural and pardonable wish on his part, that his name should be handed down among the benefactors of the university in such a way as to keep the memory of his father's labours fresh before our eyes. This result is precluded by the course now proposed, and the 'some respect,' which Mr Kerrich fondly hoped the Syndicate would pay, shows itself only in ungracious silence.

"It would have made the proposal a little less unpalatable if the Syndicate had even taken the trouble to lay before the Senate the principal results of their examination of the collection in the form of a report, instead of dismissing the matter in the present summary manner. The only satisfaction is, that we are now happily prevented from knowing the names of the individual Syndics on whose recommendation this ungenerous proposal has been brought before us.

"I have spoken of the bequest being declined, because it is clear that if the terms of the will are not accepted, any such arrangement as that contemplated by the proposed Grace is simply a bargain in which the university proposes to renounce the entire bequest, *as a bequest*, if Mr Kerrich's representatives will consent on their part to make a gift of the more valuable portion of the collection to the university. This mode of bargaining is at best unsatisfactory; it is a request which many must think we have no right to make; and it is doubly hard that one who has lived so long amongst us, and has wished so well to the university, should not be allowed a place among our benefactors.

"It is a rare thing for the university to receive a bequest of such value, and a very rare thing to receive one wholly free from those vexatious stipulations by which the vanity of the owner is sometimes but too apt to impair the value of the gift. Knowing, as I do by some experience, how often the churlish reception of one gift has damped the enthusiasm of those who would gladly have offered their good things, but have shrunk from the prospect of similar treatment, I cannot but protest strongly against the proposed mode of dealing with Mr Kerrich's bequest. In all collections there must be a certain number of articles of little value; but all things need not have the same place of honour, and it is difficult to believe that it would be impossible to find sufficient accommodation for the whole collection.

"It will be said by some that this is a case of sentiment *versus* business; but there are occasions—and I should not speak unless I believed this to be one—where the hardheaded men of business in the university, who carry everything before them, are apt to overreach themselves, and bring about results which they could not foresee, and which they would be themselves among the first to deprecate. I hope it may not be so now.

"HENRY BRADSHAW."

There were, perhaps, some remarks in this letter which in cooler moments Bradshaw would have been inclined to modify, but most persons will probably now agree that a protest of some kind was required. The shortness of the notice given, and the apparent want of deliberation with which the proposal was made, were, at all events, sufficient reason for deferring action. The grace was accordingly rejected by a majority of nearly three to one. The Syndicate were, however, not to be beaten. During the long vacation the pictures and engravings were exposed to view in the Fitzwilliam Museum; and early in the Michaelmas Term the proposal was again brought forward, the only modification being that "competent advice" should be taken in the selection of the articles to be retained by the university. This time there was no opposition, and the proposal was accepted by the Senate. The legacy of £1000 was given up, together with the greater part of the collection. Among the books thus rejected was one which was sold shortly afterwards for the sum of £200, as well as a complete collection of Stephen Weston's tracts, many of them of the greatest rarity, given by the author himself to Mr Kerrich.

In the autumn of this year Bradshaw was again at

Bournemouth, with his eldest sister and two of her children.
One of his younger nieces was left at home, and while
they were away, he wrote her daily letters, full of enter-
taining news, to comfort her in her loneliness. Here are
two or three extracts, which show that it was as easy for
him to gossip with a child as it was to decipher a manuscript or to puzzle out a problem in bibliography :

> "MY DEAREST MAUD,
>
> " I am very glad I did write yesterday, as in
> the end our arrangements went all nohow or contrariwise
> (as Tweedledee would say), and it ended by no more
> letters being written. However, a good budget came this
> morning from Fairchildes, and, desolate as you are, it is
> a great comfort to think you are well and flourishing. It
> is a great disappointment not to have Arthur, but it is
> much happier to think of his taking care of you and father.
>
> ". . . We saw Miss —— this morning after service, and
> she walked home part of the way with us. I don't know
> how to account for it, but her hair, which used to be snow-
> white, is now a beautiful pale gold, in parts a shade darker
> than Arthur's. . . . Tell father I have sent him, by this post,
> the new Macmillan, which contains the next chapter of
> the Phaeton story. I brought it away from Cambridge on
> Saturday, with the new part of Middlemarch, which I am
> reading aloud to [your] mother. . . . Write if you can find
> time from Jenny Jones and its variations, and give my
> kind regards to Miss Breguet. I must try and see you, even
> if it be only for a few hours, before I go back to Cambridge
> again. Best love to father and Arthur, and pray comfort
> Nanna about the boy,* and tell her he is all right.
>
> ". . . I needn't tell you what a pleasure it was to me to
> get my first letter from you. I hope very much it won't be
> the last ; but don't bother yourself to write when you don't

---

* A small nephew, who was in rather weak health.

feel inclined, for it is no trouble to sit down and talk to you for a few minutes after tea. . . . I am sorry to hear of the death of poor Jenny Jones. I wonder whose turn it will be next. I have that minor variation running in my head now, going in and out all round the original tune in the most doleful way. . . . Now good-bye, dearest Maud, with best love from everybody, and especially Boykin [her youngest brother], who is standing opposite to me at the table in the study.

"Ever your most affectionate,

"Henry Bradshaw."

Towards the end of the year 1872, he received a visit from his friend Professor ten Brink, the well-known Chaucer scholar. They had never met before, and the pleasure which the meeting gave was mutual. I cannot do better than let Professor ten Brink give his own account of it.* He writes as follows:—"The unselfishness, generosity, and helpfulness which are displayed in Mr Bradshaw's letters were equally apparent in our personal intercourse at Cambridge. For a whole week I enjoyed his hospitality in King's College. I conversed with him several hours every day; we had our meals and took walks together. He showed me over the chapel, the library, and the gardens, both of his own and other colleges; he made me acquainted with the treasures of the University Library and with the neighbourhood of the town. In his rooms he read aloud to me his favourite passages from Browning's poems; we talked about English literature and the laws of Latin prosody. The conversation naturally turned very often on Chaucer; and one Sunday we made a pilgrimage to Trumpington, without indeed seeing much trace of Chaucer or his miller. We discussed many Chaucerian

* I translate from a letter to myself. For the origin of their acquaintance, see below, chap. vii.

problems, and inspected a number of manuscripts and ancient books. I had a great wish to see the Lichfield manuscript of Chaucer, but had no time to visit that town. He accordingly sent for the manuscript, and I was able to examine it at my leisure in his rooms."

The companionship of so congenial a spirit was, perhaps, the highest pleasure which ever fell to Bradshaw's lot, but he was seldom able to secure it. Fortunately, he was not without other friends, who made up for their incapacity to enter fully into his intellectual pursuits by the warmth of their personal attachment. The short Whitsuntide vacation of 1873 was spent in the Lakes, in company with one of these friends, N. E. Muggeridge, then an undergraduate at King's. I shall be pardoned, at any rate by members of my college, for saying a few words in memory of this young man, who will long be remembered by his contemporaries as one of the purest and brightest characters that they have known. Modest and unassuming, but by no means devoid of general ability, and endowed with remarkable artistic gifts, he was not perhaps calculated to shine in university competitions, but was capable of binding very closely to him the affections of all who passed the barrier of his natural shyness and reserve. His sweetness and geniality of disposition, his transparent honesty, his steadiness of purpose and capacity for self-devotion, were soon discovered by Bradshaw, who had a unique gift for getting at the best side of his friends, and for encouraging the diffident into some belief in themselves. Of this kind of support, Muggeridge was much in need, and his brief life was rendered infinitely happier by the stimulating effect of Bradshaw's friendship. After a short time of study under Dr Vaughan at the Temple, he took orders, and accepted a curacy in one of the poorest parishes in South London. The devotion with which he threw himself into his work was too much for his delicate system. He broke down in health, was ordered as a last hope to take a sea-voyage round the world, and died at Hong-Kong in 1879.

The beginning of 1874 found Bradshaw at work on the earliest traces of Breton, Welsh, and other Celtic languages, and engaged in an active correspondence with Professor Rhys and Mr Whitley Stokes on these subjects. To the former he sent notes of Welsh words and proper names in the manuscripts which he had been examining for the purpose, in the "Liber Landavensis," the Book of St Chad at Lichfield, the Black Book of Caermarthen, and others.* In order to throw light on the age of the charters and other matters contained in these books, and on that of the manuscripts themselves, and so to elucidate the growth of the Welsh language, he was working carefully at the early records of British history. "I have been going through Gildas and Nennius and Asser to some purpose," he says. The fruits of this study, as shown in his knowledge of Gildas and Nennius, astonished Professor Mommsen when he visited Cambridge ten years later. Anxious to arrange the different sources of knowledge on the subject in their chronological order, he brought to bear on the problem his knowledge of the language, of history, and of manuscripts in general. "All materials," he says to Professor Rhys, "existing as entries in books, whether charters, notes, or glosses, earlier than this [the beginning of the twelfth century], ought to be most carefully and systematically collected and arranged ; and your stones [*i.e.* inscriptions] form a parallel and invaluable series. . . . The ground is clearing pleasantly, and I look forward to the results." The charters in the "Liber Landavensis" puzzled him much. They were evidently forged, but his knowledge of the

* The "Liber Landavensis" (Cartulary of Llandaff Cathedral) was edited by Rev. W. J. Rees in 1840. It was compiled in the first quarter of the 12th century. For the Book of St. Chad, see below, p. 243. The Black Book of Caermarthen, containing fragments of early Welsh poetry, has been edited by Mr. J. G. Evans (1888). It belongs to the end of the 12th century.

language showed him that there lay imbedded in them
remains of Welsh much older than the date of the forgery,
so that they must have been based on some more ancient
originals. "There is an ample field here," he writes, "for
a good charter antiquary. It will be a good thing for
Wales when it begins to produce a few Joseph Robertsons."

At the same time he was puzzling out the barbarous
jargon of the "Hisperica Famina,"* a poem written in very
debased Latin, and full of words found nowhere else. This
poem being of Celtic origin, he made the Celtic glosses
from different manuscripts and the Latin of the "Famina"
throw mutual light on each other, and was eventually able
to construe the whole of the latter by this means. The
style of the "Famina" may be illustrated by the opening
line—

"Ampla pectoralem suscitat vernia cavernam."

A gloss gives *vernia* as being equivalent to *lætitia*, and
the line is shown to mean "Great joy agitates my breast."
But he had only a transcript of the Luxemburg fragment
of this poem, with a collection of glosses at the end, to
work from, and he could not trust the copy. "I am dying
to see the original," he writes. His wish was gratified in
the following year, when he visited Luxemburg, inspected
the fragment, and afterwards had it sent over to England
to examine at his leisure.

While carrying on this correspondence with Professor
Rhys, he was also helping Mr Stokes by sending him
photographs which he had had made of the Juvencus
manuscript and of other documents throwing light on the
development of the Irish language. In a long letter, too
technical to be quoted here, he works out the whole history
and construction of the Dunstan† manuscript preserved

---

* The chief manuscript of this poem is in the Vatican Library. Another
manuscript, containing a fragment only, is at Luxemburg. See below, chap. xi.

† Bodl. Auct. F. iv. 32. So called from its having come to the Bodleian
from Glastonbury, and from its containing a portrait of St Dunstan, who
was abbot of that monastery. See a paper on it in Hermes (1880), p. 425.

in the Bodleian, showing of what parts it consists, and with which branch of the Celtic family of languages each part is connected. After filling three sheets with closely written remarks on these and other kindred matters, he concludes, " I cannot tell you what a relief it is to have some one to pour out crude thoughts to as they come up." In the same spirit he writes to Professor Rhys. " I cannot help writing whatever comes uppermost in my mind, and as I have no one else to write to [about Welsh subjects], you are necessarily the victim." The desire to communicate his pleasures and interests was at times quite overpowering with him, while at others he would remain for months without writing a word to old correspondents, who longed in vain to know what he was doing.

These studies, and other work of a similar kind, must have been a welcome relaxation to him when he could find any leisure from his official labours. There is no doubt that the care of the library lay very heavy upon him about this time. The changes necessitated by the enlargement of the library in 1867 had involved much labour in addition to the ordinary work of the institution, and the staff, although more numerous than formerly, was not large enough to meet the unusual pressure. A large number of books had been shifted from one part of the library to another, and the work of re-cataloguing had not kept pace with the process of removal. The additional space which had been gained a few years before, was almost immediately filled, and the chronic congestion due to want of room had reappeared. Bradshaw worked hard to overcome these difficulties. In the summer months he was constantly in the library for a couple of hours before most people were out of bed ; he hardly enjoyed, on the average, a month's holiday in the year. But he laboured under the disadvantage of an insufficient staff, and it must be allowed that he did not possess the knack of working through subordinates. He never kept a secretary; he never in his life, so far as I am aware, dictated a letter to a shorthand writer. When the early books and manuscripts were moved to their new places, he carried them down, for the most part, with his own hands. This was doubtless due to his love of the books, and to a fear lest they should suffer any damage by careless usage. But the action was characteristic of his whole management of the library. He could not confine himself sufficiently to the work of direction and supervision, but spent much time on details which others in his place would have left to an assistant. Moreover, it must be said that, in the management of the library, he now and then encountered difficulties, not of his own making, which were extremely painful to a man of his delicacy and sensitiveness, and which rendered his position, already onerous enough, doubly difficult to maintain.

In a library to which the public are not admitted, much confusion may exist without any news of it reaching the outer world. When readers have to wait patiently till an assistant brings them the book they want, no one but the assistant need know that it is absent from the spot assigned to it by the catalogue. But the University Library at Cambridge, alone among great libraries, is open to several thousands of persons. This fact alone immensely increases the difficulty of keeping things in order, and, what is more, it ensures that any instance of disorder shall at once be known. An occasion for grumbling is a luxury of which few persons refuse to avail themselves, and university society is no more exempt than other societies from a tendency to exaggeration. In this case there was, no doubt, some cause for complaint, and the Syndicate felt compelled to listen to remonstrances from outside. In December, 1872, they appointed a committee to inquire into the state of the library and to report on the best measures for the remedy of "existing evils." The committee reported early next year that, however desirable it might be to arrange the books in the library according to their subjects, the inconveniences involved in the process were such that "they could not recommend any attempt to develope further the principle of exact local classification." An appendix furnished by the librarian himself showed that confusion existed in many parts of the building. The committee proposed certain regulations which were carried into effect, but it was some time before the difficulties were overcome.

During all this time it should not be supposed that Bradshaw's relations with the Syndicate were anything but consistently friendly and harmonious. The measures which were adopted by the latter were adopted with the approval of the librarian, and sometimes at his suggestion. He even welcomed them, quite honestly, as a sort of support, and as supplying a stimulus which he felt to be beneficial to himself. But he cannot have been happy in the state of things which rendered such steps desirable ; on the contrary, it is clear that it weighed upon his mind, and sometimes produced a feeling akin to despondency. The fits of depression, to which he was always more or less subject, grew upon him. For a time he seemed to be losing his power of making new friends, while his craving for companionship did not grow less. To a friend who had sent him letters on Christmas Day (1873), and his birthday (February 2, 1874), he wrote in terms which show that he was not in the best of spirits. "I cannot thank you enough for your two letters. There are so few now who have any recollection of my birthday, that what do remain are all the more precious." After mentioning the names of one or two persons who still came now and then to see him, he continues, " Otherwise almost nobody comes, and I have no friends at all—not one soul to whom I can talk, so

you can believe that your coming up will be a real blessing.
Most of the people in the place [King's] I hardly know to
speak to, many not even by sight, and the Sunday mornings
are quite a thing of the past." *

At Easter, 1874, he paid a flying visit to Bonchurch,
which he had never seen since he had lived there as a child.
In a letter to one of his nieces he laments the fact that
almost all the old landmarks were hopelessly swept away.
It was a very short holiday, and less enjoyable than it
might have been, for—a most unusual thing—he was quite
alone.   The death of G. R. Crotch,† shortly after this, added
to his sense of loneliness.

He had just started for his Whitsuntide holiday in the
Lakes, when he heard of Crotch's illness, and at once
hurried to Liverpool to see the latter's brother and sister,
before their departure for Philadelphia.   During the previous year he had received several letters from his friend,
full of life and vigour, and of hopes and plans for the future.
He was hard at work in Texas, California, and elsewhere,
adding to his collection of Coleoptera, and afterwards in
the museum of zoology at Harvard, sorting and cataloguing
his captures, till he was laid low by the fatal disease.   Even
up to the last few weeks he wrote with such courage and
hopefulness as to conceal the real state of things from his
friends, and his brother and sister arrived too late to find
him alive.   His death was a grievous loss to Bradshaw.
Writing shortly afterwards to a friend, he says, " You will
not, I know, believe that I have felt the kindness of your
letters any the less from my having written so little in
reply.   I have been in no mood to write pleasant letters.
Crotch's illness upset me very much.   His death, on the
other hand, has, I hope and believe, done more than upset

* The allusion in the last clause is to the Sunday breakfasts in his rooms,
at which some four or five intimate friends, graduate and undergraduate, used
for many years regularly to assemble.

† See above, p. 89.

me. It seems to have given me in many ways new views of life, which I hope may be more lasting than such changes are wont to be. It is not often I express my real thoughts to any one, so you must not be surprised if, after all my efforts, you find me still falling back. I have felt much in the past few years the want of a friend to talk to. You will say that a wife is the only such friend a man ought to have when he comes to my age; but as that is quite out of the question, I cannot help sometimes, or indeed often, feeling the want very keenly. It is the only thing to keep one up to the mark."

Illness was added to other causes of depression. He was ill both in 1872 and 1873. His constitution, naturally robust and vigorous, was beginning to feel the effect of continuous wear and tear. Relying upon his unusual powers of endurance, he took no care of himself, but worked on regardless of results. "During the whole spring and summer" of 1874, as he tells a friend, he was disabled by "a tedious illness." He attributed it himself to want of holiday. Two days were all that he had at Easter, 1874; his Whitsuntide holiday was cut down, as I have already said, to one day, by the news of Mr Crotch's illness. In July he went again to Liverpool, to meet the brother and sister of his dead friend on their return to England, and thence he went again for a few days to the Lakes. He had been suffering in the interval, but his short outing appeared to set him on his legs again for a time. In August he writes, " I have managed to get on wonderfully well this month; not fit for anything but my library work, but still able to do this to my satisfaction."

In the summer of 1874 he was elected a member of the committee of the Palæographical Society, which had just been established. Mr Bond, the late librarian of the British Museum, had written to Bradshaw as far back as July

O

1869, to consult him about the formation of such a society, for the purpose of publishing facsimiles from manuscripts illustrating the characteristics of mediæval handwriting and other matters connected with palæography. The project hung fire for three or four years, but was taken up again actively in 1873. Bradshaw at first hesitated to join in it, not knowing under whose management the publication of facsimiles would be carried on. It was not till he felt assured that the conduct of affairs would really be in the hands of such competent authorities as Mr Bond and Mr E. M. Thompson, that he consented to become a member. Though elected a member of the committee of management, he seems to have taken but little share in the working of the society, and his own contributions were confined to descriptions of two of the manuscripts * of which facsimiles were published.

He was, indeed, in no condition to throw himself actively into such employment. He was still ailing and depressed. The solitude of September weighed heavily upon him. In answer to a letter from a friend, he writes, " You don't know what a luxury it [the letter] was in that most lonely of all months at Cambridge. . . . In spite of all my expectations, I was actually alone in college only for half an hour one day, but it felt sufficiently dismal nevertheless." A visit from Dr Murray, editor of the " Philological Dictionary," towards the end of the Long Vacation, was a great delight. " I enjoyed more than I can well describe," he says, " the pleasure of having Dr Murray here for some days. I relieved him of his journey to Blickling, as he found so much more than he expected to do here ; and the gain to me of meeting such a real scholar was untold." A short excursion to Scotland, and some pleasant days spent at

---

* These two manuscripts were (1) the manuscript of Bede's " Ecclesiastical History " (Camb. Kk. v. 16 : Pal. Soc. Publ., vol. ii., plates 139, 140 ; and (2) the " Book of Deer " (Camb. Ii. vi. 32 : Pal. Soc. Publ., vol. ii., plates 210, 211).

Longleat and Blickling, in exploring the treasures of those famous libraries, made him happy for the time, but did him no permanent good. Early in 1875 he writes, " I am not up to much at present ; " and again, in a fragment of a diary, " March 9–16.—Hardly any regular work done ; incessant interruptions and illness." At Easter he took a longer holiday than he had enjoyed for years, spending nearly a fortnight with a junior Fellow of his college in Milan and the Italian lakes. He was not well at the time, and an attempt to walk up the Monte Mottcrone near Stresa showed that his strength was not great. But travelling always revived him, and he was in good spirits all the time. On the way home he visited Freiburg-im-Breisgau, to see the copy of the Mentelin Bible preserved there, and spent half a day at Luxemburg in company with the fragment of the " Hisperica Famina " which he had been so eager to see. On his return to England he was again laid up. He hated calling in a doctor, but he did so on this occasion, and was completely cured. A little later he was able to write, " Since the end of May I have been at work, and better than I have been for years." A more careful regimen, and more attention to exercise and relaxation, kept him from falling back into his former state. From this time to the end of his life he was never, except on one occasion in 1885, prevented by illness for more than a day or two from doing his work.

CHAPTER VII.

I HAVE thought it best to put together in a separate chapter some continuous account of Bradshaw's work on typography and Chaucer during the first eight years of his librarianship, as these were the subjects which most fully occupied his attention during, at any rate, the earlier part of that time.

It was in February, 1868, that he published the first of his "Memoranda," a title which he gave to a series of little pamphlets, or brochures, intended to contain such outcome of his studies as he thought likely to interest others concerned in the same pursuits. The project of issuing such a series had been for some time in his mind. The germ of it may perhaps be detected in the series of "Literary Remains" which he contemplated in 1858, or in the fortnightly bulletin which he promised M. Holtrop in 1866.* In the latter year he printed what was meant to be the first instalment, but this particular paper never went further than a proof in slips. The proof before me, which belongs to Mr Blades, is headed as follows :—
" Memoranda chiefly concerning early printed books and manuscripts and the older literature of different nations ; collected by Henry Bradshaw." The paper deals with the history of printing at Bruges in the fifteenth century, but only embraces the work of Colard Mansion, Caxton's master, and of the successor who used his type after

* See above, pp. 71, 141.

Mansion's flight from Bruges in 1484. Bradshaw evidently intended to go on with other printers at Bruges, and with the history of Belgian typography in general. But he felt that his views on these subjects were not ripe for publication, and he therefore suppressed them. In his own handwriting at the head of the proof are the words, "This was done before I went to Bruges [in 1866], and must not now be taken as any authority.* No more was ever done to it."

Unfortunately, the project of a continuous series of publications was not adhered to long. Only eight numbers of the "Memoranda" were ever issued, and of these only six are on subjects connected with the original plan. The first number actually published is entitled "The Printer of the Historia S. Albani," and was issued in February, 1868. The books attributed to Ulric Zel which he bought in December, 1867, may have stimulated him to the production of this little tract, but the work of which it is the result was mainly done at Oxford in 1866. On that occasion, he says in the preface, he made "a catalogue of about one hundred quarto books, all printed (apparently) at Cologne." With respect to this paper, I will only say here, by way of explanation, that "The Printer of the Historia S. Albani" is the title which he gives to a nameless and hitherto unknown worker, whom he shows to have printed several of the books attributed, but wrongly, to Ulric Zel. Far from wishing to keep his results to himself, he states that his object in publishing these notes is to induce others to follow up the same line of research, and to add to his discoveries. Not that he expected much in this way, for in requesting Mr Macmillan to allow his name as publisher to appear on the title-page, he says, "I do not want it [the paper] advertised or anything of that kind, for there are but three people in

---

* I have consulted Mr Blades on this point. He informs me that the results arrived at in the paper are not to be considered as final, and that he cannot recommend its publication.

the United Kingdom who would care to see it, and they will see it anyhow. There are some persons abroad, however, who interest themselves in these matters, and if there is a London address visible it can be ordered without any difficulty."

For the next few years most of Bradshaw's leisure, which was little enough, was occupied with the subject of early printing in England and in foreign countries. Writing to M. Holtrop in April, 1868, he says, "You will wonder what it is that has suddenly made me put away my bad habit of silence and take up my pen to write to you. It is the unexpected discovery yesterday of what I believe to be a new fact in our common subject." After describing his discovery, he goes on, "Since my election I have hardly had a day to give to the matter of early printed books, I have had such a multiplicity of details of other kinds to attend to. . . . You must not think that I have forgotten your 'Thierry Martens.' I don't know how I can thank you sufficiently for the honour that you do me by dedicating it to me. It is an honour which I little deserve, and a recognition of fellow-working which I am never likely to receive from any one else. The book is a true *Étude bibliographique*. . . . You have inaugurated a new era in the bibliography of *incunabula*, and I hope you may yet live long to see the spread of your ideas." The hope was not to be gratified. It was the last letter which Bradshaw wrote to his old friend.

Not long after this, another recognition of Bradshaw's services to bibliography came from the Continent. In November, 1869, he was made a "corresponding member" of the Société des Bibliophiles de Belgique. Meanwhile, in the University Library he was putting his "museum," as he called it, into order; that is, he was arranging the early printed books in the new part of the library where he himself mostly lived and worked. He placed them

on the shelves according to the same plan on which he
made his catalogues, that is to say, on a plan which would
at once display their affinities and lines of development.
In a note-book for November, 1869, he writes, " Since I
was at Ghent I have fairly begun to arrange my museum
of early printing under countries, towns, and printers, and
I have done England, Belgium and Holland very satisfactorily."   In the autumn of the same year he made
an excursion to Ghent to view the Meyer Collection, which
was to be sold shortly afterwards.   Before starting he drew
up a complete list of all the fifteenth-century books in
the sale catalogue, rearranging them according to the plan
which he followed in his own collection.   This list he took
with him, and with its aid he worked for a whole day in
the sale-room, seeing with his own eyes everything he
wanted to buy.   The Syndicate placed £100 at his disposal for the purchase of books.   The books which he
bought came to nearly double the money, but the Syndics
had such confidence in his judgment that they sanctioned
the whole of the expenditure.

His "classified index," as he called it, of the fifteenth-
century books in the Meyer Collection was published in
April, 1870, as the second number of his " Memoranda,"
with a preface and notes on disputed points.   In the
preface he draws a sharp contrast between the condition
of typographical knowlege in Belgium and elsewhere.
" It very rarely happens," he says, " that a sale catalogue
is drawn up with such care and knowledge as regards
early printed books as to render the formation of such
an index as the present in any way possible, unless after
a careful verification by the books themselves.   Indeed,
Ghent is almost the only place where there seems to
be any attempt to give the attention to this subject which
nevertheless is rendered all the more necessary from the
very high prices which almost any good specimens of

early printing are sure to bring. The auction catalogues issued by the first houses in England and France are a standing disgrace to the two countries so far as this class of books is concerned, and yet there are no signs of a change for the better. The present index was drawn up at first simply for my own convenience. It is now at the service of any persons who take an interest in the subject."

Shortly before the publication of this index, M. Holtrop, librarian of the Royal Library at the Hague, had died (February 13, 1870). At the conclusion of his preface, Bradshaw pays a graceful tribute to his memory in the following words :—" I little thought, when these pages were sent to the press, that death would deprive me of one of the greatest pleasures which I anticipated from printing them. It is not for me to speak of that combination of gentleness and modesty, combined with deep research, which characterized everything which came from M. Holtrop's pen, so far as I ever had the privilege of knowing him. Those who knew him while he lived will readily understand the keen pleasure with which I looked forward to bringing him this year the firstfruits of my attempts to follow in his footsteps, and to becoming personally acquainted with one whom I had so long known only by correspondence. My desire in these studies was to be a willing pupil of his ; my pleasure, to prove to him that his work was the solid foundation on which others could stand to pursue the same inquiries to still further and clearer results."

. In February, 1870, occurred a still more important sale than that of M. de Meyer—namely, that of the Culemann Library. This collection contained upwards of seven hundred fifteenth-century books, of which Bradshaw made a classified list similar to that which he had made of the Meyer Collection. " Of course, it is only in certain groups," he writes to a friend, " that I am familiar enough with them to correct the mistakes [in the sale catalogue], but it is a very interesting collection, and I hope very much I may be allowed to buy something of interest." The Syndics placed ·£300 at his disposal, and he obtained almost everything that he wanted. Unfortunately, the index was never printed, probably because points were involved which Bradshaw was unable at the time to settle to his satisfaction. The manuscript is, however, preserved among his papers. To some readers it may appear that the making of these classified lists, to which Bradshaw devoted so much of his time, is a mere matter of arrangement, a work which any clerk would be capable of doing. But this is far from being the case. Not to mention the invention of a system of classification, which substitutes order for disorder, and elevates into the rank of a science what would otherwise be a mass of disconnected facts, the making of such lists involves not only a wide knowledge of typographical history, and a minute acquaintance with the habits and characteristics of different printers, but the power of putting facts together and making correct deductions from them. Such lists are necessarily the materials out of which any general history of typography must be built.

These two were by no means the only catalogues which he made about this time. He compiled another of the English fifteenth-century books at the Bodleian Library, which appears to have been only part of a much larger plan. Two letters to Mr Blades, written in April, 1870, throw light on his intentions. Speaking of his index to the Meyer Collection, he says, "The notes you will perhaps find some interest in, as I have propounded my views of the classification of such books as strongly as I can, and I do not despair of eventually working upon that most hopeless of all places, the British Museum. On

Saturday last, being unable to leave Cambridge, I spent
fifteen hours in constructing a complete list of all the
books and fragments of any kind printed in England in
the fifteenth century which are in the Bodleian Library,
with all the library-marks carefully given. . . . In the case
of all except W. de Machlinia, Pynson, and W. de Worde,
I have given references to my own complete classified
lists of the English presses, which I have very nearly ready
for printing. . . . You have not seen my museum of early
printing in the University Library, where I have all the
fifteenth-century books arranged by countries, towns, and
printers.   I have finished Holland, Belgium, and England,
and have my brief hand-lists ready made.   I think I shall
print these for convenience before I print a regular
catalogue.   When you are able to come down here again,
I shall have great pleasure in showing you our Colard
Mansion's 'Boece' of 1477, with a miniature to each of the
five books by a contemporary Bruges artist.   How little
I dreamt three years ago of ever getting or being able
to get such a thing !

"As soon as I have done the Bodleian, I think I shall
make bold and attack the British Museum. . . . If I can
persuade the people at the Hague to publish annual
supplementary catalogues of their additions for Holland,
and the Royal Library at Brussels to do the same for
Belgium, then I think there will be little difficulty in
doing the same for England, and with these three countries
thus done, we may be able to shame France, and eventually
Italy and Germany, into doing something at least for
themselves. . . . When I have got the types all settled,
I want to attack the woodcuts, and to give an account of
all the series cut, stating for what books they were cut,
and where they were used afterwards for other books.
Some very curious things would come out in this way.
I have got a good mass of material ready.   I shall be

very glad to see you whenever you can come down, though you will necessarily think my poor museum very pretentious, seeing how poorly provided we are in everything almost, as compared with either Oxford or the British Museum."

Writing to Mr G. I. F. Tupper about the same time, he says, " Having got my types pretty fairly sorted, I want to attack the woodcuts, and first those produced in England. All I can do myself is to make lists of them, and trace out what the series in each case consists of, and what book they were cut for. This is most important, but it is not enough. Now, to have a regular lithographed series would cost very far more than I or any one I know could afford, but if I could get even less elaborate tracings of them, which I could place side by side and *use*, I think a great deal might be done. The album would, of course, be a unique collection ; but then, after having had the benefit of seeing the things side by side, and so educing results which can only be obtained by that process, a selection might perhaps be made, or something in the nature of a typical collection, which might be published. . . . The danger with me is, as you know only too well, my stopping midway from some fastidiousness, and this is just what I wish to avoid, for in the case I mention, what was done would be, so far as it went, whole and complete in itself." This project was, unfortunately, never carried out.

The list of fifteenth-century books in the Bodleian alluded to above came to an untimely end, having been the unlucky cause of almost the only unpleasant episode which, so far as I am aware, marred the general harmony of Bradshaw's relations with other learned men. He had paid a short visit to Oxford in the autumn of 1868 and in a final search in the Bodleian had discovered a new Caxton, entitled " Ars moriendi, that is to saye

the crafte for to deye for the helthe of mannes sowle." *
He found this little work in the middle of a thick volume,
lettered on the back "Tracts," and belonging to the
Tanner Collection. He now apparently felt that he
had mastered the contents of the Bodleian in this department, and accordingly drew up from his own notes a
classified list of all the books printed in England in the
fifteenth century preserved in that library. He sent it
to Mr Coxe in April, 1870, with a letter, in which he says,
" Being disgusted at not being able to get home for Easter,
I spent my Easter Eve in constructing a list of your
fifteenth-century books in the Bodleian from my pencil
notes taken when I was with you in 1866. It took me
between fifteen and sixteen hours hard writing, and I was
pretty well tired when I went to bed. On Monday I gave
it to my binder, who has just brought it back. I send it
you for your instruction and amusement, . . . but please
take care of it, as I have no other copy. . . . If you allow
me to print the list, . . . I would come over and verify the
references without wasting more of your Assistants' time
than I can help. . . . I have no leisure for any work of this
kind now except at odd moments or in holiday time, but I
want to stir up our leading libraries to take some interest
in the matter. People give enormous prices for books
simply because they are printed by this or that man,
but no one takes the trouble to put the knowledge of
these things on a sound footing." A few days later
he wrote again, " It would be a great convenience if you
could print [the list], because it is not elaborate, and any
brief list of the contents of a great library is such a great
help towards seeing best how to make a fuller list if
needed." The list was intended (though perhaps this is

---

* This book is not to be confused with another work from Caxton's press,
"The arte and crafte to knowe well to dye." The discovery was reported,
not, we may be sure, by Bradshaw himself, in the *Guardian* and the *Bookworm*.

not clear from the above letters), as a gift to the Bodleian. "I thought," Bradshaw wrote years later, "that I was offering a little return for much kindness."

Unfortunately, the introductory remarks which he prefixed to his list appear to have contained some words reflecting on the management of the Bodleian * in regard to early printed books, which not unnaturally produced some resentment. Mr Coxe received the catalogue coldly, hinted that it was superfluous, and demurred to publishing it, at all events as it stood. "All this may be true,". he said, "but you must not expect me to thong the whip wherewith we may be lashed." Bradshaw had not in the least anticipated this reception, and no one ever felt a snub more keenly than he. In a fit of discouragement and vexation, he sent for the list again, and no sooner received it than he tore it up and threw it into the fire. It was the only copy that he had ; he never made another, nor has any one hitherto attempted to make good the loss. It was an unfortunate incident, not only for the destruction of a valuable piece of work, but still more for the estrangement which it produced between two excellent men, who mutually liked and respected one another, and neither of whom, we may be sure, had the smallest intention of inflicting a wound. It is pleasant to reflect that within a short time Bradshaw's relations with Mr Coxe were again to all appearance as friendly as before. Nevertheless, on one side at least, the wound was never completely healed. Twelve years after the event, Bradshaw was still obliged to write, "I have never *enjoyed* the Bodleian since."

What was in Bradshaw's mind at this time is illustrated by a letter which he wrote to Mr Winter Jones, librarian of the British Museum, in April of this year. "Dear Mr

---

* The only fragment of the list which I have been able to discover is a page which clearly forms part of a draft of the introduction.

Jones, for nearly two years past I have been most unfortunate in not being able to see you. . . . I was at the Museum for a few hours yesterday, and had a long conversation with Mr Rye on a subject which interests me very much, and I am induced to write to you on the subject. What I want is to ask if you can give me any encouragement to hope that some steps will be taken towards a systematic method of dealing with the vast treasures which the Museum contains in the way of fifteenth-century books. . . . Of all the national libraries I have any knowledge of—Paris, Brussels, the Hague, Copenhagen, Vienna, and our own—the Museum is the only one where one can get no information, *except as it were by accident,* as to what specimens of early presses are to be seen there. . . . I cannot help feeling that it would be real economy of power, as well as of funds, if you could have one of your staff told off to this branch of work, some one whose *business* it should be to deal with this class of books—books which belong to a period when printing ranks rather with the fine arts ; when, from so many printers being their own type-founders, the schools of type and woodcut are as capable of being grouped by locality or country as pictures or engravings ; and, as it is sometimes of great importance to know where and when a particular book is printed, it often happens that the volume which alone gives the clue is itself of no importance or interest from a literary point of view. For instance, in turning over a volume of fragments yesterday, I found a bull of Sixtus IV, dated 1478, in the type of the famous ' R ' printer, so often confounded with Mentelin. His books are commonly put down to 1470, or earlier ; and I believe no one ever thought of putting his books so late as 1478. Yet this little piece is almost the only certain date which is known in connection with this whole series of books. This is only one instance of a thousand. I have been at work for years trying to reduce the matter to a more scientific basis ; to be able to look at the treatment of these books from a *natural history* point of view—and here your own little blue lists of *genera* in the zoological department have been of material service to me—my object being to avoid the enormous amount of *talk* which has for years past been associated with descriptions of early printed books, and, by putting facts side by side in their natural order, to let facts speak for themselves." He then goes on to say that if the work were to be done, Mr J. H. Hessels, "who has been aiding me, as well as working under me, for several years past," would be the best man to do it. He had lately been employing Mr Hessels to make "a skeleton list of the fifteenth-century books in the Grenville Collection, arranged according to the method I always adopt [countries, towns, presses, etc.], and he has succeeded beyond my expectations. All sorts of interesting results have turned up already. Every collection I can do like this is so much experience gained ; and I should be glad to print the Grenville list as a specimen for criticism, unless there was a chance of seeing the work seriously undertaken at the Museum." This letter, unfortunately, produced no effect. Mr Winter Jones regretted that, owing to want of funds, its suggestions could not be carried out.

The rebuff which he had received in a quarter where he did not expect it, sharpened, no doubt, his sense of the loss which he had sustained in M. Holtrop's death. He felt himself lonely and unsupported in the pursuit of his favourite studies. Writing to M. Campbell, who succeeded M. Holtrop at the Hague, he says, " I cannot help feeling a sort of loyalty to him *as my chief* in these things, in a way that I feel towards no one at all in England or elsewhere, because there is no one, except yourself, to whom I can look for the least help and sympathy in these studies in the way that they really demand. . . . Pray be good

enough to present my sincere condolence to Madame
Holtrop. I hope I may yet be enabled to express to her
in words some of the debt which I owe to her husband,
whose memory will always be sacred with me." The
answer which he received from M. Campbell contained
welcome expressions of sympathy. "Your letter," says
Bradshaw in reply, "has given me more pleasure than I
can find words to express—that assurance of sympathy in
work as well as personal friendship, which is enough to
encourage the dullest to take heart and go on working."
He was still anxious to obtain the co-operation of other
libraries, in furthering the study of bibliography. Writing
to M. Campbell in May, 1870, he says, " I wish very much
that it were practicable to publish what the Germans call a
Jahresbericht, giving an account of what has turned up
during the year past in relation to these fifteenth-century
books. Of course, it would be impossible for any one to do
all the countries, but I cannot help thinking that something
might be done for one or two countries in the national
library of that country ; and by thus registering our knowledge, there would be some chance of turning it to better
account afterwards." He concludes a long letter of
remarks and queries about their common subject with the
words, " As all these things are now only the amusement
of my leisure hours, you can believe that I cannot give
very much attention to them ; and I am sure that you
cannot afford much time to read half what I should like to
write. Still, for all that concerns your own country, I am
bound to report to you any news that I have, as you are
my natural chief in this subject, and I feel bound to report
all new facts to head-quarters. Meantime, command my
services when you will, but do not let my letters become a
burden to you."

In June, 1871, Bradshaw published the third of his
" Memoranda," a pamphlet entitled, " A list of the founts

of type and woodcut devices used by printers in Holland in the fifteenth century." This list was based on the "Monuments Typographiques" of M. ·Holtrop. It begins with a table showing the order in which the different countries of Europe, and Holland among them, adopted the invention of printing in the fifteenth century. Then follows a list of the towns of Holland at which books were printed before 1500 ; and, finally, a list of the different presses, and of the types and devices (if any) used at each press, with the name of a specimen book in which each type is used. Four facsimiles of leaves from books, not given in the "Monuments," are added as an appendix to this little pamphlet of four and twenty pages, into which an enormous amount of labour and knowledge is compressed. The list, in fact, gives a complete outline of the history of typography in Holland during the first thirty years of its existence. It is only an outline, it is true ; but in order to draw it, every book, and every fragment of a book, printed in Holland during that period had to be examined, either in the original or in facsimile, and placed in its proper position in the full catalogue of books, of which this is only the essence or the skeleton. The whole development of the art in this one country is here for any one at all con-versant with the subject, the life and death or retirement of each printer, the work of each fount of type, and its transfer from one press or one master-printer to another.

With the exception of a "Notice of a fragment of the Fifteen Oes and other prayers printed at Westminster by W. Caxton about 1490–1491," published as a "Memo-randum" in 1877, the list mentioned above was the last piece of work on the subject of early typography which Bradshaw completed. The intervals of leisure which he could spare for working at the subject became shorter and shorter. The appearance of M. Campbell's book, "Annales de la typographie néerlandaise au xvme siècle," stimulated him for a short time to fresh activity. He had anxiously awaited the appearance of this book. Writing to M. Campbell in June, 1873, he says, "I am delighted to hear that you are really going to press this autumn with your account of Dutch and Belgian fifteenth-century books. I believe I have never looked forward to a book with so much interest and anxiety. . . . What would I give for a month at the Hague! only I should tire you to death."

The book appeared in the autumn of 1874, and Bradshaw, having devoured it with his accustomed avidity, at once sent off a letter of congratulation and criticism to M. Campbell. "I indeed congratulate you heartily," he writes, "on having brought out your book. In publishing it you have presented me with what I have desired with a greater desire than any book that I could name during all my previous life; so please accept my warmest thanks as one of the public. I received it on Tuesday morning, and I read it straight through, from title-page to errata, by Saturday, and during the last week I have been going through it backwards and forwards in search of all sorts of things. I have never in my life written a notice of any book in a periodical, but I must try and write some notice of this before long. . . . I have felt always that any work of mine upon this subject was fruitless unless I had all the facts before me, or at least the means of placing them before me as you have at the Hague; but now your book gives me a fresh starting-point, and my only regret is that I have so little leisure to work the subject. . . . I have delayed doing anything towards regularly cataloguing our fifteenth-century books till your book came out, but now I shall soon hope to undertake it."

The catalogue alluded to in this letter was never completed. Indeed, from this time onward Bradshaw did but little work on early typography. Not that he lost interest in the study, for a subject once taken up never ceased to interest him; but leisure was wanting. The attractions of other studies—especially that of Chaucer—the lack of sympathy and co-operation in his typographical researches, and, more than all, the growing pressure of his official engagements at the library, combined to make him gradually give up a subject on which, under more favourable circumstances, he might have produced a great and exhaustive work.

The history of early printing, although it occupied most of Bradshaw's leisure, did not engross the whole of it during the years immediately following his promotion in the library. For several years—in fact, ever since they first became acquainted—he had carried on a correspondence with Dr Furnivall. Hitherto the chief subject of this correspondence had been the selection and editing of works for the Early English Text Society. This society was founded in 1864, for the purpose of printing and publishing the less-known remnants of early English literature. Dr Furnivall submitted the prospectus of the society to Bradshaw in February, 1864, and received his assistance in arranging a plan of publication. He also frequently consulted him on points connected with the works to be published, and the latter went so far as to promise to edit "William of Palerne."* But other engagements, as usual, interfered. In vain Dr Furnivall wrote, truly enough, in May, 1865, "You can edit 'William of Palerne' quite well, and you know you can; only you like doing bits of twenty-five things instead of finishing one; and so you must be bullied and taunted till you stick to your William, and do what you have promised." As, however, no one ever lived on whom pressure of this kind had less effect than Bradshaw, Dr Furnivall's efforts were fruitless, and he was forced to look for an editor elsewhere.

* This work, also known as "William and the Werewolf," was afterwards edited by Professor Skeat, for the Early English Text Society.

From 1867 onwards the correspondence was chiefly about Chaucer. That Bradshaw had been devoting a great deal of his spare time to the study of Chaucer is clear from the contents of his note-books. In August, 1867, for instance, he notes the results of reading through Chaucer's "Boecius." He found in this work the source of the balade of "Fortune and the Pleyntyf," "almost the whole of which is here in substance." Here, too, he discovered the origin of the "Etas prima," and of the "sixteen stanzas of argument on predestination which Chaucer puts into the mouth of Troilus." His note-books during this period abound with remarks about the rhyme-endings, pronunciation, and orthography of the poet.

On the question of orthography, he writes to Dr Furnivall (August, 1867) as follows:—"About the Chaucer affairs, of course my whole object is to be upset or confirmed by Morris, Ellis, and others. What I insist on is that until some of you begin to *edit* books, there is no chance for any of us learning anything. When I give you my skeleton of the 'Canterbury Tales,' in my spelling, you will be able to say, 'What gross ignorance! He doesn't even know that the imperative singular in that verb has no *e* at the end;' and so on. For instance—

"' Stryve not as doth the crokke with the wal.'

Out of seventeen copies, sixteen read *stryve* and one reads *stryf* (which Morris says is the right form), and that not one of the oldest manuscripts of the poem. This is only one instance in a thousand to show that you cannot trust the best manuscripts for spelling rightly. . . . What do you think of this? Suppose, to begin with, I take particular terminations, as ēe, ȳ, āy, ēy, ōy, ȳĕ, āyĕ, ēyĕ, ōyĕ, and extract all the words in order as I find them in Chaucer, then group them according to their origin, and give the references, arranging the words in grammatical and alpha-

betical order. Then, beginning with these endings, one
might go on to the others, and by means of a series of
papers at the Philological Society, with discussions thereon,
we might come to some determination. The Philological
Society is the only place I can think of where one would
be able to meet Ellis and Morris, and others sufficiently
interested to take part in the discussion. It seems to me
that by some such process we might make some solid
advance in English grammar, and I should be very glad to
bear my part in the work." His theory was that by a
close analysis and comparison of Chaucer's rhymes it
would be possible to ascertain the contemporary pronunciation of many doubtful words. The pronunciation would
throw light on the derivation, showing whether the words
came direct from the Latin, or through the French,
or from some other source; and this in its turn would go
far to fix the orthography and give a philological explanation of the growth of the language.

In 1867 he had gone far enough with his Chaucer work
to feel himself justified in putting something into type. He
accordingly printed a short paper, entitled, "The Skeleton
of Chaucer's Canterbury Tales: an attempt to distinguish
the several fragments of the work as left by the author."
In the preface to this paper, dated September 8, 1867, he
says, "My purpose in printing these sheets is purely temporary; but it has struck me that by printing a few more
copies than were necessary for my immediate object, and
circulating them among those who take an interest in the
textual criticism of our early authors, and especially of
Chaucer, they might see how very far we are as yet from
the possibility of a satisfactory edition of Chaucer, and
how much it lies in any scholar's power to lend a helping
hand." But he still hesitated to publish what he had
written. "I came to the conclusion," he says later, "that
the remarks were too crude even for such a temporary

publication as I then contemplated." He accordingly
suppressed it for several years, and when at length, in
November, 1871, he published the paper as No. 4 of the
Memoranda, it was with a sort of apology for its appearance. I reserve an account of the contents of the paper
for another place.*

In the autumn of 1867 the Chaucer Society was
founded. In his own mind, Dr Furnivall tells me, one
of its principal objects was to collect the materials on
which Bradshaw might base a standard edition of the poet.
Writing to him in September, 1867, Dr Furnivall says,
" The more I think of the Chaucer Society the more I like
it, and if you'd say that you'd help, in choice of texts, etc.,
and on committee, I should start it at once." The circular
proposing to issue the six best texts of the " Canterbury
Tales " in parallel columns, was submitted to Bradshaw, and
received his criticisms. His opinion was distinctly against
the six-text edition, and in favour of editing each of the
selected manuscripts separately.† Writing to Dr Furnivall
nearly a year later, he says, " When you determined to
start a Chaucer Society, you remember we discussed the
way of printing. You were for doing what you still insist
on doing—printing six copies parallel. I urged what I still
consider the only rational way—printing a manuscript as it
stands, only with all the divisions and subdivisions marked."

In September, 1868, Dr Furnivall visited Cambridge,
and apparently induced Bradshaw to promise regular
assistance. During the rest of this year their correspondence was very active, and under the stimulus of Dr
Furnivall's sympathy and enthusiasm, Bradshaw for some
time threw himself warmly into the work of the Chaucer
Society. Letter followed letter in rapid succession, as was
his wont when he was in the mood for writing. In one

---

* See below, p. 221, and chap. xi.

† The six texts were first published collectively, afterwards separately.

of these letters he visualises the whole of the journey to
Canterbury in his mind's eye. Speaking of the hill above
Boughton, on the Canterbury Road, he says, "It is the
difficulty of this hill which no doubt caused the danger to
the sleepy Cook * which causes the fun of the Manciple's
prologue, just as it caused the break of the narrative
between the Chanoun's Yeman and the Doctor, on the
journey to Canterbury the day before. No doubt you
will say this is carrying the matter much too far. But all
I want is to picture to myself the thing as it was, and
anything which helps me to do this interests me." In
another letter, he quotes a contemporary description of what
the pilgrims do at Canterbury.† "You will see that the
pilgrims arrive at Canterbury 'at mydmorowe.' They go
straight to the inn—the Checker or the Hope—see to their
lodging, take rooms, etc., and at once go off to the shrine
in their travelling-dress, and are duly anointed by the
monks at the cathedral. This must have been in the fore-
noon ; at any rate, not late. Then they go back to the inn
and have their midday meal, the gentles putting on a
change of clothes, and all of them spending the afternoon
and evening to their hearts' content, only taking care to
get to bed in very good time so as to be ready to start
off on the return journey at the first approach of dawn."
The imaginative sympathy which these passages display
must have been of great use to Bradshaw in dealing with
such problems as those connected with the reconstruction
of the "Canterbury Tales." · Dr Furnivall was quite right

---

* An allusion to the host's words :

> "Is ther no man for prayer ne for hyre,
> That wol awake our felawe al behynde?
> A theef him might ful lightly robbe and bynde.
> Se how he nappith, se, for Goddes boones !
> That he wol falle fro his hors at ones."
>   "Manciple's Prologue," lines 6–10.

† From the Prologue to the "Tale of Beryn" (Chaucer Soc. Publ., 2nd
series, 1876).

in saying to him, "—— cares for language, —— for metre,
I for neither, only story and social life and opinion ; you
for all, and that's best."

During part of the time while this interchange of letters
was going on, Bradshaw was also corresponding with Mr
W. M. Rossetti. One of the questions on which their
discussion turned was the meaning of Chaucer's phrase in
the Troilus, "myn auctour Lollius."* Whom did Chaucer
mean by Lollius? Mr Rossetti believed him to mean
Petrarch, who was familiarly called Lælius. Bradshaw,
on the other hand, maintained that Chaucer, in naming
"Lollius" as his authority, was merely carrying out his
habitual practice of concealing his real authority and sub-
stituting the name of some other author, often, as in this
case, one whose works were entirely lost. Similarly, in a
passage in the "Monk's Tale,"† when he introduces an
incident not found in either of the sources whence the rest
of the tale is drawn, he supports it by citing another lost
author, "as seyth Trophee." This, says Bradshaw, has
nothing to do with "trophy," or, in other words, Filostrato,
who is defined by Boccaccio as "a man conquered or made
a trophy of by love," but refers to "ille vates Chaldæorum
Trophæus." "Later people," he remarks, "have been
bitten with a taste for a library of lost authors, and I think
Chaucer may fairly be said to have led the way in this
kind of work."

In proving his point, Bradshaw spared no pains to
convince his correspondent. "I am quite ashamed," he
says, "of making you read so much, but I cannot help
myself when I am deeply interested in a question." With

---

* "Troilus and Criseide," book i., line 394. The passage in question is
undoubtedly translated from Boccaccio's "Filostrato," which, according to Mr
Rossetti, was in early times attributed to Petrarch (See Chaucer Soc. Publ.,
xliv., lxv.).

† "At both the worldes endes, as saith Trophee,
   In stede of boundes he [Hercules] a piler sette."
                              "Monk's Tale," lines 127, 128.

Dr Furnivall there was always the work of the Chaucer Society or some proposal for publication to discuss. But when urged to publish something, Bradshaw persistently hung back, and pleaded for delay till something certain and final could be produced. "There is one thing which is always present with me," he writes : "I look forward to a standard edition of Chaucer's works, which now does not exist ; and if one's work is so far advanced that it is possible to anticipate conclusions now, I am, of course, for adopting those conclusions in whatever work of the kind the society does ; for it is a great evil in my mind to have all the editions, or quasi-editions, different. . . . It is this that makes me anxious to discuss with Rossetti and you and others before going to press. In plain words, I cannot bear the thought of any publication *coming forth with authority*, when it is merely the result of a few hasty and crude speculations, which a little fair preliminary discussion would get rid of."

This fundamental divergence on the principles of publication led to some harmless passages of arms between the two friends. Dr Furnivall came in for a good deal of scolding, which, it must be allowed, he accepted with admirable good temper. Not unfrequently Bradshaw expressed his opinion of Dr Furnivall's ways with remarkable plain-spokenness. For instance, in April, 1869, he writes :—

"DEAR FURNIVALL,

"You are very aggravating sometimes, particularly about the poisonous way in which you insist on editing and prefacing your books, but I am afraid I cannot take away my subscription from you. I shall want all my four Chaucers. I must have two myself ; and of the other two, one goes off to Sweden, and the other somewhere else. . . .

"Ever yours,

"HENRY BRADSHAW."

Dr Furnivall was anxious enough to get him to do the work which he found fault with. " I wish to goodness," he says, " you would write the temporary prefaces to the six texts ; it would be no end of a relief to me. . . . If you did but live in St George's Square, or we at Cambridge, things would go on smoothly. And if you were producing, and getting produced, as much as I am, and getting as much pitched·into, you'd be less particular about little matters, and more tolerant. It's wearing boots and coats, I suppose.* If you'd leave 'em off again, you'd be all right.

" Yours ever,

" F. J. F."

But Bradshaw could not work to time. It was not his way, and if it had been, he had not leisure enough. " I wish I had head to work at this now," he writes at Easter, 1869, "but it is out of the question. I looked for peace this vacation, but I have been more incessantly at work than during the last two terms. . . . I have begun again to-day going to the library at a quarter to six, so as to get a good two hours before breakfast. I got through a great deal in three months last year by doing so. I hope I may be able to continue it now." Under such circumstances it was no wonder that he was forced to allow others to go on without him. The editor of the *Edinburgh Review* wished to have an article from him on Chaucer ; he had no time to write it. The Philological Society wanted to make him a member of their council, but he could not have attended meetings, and would not undertake duties which he could not discharge. It was not surprising if he was sometimes despondent, and talked of giving up his Chaucer work. But he still looked forward to taking it up again by-and-by. " As soon as I can get my museum in order," he writes in April, 1870, " I shall take to manuscripts again,

* This refers to the incident narrated on p. 109.

and work at my Chaucer. I find I cannot do two things heartily at the same time, and it has been absolutely necessary for me to work at these things lately."

It might have been expected that he would have manifested some disappointment when others stepped into the place that might have been his. But when Dr Bernhard ten Brink, then Professor at Marburg, brought out his "Chaucer-Studien," * there is not the slightest atom of bitterness or jealousy in the single-hearted welcome which he gave to the book. Writing to Dr ten Brink, on July 1, 1870, he says :—

"MY DEAR SIR,

"At last I have found—in yourself—the man whom I have been longing to see for many years past, and I feel sure that you will forgive me for my boldness in writing to you direct, to thank you most warmly for the first part of your 'Studien' on Chaucer, which I have been feasting on for a week or more. You have taken up so entirely the lines of investigation which I had marked out, and your preface so thoroughly expresses my own feelings on the subject, that I am anxious to persuade you, if possible, to come over to England, even for a week or a fortnight, this summer, and see with your own eyes many things which now you can only learn at second-hand. For the most part, as you know, people content themselves with criticisms on the 'Canterbury Tales,' and all those who have touched the other poems have shrunk from anything but a superficial study of them. Your division into periods marked out by the first Italian journey, and the composition of the 'Legende,' shows at once the hold you have upon the subject. Some years ago I announced a book called, 'An attempt to ascertain the state of Chaucer's Works at

* This work was published in 1870. Dr ten Brink's work on "Chaucer's Sprache und Verskunst " was published in 1884.

his death, with some account of their subsequent history,' but since I became librarian here, at the commencement of 1867, my leisure has been so limited that I have found it quite impossible to put what I wish to say into print, and I must content myself with the humbler duty—which belongs to a librarian—of helping those who write. There are many papers which I would gladly place at your disposal, and there is much I should like to say, and I want you also to see the manuscripts yourself, and so get additional ideas, which, if they modify at all your present conclusions, will only confirm them in the main. . . . But I must write no more to-day. I hope you will be able to come and satisfy

"Yours most sincerely,

"HENRY BRADSHAW."

I cannot refrain from giving part of the letter with which Dr ten Brink answered this unselfish recognition of his work.[*]

"MY DEAR SIR,

"Your friendly letter of July 1 was longer on the way than might have been expected, as it had to follow me from Münster to Marburg. This is one of the reasons why my answer has been delayed—one of the reasons, but not the only one, for I must confess that, after reading through your letter, I took some time to collect myself, so great was my surprise and delight at receiving it. To find on the other side of the Channel such a recognition, so warm a sympathy for my studies, such a friendly welcome at the hands of one of the most thorough, or rather, *the* most thorough, of all living Chaucer scholars— this was more than in my boldest moments I dared to hope for in connection with my book. I had good reason

---

[*] Dr ten Brink's letter is in German, which I have ventured to translate.

to be proud, and, more than that, I had good reason to
rejoice, that my literary efforts had won me the friendship
of so noble a character. For it is friendship which you
offer me, and that, too, a friendship of the highest kind,
resting on affinity of scientific aims and common admiration for your great old poet. With all my heart I clasp
the hand you hold out to me, and wish only that I may be
able to make the one return for your goodness which is
worthy of you, I mean by actively promoting the knowledge of Chaucer, and making the right use of the abundant
help you offer me. I cannot indeed avoid regretting that
want of leisure hinders you from drawing out of the
fulness of your knowledge and the depth of your research
instruction for the literary world, and from doing the work
which in its defective foreign shape you judge worthy of
your generous approbation, but which you could do far
better. On the other hand, I am compelled all the more
to admire a spirit so entirely free from egotism—a spirit so
careless of thanks and rewards, and so wholly devoted to
furthering the cause of science. . . . In conclusion, my dear
sir, be assured of the hearty admiration and gratitude of
your friend,

"BERNHARD TEN BRINK."

More than a year after this episode, in November, 1871,
Bradshaw published his "Skeleton of the Canterbury
Tales," which had been written as far back as 1867. In a
note appended to it he says, "Four years have witnessed
a considerable advance in the study of Chaucer, both in this
country and elsewhere ; and Dr Furnivall's labours during
that period have put far out of date any work that I have
done upon this subject. Nevertheless, as the sheets are
still standing in type, and as they represent a certain
amount of thought and labour and the views which I held
at that time (since, of course, very much modified), I have

thought it worth while to have a few copies struck off, rather as a memorial of past work than as an earnest of what is to come. Every day seems to render it less likely that I shall ever put my hand again to any work of the kind." It was in vain that Dr Furnivall and other friends urged him to set to work and publish his results. The following letter from Dr Furnivall, dated March, 1872, has a melancholy significance in the light of after-events :—

"MY DEAR B.,

"Goldstücker's death,* with none of his powers, none of the produce of his work, put into print for the help of others to follow him, makes me write to you once again to urge you to edit your Globe Chaucer at once, and do justice to your work, that people may know it and be helpt along by it. Not that you're likely to die, or that strong you won't see weak me into the grave ; but if you go on refusing to set down and produce your results, you'll leave friends to lament, when you do die, the waste of power in you. You can help, as Goldstücker could have helpt, this time and after-times along. Why shouldn't you? You are something more than a librarian. Do leave a record of it.

"Yours always,

"F. J. F."

But it was not to be. The pressure of work in the library prevented Bradshaw from continuing his researches, except at rare intervals, and still more from maturing his conclusions for publication, while incompatibility of temperament and principles hindered him from taking much part in the work of the Chaucer Society. The correspondence with Dr Furnivall never ceased during Bradshaw's life. Now and then, when anything struck him, or when

* Dr Goldstücker, Professor of Sanscrit at University College, London, died early in 1872.

any circumstance led him to recur to his old studies, he would communicate it to his friend ; but letters after about the year 1873 were comparatively few and far between. After that time, though for several years more he contemplated an edition of Chaucer, Bradshaw practically relinquished the study of the poet.

It will not be amiss, perhaps, to bring together here all that passed between Bradshaw and various persons respecting an edition of his favourite poet. In 1864 Professor Earle undertook to edit for the Clarendon Press a standard edition of Chaucer, to range with that of Shakespeare. It was proposed that Mr Aldis Wright and Mr Bradshaw should act as his collaborators. At first the latter hesitated, according to his wont ; but he eventually acceded to the proposal. Mr Earle paid him a visit at Cambridge in 1866, and induced him to promise to collate the Cambridge manuscripts for the work. In March, 1866, Mr Macmillan writes to him, " I am really delighted to hear that the great Chaucer is in so prosperous a condition, and very willingly abandon my idea till after the completion of that." The idea alluded to was that of publishing a small edition of the poet, to form part of the well-known Globe series. A year or two later it became apparent that the prospect of a large edition was becoming very uncertain, and the idea of a Globe Chaucer was revived. Bradshaw undertook to edit it. " There is no doubt," writes Mr Macmillan in March, 1866, " that your decision to do this Globe edition is the right one. No pamphlets or partial publications will do anything at all to give you your right position as *the* Chaucer scholar, and the true Chaucer to the public, like this."

In 1870 Professor Earle resigned the task which he had undertaken. Professor Bartholomew Price, acting on behalf of the delegates of the Clarendon Press, applied to Mr Aldis Wright, who, however, declined the offer. An

application to Professor (then Mr) Skeat was equally unsuccessful. Professor Skeat, in his reply, wrote, " I have little
doubt that the man who knows the subject most thoroughly
is Mr Bradshaw, and I should not be justified in putting
myself before him." Thereupon Professor Price applied
to Mr Bradshaw, who, having first obtained a promise of
assistance from Mr Aldis Wright and Professor Skeat, wrote
immediately to accept the offer. Together with his answer
he sent a scheme of the edition as it seemed to him that it
ought to be. It was to be in six volumes, the first five
containing the text, the last consisting of excursuses,
indices, glossary, etc. The works of Chaucer were to be
arranged under the following heads :—(1) the larger undoubted works, in chronological order ; (2) the minor
poems ; (3) doubtful works, that is, pieces doubtfully identified with works known to have been written by Chaucer ;
(4) works attributed to Chaucer in manuscripts of the
fifteenth century, but yet of questionable authority. The
plan appears to exclude several works attributed to Chaucer,
about the spuriousness of which Bradshaw had no doubt.
The " Canterbury Tales " are called in this scheme, " Twelve
Fragments of the Unfinished Canterbury Tales." The
" Romaunt of the Rose " is included under the head of
doubtful works.

He had, however, no sooner accepted the offer than he
began to draw back. A week later he wrote to say that
he was afraid he had promised too much. He was unwilling to undertake so large a work without at least a
year's preparation ; he thought it would be better to publish
the Globe edition first ; and lastly, " If I were free for the
bulk of the day, I should like nothing better ; but the best
seven hours of the day are devoted to university work. . . .
The fact is, the work would require an amount of *daylight
leisure* which I can't give, and which no amount of money
could enable me to buy." A few more letters passed, and

then the matter dropped. The edition was supposed to be only temporarily deferred, but the project was not revived, so far as I am aware, during Bradshaw's lifetime.

Nor did it fare better with the Globe edition. From time to time Mr Macmillan and Dr Furnivall stirred Bradshaw up, but to no purpose. At length, in 1879, it was suggested that Bradshaw and Furnivall should do the edition together, and Bradshaw assented. They got as far as discussing the title-page, on which Bradshaw wanted his partner's name to stand first ; some specimen pages were put in type, and the heads of an agreement with the publishers were drawn up. A library edition, to be published by the same firm, was also discussed. The plan of this, as made out by Bradshaw, does not differ essentially from that laid down for the Oxford edition. But, alas! nothing came of it, and neither Globe nor library edition is yet in existence. Bradshaw could not even find time for an article on Chaucer in the " Encyclopædia Britannica," though repeatedly pressed by the editor to write one.* His only publication on the subject is, therefore, a solitary " Memorandum." †

* The article was eventually undertaken by Professor Hales.

† Mr Aldis Wright tells me that he believes one of his reasons for stopping short in his project was his inability to account for the wide divergences which distinguish the Harleian manuscript (7334) of the " Canterbury Tales " from all the other manuscripts.

CHAPTER VIII.

THE later portion of Henry Bradshaw's librarianship was, it can hardly be doubted, happier than the earlier. His health was improved ; the condition of things in the library was more satisfactory ; he was becoming better known and more widely appreciated in the university at large. Events occurred which gave him more confidence in himself; as president of the Library Association, as a member of the Council of the University and the General Board of Studies, he gained a reputation which he had not hitherto antici- pated, and friends seemed to multiply as these causes led him to abandon more and more his former position of reserve. In one respect only had he reason for regret—to the day of his death he never obtained the leisure which he craved, and without which it was impossible for him to lay the results of his literary researches before the world. He never ceased working at his favourite subjects, but the calls of public duty grew more exacting every year, and when at last he began to shuffle off the encumbrances of office it was too late.

At the time of which I am speaking, about the year 1876, his Celtic studies were uppermost in his mind. Re- turning health, and the conviction that a fruitful field lay open here, stimulated him to new exertions. A letter to M. Vanderhaeghen, of the University Library at Ghent, written in November, 1875, shows that he was on the track of

another discovery, that of the "Echternach * Martyrology."
" I am very much interested," he writes, " in the Plantin
Library,† from many points of view. . . . One thing especially I am anxious about. Herbert Rosweyd was engaged
upon a facsimile reproduction (engraved on copper) of an
eighth-century manuscript ' Martyrologium,' borrowed by
Bollandus from the Abbey of Echternach. On Rosweyd's
death the work must have been suspended, when it had
proceeded as far as July. D'Achery obtained (about 1662)
from Moretus a copy of the facsimile sheets as far as July
from the unpublished stock at Antwerp, and Bollandus sent
him a transcript of the remainder from the original manuscript, which was still in his keeping. The original manuscript did not go back to Echternach and with the rest
of that collection to Luxemburg, and it is now probably
lying buried in some library. . . . The manuscript was the
earliest known copy of the ' Martyrology,' and must have
come from Ireland, as is clear both from the handwriting
(which is to be seen in the ' Acta Sanctorum '), and from the
mention of Irish saints otherwise unknown."

His object in writing to M. Vanderhaeghen was to see if
he could discover, in the Plantin collection, the stock of
plates whence the facsimile of the manuscript was printed,
but he had little expectation of lighting on the manuscript
itself. An accident, it would appear, led to his doing so.
In March, 1876, he remarks in his note-book that Dr
Wasserschleben's " Irische Kanonensammlung "‡ has just
come. " I see at once that his manuscript 3 (at Paris) is
clearly from Brittany, and that it contains two Breton
glosses." He resolved to go to Paris to see the book in

---

* Sometimes spelt " Epternach." Echternach is a place on the eastern
frontier of the Duchy of Luxemburg.

† In the Musée Plantin at Antwerp. The family of Plantin is distinguished
in the history of typography. Christopher Plantin, the well-known printer,
lived in the middle of the sixteenth century.

‡ Published in 1874.

question, and not only examined it thoroughly, but discovered in the Bibliothèque Nationale the "Echternach Martyrology" which he had so long been in search of.* He at once communicated the discovery to his old friend, Dr Reeves, who says in his reply, " I am rejoiced to learn that you have hunted down the 'Epternach Martyrology,' and I feel intense satisfaction in having set you upon the pursuit. Great value will, I hope, result from the discovery under your able development. . . . For years and years I have longed to know something substantial about this precious document, and the more of its Irish character you can establish the more dear will it be to my heart. It is, I should suppose, the most venerable and important Christian calendar in existence, even on common grounds ; but if its extreme value can be associated with the Irish element, its interest will be vastly enhanced."

From Paris Bradshaw went on to Brittany, where he enjoyed the company of his friends Mr and Mrs F. W. Cornish. On the way he called at Chartres, but could see nothing in the library there, every one in authority being away. He visited Quimper, and at Rennes he with great difficulty obtained a sight of the cartulary of Redon. I quote from his note-book an account of how he overcame the obstacles that stood between him and this object of his affections. " I went to the sécrétariat directly after ten, and saw the under-secretary, M. l'Abbé Querard. He was very busy and very kind ; told me he could do nothing ; recommended me to call on M. l'Abbé Houet, of the Oratorians, in the Rue des Dames. I went, but he was at the great funeral in the cathedral. I went again after *déjeuner*, but could not get in ; then to the public library for a few

---

* The manuscript is No. 10,837 Lat. in the Bibliothèque Nationale at Paris. It was briefly described by M. Delisle in a catalogue published in the *Bibliothèque de l'École des Chartes* (1863), where it is called "Martyrologie de S. Jérôme ;" the date is said to be eighth century, and the writing "Écriture saxonne." Bradshaw's "discovery" appears to be the identification of this manuscript with the "Echternach Martyrology."

minutes ; . . . then to the Oratorians. Houet simply charming. He told me to go and ask for M. Combes, one of the
grands vicaires, and entreat to see Monseigneur even for
an instant. The porter went and brought him [M. Combes].
Could I see Monseigneur ? Quite impossible ; quite. No
reception to-day ; no seeing the archbishop otherwise. I
was miserable ; my whole journey fruitless. Write ever
such a scrap. Where ? At the porter's lodge. Tore a
leaf out of his register and began a letter humbly, when
M. Combes came in and said Monseigneur had given him
the manuscript, and I might use it in his chamber. He
had deposited it on the gravel walk (drizzling rain !) while
he came to tell me ; would see what I had written ; amused
enough. Went upstairs. After a few minutes Houet came
and sat by me while I went through it. He is better than
any English ambassador's letter. Come in the summer ;
' good-bye.' And so in easy time to the Hotel de France
to be off by the train to St Malo, to meet the boat for
Southampton." His successes on this short expedition,
and the pleasant company of his friends, made him very
happy. " The weather was mostly very bad," he writes ;
" but I enjoyed my time immensely and did good work
(what I had to do), and saw many quite fresh places and
people. Brittany is so different from ordinary France : no
endless rows of poplars by the roadsides ; and the gorse
was out for acres in a way that I never saw anywhere
before in my life."

He had for some time had it in his mind to publish the
results of his Celtic researches, and he was now on the
point of putting this plan into execution. " I am really
printing my paper at last," he writes to Professor Rhys in
September, 1876. " I give an account of all my harvesting
up to now, including all my Breton discoveries made in
March and April. Besides the new Bodleian Cornish
glosses, and the new Bodleian and Corpus manuscripts

with Breton glosses, I have got two Paris manuscripts, one ninth to tenth, the other eleventh century, with Breton glosses; also one in the British Museum with ditto. Also I have been to Rennes and seen the cartulary of Redon, and been to Quimper and seen the 'Book of Landevennech.' Did I tell you all this? Meantime I am glad to hear you are likely to allow the Breton origin of the Luxemburg 'Hisperica Famina'* and of the Oxford 'Eutychius.'"† A month or two later, however, found him apparently no nearer publication. "I am determined to do what I can," he says; "but this term is always so frightfully full of work that I am afraid to promise anything." He actually went so far as to put a sheet or two into type, but no trace of what he printed is now to be found.

His correspondence about this time shows that he was in a happier mood than he had been in for some years. The following is from a letter to a friend in Scotland :— "Scotch air must be most delicious. I have no cause, however, for complaining, as I now work at the far end of the big room in the library, looking down over our lawn to the bridge and the trees beyond, while the open window brings in all the air that could be wished. Still, my correspondence is a little oppressive at times. What is to be done with a lady who writes poetry and calls herself an authoress, and takes the opportunity of enlarging to me about 'the flowers and foliage of her glorious youth lying folded up deep down in the innermost strata of the palæozoic days of the golden past, ere genius meant sorrow, and life was but the veil of death'? I give it you word for word before tearing it up; but really one ought not to have to deal with such stuff in this hot and melting weather." Sometimes, but rarely, he speaks of the lack of friends. "Now

---

* This is not incompatible with what he says later on about the "Hisperica Famina" in a letter to Mr Hessels (March 9, 1874) : "It [the poem] is by an Irishman." See below, chap. xi.   † Bodl. Auct.

that I am growing old," he says in another letter, "I am almost out of all acquaintance with the undergraduates ; and the greater part of them I don't know even by sight, and very few indeed to speak to." But, in spite of occasional remarks of this kind, the sequence of friends among the younger members of the college was never altogether broken.

Soon after this Bradshaw was again at his old haunts in the Lakes, with an undergraduate friend. Writing from his favourite halting-place at Thirlspot, as he made a practice of doing, to the friend who was with him there on his first visit in 1869, he says, " You cannot really imagine how lovely everything is. The sky is and has been perfectly cloudless, and the lakes one and all are as blue and sparkling as sky and light airs can make them. Yesterday morning we went in from Grasmere to Ambleside, and then back the old way along the other side of Rydal ; and here we sat under the birch trees for many hours, while I read my ' Mézélie,' and Newton sketched. . . . Fancy my delight, in the middle of all this heat, at finding no flies at all ! "

He came back to London to be present at the wedding of Mr and Mrs R. T. Ritchie, both old friends of his. " There was no ceremony," he writes, "no wedding breakfast, and the result was that, instead of being a dull and miserable affair, as weddings too often are, it was one of the liveliest I have ever known. Having been ' best man ' four times in one year, I have had some little experience." From London he went on a short visit to Mr and Mrs Tennyson at Aldworth. "I have had a delightful time there," he writes. " I never breathed such delicious air in England." And in another letter, " Mr Tennyson is very fond of walking, fortunately for me, and we were on the downs the better part of the day. . . . I don't talk to him about his poems, not being myself up to the high level in such

matters. Still, I was very glad wHen he read me several
things which he is going to publish in his next volume."
Though too shy to talk to the laureate about his own
works, there were few who knew them better or admired
them more than Bradshaw.

In the autumn of 1877 was celebrated the four hun-
dredth anniversary of the beginning of printing in England.
It was in November, 1477, that Caxton published "The
Dictes and Sayings," the first book, so far as we know,
that was ever printed on English soil. Bradshaw was
naturally one of the first persons consulted by the promoters of the "Caxton Celebration." Writing in November, 1876, Mr Blades asks him to become a member of
the committee. "I hope you will accede to the request,"
he says, "as it [the committee] will be incomplete without
the presence of the chief apostle of palæotypography."
Bradshaw did not, however, become a member of the committee, but he was much interested in the exhibition, and
sent several of his treasures from the University Library to
be exhibited.

A mistake in returning the books, through which one
belonging to the library of the Baptist College at Bristol
fell into Bradshaw's hands, led to the publication of his
fifth "Memorandum," entitled "Notice of a fragment of
the Fifteen Oes and other prayers printed at Westminster
by W. Caxton about 1490–1491." This little paper fur-
nishes a good illustration of the methods which he followed
in the study of early printing. In the binding of the
Bristol book, a copy of Caxton's translation of the "Mirror
of the World," was a fragment of printed matter, which
had been used as a lining for the boards with which the
book was bound. This fragment he soaked off and examined. It proved to be a portion—two quarto leaves—
of Caxton's "Fifteen Oes and other prayers," of which a
unique copy is in the British Museum. It was not, how-

ever, the nature of the scrap in itself, but the deductions
which he was able to make from it, which gave it a special
value in his eyes. "The Bristol fragment," he writes,
"affords so much interesting evidence of the way in which
compositors of that day worked, and illustrates so many
points in connexion with early printing in England, that
I have thought it worth while to put down a few notes
on the subject." Among other things, this fragment, only
the half of an ordinary folio sheet of paper, is made
to show how rudimentary in some respects the art of
printing was in Caxton's time. Nowadays, a printer thinks
nothing of having a whole book standing in type at the
same time, before the sheets are finally printed off, but
"Caxton had been fifteen years at work before he arrived
at the point of printing four pages at once." Further, the
fragment in question appears to have been a bit of
"printer's waste," that is, a piece of work in some way
defective, which was therefore thrown aside as useless for
its original purpose. But it was not useless altogether; if
it could not form part of a book, it might be turned to
account for binding. This is what happened to the fragment—it was used to line the binding of another of
Caxton's books. Hence it is clear that Caxton, like many
other early printers, was his own binder, a fact which may
often enable the bibliographer to fix the date of a book or
to name its printer when all other indications are wanting.

Again, on both sides of the fragment Bradshaw found
what is called a "set-off," that is, the marks of printer's ink
from wet pages of some other book which has not been
preserved. These were very difficult to make out, for the
letters were, of course, reversed, and they were also much
blurred. In his diary, in which he notes down roughly
the process by which he got at the results given in the
"Memorandum," he remarks, "By the aid of a looking-
glass, my lamp, and my new magnifying glass, I can make

out one or two words, as *misericordia.*" He at once recognized the type, and, from these and other indications, arrived at the conclusion that the fragment had come in contact with a waste leaf of the octavo Primer, "at present only known from the fragment found by Mr Maskell in the binding of a book, and given by him to the British Museum in 1858." Hence it may be inferred that the Primer in question and the book to which the fragment belongs, were passing through the press about the same time. "Mr Blades and myself (continues Bradshaw) had come independently to the conclusion that both books belong to the last year of Caxton's life (1490-91); so that this fragment affords an additional mite of evidence."

Bradshaw gives several other instances in which he has extracted similar results from fragments such as this. He justly remarks, "After all that has been said, it cannot be any matter of wonder that the fragments used for lining the boards of old books should have an interest for those who make a study of the methods and habits of our early printers with a view to the solution of some of many difficulties still remaining unsettled in the history of printing. I have for many years tried to draw the attention of librarians and others to the evidence which may be gleaned from a careful study of these fragments; and if done systematically and intelligently, it ceases to be mere antiquarian pottering and waste of time."

Another happy result of the Caxton Celebration was a visit from M. Campbell, librarian of the Hague. Long as Bradshaw had been in correspondence with M. Campbell, he had never yet seen him. "I cannot tell you," he writes in August, "how delighted I am to hear this morning of your being in London, and giving me a chance *at last* of making your acquaintance in person, especially after having missed you by half an hour in Brussels in 1875." The visit, like that of Professor ten Brink, was productive

of as much pleasure on one side as on the other. Bradshaw
and his friend naturally spent the short time—only a day—
which they had together among the old books in the
University Library. "It was quite a sight," writes M.
Campbell, "to see the worthy librarian walking round his
shelves, picking out a volume here and another there,
bringing it to me with a smile and the remark, 'You will
be pleased to see this,' and showing me in this way all his
treasures." Soon afterwards Bradshaw wrote to him as
follows :—"Your visit has given me an impetus to go on
with these studies, which I have for some time been so
much inclined to neglect. Have you no young man whom
you can train to work at these things ? Now that your
book is out, I can proceed in quite a different way from
that which I was obliged to adopt when I made my list
of founts of type used in Holland. I should like to do
Holland over again, and I should much like to do
Belgium."

It was in the autumn of 1877 that the first Conference
of Librarians, which has since become an annual institution, was held. The project originated in an article
published in the *Academy* early in the year by Mr
E. B. Nicholson, now Bodley's Librarian, in which he
suggested that a conference should be held for the mutual
communication of experience and suggestion on all points
of library management. Mr Nicholson, naturally anxious
that Bradshaw, among other heads of large libraries, should
support his scheme, asked him to become a vice-president.
Bradshaw was, however, reluctant to pledge himself in any
way, and declined the honour ; nor did he take any part in
the proceedings of the conference for several years. That
he approved of the scheme in a general way is clear from
a letter to Mr Nicholson, dated July 28, 1877, in which he
says, "The programme which you have circulated of the
proposed proceedings has given me the liveliest satisfaction,

and I look forward with great pleasure to the printed reports of the conference. It is unquestionable that great good must arise from such a conference, and we all owe you a debt of gratitude for originating it in this country."

Considering the interest which he subsequently took in the meetings of the librarians, it is a little difficult to understand why at first he held aloof. It was partly due, no doubt, to his dislike of conferences in general. He regarded them as, for the most part, merely occasions for airing crotchets and otherwise wasting time. He was also influenced, we may imagine, by his habitual, almost morbid, reluctance to put himself prominently forward. He knew he would be expected to give his "views" about all sorts of topics dear to the heart of the organiser, and "views" he was always reluctant to give. He distrusted his oratorical powers, and expected, in such a gathering as was anticipated, to be completely out of his element. In all this there was, it must be allowed, a spice of that perversity which was a strong ingredient in his character—a perversity which sometimes irritated strangers, but more often amused his friends.

Another motive probably weighed with him on this occasion, and that was the prospect of speedily resigning his post as librarian. The impossibility of combining literary work with the duties of his post, as he understood them, was his principal inducement to take this step. Writing to a friend in July, 1877, he says, "I cannot go on at the library much longer, and then, if I live, I ought to bring out some of the many things for which I have been collecting materials all these years ; otherwise they will never come to anything." Added to this was the sense of his own shortcomings as a librarian, which was strengthened at this time by a step which the Syndicate had lately taken. It had been resolved that the library should be annually inspected by some person of reputation as a

librarian, who should be able to report frankly and im-
partially on its condition. Bradshaw could not help
approving of this scheme in principle. He wrote to Mr
H. B. Wheatley, who was the first inspector appointed,
"The inspection of the library—intelligent criticism from
a competent outsider—is in my mind of all things that
which we here need most." Nevertheless, the project was,
perhaps not unnaturally, at first very distasteful to him,
and in conversation with intimate friends he made no
secret of his feelings. It was disheartening to think that
such a corrective was considered necessary. Under these
circumstances, he would naturally shrink from appearing as
the permanent occupant of a position from which he was,
he believed, so soon to retire, or from taking part in
arrangements for future meetings which some one else
would have to carry out.

Whether the reasons suggested above were sufficient to
account for his abstention, or whether there were others in
the background, I cannot say. Be this as it may, he
shirked the conference of 1877 altogether, and went gloss-
hunting instead. It was not, as we have seen, by any
means the first occasion when he made an expedition of
this kind. He had hunted glosses in the Bodleian as well as
in his own library, among Archbishop Parker's manuscripts
at Corpus, and in the British Museum. Unlike most other
hunters, he rarely, if ever, returned empty-handed, for he
marked down his game before he started on the chase. A
gloss-hunt was a genuine relaxation to him, and he could
always count on sport, for he brought to bear upon his
object all the zest and keenness of a boy, combined with
the cunning of an experienced hunter. On this occasion
the valley of the Loire was his happy hunting-ground, and
his efforts were rewarded by the largest bag which he ever
made. He had paid a preliminary visit to this district at
Easter, 1877, and had seen enough to show him that an

exhaustive exploration would be amply repaid. The reasons which induced him to examine the libraries of Tours and Orleans are worth noting, for they show that his discoveries were not fortuitous, but the result of following step by step a clue which pointed to success.

The finding of these glosses, it should be remembered, was only one object and outcome of his researches among the remains of Celtic antiquity. The glosses were in themselves of the greatest value to the philologist, but Bradshaw was far from being interested in the language alone. He was engaged on a general inquiry into the early literature and history of the ancient collection of ecclesiastical canons known as the "Hibernensis." * It appeared, from the glosses contained in the two Paris manuscripts of the "Hibernensis," and from other indications, that these manuscripts, which had long been in the great monasteries of Fécamp and Corbie, were of Breton origin. The transfer from Brittany had probably taken place during the monastic revival of the twelfth century, and the final migration to Paris was the result of the Revolution. Now, in the Communal Library of Orleans is a manuscript (No. 193) containing the "Hibernensis," together with other documents. This manuscript formerly belonged to the Benedictine Abbey of Fleury, on the Loire, whence, at the destruction of the abbey about 1789, it was transferred to Orleans. What could be more probable than that this Orleans manuscript, like its fellows at Paris, should have found its way originally from Brittany, and like them should contain valuable matter in the shape of Celtic glosses? If so, not only would the philologist gain an addition to his materials, but further light would be thrown on the origin of the canons which the manuscript contained. The supposition was rendered the more plausible by the fact

* Edited by Dr Wasserschleben in "Die Irische Kanonensammlung," 1874 ; second edition, 1885.

that other Fleury books had long ago found their way to the Vatican, and among these were probably the Vatican "Gildas" and "Hisperica Famina," both of Celtic origin and most likely connected with Brittany.*

Accordingly, when Bradshaw visited Orleans in the spring of 1877, he knew what to expect, and he found what he expected. The manuscript contained glosses, and the glosses turned out to be Breton. He had not time to examine them thoroughly on that occasion, but resolved to return in the autumn. The manuscript was certainly Breton, and the glosses were sprinkled over the pages in liberal profusion. Here was something to look forward to. On his way out Bradshaw visited Cambrai and Amiens, in order to examine the manuscripts of the "Hibernensis" which existed at those places. At Amiens he found nothing of interest, but he discovered that the Cambrai manuscript almost exactly resembled one of those at Paris. At Orleans he was met by an unexpected difficulty. The library was closed, the librarian away; nothing could be seen for another ten days. The old lady who acted as custodian was for a long time obdurate, but Bradshaw's good-tempered persistence at length prevailed. The better part of two days was occupied in copying out the glosses. Fortunately, in this task he had the assistance of an old friend and travelling-companion, Mr Yeld. While at work in the library, they were joined by M. Bimbenet, president of a learned society at Orleans, who was conversant with the treasures of the library. M. Bimbenet showed Bradshaw an early printed Bible. "How nice!" he exclaimed at once; "printed at Paris in" such and such a year. M. Bimbenet looked up astonished. "You will find the imprint at the end," he continued, and the date was as he said. M. Bimbenet then

* The above is taken partly from Bradshaw's diary and note-books, partly from his published letter on the "Hibernensis" ("Memorandum," No. 8).

brought him a second Bible, and then a third, and Bradshaw, without hesitation, gave the place and date of each. When asked how he could know them so accurately, he replied, looking at his friend, "Just as I know *him*. I know every line of his face, and could never mistake him for anybody else;" and then, placing the Bibles side by side, he pointed out the minute variations in the form of the letters which sufficed to enable him to distinguish them at a glance.

From Orleans Bradshaw went on to Tours, and spent a whole day examining the manuscript of the "Hibernensis" in the Communal Library there. Thence to Paris, where he spent a day or so in getting the glosses from the Orleans manuscript into proper order. "Finished my glosses," he notes in his diary, "so as to make their sequence clear, and numbered them up to 320!" The work had told upon him. "My eyes are very weak," he writes; but nevertheless next day "did good work on the Corbie and Fécamp manuscripts," as well as on another book. Two days afterwards he was again in England. The glosses were sent to Mr Whitley Stokes, who writes in the preface to his separate edition of them,* "The following old Breton glosses were found in 1877 by the late Mr Henry Bradshaw. . . . When I was leaving England for India in 1880, he presented me with a copy in his own hand, not only of the glosses, but of the context of most of the Latin words glossed; and I seize this occasion to express my gratitude for a generosity as rare as it is precious. In 1881 I printed them privately in Calcutta, with a commentary, and in 1882 Mr Bradshaw recollated them with the manuscript. . . . There are 322 glosses, but of these no less than 109 are only portions

* "The Breton Glosses at Orleans," by Whitley Stokes, D.C.L. See also Kühn's *Zeitschrift*, vol. xxvi. pp. 423–497; and Loth, "Vocabulaire Vieux-Breton avec commentaire" (Paris: 1884), pref. p. ix., etc.

of words intended by the glosser. . . . These 109 abbreviations do not, of course, add much to our knowledge
of Old Breton, but the remaining 213 glosses are of great
value, not only from the point of view of the lexicographer,
but also from that of the grammarian."

A diary which Bradshaw kept with great assiduity for
a few months during the autumn of 1877 shows him
engaged, as usual, on a variety of occupations.   He was
making inquiries into the order of Caxton's books, and
the history of the early Bibles published at Strassburg
and elsewhere ; he was tracing the origin of the " Hibernensis," and making notes on the " Hisperica Famina,"
" Gildas," and the date of the death of Bede ; he was talking over Chaucer with Dr Furnivall, and discussing astro-
nomical difficulties in the "Canterbury Tales" with Professor
Adams ; he was helping Mr J. W. Clark with his work
on the architectural history of Cambridge by reading over
manuscripts with him and revising his proof-sheets ; and
he was superintending, with as much care as anything
else, the painting and papering of an absent friend's rooms ;
—all this, and much besides, in conjunction with his heavy
library work.

He was still thinking seriously about giving up the
library. " I know," he writes to Dr Luard, who had
dissuaded him from the step—" I know I do not leave
from any feeling of pique, and it is an untold source of
happiness to me to think that during the ten years and
more that I have been in office, I have never been on
the remotest approach to bad terms with the Syndicate.
But I do feel two things most strongly : (1) that the time
is such that the university ought to have for its library
a better administrator than I could ever be, one who has
the power of dealing with *men;* and (2) that I owe to
the university to produce some of the many results which
their endowment of me in past years has enabled me

R

nearly to work out, but which I see not the slightest
prospect of working out while I remain in office. . . . I
feel also that in the last month even I have made such
a fresh start in self-government as I have not made for
many, many years before, and this gives me hope and
encouragement to think that if I do resign, I shall not
wholly waste my time as I might have done had I given
up sooner.   But I cannot *write* about these things."   Six
months later he was of a different mind, and could write
to another friend, "When I have reached the autumn,
I shall know better what my prospects are of going on
at the library at all.   I am beginning to feel that it would
be singularly foolish to give up at my age what is really
and must be my life's work, for what would be at best
but *dilettante* work."   As time went on, he grew happier
in his place, and the feelings which had prompted him
to resign gradually wore away.

In the winter of 1877-8 much debate was going on
in Cambridge over the reform of college and university
statutes, in accordance with the Universities Act of 1877.
In King's a sort of three days' parliament was held during
the Christmas vacation to discuss the changes proposed.
Bradshaw attended the meetings, though he did not take
that vivid interest in the proceedings which he displayed
on a similar occasion fourteen years before.   " I grudged,"
he write, "having to come away [from Fairchildes] for
this college meeting, about which I hardly care a single
straw, though it is very wrong to say or feel this."   Nevertheless he took an active part in the discussion, and his
remarks, strenuous and pointed as they always were, had
considerable influence on the voting.   " They attribute to
a speech of mine," he tells a friend, " the unexpected total
abolition and sweeping away of celibacy as concerning
in any way the tenure of a fellowship.   It was almost the
only thing I cared about effecting, but I did not expect
it would come so soon."

Not long after this, in May, 1878, he was elected an honorary member of the Royal Irish Academy, in the department of Polite Literature and Antiquities ; and in the same month he was made a corresponding member of the Bibliographical Society of Antwerp (Antwerpsche Bibliophilen), whose motto, " Labore et Constantia," he might fairly have taken for his own.

Later in the summer, in addition to the work which he was doing for Mr Christopher Wordsworth, to be described presently, he helped Mr Seebohm in the investigations preparatory to his book on the " English Village Community."   Mr Seebohm had just worked out, from the Winslow Court Rolls, the average " virgate," or villain's holding of thirty acres.   On his showing Bradshaw his results, the latter at once produced further illustrations from a manuscript * " terrier," or description of land, which he had lately purchased.   " On another occasion," says Mr Seebohm, " I was studying the Welsh tribal system of land-tenure.   There are two or three records of early grants of land in the copy of the Gospels known as the ' Book of St Chad.'†   But when were these records made, and what was the date of the manuscript itself ?   Who could tell me better than Bradshaw ?   To Bradshaw I went, and found him in his rooms.   When informed of my object, he said, ' You have done quite right in coming to *me*, for I happen to have the Book of St Chad in my possession just now, and, moreover, this is St Chad's day ! '   Then he took up the volume, and, turning over its pages, showed me how, by a mark here and a few words there, he had made out its history, and could say with some confidence

---

* The manuscript in question, now in the University Library (Add. 2601), describes the district to the north-west of Cambridge.   It appears to belong to the fourteenth century.

† This book belongs to the chapter library at Lichfield, and is called after the patron saint of that see.   It is a manuscript of the eighth century, in Irish writing, and in the tenth century belonged to the church of Llandaff, whence it was removed to Lichfield about the year 1000.

what was its date and that of the entries in the margin."
Coincidences of this kind will recur to the mind of every
friend of Bradshaw.

Early in the year 1879 two events happened in which
members of his family were concerned, and which gave
him the keenest gratification.   His eldest brother, Mr
Thomas Bradshaw, then a county-court judge at Newcastle,
was requested to arbitrate in a dispute between capital
and labour which threatened to produce a disastrous
quarrel.   He settled the dispute in a manner which satisfied both masters and men, and the strike was happily
averted.   Shortly afterwards, his second brother, Captain
Richard Bradshaw, then commander of the *Shah*, being
on his homeward voyage and touching at St Helena, heard
of the catastrophe of Isandlwana.   Without waiting for
orders, he took on board what troops he could find and
sailed straight for Natal.   Every one will remember the
applause with which the act was greeted throughout the
country.

A little later Bradshaw received tidings of a very
different kind.   It was in March, 1879, that the news came
of the death of his friend, Ernest Muggeridge, at Hong-
Kong.   "No one can ever know," he writes to the common
friend who told him of their loss, "how much I owe to
Ernest, and I know you owe much also, as any one must
who saw much of him, and did not find the strength
in himself to do the right which he knew he ought to
do.   No relation is like a real friend. I do not mean
that one is better than another, but a friend is a different
thing.   And the *memory* of such a friend is a thing to
help one on in life, as few other things except his living
self could do.   You remember what you said about not
caring to send his letter round, to be read by perhaps
indifferent people.   It is no mere *sentiment*, but there
is a *sacredness* about such friendship which one cannot

talk about." Two months later the body was brought home, to be laid in the Brompton Cemetery. Bradshaw was prevented by business from being present at the funeral, but he was able to go to London in the afternoon to see the grave before it was closed. " I cannot resist the opportunity," he says, " of once looking at the place where he lies, who has formed such a part of my life during the past eight years." " We two went together," he writes to another friend, " to the cemetery, where the boy lies close to his favourite uncle, and we stayed to see the simple great slab of Aberdeen granite closed over him. It was not an afternoon to forget. Though it had been raining heavily, it cleared and the sun came out by the time we got there, and everything looked bright. We found the man who manages the whole place, and the three workmen came. There were no undertakers, no sham mourning, no vulgarity ; simply ordinary labourers doing ordinary work. There was nothing whatever to *jar* upon one. And then until the very last moment one could see the flowers which lay upon the coffin, which was of scented camphor-wood ; and when we had seen this done, we came away quietly, and I came down home the same evening."

But if death took from Bradshaw friends of this kind, there was in him a never-failing spring of affection which constantly won him others in their stead. The episode which has now to be related cannot be better told than by the person principally concerned, Mr W. M. Conway, lately professor of fine art at University College, Liverpool, who writes to me as follows :—

" You ask about my relation to Bradshaw. It was briefly this. The term after I went in for my tripos I was working in the Fitzwilliam Museum at the engravings there—Schöngauer, Dürer, etc. That was the Lent Term, 1879. I then wanted to study the woodcuts of the same period, and Colvin introduced me to Bradshaw, because, of course, most woodcuts are in printed books, and the library was the place to work in at them. The entry in my diary of March 24, 1879, is, ' Spent three hours in the University Library with Mr Bradshaw, who put me in the way of studying and cataloguing the woodcuts in the fifteenth-century printed books (of the Low Countries).' I judge from the word 'cataloguing' that on this very first day of our acquaintance he involved me in his enthusiasm, for certainly when I went to him I had no idea of doing anything of the kind.

" I well remember the friendliness with which he received me, and how he said that he had been studying the bibliography of the subject for years, and had never once had any one come to him in Cambridge to look at, still less to study, the things which had been so much to him. He said that the woodcuts had interested him, but that he never had either the time or the qualifications for studying them. Then he went to the shelves and took down book after book, and showed me the same cut turning up now in the possession of one printer, now in the possession of another. He showed me the wanderings and developments of founts of type ; he showed me the structure of books, and I know not what besides. For three hours I followed him like a dazed person into a new world—a world of what I had before thought to be dry and dusty things, but which his illuminating speech showed to be a very kingdom of romance and surprise. Next day he had a table set up for me by his own, and I came then and worked there day after day at the books he gave me, finding out a method for myself as I went along, but always guided, prompted, and controlled by him. The first book he gave me was an edition of the ' Dialogus creaturarum moralisatus' printed at Gouda by Gerard Leeu, about 1482. It was full of little cuts, and I began to measure them. The measurements showed that

three or four consecutive cuts had usually been made upon
one strip of wood, and then divided. This little discovery
pleased Bradshaw immensely, and from that time his
interest in my work increased. We usually spent five or
six hours a day together, and often I remained in his rooms
till long into the night.

"In the vacation I went to the British Museum, and
worked at the books in the library as I had done at Cambridge, and the next term I continued the same course.
That would naturally have been my last term at Cambridge,
and I was faced by the problem of what to do afterwards
as a life-work. I wanted to devote myself to some combination of art and letters, but my friends were naturally
opposed to any such vague profession, not knowing in the
least what it meant or whither it tended. Here then
Bradshaw stepped in. He said it might be possible to get
a grant from the Worts Fund to send me abroad to continue my investigations, but that the thing would take
time ; so, instead of that, he offered me out of his own
pocket fifteen pounds a quarter, as an earnest to my friends
that what I was doing was really work which some one
thought it worth while to pay for.

"Matters were thus smoothed over. I started off for the
Continent, travelled to all the libraries where fifteenth-century Netherlands-printed books were to be seen, and wrote
continually to Bradshaw of the progress of my work. He
found me getting into the dumps, and as an encouragement
he wrote, telling me that I was to have twenty-five pounds
a quarter for the future. I was to consider him as an
employer in place of the library, he said. The library had
given him some kind of endowment-of-research post when
he was younger, and he always stated that the fact that he
had been able to do the bibliographical work he did was
due to that appointment. The library, he said, could no
longer afford to do for another as it had done for him, so

he felt it a pleasure to step in personally in its place and do what he should like to see it do if he could."

While Mr Conway was abroad he frequently received long letters from Bradshaw, congratulating him upon his progress, telling him what to see and do, giving him plain and wholesome advice. "I was delighted," he writes, "with the Erlangen discovery, and still more with the mode of it. You can feel with me now in what I have so constantly experienced in going into a strange library in search of a thing which something slight led me to suppose was there, and yet which people in general would never think of. It has happened so constantly in my Welsh and Breton discoveries. . . . You must manage to let us have some real time together in January, to go over certain things, and to fight out our own views, and, if necessary, to knock each other down in more than one point." Again, "'I used to feel sure that as long as I worked steadily at whatever had to be done, things paid themselves.' This is what you say in your letter this morning, but your only failing here is that you do not put sufficient emphasis on the word *done.* It has been my curse all through life that I want the power or gift, or whatever you like to call it, of *finishing* what I work at ; and all the minute research in the world is only rendered more hopeless by this one failing. . . . The upshot of all this is that you are perfectly miserable, and I am not surprised to hear it. My dear boy, you really must begin and see what depends on yourself, and what on others. I do not like quoting poetry when people are in the dumps, but Matthew Arnold's 'Self-Dependence'* has had such a deep and lasting impression on me in connection with this very subject, that I cannot

---

* The lines beginning—

> " Weary of myself, and sick of asking
> What I am, and what I ought to be,
> At the vessel's prow I stand, which bears me
> Forward, forward, o'er the star-lit sea."

help putting it to you to look at it when you next come upon it. . . . Good-bye, my dear boy. Do not lose heart, whatever you do, but look to yourself always as the only person who can possibly be at fault when anything goes wrong with you, and then you will have the whole control of the situation."

The result of Mr Conway's journey was his book on " The Woodcutters of the Netherlands." Not content with enabling him to write the book, Bradshaw, who was delighted with the thorough and exhaustive nature of the work, persuaded the University Press to publish it, and revised the proof-sheets. In fact, throughout its production he watched the progress of the work as if it had been his own, which indeed, as the preface acknowledges, to a great extent it was. Nor was this the only book in the making of which he had a hand about this time. It was partly at his suggestion, and owing to his encouragement, that his friend Dr Norman Moore translated Professor Windisch's grammar of Old Irish. When the translation was completed, he got the University Press to undertake its publication, and he assisted the author in seeing it through the press.

His Easter holiday in 1880—he had none the year before—was spent in a tour through Southern France. On his way back through London he attended a meeting of the Society of Arts, at which his friend, Mr H. B. Wheatley, read a paper on the history and art of bookbinding. Bradshaw took the opportunity of urging that a collection of specimens, showing the styles of binding at different dates, should be brought together, and emphasised the importance of binding in connection with bibliography. Nor did he lose the chance of having a fling at his old enemies, the binders of the present day, for the damage in which old books too often undergo in passing through their hands.

It will be in the recollection of many Cambridge men

that, shortly after the regulations for the Classical Tripos were modified so as to include classical archæology as a distinct study, a member of the Senate, who wished to remain anonymous, offered two hundred pounds to endow for one year a lecturer in that subject. There are probably very few even now who are aware that this anonymous donor was Henry Bradshaw. I give here some extracts from the letter in which he laid before his intermediary, Dr Thompson, late Master of Trinity, his reasons for this act of generosity. The letter is dated May 24, 1880.

"MY DEAR MASTER OF TRINITY,

"You ask me to put on paper the main points which I tried to place before you to-day. They are briefly these. The recognition of archæology as a definite study in the new rearrangement of the Classical Tripos makes it very desirable that those who take up the study should find a good teacher to aid and direct them in their training. . . . It is difficult to find the right man at the right moment; and it is not easy always to find the necessary funds even when the right man is within reach. Nothing, you must well know, could be further from my mind than any the least resemblance of dictating to the Board. It was the simple conviction that, if only they could assure themselves of the worth of Dr Waldstein's work in such a post, they would have no reason to regret the appointment, that led me to-day to place the sum of two hundred pounds in your hands. The university has, we all know, to husband its own resources, and I feel sure it would not take such an offer unkindly. . . . I have written to you more freely than I could to any other member of the Board. But I must trust you not to use any language which might lead people to infer that the offer came from me. It is not a mere figure of speech, for I have an extreme repugnance to coming forward as doing anything of the kind. But the generous treatment I received at the hands of the university for so many years (1859–1867) makes me ready to do what I can—when I can. So pray keep my counsel.

"Yours most sincerely,

"HENRY BRADSHAW."

It is hardly necessary to add that the secret was kept, and the anonymous donor remained completely shrouded in the obscurity in which he had wrapt himself. The Classical Board unanimously passed a resolution expressing their "grateful appreciation of his munificent proposal;" the Council, with equal unanimity, brought forward a grace, which the Senate accepted; and Dr Waldstein was duly appointed to the post thus temporarily created, which was afterwards converted into a permanent appointment.

Some extracts from a correspondence which Bradshaw kept up with an intimate friend during part of this summer may be of interest.

"June 7, 1880, 11.15 p.m.—Conway just got away, after reading me his chapters on the woodcutters of Schoonhaven and Schiedam, the last in his whole series—talking about prospects, and how to bring out his book in the most wholesome manner. T., W., and one or two others in for a little and wondering what it all means, what sort of things *cutters* are, and so on.

"Frank Balfour and Taylor over annual Library Report from 4 to 5.20. Then home and copying out, digesting, and rewriting report till hall at seven; no five-o'clock tea, no coffee after hall, but straight upstairs after dinner to finish report and send off to press, which done, Conway appears. . . .

"June 8, 9, 1880.—You seem to think egotism is a fault in your letters. On the other hand, I should say precisely the opposite, and I have set you the example, which is better than any advice, which, further, is a thing I detest doing. What you should, seriously speaking, avoid is the *twistic* form of letter. I know that I rise several pegs in your estimation by coining a word, provided it is really wanted, as in this case. . . .

"June 12, 1880.—A quarter-past ten, Saturday evening, and —— has just gone away, having drunk his tea here and talked about his prospects, which I fear are none of the brightest. I am quite used up with library work from 9 this morning to 5.30 this afternoon, except one short interval in the middle of the day. . . . You were so highly amused with my pleasure at seeing the new moon for the first time and raising my hat to it. The old idea is that the first wish that comes *naturally* into your mind at the moment will turn out happily. Now, what pleases me is to notice what it is or who it is that *naturally* occurs to me first. Yesterday the merest thread was visible in the sky after hall, and you both, you and Ernest Muggeridge, came naturally and at once into my mind. I do not like to write all this ; but after a few more letters there will be no necessity for talking in the same way, and you will find that I only write when I really want something. . . .

"Sunday evening, 9.35, June 13, 1880.—I have nothing at all to say, but I merely want to talk. I went to chapel morning and afternoon, and I also went to St Mary's and heard an excellent sermon from a young man on self-gratification, self-confidence, and self-assertion. It touched me in more than one point. J. W. Clark here for an hour working in the morning,* and Conway here to luncheon. . . .

"June 15, 1880.—I had an excellent and most satisfactory afternoon on Saturday at my Report work, but I have done absolutely nothing since, so you will see I must be in a bad

* Mr J. W. Clark was at this time at work on his " Architectural History of Cambridge," and Mr Conway on his " Woodcutters of the Netherlands.'

condition of body and mind. . . . I continually hunger after some one really congenial to talk to about all imaginable things, and I suppose this will go on for a few days, and then I shall be able to look forward to three months' blank and steady work. . . .

"June 18, 1880.—The curfew and the day of the month again.* We have just come up from the garden, where we have been smoking and watching the white cat and the brown owl and the sunset clouds, each having his own thoughts and not talking over-much. I picked a bit of my favourite plant in the whole garden—the Carolina Allspice ; I don't know what you call it. It scents my whole room now, and I send it on the bare chance of its not losing all its power before it gets to Frankfort.

"June 21, 1880.—Again the curfew. I have been writing for half an hour and more, and yet I just happened to be beginning a letter to you as this blessed bell is going, bringing such endless pleasant memories to my mind, all doubly pleasant by the fact of my writing this letter at the same time. As I sit I can just see half the nearly full moon rising above the library of St Catherine's opposite my window, and it seems an age since I wrote at this time, though it was only on Friday night. . . .

"July 6, 1880.—You ask my advice, and you know how I hate giving such stuff. As I was reading somewhere yesterday, the only wise men are those who never give advice and never take it. If you must have my feeling about the Sunday lectures, I should repeat *Punch's* advice to people about to marry : 'Don't.' It is quite easy for you to earn five pounds in another way, and if you want to be a great man you will keep clear of these controverted movements. Next as to the paper ; if you are going to write it, make haste about it. You know perfectly what your dis-

* The curfew is the bell which rings from the tower of Great St Mary's Church every evening from 9 to 9.15 p.m. After it has ceased, another bell tolls the number of the day of the month.

satisfaction means. Did any man ever write anything and lay it aside, and take it up again some months after and re-read it with satisfaction? Only as it has to be published, sit down and do the re-writing at once; sleep over it, and send it off hot next day. Don't allow yourself to cool over it, or you will be miserable as before. . . .

"July 27, 1880.—I have been all day at humming-birds (*Oiseaux mouches*), collating and arranging plates, which the great man * could not be bothered to number as they came out; and it is sometimes a refreshment to me to master a bibliographical puzzle, and bring it out all neat and clean where my neighbours have all failed signally. 'Vanity,' I hear you say; but we all have our little vanities, and even your excellency is not quite free from such weakness sometimes. One stall of my Augean stable is clean; I finished it this morning between nine and ten. I look at the ten which ought to be done in the same way before October, and, though it is enough to make one despondent, I do not quite despair. For one thing, I do not set myself in a week a greater task than I think possible to be done, and in this way I am happy. My power of leaving work unfinished is so enormous, that to feel a week's promised work *done* is a sensation which is both new and invigorating. But why do I talk nonsense when I ought to be in bed? Good night now, and forgive me for my long silence. You know it has not been from my not thinking of you.

"Ever your most loving friend,
"HENRY BRADSHAW."

Early in 1881 Bradshaw gave some assistance to Mrs Guest, who was then preparing a collective edition of Dr Guest's archæological papers.† He drew up at her request

---

* The "great man" is John Gould, who issued Part I. of a supplement to his work on Humming-birds in 1880. He died in the following winter.

† Dr. Guest's papers were published in 1883, in two volumes, under the title of "Origines Celticæ," etc.

a list of the papers read before the Archæological Society and published in the *Archæologia Cambrensis* and elsewhere, as well as of the letters in the *Athenæum* to which these papers gave rise. In sending the list to Mrs Guest, he writes, "I enclose a paper which gives a first clean result of a good deal of work. I hope you will like the look of it, as it contains a fair statement of Dr Guest's archæological activity during the twenty years 1849–1869. . . . I cannot tell you what a real pleasure it is to me to help to work out a bibliographical problem of this kind, especially in the case of one who was always one of the very few who gave me intelligent encouragement in my own work."

During this period he was so much engaged on special tasks, to be presently described, that he was unable to spend much time on anything else, but he did not altogether lose sight of his old studies. An error in Mr Thackeray's account * of the Mazarine Bible at Eton set him working for a while at the early German printers, and this led him on to their English followers. "I am delighted," writes Mr Blades in September, "with your interesting discovery of what I take to be a portion of a new indulgence from Caxton's press.† . . . I don't envy much our bibliographical posterity if they go on a-gleaning after you. Your insight is so exceptional that your predictions seem to bring their own fulfilment." In the autumn of the year Mr Blades sent him a copy of his new edition of the "Life of Caxton." "Will you kindly accept it," he writes, "and give it board and lodging? You ought to do so, for in truth you had no small share in begetting its grandfather, and some, or rather a good deal, of your own blood is in its veins."

---

* *Notes and Queries*, February to July, 1881. Bradshaw's correction is in the number for May 14, 1881. He took a journey to Eton on purpose to see if the name which Mr Thackeray stated to be on the binding of the book was correctly given or not.

† In the library of Trinity College, Dublin.

In July, 1881, the office of Bodley's Librarian became vacant through the death of Mr Coxe. There was naturally much talk at Oxford about his successor, and not a few fixed on Henry Bradshaw. An intimate friend, who was in a position to know the chances, wrote to urge him to stand. "Your name is in people's mouths," he says, "and you would be very acceptable here." The idea of standing does not appear to have occurred to Bradshaw till he received this letter. For a moment the prospect was so alluring as almost to overpower him. "As to the main point of your letter," he writes in reply, "it has completely upset me. . . . To think of my saying to you in the vestibule of our college library, looking at the print of Thomas Hyde, the Orientalist, Bodley's Librarian in Charles II's reign, 'When will another fellow of King's go to Oxford in that capacity?' Honestly, the possibility of such a thing in my own case never once so much as crossed my mind. . . . Of course, it is a much greater library than ours, and a much higher position in every way, because, whatever happens, Oxford must always stand much higher than Cambridge in the general estimation, and yet Cambridge men may, nevertheless, be quite content to be Cambridge men. My own fearful indolence and want of energy, to say nothing of my total ignorance of German, would to my mind be an absolute bar. . . . But you don't know what a shock your letter has given me. The very idea of any one thinking such a thing within the bounds of possibility is enough to turn a stronger head than mine."

The letter alluded to above was followed, at the beginning of the Michaelmas Term, by more direct overtures on behalf of influential persons, and it is clear from Bradshaw's correspondence that for a short time he had some thoughts of standing for the post. But calm consideration and the counsel of one or two intimate friends enabled him to resolve on what was probably the wiser course. On October 30, 1881, he wrote to the friend who had first suggested the idea, " I have had a very anxious time of it, and I know I ought to have written to you before. But such a crisis in one's life does not often occur—of course, nothing resembling it has ever occurred to me before—and I cannot bear to decide on the spur of the moment, even though my final decision may be identical with my first impression. There are, of course, many things to be thought of and well weighed ; but I cannot have the least hesitation now in making up my mind that to stay where I am is the wisest and best course for myself, and certainly the best thing that could happen for the other people as well."

To one of the most influential of the curators he wrote at the same time, "Bodley's Librarian is, in my mind, beyond any doubt, the head of my profession in this country, and there are abundant reasons which would tend to make me covet the honour. But the more I weigh the matter the more I am convinced that I could do more good here than I could possibly do there ; and this alone has sufficed to bring me to a deliberate decision to remain here." When Mr Nicholson was appointed, Bradshaw wrote to congratulate him in the warmest terms. " I am happy and at ease," he says, " in the conviction that they have found a man who, while there is no fear of his working slavishly in a groove, will, on the other hand, not despise the traditions of a place, where *good traditions* are of such vital importance, if that aroma is to be preserved which gives the charm to the Bodleian and places it at the head of all the libraries in Europe."

Towards the close of 1881 Bradshaw was able to announce to the members of his college the completion of a work in which he had taken great interest, Mr Herkomer's portrait of Dr Okes, Provost of King's College. The value which he set on such memorials was shown by the attention which he devoted to the portraits in the University Library. He had some time before this been at much pains to trace their history, and under his supervision and that of Professor Colvin they were cleaned and repaired, and hung in the position in which they now are. Some four years back he had been instrumental in obtaining for the college a portrait of Lord Stratford de Redcliffe, perhaps the most distinguished Kingsman of the century, and had given £100 towards it. The success of this portrait, painted by Mr Herkomer, made him desirous that the college should possess an equally good memorial of the provost, who had thirty years before led the way to reform by freeing it from the unwholesome privileges which it then enjoyed,* and who had presided over the society during two successive epochs of change. His proposal was warmly taken up, and the requisite funds were easily obtained. In the summer of 1881 Mr Herkomer came to Cambridge to paint the picture, and stayed in King's as Bradshaw's guest. The portrait met with universal approval, and was presented to the college in October of this year.

Shortly after this Bradshaw was elected a member of " the Family," a select Cambridge club, consisting of a dozen congenial spirits, chosen rather for their social gifts than for academical distinction, but generally combining both qualifications. The club dates from the last century, and is said to have begun by meeting to toast " the family over the water." It no longer has any political bias, but meets for dinner once a fortnight. To be a member of it, one must, at any rate, be regarded as " a good fellow," and the distinction thus bestowed was a source of real gratification to Bradshaw. His first dinner, it may be noted, was in Francis Balfour's rooms.

In January, 1882, was published the first number of

* See above, p. 21.

the *Bibliographer*, a journal edited by Mr H. B. Wheatley. This number contained an article * by Bradshaw on " Godfried van der Haghen (G. H.), the publisher of Tindale's own last edition of the New Testament in 1534-5." The article cost him a good deal of trouble. " I shall take good care," he writes to Mr Wheatley, " never to promise any one an article again, until I can hand it over to them then and there. I would not go through the last ten days again for much. With a very heavy cold on me, which muzzed my head, and a mass of work by day, and people to attend to, whom I could not get rid of, almost every evening, and the knowledge that you *really* wanted the copy for the printer, I have been very far from comfortable. . . . I feel inclined to envy you light-hearted Londoners, who don't care a straw what you write. I hope honestly, both for your sake and mine, that it may be my last as well as my first contribution to any magazine of the kind."

The question to be solved was the following. Tindale's† first attempt to publish his version of the New Testament was made in 1525, but the work was interrupted before it had gone far. His first complete edition was printed later in the same year, and his second nine years later. The third edition, which contains his final revision, was printed at Antwerp in 1534-5. It is not known who printed this edition, but the publisher's name is indicated by the initials " G. H." on the title-page. Who was this " G. H." who was bold enough to undertake the publication of so dangerous a work as the first English version of the New Testament? To all interested in the early history of the Reformation, this was clearly an inquiry worth following up. Mr Fry, in his " Bibliographical Description

---

* This article has since been reprinted by Mr Blades.

† Bradshaw shows conclusively that this, and not Tyndale, is the way in which the reformer habitually spelt his own name.

of the Editions of the New Testament," etc. (1878), had adopted a suggestion of Mr Henry Stevens, that " G. H." stood for Guillaume Hytchins, "the assumed name of William Tyndale," thus referring to the translator, and not the publisher of the book. After showing that this explanation is impossible, Bradshaw offers his own suggestion, which is that " G. H." stands for Godfried van der Haghen, an Antwerp publisher of the day. This man, like so many others of his time, was in the habit of putting his name into a classical form, and when so Latinised it appeared as Godfridus Dumæus. Bradshaw not only shows that Godfridus Dumæus and Godfried van der Haghen are one and the same person, but he traces a close business connection between him and Martin de Keyser, the printer of Tindale's second edition, the immediate predecessor of the one in which the mysterious initials appear. It is impossible here to give the steps by which Bradshaw arrived at his conclusion, or the proofs by which he established it. A happy accident—one of those accidents which the skilled eye and the constructive mind can turn into opportunities—gave him the first hint, to be followed up, as he says himself, by "putting the book among its fellows, that is, among the productions of the same and neighbouring presses," and "allowing facts to speak for themselves." The conclusion, when arrived at, was irresistible, and the name of a worthy who took a part, and no unimportant one, in furthering the work of the Reformation, was rescued from oblivion.

This little paper was almost his last publication of the kind. Work in other lines increased upon him, and with the introduction of the new statutes, he was dragged into the vortex of university business, from which he had hitherto kept comparatively free. In April, 1882, he writes to his friend Mr Stephen Lawley, " I was away from Saturday evening till Tuesday at Christmas, and I have not stirred from Cambridge since. Every day and every night has brought its work, and I have been in one constant round, at the library by day and in my rooms by night. . . . My head is crammed full of work of various kinds, and I seem to have no knowledge of everyday outside-world interests."

One of the pieces of University business which occupied most of his attention about this time was the elaboration of the schemes for the Special and Tripos examinations in Mediæval and Modern Languages. He had been made a member of the Board which controls the teaching of those subjects in November, 1881. In February, 1882, the Board issued its first report, recommending the establishment of a special examination (*i.e.* an examination for the ordinary degree) in Mediæval and Modern Languages, and this report, with some alterations, was accepted a year later. Meanwhile they had been engaged in the more difficult task of formulating a scheme for a Tripos examination in the same subjects. Their first proposal was issued in March, 1883, but the plan had to submit to large modifications, and was not finally passed till May, 1884. When it is remembered that Bradshaw had devoted a great part of his life to the study of early English writers, and that his "Memoranda," as first projected, were to contain the results of his work on the mediæval literature of our own and other countries, it is easy to understand with what interest he watched over a scheme which was for the first time to include these subjects in the recognised curriculum of university studies.

I will conclude this chapter with a few extracts from his correspondence during the summer of 1882. Writing to one of his sisters on her birthday (July 30), he says, " I have been reading Mozley's 'Reminiscences of Oriel College and the Oxford Movement,' which is full of Moreton Pinkney. But it is a very uncomfortable book, every story, where possible, being told just wrong." It will be remembered that, having been at one time intimate with Dr Pusey, he was likely to have heard many of the stories correctly told.

On the same day, the first anniversary of the wedding-day of a young friend, he writes, " Bad as I am, I cannot let to-day pass by without writing just to tell you that I have been drinking your healths and wishing you (in silence) many, many happy returns of the day—a day I shall not easily forget. . . . I have just lost a month by a violent attack of cold, which I could not shake off till a few days ago, and the result is that I have a mass of arrears to work off. . . . When I could do nothing else, I have been destroying thousands of letters and papers of the last few years. It brings back so many things. But I could not bring myself yet to destroy the least scrap of Ernest's * or yours. The picture they all bring back is so vivid ; the varying tone of illness or health, of brightness or despondency, in both of you—all this is a thing I cannot throw away. My own hands are pretty full just now. I have the Library Association coming here at the beginning of September, and a great deal of the work falls upon me as president, and I am not much accustomed to this kind of thing. However, I hope it will go off well."

To another friend, who had declined to deprive him of a valuable book which he had offered him, he says, " I agree wholly with what you say of presents. Emerson's idea is good, that nothing but fruit or flowers, or something equally perishable, should be given. . . . Only consider that, as the offer implies no sacrifice whatever, so the refusal involves none of the churlishness which you seem to think it must imply in my mind. I know you a little too well. I am rather *down* at this moment about other things, so you must not misinterpret the dull tone of my letter."

On Sunday, July 23, 1882, Cambridge was saddened by

* N. E. Muggeridge.

the news that one of the most distinguished of her younger scholars, Professor Francis Balfour, had been killed, on July 19, by a fall on the Aiguille Blanche de Peuteret. Bradshaw felt the loss very deeply, both on personal and public grounds. Writing to Mr Seebohm on August 6, he says, " I don't think you had met him, or you would inevitably have felt something of the loss he will be to the whole university, and not only to his own near and personal friends and more immediate fellow-workers. For a man of only thirty, his influence was extraordinary ; but the secret of it lay in an indomitable energy, coupled with that Darwin-like singleness of aim, which never let him spend any of his energy, as so many of us do, in irritation at other people's shortcomings, or in abuse of his neighbours where they happened to differ from him."*

* I may mention here that Bradshaw contributed the sum of £50 to the Balfour Memorial Fund.

CHAPTER IX.

I HAVE thought it best, as in a previous instance, to give in a separate chapter some account of the work which occupied most of Henry Bradshaw's leisure during the last seven or eight years of his life. During this time he was principally engaged on two lines of investigation : first, his bibliographical researches in connection with the Cambridge edition of the Sarum Breviary ; and, secondly, his inquiries into the history of the statutes of Lincoln Cathedral. I will take these in order.

It was in the year 1878 that he began to help Mr Procter and Mr Wordsworth in the preparation of their edition of the Sarum Breviary.* His contributions are for the most part printed in the introduction to the third part, or "fasciculus." Mr Wordsworth had been for some time acquainted with the librarian when he began his work, for the latter had already given him assistance when he was composing his " Scholæ Academicæ," a book on the studies of the university in the eighteenth century. Mr Words-worth invited him one day in 1878 to his house in order to talk over the breviary. "Report," writes Mr Wordsworth, " said that Bradshaw would not accept invitations ; how-ever, he walked out to Castle End, where I was curate, to dine with us, and to give us his ideas about the proposed

* Of this edition (which is based on the Paris folio of 1531, by Chevallon and Regnault), the first part published was fasc. ii., containing the Psalterium and Commune, with Officia Missalia, in 1879 ; fasc. i., containing the Kalen-darium and Temporale, followed in 1882 ; fasc. iii., containing the Sanctorale and Accentuarius, with the bibliographical and other apparatus, in 1886.

book. You can imagine how he sat on the sofa, nursing
Dr Laing's Aberdeen Breviary, and illustrating his recommendations with his usual readiness and practical good
sense." On another occasion, when a senior member of
the university remarked in hall that he had seen Bradshaw that afternoon "discoursing plain truths to a ritualist,"
"he was really," Mr Wordsworth says, "pointing out to me
the superiority of the Prayer-book of 1549 over that of
1662, because of the disadvantage which Cosin (as well as
Laud and Overall) laboured under, with all his desire to
be correct, as compared with Cranmer and his contemporaries, who could not help being familiar with the old
services, which as priests they had been obliged to know
almost by heart." Mr Wordsworth left Cambridge shortly
after this, and henceforth the assistance which Bradshaw
gave him was mostly conveyed in a voluminous correspondence extending over a period of eight years.

In preparing the text of the breviary for publication, the
editors were not often obliged to have recourse to Bradshaw, but the introductions and appendices bear the mark
of his hand on almost every page. The editors gratefully
acknowledge that the most valuable of these supplements to
the text are the chronological lists and descriptions of all
the printed editions of the breviary and other service-books
belonging to the Salisbury use. These lists are almost
entirely Bradshaw's work. To draw them up was one of
the toughest bits of bibliographical research which he ever
undertook. The service-books are arranged under nine
heads—breviaries (of which three classes are distinguished),
special services for certain feast-days, antiphoners or anthem-
books, psalters, hymnals, etc., for a detailed account of
which I must refer my readers to the pages of the Cambridge edition. Some notion of the onerous nature of the
task may be derived from Mr Wordsworth's statement—a
statement borne out by several passages from Bradshaw's

correspondence—that he examined no less than 210 out of
the 277 volumes or fragments of Sarum Breviaries known
to exist, besides 58 volumes of other choir service-books
of the same use. Not content with inspecting one copy
only of any particular edition, he examined, so far as he was
able, every copy which there was the slightest reason to
suppose contained any variation. The copies so examined
are scattered up and down the country, in England, Scotland, and Ireland, in private as well as public libraries.
Some are abroad, in Paris, Antwerp, and elsewhere. The
examination of them entailed much correspondence and
not a few journeys, for he insisted on doing the work himself, and would rely on no second-hand evidence.

The result is to be seen in these lists, lists like those of
his fifteenth-century books, devoid of all ornament and
unnecessary detail, and compressing into the barest possible
statement the outcome of years of toil. They state the
edition, the date, size, printer's name, and place of printing
of every copy known to exist, as well as the name of present owners. It is needless to say that the result, small as
it appears on paper, would have been unattainable had not
Bradshaw been familiar with the services of the mediæval
Church from his youth up. Writing to Mr Maskell in
1882, he says, "I think of all my favourite fields of work
this is my special favourite. . . . I only wish I could have
had you here for a week or a fortnight, to go through the
books one by one. It is impossible to put into the com-
pass of letters the results of twenty years' anatomical study
of these books."

During all the time while the edition was preparing,
Bradshaw was engaged in constant correspondence with the
editors. His letters touch on a multitude of obscure points,
such as the terminology of mediæval service-books, the
origin and connection of different parts of the services, the
order of the various portions of the breviary, liturgical

survivals from remote periods in the history of the Church, and kindred subjects. " I know next to nothing," he writes to Dr Littledale, "about what the young men call liturgiology," but those who have perused these letters will hardly agree with him. The correspondence is naturally, for the most part, too technical to be given here, but I may quote a few passages. The preface spoken of in the following extract from a letter dated February, 1879, is the preface to the first fasciculus, and the list alluded to is the list of breviaries, for which " one day in London and one in Oxford " were eventually not found to suffice.

" I have read your proof [of the preface] over and over again, and have made many alterations. I will send it you as rewritten in some parts by me, that you may use it as you think fit. It will come in a day or two, I hope. Where do you find that odious word *portuary ?* That and *portfory* are words used by modern liturgiologists which I cannot abide, until I find the old people using them. The title-page is frightful, as most titles are.* . . . I am very anxious indeed about the bit at the end. It is a great pity to leave it as it stands without a revision of certain things, which one day in London and one at Oxford would suffice for, both of which I would gladly give, in spite of all library work here, if you would accept of such a contribution. . . . The list ought to begin with my fragments of an edition † of 147—, probably printed at Cologne, at least ten years earlier than your first. Your first ought to be ' formerly University Library, Cambridge,' instead of ' formerly McCarthy.' It was stolen from here, and still bears our library class-mark." ‡

---

* Mr Wordsworth says that the title-page eventually prefixed to the Kalendarium was "sketched by Bradshaw one morning in bed, when he had been up a great part of the night with some manuscripts which I had to carry back to Lincoln."

† These fragments are dated in the published list " 1475 ?"

‡ This is the Venice edition, on vellum, of 1483, the rediscovery of which I have narrated above, p. 101.

"April 5, 1879.—I have done a good deal to most of the books, but I have done more than this in the breviary. I have begun at the end, and am examining everything I can find before going to Oxford. The fearful mess of Marian Breviaries I have wholly and satisfactorily cleared up, except only the two editions of Kyngston and Sutton, which will present no difficulty when I can examine one or two copies which have not been tampered with in modern times." After giving a classification of the Marian Breviaries, the results of which are printed in the appendix to the Cambridge edition, he continues, "I am very anxious to get to the bottom of this. I have mastered the real 1535 edition, which is of some consequence, and every step backward becomes very much easier. I must print somehow what I do now, as it would be so much waste, and it would be much more satisfactory, of course, to get it into a standard book such as yours must be.

"April 8, 1879.—I hope I have said or written nothing which *grates* upon you. As far as I can see, our habits of thought are equally *Anglican* of the last generation, and not at all the *independent* of the present generation. It is a great comfort to find some one of the present generation who retains this tinge. I know no one in Cambridge who does it at all.

"June 26, 1879.—I have told Mr Procter of a *monastic English supplement* to a breviary printed at York about 1513, which I have just turned up. . . . I have written to see if I can get any further information, and meantime I have copied it all out. It is very interesting to me from all sorts of points of view, both what you would call li-tur-gi-o-lo-gi-cal as well as pa-læ-o-ty-po-gra-phi-cal, if these words are long enough."

In August, 1879, he made the visit to Oxford which he promises in one of the previous letters. The special object he had in view was to work out the relations of the Marian

Breviaries, and this he satisfactorily accomplished. On his return to Cambridge he writes (September 6, 1879), " I send you a variety of things. I hope you will not be very much shocked at the amount. After thirteen hours yesterday at it, and twelve the day before, and a good deal of tolerably constant work before that, I am glad to have something to show."

In September, 1879, he paid a visit to Longleat, whence he writes, " I had not been a quarter of an hour in the house yesterday before I ran up to the old library at the top of the house (the room where Bishop Ken spent so much of the latter part of his life), to see again a volume of the Sarum Breviary, which I knew I could put my hand upon in the dark. I knew it was a P. E.,* bearing the imprint of Regnault, 1535 ; but I had written it down in my list a Caly (*i.e.* the pseudo-Regnault). Imagine my delight at finding it a *real* Regnault, quite complete as far as P. E. goes, and just exactly settling my question." A few days later he writes again, " I had a delightful day over at Mells † yesterday, and saw all the Horners and all the breviaries, and a heap of most lovely and interesting things besides."

In October, 1879, he was at Dublin, still engaged principally on breviary work. While there he wrote to Mr Wordsworth, " Here I am, after three days' work, and crammed full of breviary collations. When I wrote to you from London, I hardly knew where the next hour would start me for—whether for Paris, to master the 1483 edition ; to Antwerp, to see for the first time the long-lost Louvain edition of 1499 ; to Edinburgh, to examine for myself the Great Breviary ‡ of 1496, which —— and ——

---

* Pars Estivalis, *i.e.* for the later or summer half of the year. P. H. stands for Pars Hyemalis, the winter part, beginning with Advent.

† A house belonging to Mr J. F. F. Horner, who possesses copies of several of the Marian Breviaries.

‡ A Great Breviary, as distinguished from the Portiforium or Common

combined have made such a hopeless fog about; or, finally, here to master the editions of 1494 and 1516, as well as the Rouen edition of 1556. Three days' steady work—from ten to six—have enabled me to do something towards clearing my way. . . . When I am tired out with such work I take a short interlude of Irish books, which are of all my special hobbies the most special; and, as I am here at head-quarters, it is a perfect holiday for me, as you may well believe."

Not long after this, Mr E. M. Thompson, of the British Museum, knowing the interest which Bradshaw took in Celtic remains and in service-books, presented him with a Christmas dish combining both these dainties. He had lately seen at Salisbury a manuscript * containing a Psalter and Litany, with several entries in a Celtic hand, and he wrote to inform Bradshaw of this treasure. Bradshaw's answer is dated December 31, 1879.

" My dear Thompson,

   " What an angel you are, and how many happy new years do I wish you in return for your most welcome letter just received! The Litany does indeed interest me. . . . Cutberct, of course, is northern English, and Iltutus Welsh; but every other man among them is *pure Breton,* and therefore gold to me, and I must see the book as soon as I can."

Besides this enchanting book, there was in the same library a Sarum Breviary of 1556, which he was anxious to see. With this object he went off to Salisbury one cold, wet January day, returning as far as London the same evening, in order to look at the books with his own eyes, and he afterwards sent a special messenger to Salis-

Breviary, is a large book adapted for use in church. All known editions of it are in folio; the Common Breviaries are in quarto, or a smaller size.

 * No. 180 in the cathedral library.

bury to bring away the Psalter, so that he might examine it at his leisure at Cambridge.

In the course of the next year (1880) he extended his investigations so as to include several classes of service-books beyond those to which he had at first intended to confine himself. In reference to this, he writes to Mr Stephen Lawley, the editor of the York Breviary,* about the same time, " Here is one [letter] which I wrote an hour after you left, but did not send, because later on, before post-time, I had advanced in my ideas to include all the printed service-books, and the matter was so fully in my head that I sat down in my room, and, after thinking in peace for an hour, I put my work down on paper, and it was half-past five in the morning before I knew where I was. Fortunately for me, it is not often nowadays that I give way to such impulses, or my life would not be good for much."

A short visit which he made to Paris in January, 1881, had for its principal object an examination of the unique Sarum Breviary of 1483 preserved in the National Library. He speaks afterwards in the warmest terms of the kindness which was shown him on this occasion by M. Leopold Delisle, the librarian. For some years after this his time was so much occupied with other things, particularly with his work on the statutes of Lincoln Cathedral, and his edition of the university and college statutes, that he was able to make but slow progress with the breviary. He continued, however, to work at the subject at intervals, and the editors, it must be allowed, showed considerable patience in waiting for his results. The pressure of public and private engagements, which increased very largely during the last five or six years of his life, was beginning to tell upon his strength, and he felt that he had undertaken too

---

* The York Breviary was edited by Mr Lawley (from the 8vo edition of 1493) for the Surtees Society, in 1880–83.

much. At one time he was on the point of putting aside
all the work that he had done, and allowing the breviary
to appear without his additions. That his task was weighing heavily upon him is clear from the following letter,
addressed to Mr Clay, of the University Press, in September, 1884 :—

"MY DEAR CLAY,

"I have put everything aside this Long Vacation to get my list ready for the appendix to the preface
to the breviary ; but I do not hesitate to say that the
labour all along (and skilled labour too) has been far
greater than any editing of the text of the breviary could
possibly be, apart from journeys to Paris, Edinburgh,
Dublin, and a score of places in England. I will do my
very best to see what this week will enable me to do,
which I can print with as little discredit as possible. . . . It
is work I find extremely difficult to do for another, when
every day I feel the curse of keeping others waiting.

"Yours very truly,
"HENRY BRADSHAW."

Mr Clay offered him the services of an amanuensis,
to which he replied, "Thanks for the offer of an amanuensis, but I fear that would be of little use at present.
I never know how to deal with such a person, and it
generally ends in my wasting both his time and mine."

He was fortunately dissuaded from putting aside his
work, and he continued his researches whenever he could
find time. Writing to Lord Beauchamp in 1884, to ask
him for the loan of some of his breviaries, he says—

"DEAR LORD BEAUCHAMP,

". . . The University Press edition of the book
(by Procter and Christopher Wordsworth) is now waiting for

my account of the printed editions, and this I have worked
out almost entirely to my satisfaction.   I am most anxious,
for the sake of future investigators, to sèe all the copies
I can see, and so to settle clearly what each copy contains."

After asking for the loan of Lord Beauchamp's copies,
he concludes—

"I know you will forgive me for asking such a favour,
whether you see your way to granting it or not. As I
cannot get away from home at this time, and I really do
want the books, I feel sure you will do what you can.
I can never forget that it was by you that I was first in-
doctrinated with these studies long ago.

"Yours very sincerely,

"HENRY BRADSHAW." .

A few days later, after receiving the books, he writes
to Lord Beauchamp again, "Your letter and the books
which followed it are both delightful. . . . I have not half
expressed my thanks for your kindness.   You naturally
forget these things, but there is no doubt you were the
very first, as a boy at school, to give my mind a turn
towards *Church* ideas and Church things.   It was an
epoch with *me*, and one does not forget these things easily."

Throughout the next year (1885) he continued to ex-
amine the books necessary for the completion of his list.
In January, 1886, he had very nearly completed his task.
His last letter to Mr Wordsworth, is as follows :—

"King's College, January 18, 1886.

"MY DEAR WORDSWORTH,

"I trust your extreme gentleness and forbearance will shame me into doing what much louder expostulation would fail in doing. I dread making promises,
or talking of the future, when I have failed so egregi-
ously before in keeping to my word. But I have to-day

T

written to Lord Spencer and to Mr Ellis to ask them
to let me see their two books; and when I have seen
them I see no possible excuse which I shall be able to
allege for not finishing my work. I have been better all
to-day, in consequence of your letter, than I have been
for two months, and I seem to have gained heart to take
the necessary steps. But I dare not say more. Be urgent
and do not listen to any excuses on my part. I have
cleared my rooms of service-books, and have given every
scrap to the library, this Christmas. I hope they will not in-
fect all who use them hereafter with my own dilatory spirit.

"Ever yours affectionately,

"HENRY BRADSHAW."

His requests to Lord Spencer and Mr J. H. Ellis were
naturally granted. In writing to thank the latter, he says
(January 22), "Your precious little book has come safely.
I am delighted to see your careful way of packing it. It
more than answers my expectations, as it at once explains
my troubles about Regnault's books. . . . Your book has
been very slightly cut by the binder, nothing really to
hurt; but I regret to find that he has misplaced the first
sheet of the *Proprium Sanctorum* . . . From the very
minute worm-holes which exist in some parts, it is perfectly
clear that the sheets were correctly placed before it came
into the recent binder's hands. If they possibly can ruin
a book, they will do so, and I know no binder free from
such habits—certainly none of the great London binders."
The books from Lord Spencer's collection were deposited
in the British Museum for Mr Bradshaw's use, but he did
not live to use them. They were the only Sarum Breviaries
in England which remained for him to examine. At his
death he left the lists of breviaries and other service-books
so nearly complete, that his friends were able to fill up
the few gaps and to print the lists almost as they stood.

I now pass to Bradshaw's work on the Lincoln statutes.

In September, 1880, he paid a visit to Lincoln, in order to examine the documents in the chapter muniment-room, as well as some books in the cathedral library. This visit was the beginning of his investigations respecting the statutes of Lincoln Cathedral, the results of which he, unfortunately, did not live to publish. It is to be hoped that they will shortly, however, see the light under the editorship of his friend, the Rev. Christopher Wordsworth. Without anticipating his fuller statement, I must give some account of them here.*

The circumstances which gave rise to these investigations were as follows. When Dr Wordsworth, having been enthroned as Bishop of Lincoln, in 1869, was inducted, as the custom is in that cathedral, into a prebendal stall, in order to gain a voice in the chapter, he promised to observe, among other things, all the statutes, customs, and ordinances contained in the "New Registry," and in the "Laudum," or award, of Bishop Alnwick. Up to this time these documents existed only in manuscript. Bishop Wordsworth, thinking it well that they should be more accessible to the persons interested in them than they could be while in this condition, printed a copy of each document in a volume which appeared in 1873.†

A few words are necessary here, in order to explain to the reader the relations of these and other documents which formed the subject of Bradshaw's investigations. The older customs and ordinances of Lincoln are contained in a book known as the "Liber Niger," a document compiled in the early part of the thirteenth century, but based

---

* I ought to say that I am specially indebted in what follows to Mr Wordsworth, who was kind enough to read over and correct this chapter, and to entrust me with the papers (or copies of them) by Bradshaw which he intends to publish, as well as with notes of his own.

† In printing this volume, Bishop Wordsworth had the assistance of Canon Venables and of Dr. Benson, then Chancellor of Lincoln Cathedral.

upon still older documents which have long since disappeared. That these customs were not clearly laid down or that all cases which might occur were not provided for, is evident from the fact that there arose in the first half of the fifteenth century a great dispute between Dean Mackworth and his chapter. This dispute, which lasted many years, was settled by Bishop Alnwick in 1439, after a unanimous appeal from all parties concerned. The episcopal award is contained in the "Laudum" mentioned above, and is undoubtedly of statutable authority. Not so the "Novum Registrum." Bishop Alnwick, anxious to provide against such disputes in future, proposed that the existing laws and customs of the cathedral should be brought together and clearly stated in a new book, and that this collection should supersede all earlier documents. The dean and chapter consented, and a "registrum" or collection was drawn up. This "registrum" was discussed at a length which even a parliament of the present day might almost envy, and with a result which not unfrequently closes the lengthiest parliamentary debates. After no less than thirty-six "convocations," the matter was brought to a close by a solemn protest * from Dean Mackworth against the acceptance of the bishop's proposal. It therefore fell through, and the "Novum Registrum," not being accepted, remained of no effect.

But the efforts of Bishop Alnwick, though frustrated at the time, eventually bore fruit. Towards the close of the seventeenth century, two hundred and fifty years after its first appearance, the "New Registry" was revived. By a process, the history of which was not preserved, it became customary at that time, and has been customary ever since, to exact from every member of the chapter on taking possession of his dignity a promise of obedience to

---

* It appears to have been Dean Blakesley who unearthed this protest, and thus threw the first doubts on the validity of the "New Registry."

the rules therein contained. For nearly two centuries after this, it appears that no one doubted the authority of the "Novum Registrum." In recent times, however, doubts began to arise, and Dean Blakesley, in his answer to the questions addressed to the dean and chapter, in 1879, by the Cathedral Commissioners, plainly expressed his belief that it was invalid. What Bradshaw did was to trace out the history and connection of the documents mentioned above, and of others still older, and to establish beyond a doubt what was already matter of suspicion—that the "Novum Registrum" is a document of no authority beyond what the custom of the last two centuries may have given it.

A contemporary copy* of the "Novum Registrum" was carried off, a century after Alnwick's time, by Matthew Parker (afterwards archbishop), when ejected from the deanery in 1553, and deposited at his death, with the rest of his books, in the library of Corpus Christi College, Cambridge. Bishop Wordsworth, being anxious that the inquiry which he had set on foot should be prosecuted further, requested Mr Lewis, librarian of Corpus Christi College, to give him some information respecting the copy of the "Novum Registrum" preserved in the library of that college. Mr Lewis brought the letter to Bradshaw, who examined the book. "I was not long," he writes in the introduction to his unpublished memorandum on the subject, "in making the unexpected discovery that it was no mere transcript of Bishop Alnwick's book, but an original copy of the most precious description, and full of a living human interest possessed by very few books of the kind. What with the amendments of the hot-tempered

---

* Mr Bradshaw, judging from internal evidence, considered that the Corpus copy was not the absolute original draft, but a contemporary transcript, a sort of fair copy, made immediately from the original used in the discussions, and therefore of all but equal value with the absolute original, which has disappeared.

precentor and others, and the running comments of the
bishop, accepting or rejecting them, the whole scene in the
chapter-house at Lincoln was brought up so vividly before
one, that the very life of the people of the time seemed
to be in the book :

> "'A book in shape, but, really, pure crude fact
> Secreted from man's life when hearts beat hard,
> And brains, high-blooded, ticked *four* centuries since.' *

The temptation to pursue the subject was irresistible."

In order to pursue it, he made the visit to Lincoln to
which I have already alluded.   On his return to Cambridge,
he wrote to Mr Wordsworth, "My brain was seething with
the results of my six hours' work in the muniment-room all
the time of my journey back, and a good while after I
got to bed.   I have come to a few very satisfactory results
in my own mind."   This first visit enabled him to take
a general view of the subject, and to draw up a rough list
of the documents with which he was concerned.   A couple
of months later he visited Lincoln again, and made a more
searching examination, the results of which he wrote out
soon after and put into type (November, 1880).   The
printed matter occupied nearly fifty pages, but he afterwards became dissatisfied with it, and cancelled the whole.

The work which Bradshaw had already done on these
and other cathedral statutes enabled him, in the spring of
1881, to draw up a letter on the cathedral system addressed
to Archdeacon Norris, which I have printed in the appendix.
Dr Benson, now Primate, then Bishop of Truro, in writing
to thank Bradshaw for allowing him to see this letter, says,
"It is simply the most important paper on chapters and
their modernisation which I have ever read ; " and he goes
on to remark that he had found the statements and suggestions of the letter most useful in elaborating the ecclesi-

* "The Ring and the Book," i. 86–88.   "Four" in the last line is sub-
stituted for "two."

astical machinery which he desired to establish in his new diocese.

Bradshaw paid two more visits to Lincoln in 1881, and the second time carried off with him the famous "Liber Niger." He copied out the whole of this book, which in many places is very difficult to decipher, and put it into complete order. Finally, he had it rebound under his own direction, a process of which it stood much in need. The chapter passed a vote of thanks, when they received the book back in 1883, "for the pains and skill bestowed by him on one of the most valuable of their muniments, which they could not have found in any other quarter, and which have made the document in question readily available for consultation."

Early in 1882 he sent to Bishop Wordsworth an elaborate analysis of a volume called, "The Bishop's Statute-Book," as being always in the possession of the bishop for the time being.* In the letter enclosing this analysis (which Mr Wordsworth intends to publish), Bradshaw says, "My only wish has been to collect facts, in order that others may form a judgment upon them. As a Fellow of King's College, I cannot feel that there is anything incongruous in my contributing my share towards the elucidating the history of the Church of Lincoln.† Only a few months ago Canon Robertson brought me an undoubted autograph signature of Remigius, the founder of the see of Lincoln, to examine; and I confess that to one like myself, whose life is spent in the care of books, the very sight of such a document is enough to stir me to do my best to clear the ground for those who want a knowledge of the historical facts, in order to form a just judgment on

---

* This volume, says Bradshaw, was compiled about 1540, and contains transcripts of the "Black Book," the "Laudum" of 1439, the "Novum Registrum" of 1440, and the "Statuta Vicariorum."

† The Bishop of Lincoln is Visitor of King's College.

what is put before them." And a few days later, " How far the continuous acceptance of a body of statutes (which were first acted upon two hundred and fifty years after date, under an erroneous conviction that they had been ratified at the time of their composition) is a tenable form of acceptance, is a *legal* difficulty upon which, of course, it does not concern me even to offer a suggestion. But having a very great love for anatomising books, and for working out what I may call the *bibliographical* elements of a problem of this kind, so as to ensure to those who wish to form an opinion a sound basis on which to form it, I have been unable to resist the temptation to work out the results of my various searches. This, I hope, now very soon to have finished. I wish much that I could write briefly ; but when my heart is full, I cannot help myself."

To Dr Benson he writes a little later (March, 1882) :—

" I am beginning to see daylight about my own little book. I am making it simply a *guide* to such things as are to be found in the Lincoln muniment-room and else-where, illustrating or containing statutes and ordinances affecting the chapter. . . . It will be very imperfect at best, but I think the lines will be drawn which others can fill in. . . . I have made a thorough chronological tran-script of every atom of writing that is to be found in the Black Book, copying everything in the order in which it was written into, or came to form part of, the book. This I should like to print directly I can get the other out of my hands. I hate shovelling in a mass of old documents, with no clue to what they mean, what they consist of, or how they came there. But, intelligently printed, I feel sure it would be found of some use. Having done this, which would please the Bishop of Lincoln, and enable the people there who differ to see and understand what they are differing about, I should like to print a little volume

containing as good a text as can be got, of the five or six
sets of *consuetudines* (you will be surprised at the number)
with which Lincoln was provided in the thirteenth century,
or a hundred years before the Mackworth-Alnwick period.
These I have got into shape, and I am working hard to
understand their history and their connections with the
consuetudines of other churches. I can truly say that
I have never been engaged in such an intensely interesting
piece of anatomical work.

"Salisbury and Lincoln are two sister churches, children of Rouen. . . . Just before Salisbury came to the
front under Richard Poore,* who built the cathedral and
drew up (to all appearance) the Consuetudinarium which
all the world quotes, Lincoln was the most prominent
church in England, and sent its customs to Scotland,
where Moray, Aberdeen, and Caithness all bear marks of
its influence. Then the new Salisbury book goes to
Lincoln, to Lichfield, to Wells, to Exeter, to Dublin, to
Glasgow, to York, and Hereford, and leaves its mark.
Lincoln uses it and modifies it, and hands it on to
St Paul's. I now find, to my surprise, that whereas
Alnwick's book is based on St Paul's, so St Paul's is
based again on Lincoln, having got nothing (apparently)
direct from Salisbury. But I need not go on with this.
I will only say that the erasures in the dean's oath in the
Black Book of Lincoln I was able to read only by going
to the Dublin and Lichfield books. . . . Your letters
always stir me up, and give me renewed life and heart
for work ; and if I can only keep from side work, I hope
to be able to do something to help you to clear the ground
to build upon. It requires endless patience, but it is its
own reward.

"Ever yours most affectionately,

"HENRY BRADSHAW."

* Bishop of Salisbury from 1217 to 1228.

That these historical researches were, in Bradshaw's mind, connected with the problems of modern ecclesiastical organization is clear from a letter to Dr Benson, written shortly after the above, with respect to his work in the new diocese of Truro. " I wish it were not too late—as you are reviving old ideas, and are presenting to men's eyes and minds a thing which is very different from the vague ideal they had formed of a cathedral chapter and its constitu-tion—to restore the real body." He goes on to speak of the large body of canons which formerly existed at Lin-coln, the bishop himself being one, together with other officers, dean, chancellor, archdeacons, etc. The canonry, or position of a *canonicus*, is the bond which binds all together in one brotherhood. " The fact of having one common symbol of membership, the canonry, seems to give a notion of corporate unity—the one body, and many members—which I should dearly like to see brought to light again."

To Mr Lawley he writes in April, 1882, " I am at pre-sent in a great state of delight at having finally knocked the Sarum Consuetudinary on the head. I have been very sick, for some years, of hearing it called St Osmund's work, and I felt sure it was really the work of Richard Poore. And now at last I have got the actual constitution of Osmund * himself, dated 1091, and it is altogether the most interesting document I know, or have ever heard of, for my purpose. It seems the three great churches where this four-square arrangement of chapter—

Treasurer.		Chancellor.
Chanter.		Dean.

was established, were your own beloved York, Lincoln, and Salisbury. All the others gradually adopted it, except London ; but these are the three primitive establishments,

* St Osmund was Bishop of Salisbury from c. 1078 to 1099.

and they are almost coincident. York is *said* to be 1090. I wish I could find any document anywhere, or anything which would give me certain information. Lincoln was September 1–8, 1090, Thomas of York and Osmund of Salisbury both being witnesses. Salisbury was early in 1091, Thomas of York and Remigius of Lincoln both being witnesses. You read a great deal nowadays of this constitution being of the usual Norman model (a vague phrase), so I was at the pains to take all the churches (forty-four of them) within a considerable range of Normandy, and see what their constitution was, in the 'Gallia Christiana,' as a rough indication. The only one which is precisely Osmund's *institutio* at Salisbury is Bayeux. . . . Now, Thomas of York was himself *Treasurer of Bayeux*, and Bayeux was a church with greater prestige in some respects than even Rouen. Is it not pretty? I should like you to see my schedule of the different constitutions, showing how they tell their own story."

In the year 1882–3 Bradshaw was much occupied with his work on another body of statutes, namely, those of the University and the colleges of Cambridge. He managed, however, at intervals to carry on his Lincoln work. In the summer of 1883 Mr H. E. Reynolds advertised an edition of the Lincoln "Consuetudinarium," which was to contain some work of Mr Wordsworth's. "I sent him [Bradshaw] the proofs," says the latter; "I received them carefully annotated, but with a candid admonition as to the crudeness of the production." "I am," writes Bradshaw, "in a state of very half or quarter knowledge on the subject myself, and I naturally look eagerly everywhere to see fresh light. . . . I cannot put down on paper for you my views, merely because they are thoroughly provisional. Ever since I began to print in 1880, I have felt bound (not only to you and to Wickenden,* and to your

* The late Rev. J. F. Wickenden, Prebendary of Lincoln, had for several

father,* but especially to the dean [Blakesley] for all his kindness and hospitality to me while at work, and to the chapter for lending me books) to do my best to work out the subject, bringing to bear the familiarity with anatomising manuscripts which my work here has forced upon me. It is a very serious work, and my leisure is small, but the work progresses, and if I live I hope it will not be long before I have something to show, both for my own labour and for other people's exceeding kindness." He did not live to accomplish this task, though he made large preparations for it. In 1884 he made with his own hand an inventory † of a great portion of the contents of the muniment-room at Lincoln, " as a first attempt to take stock (so he modestly described it) of the patient and loving work bestowed upon these treasures " by Mr Wickenden.

The work which he left on the subject of the statutes can only be regarded as containing his provisional, not his final, judgment. Nevertheless it is not probable that any but a few details will need alteration. He seems to have been dissatisfied more with the form than the substance of what he had put into print. As his work, so far as it was put on record, will be published by Mr Wordsworth, I need only give a brief summary of it here.

The object of the paper which Bradshaw intended in 1882 to publish was, as he states himself, " to clear the ground for an investigation into the growth and subsequent history of those documents which either possess, or have been supposed to possess, more or less claim to be considered authoritative statutes of the Cathedral Church of Lincoln." He goes on to point out that, " strange as it may appear, there is not yet the slightest evidence to be found that the chapter has ever been provided with a body of

summers been engaged in arranging the contents of the muniment-room at Lincoln. He died in 1883.

* Christopher Wordsworth, D.D., Bishop of Lincoln 1869–85.

† This inventory has since been completed by Mr C. Wordsworth.

statutes under seal," and that there is "grave doubt, at the present moment, as to what are strictly to be considered statutes of the church, and what are not." For the purpose in view, he divides the history of the Church of Lincoln into two periods : from its foundation soon after the Norman conquest to the early part of the fourteenth century ; * and from that date to the present time. He intended to take the latter period first, and to trace the history of the " Novum Registrum " from its promulgation in 1440, through the stages by which it gradually crept into recognition and acceptance, to its publication as an authoritative document by Bishop Wordsworth.

Secondly, he contemplated printing the contents of the " Liber Niger," the book of statutes which the " New Registry" was intended to supersede ; and, in the third place, he hoped "to print as accurate a text as can be found of the several collections of statutes, or *Registra consuetudinum*, of the Church of Lincoln, which were in existence before the compilation of the Black Book, adding such illustrative documents as may serve to show the position of the Lincoln statutes by the side of those of other cathedral bodies." He intended, moreover, not only to print but to describe and analyse, and, where possible, to date, these documents. Such a scheme, if only it could have been executed, was calculated to throw a flood of light on the mediæval history of the English Church. Unfortunately, only the first, and perhaps the least interesting part, of the programme was—even provisionally—carried out, though extensive preparations, including a transcript of the Black Book, were made for the rest.

The question to be answered in the first part of this plan was, How did the " Novum Registrum," in reality

---

* In the (manuscript) introduction to his memorandum, dated 1882, he adopts another division, breaking the history at the early part of the fifteenth century, the date when Mackworth became dean.

nothing more than an abortive proposal, come to be recognised as possessing statutable authority? Bradshaw solved this problem by examining in order, first, the oaths taken by members of the chapter on admission to their dignities; and, secondly, the copies of statutes or collections of customs made from time to time since the middle of the fifteenth century. The evidence derived from these two lines of investigation combined to show that there had gradually arisen in the minds of the chapter a misconception as to the nature of the "Novum Registrum," which ended in its adoption as a body of statutes after 1695. Down to that date, the oaths made no allusion to that document, but for two centuries previously, owing to the fact that it was frequently copied out along with the statutes contained in the Black Book and other ordinances of undoubted authority, it had been gradually creeping into an authoritative position. In 1523 "a regular Lincoln statute-book" was compiled, containing the "Novum Registrum." The increasing sense of its importance is shown by the fact that in the transcript of 1540 a joint index for it and the Black Book is provided. A few years later Parker carried off the original, and thus made it still more difficult to keep the true nature of the "New Registry" in mind. At length, after the confusion of the civil wars, the tradition of its origin had completely disappeared. The chapter suddenly awoke to the inconsistency, as they thought it, between their oaths and the laws under which they lived. "After a short period of fluctuation, the oaths of the Black Book were quietly superseded in favour of those prescribed in the newly discovered treasure, and all mention of the Black Book disappears from the official records of the chapter."

Having thus answered the question with which he set out, and explained the acceptance of an unratified body of statutes, Bradshaw proceeded to another part of his inquiry— the origin and growth of that body of customs and ordinances which Bishop Alnwick's "Novum Registrum" set aside. The Black Book itself he ascribes to the fourteenth century. Its contents, or some of them, go back a good deal further. Bradshaw proves the existence of two earlier consuetudinaries or collections of customs, known at the opening of the fourteenth century as the "Registrum Vetus" and the "Novum Registrum" respectively. The former of these he traces back to 1214 or thereabouts ; the latter to 1267.* By a delicate process of analysis and comparison, the details of which are too minute to be given here, he shows what the earlier of these two consuetudinaries contained. The fragment of his work unfortunately breaks off just as he was about to enter on a similar examination of the fuller Consuetudinary of 1267.

---

* With respect to the contents of the Black Book itself, Bradshaw (about 1884) distinguished three principal portions, viz. (1) transcribed soon after 1300 from the "consuetudines" drawn up about 1236–7 ; (2) a collection of privileges, etc., entered in the book about 1325, with the oaths and other entries inserted about 1421 ; (3) the Consuetudinary drawn up about 1260–70, and entered in the book about 1400.

CHAPTER X

EARLY in September, 1882, the fifth annual meeting of the Library Association was held at Cambridge, under the presidency of Henry Bradshaw. It was an event of great importance in his quiet life, and one which, in several ways, had a lasting effect upon him. He took' much trouble in thinking out all the details beforehand, and in the preparation of his address; he fulfilled the duties of chairman with conciliatory tact and firmness, and his attention and geniality as a host won all hearts. The consequence was that the meeting, to which he had looked forward with considerable trepidation, was a complete success. It had been proposed to hold the meeting of 1881 at Cambridge, but it was held in London instead, in order that Bradshaw, who had not attended the previous meetings, might have an opportunity of becoming acquainted with the nature of the proceedings before undertaking the duties of president. He accordingly attended the London meeting as an ordinary member, but he refused to take a place on the platform, and at first took no part in the discussions. Presently he suggested to Mr R. Bowker, who happened to be sitting next him, that they should move up towards the front, in order to hear better. He would not go alone, but was willing if Mr Bowker would support him. It was, as the latter remarks, a characteristic bit of shyness. After this he became keenly interested in the proceedings, spoke several times, and before the conference was over had made acquaintance with most of those present.

The local arrangements for the Cambridge meeting and for the reception of the visitors gave him naturally a good deal of trouble, and that, too, of a novel kind. Shortly before the conference he wrote to Mr Lawley, "The Association people come to-morrow fortnight. Most university people snub the whole thing and go away, so I have double work in the way of thought, letter-writing, and responsibility. I have asked some five and thirty people to come and stay with me in college for the week, and twenty have had great pleasure in saying yes. So you can, perhaps, believe that I have enough on my hands —what with preparing my opening address and general material for work and discussion. Besides which, I have four people all on me, clamouring for me to read their proofs and give them criticisms, every word of which they resent as soon as given. I was not made for this kind of work."

When the guests, a hundred or more in number, met in Cambridge, they found everything prepared for them, and not a hitch occurred. The meetings were held in the hall of King's College, and other public rooms in the college were also put at the disposal of the visitors. Bradshaw's opening address * dwelt chiefly on the duties of a librarian ; on the development of the library in general, from the purely utilitarian library of early times to the mixed antiquarian and practical library of our own days ; and on the history and principal features of Cambridge libraries in particular. He entertained the members of the Association at a social gathering in his own college the first evening of the conference, and two days after- wards was entertained by them in return at a dinner at the Lion. He presided at all the meetings, which no

* Subsequently printed as No. 7 of the " Memoranda."

president had done before, and more than once restored a friendly tone to discussions which threatened to become acrimonious, or by some happy suggestion reconciled discordant views. He warmly supported a proposal to institute some sort of examination or a certificate of competency for library assistants, to be granted by the Association, which would assist the provincial libraries in obtaining an efficient staff. He conducted the visitors over the University Library, and arranged for the inspection of other important libraries and objects of interest in Cambridge. Besides his address, he contributed an " Account of the organisation of the University Library ; " a " Note on local libraries considered as museums of local authorship, and printing," a subject in which he always took a keen interest ; and a " Note on size-notation as distinguished from form-notation," * at the end of which he remarks, in defence for introducing what might to some appear superfluous, that " he had not found, in the last twenty years, five Englishmen, either librarians or booksellers, who knew how to distinguish a folio from a quarto, or an octavo from a 12mo or 16mo." He had also intended to read a paper on English bindings, and to have arranged an exhibition of specimens, but want of leisure prevented him from carrying out either project.

The week during which the members of the Association were at Cambridge was for Henry Bradshaw one of unmixed satisfaction, the satisfaction which arises from the discovery and exercise of powers of which the possessor was previously unconscious, and the conviction that he was winning the gratitude and respect of all his guests. It was generally acknowledged that it had been the most successful meeting yet held, and when the mover and seconder of the vote of thanks attributed this success to

---

* These are printed in the appendix to the Report of the proceedings at the conference.

the energy and forethought of their president, and to the
tact and judgment which he had displayed as chairman,
they were giving utterance to a universal sentiment.   "His
conduct in the chair," writes Mr Nicholson, "was a model
of dignity, pleasantness, and impartiality."   Several leading
members of the conference have told me since that they
were astonished by the practical ability displayed by one
hitherto almost entirely unused to the conduct of public
business ; but no one was more surprised than Bradshaw
himself.   The success of the meeting, and the recognition
which awarded his efforts, acted upon him like an ex-
hilarating stimulant.   He said no more than he felt when,
in answer to the vote of thanks, he remarked that, in spite
of the work which the meeting had entailed, "it had been
the most perfect holiday to him which he had ever enjoyed
in his life."

Writing to a friend shortly after the meeting was over,
he says, " I only wish you could have seen us at our work.
I had five and twenty guests of my own in college, and I
had council-meetings and committee-meetings in abundance, besides taking the chair at all the general meetings.
But instead of knocking me up, as most people thought it
would do, it has had the effect of a complete holiday, and
I feel really better than I have for years past.   Every
single thing went well, and the tragedies which were expected to come off and mar the pleasure of the meeting,
every one melted away and ended in stronger feelings of
union and friendship than could have been believed.   Com-
mittees which were composed of irreconcileables (to each
other), so that no report seemed possible, ended in satisfactory reports in which people were unanimously agreed,
by people being brought to understand each other, instead
of being allowed to succeed in *getting round* each other.   I
never experienced such pleasure as I did in the sense of
power in controlling those opposing forces, especially at

the general meetings, and in doing so by uniformly taking every one at his best, and ignoring anything he might say which tended towards the irreconcileable. There had been a great deal of ill feeling for a year or two past, and by a simple determination that it should be worked out of the system (as the doctors say), it *went*, to the infinite satisfaction of all. It has made me extremely happy." He had already taken the part of peacemaker, and with effect, though in an unofficial position, at the meeting of 1881.

To one of his guests, who had thanked him for his hospitality, he writes, "My one object was to make people feel at home and at their ease ; to leave them in great measure to themselves, but yet to provide them with an opportunity of making one or two acquaintances which they would be very glad of the chance of making." And again, "Outsiders have so often in the last week remarked to me how especially humanising a librarian's work seemed to be, the people were all so genuine and friendly." To another he writes, "Work seems to increase upon me daily, but my librarians' meeting did me an enormous amount of good. It was like a three or four weeks' holiday in the Alps—the entire change, and the absence of a jar, not a shadow of a thing going wrong. I had not the face to run away after the meeting, I felt so completely set up by it ; so I remained here, and did a quantity of necessary work."

His correspondence for some time after this shows the stimulating effect which the conference had upon him, though it can hardly have been in reality the holiday which it seemed. The following is from a letter written in October, 1882, to an intimate friend, who had some notion of taking work at Cambridge.

"If you were drawn strongly towards some particular calling, I should, of course, never dream of allowing myself

to try and move you from your purpose, however much I
might regret your loss to us here. But it is evident that
your schoolmastering project is not a thing of this kind. . . .
No doubt there is too much of picking holes at King's,
and misunderstanding of good intentions ; but this is the
case more or less at most places, and nothing but a higher
tone of real work will remedy this. It is here that Frank
Balfour's death * is such a terrible loss. He was one of
those people who go on and on, working, and full of work
and vigour, and never wasting a particle of energy on
decrying his neighbours, and ready to enjoy himself in
congenial company to the very fullest. It is these Darwin-
like men that we want here, the men who go at truth
because they can't help it, and never find pleasure in weakly
picking holes in their neighbour's work. There are several
here as it is, and the more we have the more we shall
get on.

"I cannot for a moment allow your plea of want of a
real sphere of work here. So far from your absence from
Cambridge being a loss, it is a double gain both to yourself and us. Save me from a Cambridge man who has
never known any atmosphere but Cambridge. It is this
very freedom of the early years of a college fellowship
which is such a blessing. A man gets time and leisure
to find favourite pursuits, which he can carry on when he
comes and takes up his quarters here. The only thing is,
you must write—you must produce. It is that cynical
fastidiousness which destroys so many of our good men.
Don't tell me that a man of your calibre of mind could
possibly be forced to sit without employment in Cambridge. The sensitiveness which says, ' I cannot bring
myself to fight against the dead weight of philistinism, or
whatever it may be called, and sooner than it should crush
me, I will go elsewhere,' is a thing to be fought against

* In July, 1882. See above, p. 263.

in one's self, quite as much as the other thing in one's neighbour. Further than this, if you feel that you are working honestly, and are worth your salt, you cannot fail to find friends whom you never dreamt of. The very essence of university life is that friends must go, but this only means that friends must come ; and those who go are not by any means lost, while one's own sympathies are widened by the very variousness of men's character.

"All that you say at the end of your letter is a mistake. A man can be none the worse for having two very different favourite pursuits or lines of work. . . . I am not going to believe that you could not make yourself really useful in both your subjects. The soundest way of learning is teaching, provided only you enjoy the work, and that I know you would do. . . . My heart is so full that I cannot help writing all this. I must give my testimony, as the Quakers say. Who can say what a very few men, banded together unselfishly to go straight ahead in a good cause, will accomplish, or rather, what they will not accomplish ? Only bear with me for my pertinacity. My library meeting has given me a new sense of life, and stirred me up in many ways."

To the same friend he wrote in another letter, " The serious task which I have set myself is to draw people to see that the leading feature of the new day, which is beginning now with our new constitution, is that, idle fellowships being abolished, the only real meaning of this is that in the future the fellowship dividend is to be looked upon as a part endowment of the work done here, and that *all* recognised work done here is work which qualifies for a fellowship. It will be a hard task, and will require more tact than I have, but with patience and help it ought to come. When this becomes recognised, all will go right. A man holds his fellowship free as air for six years, without being compelled to make up his mind to his vocation

in life. But if, before that time is over, he comes here
and *takes work* here, his fellowship lasts at least as long
as his work lasts. Cambridge is becoming every year
more and more such a hive of workers, that I do long to
see King's possessed of some good share of these workers
in different fields. Only none of these changes for good
will ever come of themselves, or without strong individual
effort on the part of each one of us—that is certain."

The New Statutes to which this letter alludes came
into operation during the Long Vacation of 1882. Bradshaw was elected a member of the newly created council of
his college, in the affairs of which he had been unable,
since he had been Librarian, to take much active part.
A more important event was his election to the General
Board of Studies, a body which controls the various special
boards, and exercises a general supervision over the educational machinery of the university. These appointments
indicated the respect which was felt for him in his college
and in the university, but they added heavily to the weight
of his business engagements. For the present, however,
the encouragement which they gave only stimulated him
to fresh exertions.

In 1882 he undertook to edit for the University Press a
volume containing the statutes of the university and the
colleges, as sanctioned by the commissioners in the previous summer. It was a very laborious work, for he was
too scrupulous to allow any one else to look over the proofs,
and spent much time, which he could ill spare, in the
effort to obtain absolute and literal accuracy. Beyond
this result, his zeal for which was characteristic enough,
the work offered no scope for the display of his peculiar
powers, and one can hardly help regretting that he ever
undertook it. He regretted it himself when it was too late.
Writing to Mr Clay in February, 1883, he says, " I am
ready to go on steadily, but for goodness' sake don't let

your people send me the council office copy rolled up tight
and wet with paste, for the boy to jam into a small hole in
my door." Two months later he writes, " Every day
shows me more clearly that I ought never to have allowed
myself to undertake any such work, and if you can make
any other arrangements I shall be very grateful." He
went on with the book, however, and finished it in the
autumn of 1883. For all the labour expended on it, which
was considerable, he declined to accept more than a merely
nominal *honorarium*. The Syndicate offered him a certain
number of copies. He accepted two for his own use, but
the rest he refused, with the remark, " I should prefer to be
allowed to buy all such copies of the book as I want to
give away to my friends. It would be a satisfaction to me
to feel that the book had some sale, even though a portion
of the money came out of my own pocket."

At Easter, 1883, he took a fortnight's holiday in the
south-west of France. He visited Bordeaux and Bayonne,
and finally took up his quarters at Pau. He was evidently out of health. He notes in his diary that he slept
badly, and one night he " woke in pain, which nothing but
quiet made right." The weather, too, was often bad, and
rain deprived him of much of the enjoyment he expected.
Even when away he could not rid himself completely of
work. Writing to Mr Arthur Coleridge on March 23
(Good Friday), he says—

" MY DEAR ARTHUR,

       " These great Church days always have the effect
of bringing you to my mind, and I have treated you so
very badly for many months past, that I must sit down
and talk to you, if only for a few minutes, before going
out for a walk. We are away for an exact fortnight, . . .
and I, not having had a clear week's holiday for three
years, am quite content with a fortnight as things go. It

is a thorough change and holiday, and I have brought an
Augean stable of letters and papers in my portmanteau,
all wanting sifting, answering, or destroying. . . . The day
is baskingly lovely, and the pure snow-line of the Pyrenees
just out of my window, as I sit writing, fills me with all
good thoughts. We had a nice quiet service (such as
you would have liked) at Trinity Church this morning. . . .
Kindest regards to all.

" Ever your loving friend,

" HENRY BRADSHAW."

To Mr Donald Masson, of Edinburgh, he writes, " I
am just reading with very great interest M. d'Arbois
Jubainville's first course of lectures at the Collège de France,
' Introduction à l'étude de la littérature Celtique.' They
are, to my mind, extremely well worth reading, having all
the research of a German, coupled with the lucidity of a
Frenchman. He deals only with Irish, and it makes me
long to have leisure to learn something of the language,
to which I have always had such strong attractions. But
I have to content myself with the lower ground of the
palæography and bibliography of the subject."

Early in September he attended the conference of the
Library Association at Liverpool. He occupied the chair
at one of the meetings, and spoke several times. Mr R.
Somervell, with whom he stayed on the occasion, says, " He
was in excellent spirits, and used to give us, with almost
boyish pleasure, accounts of what he had done and said in
the course of the day, while he sipped the nightcap of milk
and soda-water with which he used to regale himself before
going to bed."

In October, 1883, he finished the statutes. On the 8th of
that month he wrote to Mr Seebohm, " I have this evening
returned for press the last sheet of a book of eight hundred
pages which I have been seeing through the press, and it

has taken it out of me considerably, though there is nothing that most people would not have found easy and light work. The result is that I have not been able to get even my week's 'long vacation,' at the beginning of October, as I generally do." The result, however, must have been very gratifying to him, for those best qualified to judge received the book with grateful applause. Mr Coutts Trotter wrote to him, " Your handsome and well-printed volume is a pleasant contrast in every respect to the chaotic blue-book which contained the college statutes of 1859–61 in their least inaccessible form." Dr Luard said, " I see what pains and trouble it has taken ; but this is only to say in other words that it is you that have edited it." Dr Hort wrote, " One line of warm thanks and congratulation. It is a beautiful and satisfactory book. It would be pleasant to believe that many of those for whose benefit it is intended will value as they should the care and thought which have been lavished upon it." And Professor Mayor, in a letter of thanks, remarked, " It is curious to contrast the statutes of the sixteenth and seventeenth centuries with the wisdom of the nineteenth ; the one dealing with the ends of university life, the other engrossed in the means, which, just in the nick of time, are dwindling away."

In December, 1883, the stipend of the librarian was raised, in accordance with a recommendation from the Library Syndicate, to £500. Bradshaw had held the post for more than sixteen years at the original stipend of £400 a year. It was certainly high time that some such recognition of his services, slight as it was, should be made.

Early next year there was a great sale of books, belonging to the famous Vergauwen Collection, at Brussels. The Syndicate placed £500 at the librarian's disposal for the purchase of early printed books from this library. In March he went over to Brussels to inspect the collection, having previously armed himself, as his custom was, with a

classified index of the fifteenth-century books which it
contained. Shortly after the sale he wrote to Mr Ferd.
Vanderhaeghen, of Ghent, "I went over to Brussels on
Thursday night, and returned on Friday night, having
spent a long day at Olivier's, examining M. Vergauwen's
books, as I had never had a chance of seeing them before. . . .
I sent commissions for several books, and obtained a good
many of them. Our funds would not, of course, allow us to
bid for any of the great treasures, like the Colard Mansions,
and many others of general interest. But such as I wanted
for my typographical researches I happily succeeded in
getting. Among these was a packet of fragments sold at
the very beginning of the sale, and not in the catalogue.
If I had not gone to Brussels myself, I should not have
known of their existence. . . . I felt very heartless when I
heard that it had fallen to me, because I felt that you
ought to have had it. But then, I did not feel at all sure
that it would go to you if I lost it."

The acquisition of one of these fragments, consisting of
some leaves from a " Horæ Beatæ Mariæ Virginis," in 8vo,
printed by Arend de Keysere at Ghent, gave him very
great pleasure, for the book, he says in another letter, was
wholly unknown, and he considered himself amply rewarded for his journey by having obtained it. He bought
altogether at this sale one hundred and forty fifteenth-century books, at a cost of £551. " I only lost two interesting
things," he told Mr Sandars, "and neither of them was of
real importance to me. What I need is not so much
rarities as books containing problems to work out."

In October, 1884, he attended the annual meeting of the
Library Association at Dublin. At the dinner on October
2, he replied on behalf of the members of that body to the
toast of " the Association." The next day he delivered an
address on the subject of Irish printing. He had intended
to write his paper, but when the time came he had only

put together a few notes, and his communication was almost
entirely oral.   He was listened to with great attention for
over an hour.   Unfortunately, the newspaper reports have
preserved very little of what he said, but he appears to
have given a general sketch of the history of printing in
Ireland, and an estimate of the chief authorities on the
subject.   He traced the wanderings of printers and workmen from one spot to another, and showed how the printing trade moved with other trades from place to place,
even from street to street in Dublin.   He appealed to all
interested in the study to aid in collecting materials.   Every
provincial library, he thought, should form a museum of
local productions.   Such a collection might contain much
rubbish, but for their purpose it ceased to be rubbish when
once put in order and employed to throw light on the history of typography.   His own interest in the subject arose
from the circumstance that his father and mother were
natives of Ireland, and that he had inherited from the
former a collection of Irish books.   He had, therefore, been
all his life interested in Irish literature and printing, and
his object was to get at the original sources of information,
especially the books themselves, and so to place the study
of Irish typography on a scientific basis.   Professor Mahaffy
says in a letter to me, "The flood of facts, of original
combinations, of acute inferences in his address, was quite
astonishing, and we came away so amazed that no one
thought of writing anything down."

The success of his address and the pleasure of meeting
old friends put him in high spirits.   Dr Gwynne, who had
known him in far-back St Columba days,* writes of him
on this occasion as follows :—" I was at a conversazione
[in Dublin], and I was informed that Bradshaw was in the
next room, and was anxious to see me.   I went in the
direction indicated by my informant, and saw a small

* See above, p. 55.

group of men talking together. I looked at them for a
few minutes, utterly unable to identify any one of them
as Bradshaw. At last I was obliged to turn to my friend
and ask him which was the man I sought. Even when he
was pointed out, I was still unable to recognise him in the
stout, healthy-looking man, with an air of hearty enjoyment and a manner full of animation and *bonhomie*,
whom I saw before me. When he spoke, my puzzle came
to an end. The voice was unchanged, and I felt at last
that this was the Bradshaw I had known twenty-eight
years before." Throughout the meeting he was treated
with marked respect. On his first appearance, on the
second day of the meeting, the whole assembly stood up
to welcome him, and received him with loud applause.
His remarks were listened to with attention, and carried
conviction. "I never knew before," says one who was
there, "what commanding personal influence meant."

From Dublin he went to Broomfield to stay a day or
two with Archbishop Trench. Thence he wrote to a
friend, "The meeting of the Library Association has
been very pleasant. . . . I got over my paper better than
I expected. I had put down on a bit of paper the order
in which I wanted to take the several matters, and of
course I had thought it out; but it appears that I went
on for an hour and a quarter without a break. There was
no clock to warn one, and they were all perfectly attentive.
I was amused to read in one of the papers next morning
that 'Mr Henry Bradshaw from Cambridge delivered *a
most engaging address* on the subject of printing in Ireland,'
etc. It was very amusing, and the people are coming
to me now hour by hour to ask questions, and to see how
they can help in working the matter out." From Broomfield he went to visit Dr Reeves, now Bishop of Down and
Connor, one of his oldest friends. "My stay in Ireland,"
he wrote a little later, "was most enjoyable; and it ended

up most happily with a long hoped-for visit to Armagh and Tynan. Was there ever such a man in this world as the dean?"

Soon after his return from Ireland in November, 1884, Bradshaw was elected a member of the University Council. His name appeared on the Liberal ticket, but the support given to him was very general, and in the voting he came out at the head of the poll. He was much gratified by the compliment, but, as it implied being engaged on university business several additional hours every week, it was a compliment which he could ill afford to accept. Nevertheless he attended the meetings regularly, and took an active part in the conduct of business. All this implied an increasing readiness on his part to "come out of his shell." It is certain that, during the later years of his life, a sense of growing influence gave him more confidence in himself, and broke down, to a great extent, the old barrier of shyness and reserve. As an instance of this tendency, I may mention that in June, 1884, he allowed himself to be proposed for the Athenæum by Professor Liveing, after having for many years refused to stand. He did not, however, live to become a member of the club.

Just before Christmas, 1884, he received the news of the sudden death of his eldest brother, Mr Thomas Bradshaw, a county court judge at Newcastle-on-Tyne. He immediately went north, and stayed with his sister-in-law and her family for some days after the funeral.

From Newcastle he writes to a sister, respecting the brother whom he had lost, " I never knew a man more perfectly happy within his own immediate family, and I have never known a man about whose public work, and the good unpretending high quality about it, there has been for years past a more singular unanimity of opinion. These two things I am content to take as the lesson of his life." To another sister he writes, "You know something

of what I can feel of the satisfaction of my having had
ten days here last summer. . . . ' If only,' he said so many
times while I was here—' if only we could see each other
a little oftener, as we all grow old ! We cannot see each
other many more times, in any case.' The words sunk
into me, and I made up my mind to spend a few days
with them at Christmas." Writing to one of his oldest
friends, in answer to a letter of condolence, he says, " I
have just been with them [his brother's family] for a week,
and, though a very sad Christmas, it has been in some
ways a happy one, for these times of deep sorrow somehow open up wells of comfort which might otherwise have
been unobserved."

The shock of his brother's death was all the more
severe because he was himself far from well. Unintermitted
labour was undoubtedly telling upon him. His snatches
of holiday were but pleasant moments ; they did not suffice
to recruit his waning strength. Those who saw him day
by day hardly marked the gradual change, and when long-
absent friends came to visit him, old affection and common
interests acted as a pleasant stimulus, and made him appear
the same man as he had been. His spirits were not visibly
affected. He went often into society, more often than had
been his wont some years before, and he enjoyed his growing popularity. His interests seemed as keen as ever.
Whether he had any inkling that he was suffering from a
serious disease, it seems impossible to say. He certainly
took his brother's death as a warning, and he made no
secret of his conviction that his was not to be a long life.
He more than once told me he knew he should not live
to be more than sixty. But it does not appear that as
yet he had any notion that the end was near ; nor did any
of his acquaintances, so far as I am aware, discover any
signs of its approach.

In looking back at the last year of his life, one can

recall a certain loss of the old elasticity, a shrinking from unusual physical exertion, and other symptoms of failing energy, but these were not sufficiently marked to demand attention at the time. The consciousness of fatigue shows itself, however, in his correspondence. He frequently complains of being tired out, a condition which, in former days, never seemed to occur to him as even conceivable.

At Easter, 1885, he went for a short holiday to Whitby, in company with Dr Jackson. Writing to Mr F. Madan, of the Bodleian, on April 6, he says, "I have come off here with Henry Jackson for a week's real fresh air and exercise, with no intellectual food but a portmanteau full of letters to answer, yours among the number. I was completely used up at Cambridge, and now, spending, as we do, most of our day in fighting the strong south-east wind on the sands or on the cliff, I feel getting daily stronger, and more without excuse for not answering my letters. I am delighted to hear of your discoveries at Oriel. . . . But you are really on the wrong tack when you go to a college library and look in their alphabetical catalogue. I never should have found anything in this way. The only real way is to walk right round the shelves, as I have often longed to do at Oxford, and as I so often have done at Cambridge—every time I do so, finding something which I had allowed to escape me the time before: I should dearly like to have another good time at Oxford."

Dr Jackson notes, in connection with this Easter holiday, a characteristic incident. "We broke the journey," he says, "at York, and after dinner, with his bag of letters in his hand, he joined me on the platform for a turn or two. It ended in a promenade of something like three hours, during which time, swinging his bag as he walked, he told me the whole history of his inquiries respecting the 'Hisperica Famina.' *   I was very anxious that he should

* Unfortunately, Dr Jackson took no notes of this conversation.

lose no time in publishing an account of his discoveries."
Unfortunately, he did not live to do so.

I may mention here a kind and thoughtful act which
he did about this time. When in Dublin for the meeting
of the Library Association, he was shown by the Rev. Dr
Gibbings, among some books of his which were shortly
to be sold, the proof-sheets of Dr Lingard's "History of
England" (first edition), with the author's notes and corrections, bound up in several quarto volumes. It occurred
to him afterwards that such a relic would be valued at
St Cuthbert's College, Ushaw,* and he therefore bought
it and presented it to the college. The gift was gratefully
received, and is now in the library there. Bradshaw had
no personal connection either with Dr Lingard or with
Ushaw, and his motive was simply his habitual desire
to preserve any literary memorial of interest, and to
preserve it in the place where it was likely to be most
appreciated. "As I know," he writes to the president,
"that the people at Ushaw value every relic of him [Dr
Lingard], you must let me deposit it in your library, as
some return for your kindness to me at Ushaw last year."

About the same time he was engaged in doing another
small service for the chapter library at Carlisle.† A packet
of musty and worm-eaten letters had been lately discovered by a workman engaged in the restoration of
the cathedral. They were concealed in a hole in the
wall of the triforium, and had lain there unnoticed for
more than two hundred years. On examination they
proved to be the correspondence of Lord Nithsdale, a
leading royalist partisan in the time of the Civil War.

* The famous college of Douai, broken up by the Revolution, migrated to
England, and, after several changes of abode, was finally established at Ushaw.
Dr Lingard, who had himself been at Douai, was for several years resident as
a professor at Ushaw, and began his history there.

† He had, some years previously, rearranged and superintended the rebinding of the ancient registers of the chapter of Carlisle Cathedral.

X

The chapter applied to Bradshaw, as they had done on a previous occasion. He undertook the arrangement and restoration of the letters, put together the mutilated fragments, and had them carefully mounted. Some of them were so illegible and dilapidated that this was a task of great difficulty. He was able, however, to complete it, and the letters, bound up in a volume, were sent back to Carlisle after his death.

In May, 1885, he read a paper on " Early Bibles " at a meeting of the Library Association in London. But his chief work this year was the eighth and last of his " Memoranda," on " The early collection of Canons commonly known as the Hibernensis." It was in the form of a letter to Dr Wasserschleben, who was just about to bring out a second issue of his edition of his " Irische Kanonensammlung." Bradshaw had for several years, more especially about the year 1876, been at work on the early history of this famous code of ecclesiastical law. He had been led into the investigation in the course of the search for Celtic remains, of which I have already given some account.*
It was obvious that his palæographical and philological researches would be aided by a study of the origin and sources of the code itself, and would in turn throw light on the latter. It was in accordance with his habits and training that he approached the question from the point of view ⁓ of the manuscripts, deducing his conclusions primarily, though not altogether, from the nature of the handwriting, the language of the glosses, and similar characteristics. Dr Wasserschleben, on the other hand, based his results mainly on the subject-matter. Bradshaw was anxious to prove that while, without any doubt, " the ultimate origin of the ' Hibernensis ' was Irish," the two texts, as we have them, in which the canons have been preserved, " can only have spread over Europe from Brittany." This was only part

* See above, pp. 187, 227.

of the outcome of his work on early Celtic remains, the result of which had been to show that "Brittany had been overlooked," and to restore Breton to its proper place among the dialects of the Celtic race.

When Dr Wasserchleben was bringing out his second edition, Bradshaw, to whom he had applied for the loan of a transcript of one of the manuscripts, requested him to delay the issue for a week or two till he could send him the results of his investigations. This Dr Wasserschleben consented to do, although it took Bradshaw a month before he could get his work into shape. While engaged on this task several new ideas occurred to him. In a letter to Mr Whitley Stokes, dated May 17, 1885, he asks his opinion about an ingenious emendation of a hitherto unintelligible passage, in which he discovers the name of the person who was most instrumental in transcribing or drawing up the code, and adds another proof to the evidence of its Irish origin. He writes, "My present point is about the rubric at the end of the 'Collectio Canonum Hibernensis' itself. This is the only manuscript* which has anything like a rubric with a name, and at the end of the last chapter it stands thus : ' Hucusque nuben & cv. cuiminiæ, & du rinis.' Seeing how undistinguishable *et* and *ex* are in Hiberno-Saxon manuscripts, and how easily *a* and *æ* might be confused, it strikes me that the rubric might read thus : ' Hucusque nubenetcu cuimini a· ex durinis,' and that 'cuiminus abbas ex durinis ' might well be a Cumin, abbat of Dairinis, or some such place. If so, can you see any trace or corruption in 'nubenetcu' of an Irish word which might refer to any such compilation, or *defloratio*, or series of extracts. I do not, of course, wish to force anything, and I think you will credit me with sufficient honesty

---

* This is one of the Paris manuscripts, which, he says, "is clearly the most primitive of all, and the only one which contains traces of Irish in what I should call a fossil state, the scribe [a Breton] not understanding what he is writing."

of intentions for this ; but it would be so extremely happy
a result, if this should turn out to be some disguised word,
which really made sense to any one who had the key to
unlock the difficulty."

Mr Whitley Stokes, in his reply, accepts the suggestion
that Durinis stands for Dair-inis (oak island), " a monastery
near Youghal, now called Molana, from St Maelanfaedh,
the patron saint," and, while suggesting that the letters
" nubenetcu " contain the proper name " Ruben," recognizes
Cucumne as an Irish celebrity of the eighth century more
than once mentioned in the annals of that time.*   " This
hitherto unrecognised compiler of the ' Hibernensis,' " says
Bradshaw in his published letter, " may, without any strain
either of language or of evidence, be looked upon as
possibly identical with the *Cummeanus abbas in Scotia ortus*,
to whom the penitential literature of the eighth century is
so much indebted."

Unfortunately, Bradshaw found it impossible to work
out his ideas fully, and was forced at length to put merely
his results on paper, and send them to Dr Wasserschleben
with no more than a short introduction.   At one moment
he despaired of being able to send him anything at all.
" I have been doing my utmost," he writes, " to put my
notes into a satisfactory shape that I might send them
to you, but I find that it is more than I can possibly do
in the middle of the work of the University term, with the
mass of other things that I have to do.   So I must release
you at once. . . . My health will not bear the strain of
the double work of the last three or four weeks, and I
must reluctantly give it up."   He went on with it, however,
and a week later wrote to Dr Wasserschleben as follows :—

" I could not resist sending you something of my work,

* Mr Stokes refers to the " Four Masters," ed. O'Donovan, *s. a.* 742 ;
and "Liber Hymnorum," ed. Todd, pp. 138–146.   Cucumne died about
742, and " oddly enough," says Mr Stokes, " the entry in the 'Four Masters'
next before that relating to Cucumne is the obit of an abbot of Dairinis."

so I determined to compress a part of it into twelve short propositions, which I hope some day to be able to substantiate. I wrote them out with a few preliminary pages, necessary to show how I came to find the clue to so many difficulties in Brittany, and these I finished at six o'clock this morning and sent them to the press. . . . My twelve propositions will show to some extent the aim of my work, and if you choose to say anything about them in your preface, or even to print them, I shall be encouraged to carry my intentions through, and to put my reasons clearly (or as clearly as I can) in print, when the vacation comes. . . . I think you will see that *my work* has brought me to see things which *your work* did not lead you to consider, and that there is no real antagonism between our views." *

In the paper in question, after sketching briefly the course of his own studies and the steps which led him "to bring the claims of Brittany into notice," Bradshaw gives a list of the manuscripts containing the "Hibernensis," and then lays down the twelve propositions referred to in his letter, touching the manuscripts themselves, the origin and authorship of the "Hibernensis," the chief facts in the life of Gildas, and the position of Brittany in Celtic history. Of these propositions I have given some further account below (Chap. XI.) "Until you have fuller materials before you," the author says in conclusion, "these propositions may at least serve the purpose of suggestions. They may, perhaps, lead some student to take pleasure in pursuing the investigation further, and if they are honestly pursued, light will assuredly come to clear up what is a deeply interesting, even though a most obscure question in literary history."

Another bibliographical problem, smaller and more capable of complete solution, occupied Bradshaw for a

---

* Dr Wasserschleben printed the whole of Bradshaw's letter as an appendix to the preface of his book (Die Irische Kanonensammlung, ed. 2, 1885).

short time this summer. This was an investigation of the work of the first Cambridge printer, John Siberch, who printed several books at Cambridge in 1521-2. Mr Robert Bowes had issued, in 1878, a facsimile of one of these books, Linacre's translation of Galen, and was anxious to publish the other productions of Siberch's press. At his suggestion, Bradshaw set to work on the books, and succeeded in discovering, from internal evidence alone, the exact order in which Siberch's eight volumes were published. The different copies of one of these, however, an edition of " Papyrius Geminus," displayed certain variations which could not easily be explained. The publication was therefore delayed, in order to give Bradshaw time to examine all the known copies. This he was able to do in 1885, and by putting the books side by side and patiently comparing them, he made out for the first time a complete history of this, the first Cambridge press.*

Meanwhile he gave as much attention as ever to the affairs of his office and to the public business of the university. In May, 1885, he drew up a long and elaborate report on the requirements of the library.† In this report he emphasised the increasing need of space, and the growing inconvenience which arose from overcrowding. As a partial relief he proposed the annexation of the Law School, the last of the three old public lecture-rooms which originally occupied the ground-floor of the library. But he pointed out that the relief thus obtained would be only temporary, and therefore suggested the filling up of the western side of the western quadrangle. The first of these suggestions was carried out almost immediately. Funds were at the time lacking for the execution of the larger

* His notes, prepared for press by Mr Jenkinson, are printed as an introduction to the facsimile of " Bullock's Oration," the earliest of Siberch's books, published by Mr Bowes.

† Published in the *University Reporter*, May 6, 1885, p. 679.

part of the scheme, but it has been taken up since his death, and the building which he proposed is now nearly completed. Another matter in which he took great interest was the proposal * to reorganise the machinery of the university registry, and to increase the stipend of the registrary. In support of this scheme, he issued (on June 10, 1885) a warm appeal to the members of the Senate, in which he traced the steps which led up to the proposal, pointed out the insufficiency of the existing staff, and pressed upon the university the claims of the registrary, who, "with an old-fashioned modesty which it is easier to respect than to approve, had unfortunately felt it his duty to go on and on for years unaided in the constantly increasing work of his office." The grace approving the proposal was carried by a large majority.

The day after this letter was written he received the news of the sudden death of his eldest sister, Mrs Daniell. It was the severest loss he had ever yet sustained, and it affected him very deeply. For years past her house had been a second home to him, and his letters to her show the intimate communion and sympathy which existed between them. "There seems nothing but death on all sides this year," he wrote soon afterwards to a friend. "My brother's sudden death last Christmas has broken up a very happy home, and my sister Katherine's death last month has been a blow such as I never experienced before." But on occasions like this he was not wont to express his feelings in words, and only those who knew him well saw how bitter was his grief.

It was, perhaps, some sort of foreboding aroused by these events which induced him to make an effort to set in order or get rid of the accumulations of years which lay piled about his rooms. Early in July he was destroying old letters, he writes, at the rate of a hundred a

* Published in the *University Reporter* for June 2, 1885, p. 789.

day. A little later he went north to aid his sister-in-law, Mrs Bradshaw, in the move from Newcastle to London. On his way home he took the opportunity of paying a short visit to an old Eton and college friend, Mr Booth, near Sheffield. They had not met for years, but absence never interposed a barrier between Henry Bradshaw and any one to whom he had once become attached. "While in my house," says Mr Booth, "he found the original edition of the Waverley novels, in rather a neglected condition. He gathered them together, all but one (since found), which he noted as missing, and wrote off a catalogue of them for me, then and there, in a few minutes, seeming to have all their titles and the order of their publication in his head." The meeting was an affecting one for both of these old friends. To Mr Booth it seemed like a farewell. "It was rather," he writes, "the general tone of Bradshaw's manner and conversation when he was here, along with the fact of his coming at all and of his having volunteered to come, than any particular expression, which assured me that he was aware of his precarious condition. But just before we parted company, when I had been speaking of something (I forget what) to be expected with certainty at no distant time, he said abruptly, with some emphasis, and in his cold, grave, composed tone, '_I_ shall not be alive then.' The remark only seemed to me at the time to be a summary of what had been unexpressed, but sufficiently understood between us."

Not long after this, towards the end of August, Bradshaw had an attack which alarmed his friends considerably, and appeared ominous of serious mischief. He had been ailing for some time past, when one night, just as he was going to bed, he was seized with a violent bleeding at the nose, which continued for more than three hours. There was hardly any one in college, and he tried in vain to rouse the porter in order to send for a doctor.

Thus imprisoned, and unable to get assistance, he had to return to his rooms and await the event, whatever it might be, in no pleasant frame of mind. The bleeding stopped eventually, and he got to bed. "I have at last collapsed in my small way," he wrote shortly afterwards, "and it is a thousand pities it did not happen before. It has been a very innocent thing—merely violent bleeding at the nose for three or four hours together one night, repeated to a smaller extent next day. But I did send for a doctor at once, when morning came—for the first time for ten years—and I am ordered to shut up. Professor Robertson Smith has insisted on carrying me off with him to France somewhere next Monday, and I hope to come back a wiser and a soberer man in three weeks' time. I can only reflect that my experience of the Long Vacation has shown me that I have neither done work nor had holiday, which is a very desirable sort of warning to prevent me going on with this sort of folly."

During the warm days of the latter part of August and the first half of September, he wandered from one old French town to another, seeing much and enjoying all. Even now he could not avoid doing some work. "I had a very successful hour in the library at Tours," he writes, "going carefully through a manuscript I wanted much to get an account of. At Le Mans, the only other place where I tried the library at all, I failed signally, being paid in my own coin, After waiting two hours to see the librarian, he did not come till just as I was forced to leave, and it was no use speaking to him. I wanted to see the library-marking of some of the old cathedral library books, to get confirmation about our Bede * having come from there."

Once back at Cambridge, he plunged into work again

---

* The famous contemporary manuscript of Bede's "Ecclesiastical History," preserved in the University Library (Kk. v. 16).

as before. It was at this time, the quiet fortnight at the end of September, when Cambridge is quite empty, that he made the acquaintance of Professor Mommsen, who had come to Cambridge in order to examine the manuscript of Gildas in the University Library, and to investigate the authenticity of that work. This was naturally a point on which Bradshaw was able to give him valuable assistance, for it was one on which, as we have seen, he had bestowed much attention.* "I am writing in the library," he says in a letter of this date, "attending every two minutes to old Professor Mommsen, who is here from Berlin. He has completely won my heart, and it is as good as a month's holiday to see his method of working." The respect and liking were reciprocal. Professor Mommsen told Mr Robertson Smith that he had been more impressed by Henry Bradshaw than by any other man he had met in England, and that he longed for a shorthand writer to take down the information which he poured forth on subjects of common interest. He had come to England with a suspicion that the work attributed to Gildas was a forgery, and that Gildas himself had never existed. Bradshaw succeeded in convincing him that this was not the case.

After Professor Mommsen had left Cambridge, he exchanged several letters with Bradshaw, bearing on the history and manuscripts of Gildas and the so-called Nennius. These letters are of too learned and technical a character to be given here, but I may quote some passages of general interest. "Do not scruple," says Bradshaw "to ask any number of questions about the manuscripts which you think I may be able to answer for you. It will be no loss, much less *waste*, of time to me; for I have longed for years past to find some one who will work at these books with grounded intelligence, and it is a real

* See above, pp. 120, 187.

happiness to have lived to find the man." Again, "Above all things, I feel that it is of vital importance to trace out, by all available means, what was the home of each of these manuscripts in early times, before attempting to come to any final decision about them. It is, as you justly say, an extremely complex investigation; but it is its very complexity which interests me so much, and induces me to try my utmost to clear it up. I have done something towards this end in past years, but, from not finding any scholar to whom my work could be of immediate use, I have never carried it through, as so many matters have stood in the way with more pressing claims. My primary duty as a librarian is, of course, rather to help scholars in their work to the best of my power, than .to pursue any favourite investigation of my own."

Shortly after this Bradshaw was in correspondence with Mr Talbot B. Reed, who, while engaged in bringing out his "History of Type-Founding," had written to ask him some questions about Irish printing. "I hope," he writes to Mr Reed, on October 15, "that you will not put down my silence for five days to ingratitude, but I have been absolutely unable to get five minutes' peace in which to answer a letter which has given me more pleasure than any I have received for many years past. It is a real satisfaction at last to find some one who can interest himself in the question of Irish typography from a typographical point of view." And then he goes on to write him a long letter full of information, especially with regard to the use of the Irish character in printed books, which he describes as stopping short in 1742, and not beginning again till after the Union. This letter was followed by several others, and by a long list of books (covering three large sheets) which he had examined in the course of his investigations into the subject. "To have found some one," he writes, "who will aid in carrying the matter back beyond the printers to the letter foundry is an advance which I hardly expected to see." One of his letters ends with the words, " I was very glad indeed to hear of the Belfast movement * about local books ; I wish very much I could be put into communication with those who are interested in the subject."

This wish was soon afterwards gratified, and in the early part of 1886 several letters passed between him and Mr Anderson, the author of the movement referred to, on the subject of Belfast books. These letters show that typography was with him by no means confined to the study of printers' types and habits. He brought his typographical facts to bear on the history of religion and politics in Ireland, and extracted from them new information about the spread of Protestantism or the stirrings of the national spirit. They show also the human interest which attached him to these studies. " I hope some day," he writes to Mr Anderson, " if I live, to get as far as your part of the country [Belfast]. . . . My mother came from Ballintoy, and lived till she married at Lisburn, while my father came from Newtownards ; so you cannot be surprised at my taking an interest in such matters. My father left me the Irish portion of his library, and during the last thirty years I have done my utmost to increase it, and the productions of the Irish presses have always had a special interest for me. Some fifteen years ago I gave all I had in this way to the University Library here —some five thousand books, pamphlets, and papers—but I cannot now help buying whatever I can afford to buy when it comes in my way, and I must have about three thousand more by this time ready to go in the same direction † when I can get them into some sort of order."

---

* This refers to the list of books printed at Belfast, which was then being prepared, and has since been published, by Mr J. Anderson.

† The Irish portion of Mr Bradshaw's library, together with all the early

These Belfast books were almost the last subject that he was at work upon, and his last letter to Mr Anderson was written only four days before his death. He gave Mr Anderson considerable assistance in drawing up his list of the productions of the Belfast press, and added a number of titles from the books in his own possession and elsewhere. At the same time he was corresponding with Mr J. P. Edmond about Aberdeen printing. Other productions of the Irish press were also engaging his attention. One of the last facts he elicited from this investigation was the continuance of the Cork press all through the troubled times of the Irish rebellion in 1641 and of the civil war.

In spite of the unabated scientific ardour and vigour which his correspondence with Professor Mommsen, Mr Anderson, and others, displays, it is clear that he felt his duties press too heavily upon him, for towards the end of the Michaelmas Term, 1885, he wrote to the vice-chancellor to resign his place on the University Council. A plan was talked of among his friends by which he might have been relieved of the more onerous of his duties as librarian, and have been left free to devote himself to the care of his favourite books and the pursuit of his favourite studies. He himself seemed to favour this idea, but he did not suggest it or press it on. Perhaps he felt it was too late. During the last two months of his life he lived as he had lived before, busy in the discharge of his regular duties, and enjoying the society of an ever-increasing circle of friends. He was much interested in the production of the late Dr Todhunter's work on "Elasticity," which was being edited by his friend Professor Karl Pearson for the University Press. He was aiding Mr J. W. Clark in bringing out his architectural history of Cambridge, and Dr Wald-

printed books and the service-books which he had not already given to the University Library, were presented by his family to the university after his death.

stein in his " Essays on Pheidias." His sympathies were
as keen as ever. To his friend Mr Seebohm, who had
lately lost a daughter, he wrote on December 20, 1885—

" I am indeed sorry to get your letter and to hear your
distressing news. . . . From the few times I have been
with you, I have always pictured to myself yours as almost
the happiest home I have known—all bound up in one
another, yet without any of the exclusiveness which sometimes goes with this; all full of their various kinds of
work, and so all ready with sympathy for others. I have
had so much to bring home to me sorrow of this kind
during the last twelve months that you will know, apart
from my own feelings for yourself, how much my heart is
with you.

" Ever yours affectionately,
" HENRY BRADSHAW."

He spent Christmas with his sister-in-law, Mrs Bradshaw, in London. Soon after coming back to Cambridge,
he wrote (January 4, 1886), to two intimate friends :—

" MY DEAR PEOPLE,
　　　　　" My hand is quite tired with writing twenty
letters since I came in this evening, but I have not the
face to send off such a packet without also sending a
few lines to both of you. . . . It is very stupid of me
to be in the dumps, except that I am quite stupid with
coughing, but in other respects I have nothing to complain
of. . . . I often think of you all, though I never write ;
indeed, the less I write the more I think of you, because
it weighs upon me so, not writing."

And a little later to the same—

" The weather here gets more and more disgusting.
I had to come here from the library just now in a pelting

storm of rain, and every few hours it freezes hard ; so altogether I am in no mood for seeing my way happily through the work of an unusually long term. I have not been so deeply in the dumps for a very long time. The chief moral of this is that I had better stop this, and not pour out my troubles (which are entirely of my own making) to you. With best love and thanks for both the long and welcome letters,

> " Ever yours affectionately,
> " HENRY BRADSHAW."

Towards the end of January, 1886, he was much pleased by the receipt of Mr F. Madan's edition of the " Day-book of John Dorne, Bookseller in Oxford, A.D. 1520." This day-book, or bookseller's diary, containing an account of the books sold at an Oxford book-shop ten years before the Reformation, naturally threw light on the literature of the day, and at the same time raised a number of those bibliographical problems which it was Bradshaw's chief delight to solve. He at once set to work on it, and in a few days produced what he called " A Half-century of Notes " on the book in question. These notes abound with abstruse knowledge, conclusive explanations of difficulties, and ingenious suggestions. Here is one, for instance. Dorne enters in one place, " 1018 : 1 hackum end hontigle 4*d*." On this Bradshaw writes, " You will think me very bold (or rather presumptuous), but Dorne shows himself so hopeless where he has to deal with English books, that I am quite prepared to see, through the mist of this entry, the little quarto pamphlet issues of ' Hawking ' and ' Hunting,' issued by W. de Worde about this time. We have the ' Hunting ' in our library, and the ' Fishing ' is well known. The price would suit perfectly for such a book." This is but a slight specimen of his notes, which I extract merely on account of its shortness and simplicity. Refer-

ence must be made to the whole body of notes in order
to obtain an idea of the wide and intimate knowledge of
mediæval literature and typography which they display.
What makes the production the more remarkable is the
rapidity with which it was dashed off, in short intervals
of leisure, with hardly any books at hand, the facts drawn
almost entirely from the storehouse of memory.*

When finished, he wrote out the notes quite cleanly—
they cover about thirty pages of foolscap—made an index
to them, drew out a title-page, had the sheets bound as a
book, and sent them off at once to Mr Madan. Round
the title-page is written, in a dotted border, the text, ominous
of what was close at hand, " Whatsoever thy hand findeth
to do, do it with thy might ; for there is no work, nor
device, nor knowledge, nor wisdom in the grave, whither
thou goest ". (Eccles. ix. 10). And at the foot are the
words, " Quasi morientes et ecce vivimus." The following
introductory letter is prefixed :—

> " King's College, Cambridge, January 30, 1886.

" MY DEAR MADAN,

" The care and patience with which you have
edited the ' Day-book of John Dorne,' ought to have secured
you an earlier acknowledgment on my part. The separate
copy reached me at the beginning of this week ; and, as
it happens that I have been unequal to much serious work
during the interval, the interest and amusement which such
a book naturally provides for me has come at a most
welcome time. I have been through it over and over
again, every time finding some new light which it throws
upon the subject in which we both feel a strong interest.
To show you the sincerity of my thanks, I have put down
a few notes, in which I have brought some of the entries
to bear upon one another with very satisfactory results.

---

* The " Half-Century of Notes " has been reproduced in facsimile by the
Cambridge Scientific Instrument Company.

You will be glad to have them, though I dare say many of them express rash views which may have been enter-tained by yourself for a moment, but have been rejected on the second thoughts which come before final publication. The notes are arranged in the order of your first index, and I have added a small supplementary index, in which I have endeavoured to follow your admirable method: It is not until such a book is actually in print, with the contractions and abbreviations all honestly marked, just as you have done here, that it becomes possible to inves-tigate the further problems which such a document pre-sents. It augurs well for your Historical Society, if the publications continue to show the same amount of intelli-gent care which you have brought to bear upon this.

" Yours very sincerely,

" HENRY BRADSHAW."

This was the last piece of work which he was able to complete. The end was come. On the evening of Wednesday, February 10, 1886, he dined with Mr and Mrs J. W. Clark, at whose house he met several old friends, Dr and Mrs Luard, Professor and Mrs Sidgwick, Dr Henry Jackson, and others. He seemed well, and was in excellent spirits. Dr Jackson asked him about his work on the " Hisperica Famina." He said he had done nothing at it since the May Term. " How long would it take you to get it out of hand?" " Perhaps a fortnight." " Then why not stop all other work and clear it off?" " Because there are so many other things to do." The evening passed agreeably, with plenty of genial conversation of that pleasant sort which leaves no special impression behind. When the time came to part, Bradshaw walked home with Professor and Mrs Sidgwick as far as the gate of King's. The porter who let him in was the last person who saw him alive.

Y

Next morning, when his servant came in to call him about eight o'clock, he was startled by finding that his master had not gone to bed. He brushed past him in the dark as he went to open the shutters, and at first thought him asleep ; but when he touched his hand it was cold. He was sitting in his armchair at the table in his inner room, the head leaning over to the left side, the left hand hanging down, the right in his lap. His spectacles were pushed up on his forehead, as his habit was when he was not actually at work. A little Irish book, closed, lay on the table in front of him, and near it some paper and a pen, unused. He had taken off his overcoat, but still wore his evening dress, and a blue silk scarf which he used to put on when going out in the evening hung loosely about his neck. The fire had burnt down in the grate, and the reading-lamp on the table had gone out. It seemed as if he had sat down to do a little work before going to bed, and had fallen asleep.

On the following Tuesday, February 16, his body, followed by a great concourse of persons assembled to pay him the last tribute of love and honour, was laid in the grave. He lies beneath the vault of that great chapel in which he worshipped from a boy, and by the doors of which he passed to and from his daily work for thirty years. His last resting-place is fittingly midway between the rooms which to so many were a second home, and the library where he spent his life in unselfish toil.

CHAPTER XI.

IN this chapter I propose to bring together some materials bearing on Henry Bradshaw's literary work, for which there appeared to be no special place in the foregoing pages, and to attempt a summary of what he accomplished in the various branches of study in which he was interested. The chief of these branches were bibliography, especially, perhaps, that of Irish literature; palæography, and the study of manuscripts in general; Celtic antiquities; ecclesiastical antiquities, particularly mediæval service-books and cathedral organization; early English literature, especially the works of Chaucer; and the early history of printing. This list is not exhaustive, but most of his work, of which any traces remain, will fall under one or other of these heads. It is not too much to say that in each of the subjects mentioned he was the first, or among the first, of the scholars of his day. The order in which the subjects are placed is unimportant, for it was one of Bradshaw's peculiarities that he studied them simultaneously, and there was hardly a year of his life after he first entered the University Library when any one of them was altogether put aside. The Irish books which he inherited from his father were apparently his first love, and he remained faithful to them to the end; but his employment among the manuscripts and early books in the University Library determined the main lines of his intellectual activity. He had an irresistible tendency to go to the bottom of things, and the study of manuscripts was therefore the natural basis of his work. Still, in his own mind all his favourite subjects were connected. His manuscripts opened the door to a knowledge of Chaucer and other early poets, of the Celtic languages, of the system and ritual of the mediæval Church; and from manuscripts he passed on to the study of those *incunabula* in which the printing-press first supplanted the scribe.

This "natural piety," which linked together the various branches of study which he took up, was at once a source. of strength and weakness. Of strength, for it enabled him to view things in their entirety, with all their surroundings, and to bring to bear on the solution of any problem a mass of illustrative knowledge. Of weakness, for one subject inevitably led on to another; one peak surmounted, another lay beyond ; he could not resist the fascination of discovery. Unambitious as he was, no thirst for fame urged him to publish his results, and acquisition was more attractive than utterance. His very fastidiousness, his love of accuracy, his ideal of completeness and perfection, stood in his way. He could not desist from his research till he had explored every by-path ; he could not leave any difficulty unsolved so long as any clue remained to follow up. His marvellously retentive memory was in one respect a drawback, for it enabled him to lay one subject after another aside, confident that he could take it up again at any moment. He would thus return again and again, often at long intervals, to some favourite mine, each time discovering something new, but never working out the vein. At the British Museum there is a relic of Celtic antiquity, the Bodmin Gospels, a manuscript containing entries in the Cornish dialect, in which his marks were allowed to remain for ten years and more. "Almost every time he came to the museum," says Mr E. M. Thompson, "he used to have a turn at it." What was true of the Bodmin Gospels was equally true of many other things.

His position in the library was in itself a hindrance to concentration. His intimate knowledge of the treasures under his charge laid him open to the attacks of scholars in many lines, and questions would be asked or suggestions made which constantly started him on a fresh course. There was also in him, it must be allowed, a certain natural indolence, combined with an immense capacity for work. To put his results on paper involved an effort which he was generally loth to make, and he willingly seized on the pretext of some fresh opening or some unsolved problem to defer the unpleasant task. This peculiarity was early noticed by his friends. The late Mr A. A. Vansittart was once asked what Bradshaw was doing. "Oh, he's doing something else," was the reply. Pressure put upon him— and there was no lack of this from certain quarters—produced only an effect the very reverse of what was intended. He was touchingly grateful for sympathy and encouragement, and he stood much in need of such assistance ; but he would not be driven, and the more he was pushed the more he hung back. He shrank from publicity ; he hated being pinned down to any statement of which he was not absolutely sure ; he was ever apprehensive that something might turn up to modify his best-grounded opinions. The consequence was that he published comparatively little. Had he known less he would undoubtedly have written more. How much of his knowledge died with him it is impossible to say, nor is it, perhaps, very important to discover. It was not, after all, his acquirements which were most remarkable ; it was the spirit and the method of his research. His intense love of truth, his scrupulous accuracy, the sense of responsibility which controlled his sympathetic imagination, the sobriety of his judgment, the carefulness of his deductions, his tender and reverent regard for the

past, the human interest in which he clothed the dry bones
of learning, his generosity towards predecessors and contemporaries,—these and other qualities of his work are still
more worthy of admiration than the width or profundity of
his knowledge. It is to those qualities that I am most
anxious to draw attention in the following pages.

BIBLIOGRAPHY.

Of Bradshaw's work in this department there is, unfortunately, little to record. It was one of his earliest pursuits.
Mr Alexander Macmillan remembers him well as an undergraduate, often coming into his shop at Cambridge, and
looking through his books with a bibliographical eye,
counting the signatures, saying, "This is in sixes, this in
eights," and noting cancelled pages. Mr Tuckwell, one of
his contemporaries at St Columba's, recollects "with what
skill and completeness he catalogued the library there. It
was a treat," he continues, "to see him handle a rare
volume. First the caressing clasp of the closed book in
his two broad hands; then the rapid estimate of lettering,
tooling, gilding; then the critical glance at type and
margin, the survey of title-page and colophon, and the bit
of erudition or instructive anecdote in illustration of his
judgment."

Bibliography is a subject which gave ample scope to
his love of accuracy and his minute observation, but what
he has left behind is little more than a vast collection of
facts. A long line of note-books bears witness to his
industry, and it is to be hoped that an index may be made
which will open these storehouses of information to the
bibliographer. But to Bradshaw himself the mere dissec-
tion and description of books was a matter of interest only
so far as the results threw light on the habits of writers,
printers, and publishers, and generally on the history of
any particular place or time. It was not only literature,

but the whole life of the day, which was capable in his hands of illustration from its books. " Books," he wrote to the Rev. J. T. Fowler, in connection with the Coverdale Bible,* which he bought for the University Library in 1883— " books are to me living organisms, and I can only study them as such ; so every particle of light which I can obtain as to their personal history is so much positive gain." In another letter he urges Mr Fowler "to see that it [the Bible in question] does not go to any place whatever, where they will separate the title-page from the rest, and so destroy the book for scientific purposes. . . . Whatever happens to your copy," he continues, " it is of vital importance that the whole preliminary matter should be kept together as a *monumentum* of this state of the book. Now, this is a point which, I feel absolutely certain, almost any one . . . would entirely fail to see ; and it makes me sufficiently miserable to think that the book is fated to pass into the hands of those who will certainly destroy what is really the principal feature of value in it.

"It is very hard to see these precious *monumenta* destroyed almost before one's very eyes, without being able to help it. If I were a richer man, I would not let it go from the university, because I know it would be safe here, and it would be highly appreciated—and if I had any patrimony left, I would give what I had to secure such a thing on any reasonable terms. I am aware that at present I stand almost alone in my view of the nature of these questions. But in another generation it will be different, and then the things will have been destroyed. You must forgive me for writing at this length, but you do not know how nearly this question touches my heart."

Speaking of the light which Bradshaw's observations enabled him to throw on the past, Professor Pearson justly

* For an account of this copy, in some respects unique, see *Notes and Queries*, 6th series, vol. vi., December 16, 1882.

says,* " In books which the mere bibliographer described
as reprints, he would find the local colouring, the peculiar
prejudice, or the special glory of a district, introduced by
some slight change. . . . As he handled the pages of some
early folio, and described how two presses had been employed, one working away at this point, and the other at
that ; how the first stock of paper had been exhausted here,
and the second there ; how at this point the printer had
thought to improve on his original, or had bought somebody
else's cuts, or chopped up his own—the auditor felt himself
carried back centuries, and saw the men of the past at their
work. Not improbably, Bradshaw would conclude with the
remark, ' I wish I could find out anything about that book.' "

The readiness and accuracy of his bibliographical knowledge were astonishing. Many years ago, when he was as
yet only a beginner, he gave a remarkable proof of this.
It was in the year 1861. He happened to be in Mr
Quaritch's shop in Piccadilly, when that well-known bookseller received a request from the late Earl of Crawford
and Balcarres for a "collation," *i.e.* a bibliographical description, of a very rare book, the Virginian or Massa-
chusetts Bible, a large folio in two volumes, printed in
Charles II's reign. Not being able to lay his hand on any
collation of the book, Mr Quaritch referred to Bradshaw,
who at once wrote down a complete collation of the book
from memory. It was sent to Lord Crawford the same
evening, and proved to be quite correct. Any one who
knows what the collation of such a book is, will be able to
appreciate the feat.†

The following extract from a letter ‡ to Dr Furnivall is

* The *Academy*, Febuary 27, 1886.

† I have this story both from Mr Quaritch and the present Lord Crawford,
who was good enough to send me the actual sheet on which Bradshaw wrote
out the collation.

‡ This letter is published in " Francis Thynne's Animadversions," etc.
(Chaucer Soc., series ii. 13, 1875), p. xxvi.

so neat an example of the ingenuity which he brought to bear on bibliographical problems and of the human interest he attached to them, that I cannot help inserting it here.

" We know that William Thynne [the editor of Chaucer] was 'Chief Clerk of the Kitchen,' that is, as we should now say, that he held an appointment in the royal household (the Board of Green Cloth) at Greenwich. Sir Brian Tuke was postmaster, then an appointment in the same office. When Leland tells us that Sir Brian Tuke wrote a *limatissima præfatio* to the edition of Chaucer published by Berthelet, we are all puzzled; and when Leland tells us that Thynne edited the edition, we are still more puzzled, because no such edition is known. Now, the woodcut frame round the title in Godfray's edition (Thynne, 1532) is that which, having belonged to Pynson, the king's printer, was transferred to Berthelet, his successor as king's printer; and this is enough to show that there were printing relations between Berthelet and Godfray, quite enough to allow this to be the edition meant. Curiously enough, there is a copy of Godfray's edition in one of the college libraries here, in its original binding, in which, at the top of Thynne's dedication, Sir Brian Tuke has written with his own hand : 'This preface I sir Bryan Tuke knight wrot at the request of Mr Clarke of the Kechyn then being, tarying for the tyde at Grenewich.' It would be difficult to find a prettier coincidence in all points—the tarrying for the tide at Greenwich, when we learn from quite other sources (1) that Thynne's office was at Greenwich, and (2) that he lived down the Thames at Erith. You will allow that it is not often one has the pleasure of hitting things off so prettily."

Of his work on Irish bibliography there is, unfortunately, next to nothing in print. Mr Anderson's list of books printed at Belfast owes a good deal to him, and other Irish bibliographers have received his help ; but most of his work in this department is buried in his note-books, or has perished with him. He prepared only a few notes for his address on Irish printing at the Librarians' Conference in Dublin (1884), and these notes I have been unable to find. One of the last things he was working at was Lord Orrery's romance, "Parthenissa," which was supposed, from the title-page, to have been printed in London, but which he ingeniously proved to have been printed in 1654 at Waterford, where the author was at that time staying.

Bradshaw paid special attention to the bindings of books in this connection, and he was much interested in a proposal of Mr H. B. Wheatley's for an exhibition, showing in chronological order the styles adopted at various times. He had an intimate knowledge of the styles, and could often fix a binding down to a certain decade or a particular collection. For instance, in a letter to Mr Cosmo Innes respecting a manuscript in the library of Trinity College, Cambridge, he says: "From the look of the binding I should think it had formed part of the Lauderdale collection." Acting on this idea, he looked up a catalogue of that collection, after doing which he continues: "I have very little doubt it is the volume marked nine in the list." Nor was his knowledge confined to early books; he was well acquainted with all the changes in binding that have taken place down to the present day. About a year before his death, Mr Wheatley proposed that Bradshaw should join him in a history of English binding, with facsimiles of various dates. He agreed to do so, but he did not live to take any steps in that direction. In his younger days he was very particular about his own bindings, and had his pet books clad in certain distinctive garbs.

MANUSCRIPTS.

Bradshaw's knowledge of manuscripts was, as I have already said, the ultimate basis of most of his work. His ten years' training in the University Library, before he became librarian, gave him a control of the subject which was probably surpassed by none of his contemporaries. But here again his biographer is met by the difficulty that there is little to refer to, beyond the testimony of others, in proof of the assertion. Bradshaw never edited a manuscript; he seldom described one in print; and his publications under this head are almost entirely confined to a few short papers in the Communications of the Cambridge Antiquarian Society. I have already mentioned his discoveries of the "Book of Deer," the Vaudois manuscripts, the poems of Barbour, etc., and his connection with the catalogue of manuscripts in the University Library.* His work on Chaucer, on the Lincoln statutes, and on the "Hibernensis," was based on a careful and exhaustive examination of manuscript authorities.

In his study of a manuscript he brought to bear the same human interest as in the case of printed books, and that, as was natural, in a still greater degree. The monk at work in his scriptorium, the clerk in his office, the succession of hands which have left their mark on some great historical manuscript,—all these were as real to him as the men of the present day. To see and touch the handwriting of some great man of the past, to have in his possession the actual manuscript which was written at Bede's dictation when the saint was on his death-bed, to show to a sympathetic observer the portrait of Dunstan traced by the hands of Dunstan himself, filled him with an emotion as infectious as it was real. The spirit of an ancient pilgrim was in him. Writing to Mr Stephen Lawley in 1881 he says: "How I should indeed enjoy going to St Gall and elsewhere under your guidance! All that country is entirely unknown to me, and if I could worship at the shrine of Schaffhausen, where the contemporary copy of

* See above, pp. 69, 87, 103, 134, 153.

Adamnan's 'Life of St Columba' is preserved—the patriarch (by centuries) of all Scotch books—I should be supremely happy."

The love which inspired his work triumphed over all difficulties. M. Jusserand, who on one occasion paid him a visit at Cambridge, notes in his diary his admiration of the "merveilleux flair au fait de mss. et cette sorte de pouvoir divinatoire dont il [Bradshaw] est doué." He puzzled out the most crabbed writing, and unravelled the most perverse contractions with an astonishing ease which nothing but lifelong application could give. He was as conversant with the general characteristics of manuscripts as with the handwriting of particular ages and countries, and could base the detection of a forgery or the dating of a book on observations quite out of the reach of most palæographers. I may refer here to the controversy with Simonides, and his proof that the Codex Sinaiticus could not have been the manuscript which Simonides said he wrote.* His knowledge was shown in a somewhat similar way in connection with another famous manuscript of the Greek Testament, the Codex Alexandrinus. Mr E. M. Thompson, in his preface to vol. iv. of the facsimile edition of this manuscript (1879), described it as bound up in quires of six leaves each, as indeed is now the case. Bradshaw said he was sure there was something wrong about this, and a closer examination of the manuscript disclosed the fact that the book had been mutilated when it was rebound early in this century. The binder had actually had the audacity to cut the double leaves in halves, and, after remounting them and rejoining the edges, to bind them in quires of six instead of eight, but no one appears to have been aware of this fact till Bradshaw's doubts led to the discovery.†

* See above, p. 95.
† See a paper by C. R. Gregory on "The quires in Greek manuscripts,"

The following instance, one out of many, illustrates his mastery of a science for which we in England have no special name, but which the Germans call *Handscrifts-kunde*, or *Diplomatik*. Mr C. Wordsworth writes to me, " I remember that when I showed him the manuscripts which my father sent for his inspection, he at once guessed the dates of them as 1540 and 1750 respectively. The latter, on closer examination, proved to have a water-mark relating to Culloden (1746), and the other date was verified by a memorandum at the end." A few testimonies from well-known scholars will confirm what I have said.

The Bishop of Oxford writes to me as follows :—" He [Bradshaw] knew, more than any mere critic of ink and paper, the contents of books, and had a really unparalleled power (in my experience) of critical analysis ; able to dis-tinguish *primo morsu* between the original and the insititious parts of texts, even of subjects remote from his favourite studies." Mr Scrivener, asking for some notes on the book of St Chad at Lichfield, writes, " Rough notes from you are better than elaborate treatises from others." Professor Robertson Smith remarks, " He used to say that he was very ignorant of palæography and bibliography. By this he meant that there were lacunæ in his knowledge, as there must always be in the case of a man who refuses to take things at second-hand. But it is also true that his way of dealing with a manuscript or an early printed book was entirely different from the received way, and led him to results which the 'landläufige methode' could never have touched. . . . You know, I suppose, that he was the one man who produced a great impression on Mommsen on his recent visit to England [1885]. Mommsen said to me, ' I will tell you one thing ; it is a small one, but it is charac-

in the *American Journal of Philology*, vol. vii., no. 1. The mutilation is noticed by Mr Thompson in his preface to vol. i. of the facsimile edition, published in 1881.

teristic. I told Mr Bradshaw of a contraction I had seen in a manuscript of the British Museum, which, with all my experience of Pandect manuscripts, I had never seen before. The British Museum people, who have also great knowledge, had not seen it either. When I told it to Mr Bradshaw, he said nothing, but presently brought me a manuscript and showed me the very thing.'"

Professor Robertson Smith continues, "In everything that relates to the history of manuscripts he was *facile princeps*. As to English manuscripts, he could often tell by the writing alone in what monastery they had been written. But he knew all about his manuscripts. I learned from him, for example, a very simple mark, characteristic of Arabic manuscripts written in India, which I don't think any orientalist was aware of till he discovered it." Of several oriental languages he taught himself enough to impress more than one scholar with his knowledge, and this simply with the object of being able to catalogue his manuscripts correctly. Mr Rhys-Davids writes, "At a time when the Pali language and the historical treasures recorded in it were almost unknown, I was agreeably surprised to find that Mr Bradshaw showed not only a keen interest in Pali manuscripts, but a better knowledge of them than was possessed by any one in Europe, except a few specialists who could be counted on one's fingers. But you will doubtless have many and more striking examples of a breadth of sympathy and of a rare and accurate knowledge which filled me with reverence."

Professor Wright, speaking of the Sanskrit manuscripts in the University Library, says, "I often had long conversations with Bradshaw about them, and was surprised to find how much he, though no Sanskritist, really knew about them, and how readily he could assign approximate dates and localities to manuscripts which had no indication of either. Again, as editor of the oriental series of the Palæographical

Society of London, I was anxious to give some specimens of Tibetan manuscripts. I took advantage of a visit
from Professor Schiefner, of St Petersburg, to get him to
select a couple of specimens [from the University Library]
and to describe and transliterate them for my series. Circumstances prevented Dr Schiefner from revising the
descriptions when printed, and as neither I nor any of my
colleagues had any acquaintance with Tibetan, I thought I
should have to lay aside the plates. But to my no small
surprise I found that Bradshaw knew enough of that
language to render me adequate assistance, which I doubt
if any other man in our universities could at that time
have done."

M. Paul Meyer, the first, or one of the first, old-French
scholars of the day, says of him, "Bradshaw était admi-
rablement doué pour le recherche. Il savait, dans l'ensemble
d'un sujet, démêler le point capital à éclaircir, et des re-
marques que personne n'eût songé à faire l'amenaient à
de sûres découvertes. Il connaissait tous les mss. des
'Canterbury Tales,' et en savait la valeur relative." Mr
T. W. Jackson, of Worcester College, writes, "His astonishing familiarity with the manuscripts of the library appeared,
without fail, the moment any question arose. For instance,
I was trying to work out so minute a point as the methods
of ruling Greek manuscripts up to the end of the thirteenth
century, a subject which no one else had, apparently,
attended to. Mr Bradshaw's knowledge was as full and
accurate in this as in all else. It was simply marvellous to
me to see the extent and certainty of it. He knew what I
asked, as if it had been his one speciality, instead of a
minute point among a vast number of greater things.
And he not only knew at once where to go among the
manuscripts, but to the point in any one where a peculiarity
was to be found."

At the same time, with all this knowledge, his modesty

and diffidence led him to shrink from making decided statements, even in a region which he had made so thoroughly his own, unless he had positive proof for his assertion.* Many palæographers are ready enough to assign dates or localities to manuscripts on the mere evidence of their senses. Bradshaw's instinct enabled him to say readily enough what he *thought* of such matters, but he never confused proof with probability. Mr E. M. Thompson could not get him to make a formal statement, even about a manuscript which he knew so well as the "Book of Deer." His Socratic pretence of ignorance seemed to some, who did not know how incapable he was of affectation, to be almost affected. But the limits of his knowledge were always more visible to him than its extent. When questioned about such points by experts, he would say, "Oh, I suppose it is so and so, but you know better than I." Professor Pollock remembers how "he always began by saying that he knew nothing about the matter. During this protest, if it was in talk, he would be sidling up to his bookcase, from which he would take down a book in an apparently casual manner, and produce it open at a page having on it the exact reference or information wanted."

The following letter to Mr S. Sandars (1875) may be quoted as an example of the paternal affection and the dainty care he showed for a pet book. "I am afraid you will be shocked, but as I examined the manuscript you were good enough to give us,† I found it was so precious and so interesting that I could not resist the temptation of taking it to pieces, which I did with the utmost care and gentleness. I have put it into Mr Hawes' hands to rebind in a way worthy of it. It would have been quite im-

---

* The late Mr Coxe, Bodley's Librarian, and not Bradshaw, is the hero of a story told in this connection in an article in *Macmillan's Magazine* for April, 1886, p. 480.

† A little manuscript Rosary, or book of prayers to the Virgin, illustrated with woodcuts.

possible to get at the truth about it without doing what I
have done. . . . My usual tendency, I confess, is to unbind
a thing and leave it so, but for your sake I could not do
this with this manuscript. Several leaves were cruelly
misplaced, but I have made out the whole thing clearly
now, and I shall be very glad to show you how prettily it
all comes out. I did it all on the afternoon of the day you
were here." And then follow a number of interesting
observations on the little book. A final illustration of the
wide human interest which he could attach to a manuscript, may be found in a conversation which Dr Norman
Moore has recorded. "One evening," says Dr Moore, "he
gave me an autotype of the deed * in which the Archbishop of York recognises the supremacy of Canterbury,
marked with the rough 'signum Willelmi regis,' and the
fine 'signum Matilde regine,' and he pointed out the great
Hiberno-Saxon hand of the only Saxon bishop, 'Wulfstan
Wigornensis eps̄,' and the foreign hand of Lanfranc, and
the Italian writing of Hubert, the papal legate. He remarked how one page of writing brought the whole history
of the time before us ; the great king who made his rough
cross by way of signature, and the scholarly Lanfranc of
the new learning of that day, and Wulfstan of the old by-
gone English school ; and how it showed that the old
Norman part of Lincoln Cathedral was not yet begun, for
Remigius, who was to have been its builder and first
bishop, was yet at Dorchester, while the Norfolk bishop
was not at Norwich, but at Thetford, so that the transference of bishops from villages to large towns had hardly
yet come in. He made the whole come out of that deed
without any word-painting or rhetorical ornament, but
merely by letting it tell its own story. This was the way
he learnt and taught history."

* The original is preserved at Canterbury, and is dated 1072.

I have already mentioned incidentally most of Bradshaw's discoveries in this department.* His studies in it were mainly linguistic and documentary. Though not pretending to any intimate knowledge of Celtic dialects, he could not have passed so many years in examining Celtic manuscripts, and in discovering and transcribing glosses, without gaining a considerable amount of linguistic knowledge. Though he complained of his ignorance of Celtic, "he knew enough," says Professor Rhys, "both of Welsh and Irish not to be impeded in his palæographical researches by lack of acquaintance with those languages." His "finds" in the manuscripts at Cambridge and Oxford, in France and elsewhere, added immensely to the vocabulary which had already been put together by Celtic scholars. It is hardly too much to say that he almost rediscovered the old Breton language. He not only found many traces of it previously unknown, but he distinguished its earliest remains, hitherto confused with Cornish or Welsh, from those of the sister-dialects. In tracing manuscripts, thought to be of British origin, back to their continental home in the Armorican peninsula, he based his conclusions primarily on palæographical evidence, but, having fixed his documents in a certain locality, he then brought comparative philology to bear, and elicited important linguistic results. His distinctions between Breton, Cornish, and Old Welsh have been adopted by Celtic scholars ; for instance (as Mr Whitley Stokes informs me), by Ebel, in his edition of Zeuss.† Professor Rhys, speaking of the differences between these early languages, says in a letter to me, "The difference is very small, but his

---

* For instance, the "Book of Deer" (above, p. 69), the glosses in the "Juvencus," in "Martianus Capella," the "Hibernensis," etc. (pp. 72, 178, 229, 238).

† Zeuss, "Grammatica Celtica," 2nd edit., 1871.

palæographic evidence settles it;" * and again, " There was
nobody who knew so much about Celtic manuscripts, or,
at any rate, where to look for Celtic things."

Bradshaw's work on the early collection of ecclesiastical
canons known as the " Hibernensis" has already been
noticed (p. 306). In his introduction to the " Hibernensis "
(1885), Dr Wasserschleben, while discussing at considerable
length the origin of the code, confines his attention almost
entirely to an examination of its contents, and leaves out
of sight the palæographical considerations on which Bradshaw lays so much stress. He hardly notices the connection
with Brittany which Bradshaw points out, and he dismisses
the question of authorship with the words : " It is, however, a matter of slight importance whether the author was
an Irishman or not : that the work was intended for the
Irish Church, and contains numerous ordinances of Irish
law, is indisputable, and that is the decisive point." † Into
the question *where* the code was drawn up, or where the
existing manuscripts were written, he hardly enters at all,
except in his remarks on Bradshaw's paper.

Bradshaw's attention was originally drawn to the " Hibernensis " when Dr Stubbs and the late Mr Haddan were
preparing their work on the councils. Afterwards, while
engaged in looking for traces of the old Celtic languages,
a number of copies of the book came under his notice, and
his palæographical and philological researches combined
led him to form certain theories respecting the origin of
the code and other points connected with it, which he set
forth very briefly in his " Memorandum " (No. 8) on the
subject. The chief of these conclusions may be summarised
as follows.

The existing manuscripts which contain copies of the
" Hibernensis " were all written on the Continent. Five of

---

* See Professor Rhys' "Lectures on Welsh Philology," 2nd edit., p. 259.
† " " Die Irische Kanonensammlung,' 2nd edit., 1885 ; Einleitung, p. xiv

them contain Breton, not Irish, glosses, and must have been written in Brittany; others, though not written in Brittany, are closely connected with the former. Several of these manuscripts show signs of having been derived from still older manuscripts now lost, which were of Irish origin; while the titles of certain pieces, annexed in these manuscripts to the canons, also point to Ireland. Brittany is the only district on the Continent in which certain conditions indicated by the manuscripts—for instance, the juxtaposition of British, Irish, and Frankish documents—were to be found. The books themselves were, on the decay of Celtic institutions in Brittany, transferred from their original homes to the great monasteries of the new life, in which they remained till the Revolution removed them to their present resting-places. These conclusions, which Bradshaw sets forth in the barest and briefest way, he unfortunately never lived to substantiate, though he had collected a mass of evidence for the purpose. They remain a series of assertions which it will be the duty of other scholars to test, and probably to establish.

In the course of these investigations, Bradshaw was led to inquire into the origin and nature of the curious Low-Latin poems known as the "Hisperica Famina." These poems were printed by Cardinal Mai in 1833.* He says little about them, except that they are alluded to by the grammarian Virgilius, and that any lover of classical Latin would devote them to the Furies. He does not appear to have been aware of any manuscript but that in the Vatican; at all events, he does not mention the Luxemburg manuscript. Bradshaw, who carefully examined the latter, and collated it (with Dr. Luard's aid) with the Vatican manuscript, was attracted to this strange relic of barbarous Latinity by the Celtic glosses which it contains. In order

* In his "Auctores Classicie Vaticanis codicibus editi," vol. v. pp. 479-500. Cf. above, p. 188.

to ascertain their meaning, he had first to understand the Latin. The following specimen will show that this was no easy task. It is from what appears to be a description of sunrise.

> "Titaneus olympic*um* inflammat arotus tabulat*um*,
> thalassic*um* illustrat vapore flustr*um*,
> flammivomo sectat pol*um* corusco supern*um*,
> alm*i* scandit cameram firmament*i*.
> . . . Aligera placore*um* reboat curia concent*um*,
> tinul*as* patul*is* murmurat harmoni*as* rostr*is*,
> concav*os* aurium refoculant mulcedine cliv*os*," etc.

These lines are printed by Mai as prose. Bradshaw observed that the clauses of the original are, roughly speaking, of about the same length, and that each clause contains one or two pairs of rhyming words.* He came to the conclusion that they were intended for lines of poetry, a conclusion borne out by the style and language of the production. The glosses and the words which they were meant to explain threw mutual light on each other, and eventually he succeeded in "construing" the whole poem. Writing to Mr Hessels, in March, 1874, he says: "The words I gave you are all from a poem called 'Hisperica Famina.' . . . It is by an Irishman, and must be of the ninth or tenth century. It has been an immense help to me. I have copied the whole thing out (more than six hundred lines) as verse, and I have so got the meaning of numbers of words which have been puzzling me for many years. . . . It is very queer Latin ; but it happens to have had a special interest for me. I want to print it with a commentary." Unfortunately, he never carried out this project, nor do I know whether he had any idea who was the author.†

---

* I have italicised the rhymes to make the system, if such it may be called, more apparent. What I have said in the text is based on my own recollection. I have been unable to ascertain anything further from others.

† Dr Wordsworth, Bishop of Salisbury, refers me to an epitaph in Hübner's "Inscriptiones Hispaniæ Christianæ," on a certain Bishop of Auria, in which

In the early records of British history, the works of
Gildas and Nennius, Bradshaw was also much interested.
It was in connection with the former that his erudition
and originality made so much impression on Professor
Mommsen, whom he succeeded in convincing of the
authenticity, in the main, of the work attributed to Gildas.
In his conversations with Dr Norman Moore, Nennius was
a frequent topic. Bradshaw believed that a minute examination of the Latin text would reveal the original work
imbedded in twelfth-century additions and ornamented by
phrases from the Vulgate. He projected a journey to Rome
in order to examine the Vatican manuscript, and he wished
to see the oldest Irish fragment of Nennius, which dates
from about 1100, printed at the University Press.

ECCLESIASTICAL ANTIQUITIES.

There were few things which Bradshaw worked out
more thoroughly than the history of mediæval service-
books, but almost his only published work in this direction is contained in the prefaces to the Cambridge edition
of the Sarum Breviary;* in the appendix to Mr Hope's
" Chronicles of the Collegiate Church of All Saints, Derby,"
for which he drew up a list and description of mediæval
English service-books in general; and in Mr Lawley's
edition of the York Breviary,† in which is a list of York
Breviaries drawn up by him. He declared himself more
than once to be ignorant of what is called liturgiology.
What he meant, apparently, was that he had not paid much
attention to the *origins* of mediæval liturgies. But of the
services of the Church in the later middle ages he had a
profound knowledge, and he always considered this one of
his favourite subjects. Mr W. J. Weale tells me that he

the following lines occur :—"Cuius arca tenet hæc sacra membra, inaula
Personat *esperio* illius *famine* fota." It is possible that this may give a clue.

* See above, chap. ix.

† Surtees Society's Publications, vol. lxxi p xiii.

never knew any one not a Catholic with anything like
the same knowledge of mediæval liturgies. Bradshaw's
analytical skill stood him in good stead here. He anato-
mised his books and manuscripts, and, as has been said of
Johnson's criticism, he reduced everything to its elements,
and so traced the steps by which the English Prayer-book
and its Catholic predecessors grew up. And the knowledge
thus acquired, like that of all other subjects which he had
mastered, he had at his fingers' ends. Once in conversation
with Mr Wordsworth, the talk turning on Sarum Breviaries
printed in Queen Mary's reign, he took a sheet of paper
and wrote down from memory a full and accurate list of
these editions, seven in number, with dates, printers' names,
and other particulars.* This list, I need hardly say, had
not been previously drawn up by any scholar.

His knowledge of this subject won the admiration of
many distinguished students in the same field. Dr
Henderson,† dean of Carlisle, writes, " Of these books [Eng-
lish service-books] and their contents his knowledge was
equally exact and extensive, and I never put a question
to him, that I can remember, without getting a full and
satisfactory answer. His enthusiasm about the many
Cambridge ritual treasures was most delightful ; and most
encouraging, too, was his sympathy with research among
them." Mr J. Wickham Legg‡ says, " His liturgical attainments were something extraordinary. One had to go back
to the Benedictine ritualists of the beginning of the last
century to find his equal. And his head teemed with ideas,
far more sound and fertile than those of Claude de Vert."

The sympathy of which Dr Henderson speaks was
abundantly shown in the readiness with which he communicated his discoveries to other scholars. Mr French,

---

* See the Cambridge edition of the Sarum Breviary, fasc. iii. p. xlii., note.
† Editor of the Hereford Missal (1874), the York Pontifical (1875), etc.
‡ Author of " Notes on the History of the Liturgical Colours " (1882).

of Trinity College Library (Dublin), remembers how delighted he was at finding there a copy of a York Breviary and a York Missal not noticed by the authorities. "He walked up and down the room, chuckling with delight, and saying he would have a laugh at Dr Henderson, who had not mentioned the books in his list." And he promptly wrote off to Dr Henderson to inform him of his find.

The following extract from a letter to Mr Weale gives his views on the best manner of editing mediæval rituals :— "I should not adopt a vigorously uniform spelling, or anything like it. What people ordinarily do is to modernise everything, as they call it, which is to write everything as we were taught to write Latin when we were boys—that is, neither as the real ancients did it, nor as the most modern scholars do. I should keep a normal Middle-Age spelling without being pedantic in the matter, if that is possible. . . . I mean that I should not mind being inconsistent, provided I didn't put my own crotchets in place of the old scribe's habits."

Of his work on the Lincoln statutes I have already spoken. He could not have done it without an extensive knowledge of mediæval cathedral organisation in general, and he used that knowledge to elucidate the history of other cathedrals as well. For instance, Bishop Abraham informs me that, through his intimate acquaintance with the relations between deans and canons in the twelfth and thirteenth centuries, he was able to set right the history of the Lichfield statutes in some important particulars, which Dugdale had confused.* That he could bring his knowledge to bear on modern problems, the following reminiscences by Dr Benson, Archbishop of Canterbury, will testify. Dr Benson says—

---

* See Dugdale's "Monasticon" (edit. 1830), vol. vi. part 3, pp. 12-55, *et seq.*

"The last piece of work he did with me and for me was after the statutes for a new cathedral [Truro] had been drafted in full detail, when it became necessary to re-examine and verify the precedents of everything which was old, and to make sure of the genuineness and consistency of the principles of each point of departure into the modern world. Busy as he was all day at Cambridge, how often would his cab-wheels stop at the little door of Lollard's Tower late on in the evening; and he would sit carefully reviewing point by point, illustrating with amazing and amusing erudition, and emphasising thus : 'Yes, the bishop is of course a canon among the canons; first of them, but always a canon.' 'What a misconception of the whole thing at Lincoln Exeter, etc., to have separated their prebendal stalls from the bishop and officers—all for nothing !' 'No; Bayeux, not Rouen. The three great codes of Sarum, Lincoln, and York came not from Rouen, as the founders themselves believed, but only through Rouen, from Bayeux. The real mother is Bayeux.' 'Osmund, Remigius and Thomas had conferences. It is the only way in which these exact correspondences and differences can be accounted for—and I find that they had.' 'Certainly ; no principle hinders the bishop from acting as dean, if it is convenient, nor the highest canon from being subdean.' 'Canon missioner? of course, if you want him. Quite analogical.' No labour or research was too much if it set the smallest fact quite truly. One question was of the exact relation of the great officers, or departmental heads of cathedral work, to each other. Between visit and visit he collected from authentic sources, verified, and wrote out with his own hand, all the capitular offices of the cathedral churches of France, and of other parts of Europe beside—a thickish volume of foolscap—just to exhibit how living and unmechanical such arrangements had once been, and ought to be."

Chaucer, etc.

In connection with this subject, something should first be said on the state of Chaucer criticism twenty-five years ago, in order that we may appreciate what Bradshaw did for the poet. When he began to study Chaucer, the criticism of that poet's works had hardly advanced at all beyond the point at which Tyrwhitt left it nearly a century before. The first collective edition of Chaucer, that of William Thynne, was published in 1532. It formed the basis of all subsequent editions for nearly two hundred and fifty years. Thynne was not critical, but editor after editor followed him with slavish fidelity, only adding now and then to the body of spurious poems. Modern criticism of Chaucer begins with Tyrwhitt, who in 1775–8 published his edition of the "Canterbury Tales." *

Tyrwhitt made a great advance upon his predecessors. He struck the true note of criticism by basing his emendations on a study of the manuscripts, and on the internal evidence of the poems themselves. He was the first to recognise that the "Canterbury Tales" were left by their author in an unfinished state, and that the conventional order in which they had been placed was incorrect. He restored the "Tales" in some measure to their right order; he rejected as clearly spurious the tale of Gamelyn and many of the minor poems hitherto attributed to Chaucer; and he based his sketch of the poet's life on the evidence of documents, instead of on the dangerous ground of supposed allusions in his works. At the same time he had not fully grasped the fragmentary nature of Chaucer's greatest work, and he seems to have been unaware of any test beyond the evidence of the manuscripts by which to try the authenticity of the other poems.

* A second edition was published in 1798, with a few improvements and additions.

Subsequent editors, till a short time back, were content to reproduce Tyrwhitt's edition, with very little change. The only real advance made was due to Sir Harris Nicolas, who published the first full and trustworthy life of the poet in 1843, a life based almost entirely on documentary evidence. This life is published in the Aldine (or Bell's) edition of 1866, which, however, differs in very few important particulars from Tyrwhitt's. The edition of 1866 retains Tyrwhitt's order of the "Tales," except in one instance, and inserts almost all the poems which Tyrwhitt accepted, but which are now regarded as spurious, such as the "Romaunt of the Rose," the "Flower and the Leaf," and the "Cuckoo and the Nightingale."

It was about 1866 that Bradshaw, who had for some time past been studying Chaucer, began to be known as a master of the subject. In that year he projected a treatise, which he entitled, "An attempt to ascertain the state of Chaucer's Works as they were left at his death, with some notices of their subsequent history." The introductory pages of this treatise, which are all that I have been able to find among his papers, state the author's intention of examining what works were attributed to Chaucer by himself or his contemporaries; what works we have still remaining which appear to correspond with these; what works are attributed to him before 1532, and subsequently to that date; and what works, not yet recognised as his, may reasonably be assigned to him. This being done, he proposed further to give some account of the history of the text of each work, dividing them into five groups according to their metre, the prose works being in a sixth group. Unfortunately, he appears to have gone no further with this plan.

What he ultimately did for the study of Chaucer may be considered under two heads—his work on the "Canterbury Tales," and his work on the minor poems. He was

led by the study of the manuscripts to the conclusion that
the " Tales," as we have them, are merely a series of fragments, written by Chaucer at different times, some early,
some late in life, and never compacted into a finished whole.
Chaucer went some way towards weaving these fragments
together by means of introductions, which the older editors
called prologues. Bradshaw preferred to call all these
introductory pieces " links," end-links or beginning-links,
a sort of hook-and-eye arrangement, capable of adaptation
or change. Long before the invention of printing, the
scribe-editors, finding discrepancies and gaps, had tried to
set things straight, by shifting the links from one place to
another, sometimes omitting them altogether and even
inventing fresh links of their own, in order to give the
poem the appearance of a complete and finished work.

To unravel all this confusion, Bradshaw went back to
the manuscripts, and, by means of analysis and comparison,
broke up the whole work into twelve fragments, or groups
of tales, some containing as many as five or six tales,
others only one. In his " Skeleton of Chaucer's Canterbury Tales," * after classifying the manuscripts in three
families, and pointing out the chief characteristics of each
family, he gives a table of these fragments, marking the
gaps, as shown by the want of fitting links, wherever they
occur. " The critics," he says (p. 17), " have unfortunately
looked upon Chaucer's great work as simply a collection of
twenty-four tales, each preceded by a prologue introducing
the next narrator. Until this notion is thoroughly up-
rooted, the poem must remain an inextricable mass of
confusion. On the other hand, as soon as we perceive
that the author composed the work piece-meal, with the
intention of finally working all his pieces into one harmonious whole, this confusion disappears. Every one
allows that this finishing process was never reached by the

* Memorandum, No. 8 (1868).

author, so that it remains for us to make the best of the several fragments that have come down to us. We must look upon these fragments as so many portions of the story of the Canterbury pilgrimage, into which the tales are introduced ; the so-called prologues then become the main line of the action of the poem, and in each fragment we shall see that the story is taken up at one point and dropped at another, without a clear reference to what has gone before or what is to follow."

Of his relations to Tyrwhitt on this point Bradshaw himself says, in a letter to Dr Furnivall (August 7, 1868), " As for the originality, I, of course, never laid claim to any new facts. My only point is my method, which I always insist on in anything in bibliography—arrange your facts vigorously and get them plainly before you, and let them *speak for themselves*, which they will always do. Tyrwhitt saw that certain links, like the Merchant's, Squire's and Franklin's prologues, had a much better meaning when arranged according to the best manuscripts, than they had in the confusion of the old editions ; but he was nowhere near avowing the fragment system as a *principle*, nor of distinguishing much between what was spurious and what was cast off, except in two cases, nor of seeing that, if a Tale was without a prologue in one manuscript and with one in another, it is quite possible that Chaucer may have written that prologue *afterwards*, with a view of linking two tales together, which yet might quite well stand far apart in a previous state of the composition."

After breaking the poem up into fragments, the next point was to ascertain their order. Some improvement in this respect had been made by Tyrwhitt, but the received arrangement still introduced many incongruities and ab- surdities. It was impossible to bring the mentions of time and place into accordance with the facts of a journey from London to Canterbury in the fourteenth century. Rochester and Sittingbourne, for example, were transposed, and the journey was crammed into one day. The key to this difficulty had not been found, until Bradshaw, acting on the evidence of one of the best manuscripts, shifted his tenth fragment into the third place. In a letter to Dr Furnivall, dated September 21, 1868, he suggested this new view. "Better and better," he says, "everything comes straight with the 'Canterbury Tales,' more so than I could possibly have dared to expect. I enclose you a pretty little programme of the whole affair, and see if it does not look charming." And then follow four closely written sheets, in which the change of order and an extension of the time occupied by the journey are shown to solve all, or nearly all the difficulties. "At once," says Dr Furnivall,[*] "the whole scheme came right. Rochester got into its proper place, the journey turned into the regular three or four days' one, and all the allusions to time, place, former tales, etc., were at once harmonized." Many subsequent letters passed between Bradshaw and Dr Furnivall on this and kindred points. There still appears to be some doubt about the duration of the journey, but Bradshaw's views about the fragments and their order have been generally accepted in principle, and his influence has drawn the lines on which the Chaucer Society has worked.[†]

We may now pass to his work on the minor poems. In distinguishing the spurious from the genuine, Bradshaw applied two touchstones—the evidence of the manuscripts, and what has been called the "rhyme-test." He hardly ever relied on one of these criteria alone. His criticism was irresistible when it appeared that poems, for the

---

[*] *Macmillan's Magazine*, March, 1874. See, too, Dr Furnivall's Temporary Preface, Chaucer Society's Publications, 1868.

[†] Professor Skeat's views about the "Canterbury Tales" are given in his edition of the "Prioresses Tale" (Clarendon Press Series), p. xii. What is now believed to be the correct order is set forth in the Bohn Series edition (1878), vol. ii. p. 352.

authenticity of which the manuscripts refused to vouch, gave way also under the other test. As to the verdict of the manuscripts little need be said. For some pieces attributed to Chaucer there is no manuscript evidence at all ; for others it is too slight to hold out against attack from other sides. The rhyme-test needs more explanation. Professor Skeat has been kind enough to write to me about it as follows :—

"Long before much general interest was taken in Chaucer's rhymes, Bradshaw perceived their great importance as a critical test. In order to make use of this test, he compiled a complete list of all the rhymes used in poems attributed to Chaucer, keeping each poem separate. By comparison of these lists, he was able to say, definitely, that the rhymes occurring in poems known to be genuine differed from those in poems which were probably spurious. He told us, for instance, that Chaucer never rhymes a word which, *etymologically*, ends in -*y* with a word which, *etymologically*, ends in -*ye*. This test is quite independent of the spelling adopted by the scribes, who constantly confuse these suffixes ; it depends solely on the actual origin of the word and its consequent pronunciation in the fourteenth century. All adverbs which now end in -*ly*, such as *trewely* (truly), *feithfully* (faithfully), and the like, belong to the former class. On the other hand, there are a large number of words which, in modern Italian, end in -*ia*, such as *cortesia* (courtesy), *follia* (folly). These words, in Old French likewise, had a final -*e* (in place of the Italian -*a*), which formed a distinct syllable, and the same syllable remained distinct in Chaucer's English. That is to say, these words were pronounced by Chaucer as *curteisy-e* (in four syllables), and *foly-e* (in three). And just as, in Italian, it would be absurd to suppose that a word like *si* could rhyme with *cortesi-a*, so likewise, in Chaucer's English, we cannot expect that such a word as *feithfull-y* can rhyme with *foly-e*.

But Chaucer's English is quite of an archaic character. He kept up these distinctions at a time when the language itself was rapidly losing them. Consequently, though these rules are observed by himself and by Gower, later writers, such as Lydgate, ignored them, and a large number of such rhymes, which are not found in Chaucer, constantly appear in imitations of him. To take an instance—the 'Court of Love,' a poem which some who are ignorant of the history of our language impute to Chaucer, is really a production of the end of the fifteenth or the beginning of the sixteenth century. Consequently, it necessarily fails to fulfil such a test as the above. Glancing at it, we find, in stanza 31, that the monosyllabic pronoun *I* is rhymed with the dissyllabic present tense *dy-e* (I die) ; or, to take a more palpable and easier example, we find, in stanza 164, that the word *company-e* (Old Fr. *compani-e*, Ital. *compagni-a*) is made to rhyme with an adverb in *-ly*, viz. *faithfull-y*. This is, of course, quite enough to condemn it, and it is, at the same time, an excellent example of Bradshaw's method. He was thus enabled to say definitely that many of the poems recklessly and persistently ascribed to Chaucer constantly transgress the rules which Chaucer strictly observes, and are therefore spurious."

Bradshaw was the first person in England to apply the rhyme-test to Chaucer's poems. It was simultaneously and independently applied by Professor ten Brink in Germany, and these two scholars arrived at almost identical results. Many lovers of Chaucer were naturally loth to give up their cherished beliefs on the subject. Dr Furnivall fought hard and long for the "Romaunt of the Rose," but was at length compelled to give way. Professor Skeat found additional evidence against it in the fact that it is written in a northern dialect.* Other well-known poems

---

* Cf. Professor Skeat's paper, " Why the 'Romaunt of the Rose' is not Chaucer's" (Chaucer Soc. Publ., 2nd series, 1884).

like the "Flower and the Leaf," "Chaucer's Dream," etc., had also to be surrendered. Bradshaw's own position on the subject is shown by the following letters. Writing to Professor ten Brink on July 1, 1870, he says, "About the 'Romaunt of the Rose,' I cut the knot by saying that there is no *authority* whatever for considering this version which we have Chaucer's, and therefore the *onus probandi* lies with those who make it so. Of popular works we know that there were several (sometimes four) English versions, and the rhymes, etc., exactly accord here with the laws followed by the writers of the generation following Chaucer."

On January 12, 1872, he writes to Dr Furnivall as follows :—" I am afraid you don't see my point about 'Blaunche.' When a man tells me he wrote a poem on the death of the Duchess Blaunche, who died in 1369, and I find a poem on that subject in several volumes containing undoubted poems of his, I accept that poem as his, until I know that some one else wrote a poem on the subject and that this is that. When a man tells me he made a translation of one of the most popular French works going, and I find part of *a* translation, with nothing whatever in its surroundings to point it out as Chaucer's, *I do not accept it as his* until I have better ground for doing so. But I do not deny it to be his, because denying is not my business. The experience afforded by the Troy book,* warns me against taking rashly any translation of a popular work to be the very one I am in search of. . . . The case of an original poem is surely on a very different footing from a translation of a very popular work.

" The fact is, you want me to lay down the law dogmatically, and I don't wish to do anything of the kind. I give my reason for accepting certain pieces until they are proved to be not his, and I also give my reasons for not accepting

---

* See above, p. 134.

certain things which are not proved to be his. But in no case do I lay down as a certainty either that the one set of things are his, or the other not his. . . .

"In all this you observe there is no word of the final *e* question. I had reached this point before I had any cause to look at that matter. It was only on examining the 'Parlement of Foules' and one or two other poems in the rhymes, in order to get at the normal forms used by Chaucer (however much disguised by variety of spelling), that I was led to observe a difference between the English equivalents of terminations in -*ere*, -*am*, -*iam*, and of those in -*um*, etc. The more I searched the more curious it seemed, and at last, when I had been through and through everything over and over again dozens of times, I could not fail to be struck with the difference between those poems which I had been led temporarily to accept as having authority, and those which I had been led provisionally to exclude for want of due authority. It was a coincidence of a very *taking* nature, and I confess I was very much taken by it. You must only do me the justice to allow that I never did dogmatise on the subject. I am searching for facts, and a provisional hypothesis is constantly the only possible means we have of grouping any collection of facts, for the purpose of getting us a step further.

"What you say of a life and death question, and an infallible test of genuineness, is utterly and entirely out of my beat, and appears to me utterly unscientific. We never can know for certain what pieces are Chaucer's and what are not, and yet we are never content without an infallible test on the subject. I am quite content to know that my work in that line has given me a firmer hold on what little knowledge I have of early English than I should ever have had without it."

It was like Bradshaw that he refused to claim any credit for these discoveries. Letters on this subject by

Mr Payne Collier having appeared in the *Athenæum* for March, 1869, he wrote a letter to Mr Collier, dated April 23, 1867, from which the following is an extract :—

" DEAR SIR,
          " I have just seen the *Athenæum*, with your request that I should say something about the prior critics and the ' Testament of Love ' . . .

          " I have been so constantly, for the last six years, dinning into the ears of all whom I come across—Mr Furnivall and Mr R. Morris among the number—the total want of trustworthy evidence in favour of attributing to Chaucer any of the following pieces :—' The Romaunt of the Rose,' 'The. Court of Love,' ' The Flower and. the Leaf,' ' The Cuckow and the Nightingale,' ' Chaucer's Dream,' ' The Testament of Love,' ' The Complaint of the Black Knight,' and other smaller pieces, both from an external and an internal examination of them, and that not as a discovery of my own, but as self-evident to any one who will take the trouble to apply the simplest canons of criticism on the subject,—that it seems that the writer of the Early English Text Society's report had begun to fancy that this was the recognised view.

          " Living as I do in charge of a very large library, where all I find is instantly at the service of my neighbours, I find but little leisure to put my results into print, and I have to content myself with the humbler position of helping students by oral communication ; but I am only too thankful to find, from such men as Ebert and Hertzberg and yourself, independent confirmation of my results the moment any of you apply your criticism to the point. I should be the last to wish to deprive you of the credit of being the first to notice in print the incongruity of calling the ' Testament of Love ' Chaucer's.

                    " Yours most truly,
                         " HENRY BRADSHAW."

The discoveries which I have mentioned, though they were Bradshaw's most important contributions to Chaucer criticism, do not by any means exhaust the list. To his sympathetic and imaginative criticism is due, among other things, as Professor ten Brink points out to me, "the startling discovery of the hidden meaning of the 'Complaint of Mars.'" He studied with much assiduity the sources whence Chaucer drew his inspiration, though here again he did not publish his conclusions. He only communicated them to Dr Furnivall and others, and the publication of them was anticipated by Professor ten Brink. Writing to Mr Wheatley in 1883, he says, " It was this very fact of Chaucer's uniqueness in the matter of acquaintance with Italian literature, at his own time and for more than a century afterwards, that led me first to give up the early date of the poems, and to make his Italian embassy a turning-point in his history and work. This conclusion was arrived at independently by ten Brink, while Kissner had already pointed out the Dante and Petrarch points." He brought to light more than one poem of Chaucer's previously unknown ; for instance, the " Ætas Prima," or " Former Age," published by Dr R. Morris in his edition of 1866, and the earlier version of the prologue to the " Legend of Good Women," and he was even able to add to or correct some particulars in Chaucer's life which the researches of Sir Harris Nicolas had failed to ascertain.

The bibliography of the poet was, it is almost needless to say, at his fingers' ends. " I wrote to him one day," says Professor Skeat, " with a request for information as to the old black-letter editions of Chaucer, not reckoning the editions of separate works by Caxton and others. He at once took a pen, and there and then, without a pause, wrote out a complete list, with title, date, size, and other particulars of each edition." *

* This list is published in Professor Skeat's edition of the " Astrolabe "

Scattered up and down in the publications of the Chaucer Society, and in the works of various Chaucer scholars, will be found many references to Bradshaw's labours, as well as grateful acknowledgments of his assistance. Dr R. Morris writes, "Mr Bradshaw was very helpful to me. . . . His knowledge of the early English manuscripts in the public library and elsewhere was unrivalled, and he was always willing to tell all he knew to a scholar." Dr Furnivall, writing to him in 1879, says, "In all important matters you have led me. My Chaucer work was done for you."

Nor did he by any means confine himself to Chaucer. He could not have done for Chaucer what he did had he not been conversant with the whole range of mediæval English literature. Professor Skeat received valuable assistance from him in editing "William of Palerne," and adopted that title in deference to his suggestion. He received still more aid in editing "Lancelot of the Laik," and "Piers Plowman." The intensity of his love for these studies is witnessed by the following extract from a diary in which M. Jusserand, one of the most distinguished foreign students of our literature,* noted down his recollections of a visit to Cambridge in 1878 :—"Allés ensemble à la bibliothèque de l'Université voir les mss. L'un d'eux, un ms. de Chaucer,† contient un texte complet et excellent. C'est un des favoris de M. Bradshaw. Il en parle avec amour et en touche les pages avec respect. Il m'en lit des passages et, au ton qu'il y met, on sent qu'il n'est pas si uniquement homme de faits positifs qu'il le dit. Il sent, il se délecte, il est touché."

(Chaucer Society, ser. i., vol. 29, 1872), p. xxvi. ; and in the preface to his edition of Chaucer (Bohn series), p. 3.

* Author of an Essay on "Chaucer's *Pardoner:* his character illustrated by documents of his time" (Chaucer Soc. Publ. 2nd series, 1884) ; and "Les Anglais au moyen âge, etc." 1884.

† Univ. Library, Gg. 4. 27.

In conclusion, I cannot refrain from quoting the generous
testimony contained in the following letter from Professor
Skeat, which was written on the occasion of his election to
the Professorship of Anglo-Saxon in 1878 * :—

"Dear Bradshaw,

"*Now* let me say what I wanted to say before,
but could not so well as now. You shall put your own
interpretation on your work—and I will allow you to know
best. But, at the same time, it is for *me* to know what
you have been for me and what you have done for me.
In my beginning to study, I was, with the best of intentions, all abroad. I could not read a manuscript; I did
not know what a manuscript was. I wanted to read books,
but did not know what books. I wanted to understand
Chaucer's rhymes (or rimes) and his grammar, and his
ways in general, and I had none but vague ideas. And
in hundreds of ways I wanted to know (and I still want
to know) all sorts of things more or less connected with
manuscripts or literature. Well, it is the merest truth that
it is, practically, to you that I owe all my best ideas. You
have set me thinking where I was before thoughtless; you
have helped me to read manuscripts; you have told me
of this or that book or edition, over and over again, and
thrown out hints (so thankfully received), and told me of
points, and, in fact, helped me, in and out, in hundreds
of ways and thousands of times. Your remarks have
always been *treasured ;* some have seemed wrong to me
at first, but they generally *came* right, and I can only say
that I never remember a remark of yours that was not
received with profound thankfulness and with a determination to follow it out. It is merely and perfectly hopeless

---

* Professor Skeat, in a letter to me dated August 25, 1886, says, "Of
course I fully meant and mean it [the above letter], and you are at liberty to
do as you please with it."

for me to say how much more I owe to you than to any-
one else, be the others who they may ; how I have felt
this for years ; how it has underlain all my remarks to
you, even the most combative ; and, to speak in a word,
how great is the respect entertained for you by

" Yours *most* sincerely,

" W. W. SKEAT."

EARLY PRINTING.

The subject of early printing was one which occupied
Henry Bradshaw perhaps more continuously than any
other, and in none did he accomplish more.   His retentive
memory and his extraordinary accuracy of eye were
qualities invaluable to him in this department of study.
The lapse of time never appeared to efface or even blur
the impression once made upon his mind.   He never
forgot a specimen of type which he had once examined,
and a single page, or even a tiny fragment of a page, would
often enable him to name the book to which it belonged,
its printer, and its date.   The mass of details in his mind
never led to confusion.   Each fact was recorded and
retained for years, until it fell into its place as a link in
a long chain of evidence tending to some definite conclusion.

But the acute observation of varieties in type was only
one of many ways by which he approached the problems
connected with the early history of printing.   He regarded
the printers of the fifteenth century as artists, and printing
as an art, almost in the same sense as that in which
painting and engraving are arts.   Letters in those days
were not mere machine-made symbols : the hand of the
craftsman was visible in them ; they possessed a sort of
character and individuality, like the works of Dürer or
Marc-Antonio.   Masters in the art impressed their peculiarities on their pupils ; we see Caxton using the sharp

pointed letters which Colard Mansion loved. Each country, each town, had its school or schools ; according to a favourite theory of Bradshaw's, typography followed, like trade, the course of rivers, so that books printed on the upper Danube display special characteristics—distinct, for instance, from those printed on the Rhine or Main. Each printer had his own habits, too, of following his trade, his own way of using hyphens, or of finishing his lines. Thus the study of early printing is like the study of any other art— a study of character and processes, of almost infinite variety.

Keeping the printer before him as a *man*, not a machine, Bradshaw studied all his peculiarities, his type, his paper, his water-marks, his bindings—everything, in short, that could throw light on his history and his method. "The only way," he writes to Mr Francis Fry, in January, 1882— "the only way really to find out about these things is to take all a man's books which he is known to have printed—or, at any rate, such as can be got at—and to study his habits of printing ; not only his type and cuts, but also his habits of using these materials. . . . I have done something among fifteenth-century printers, and therefore know how to set to work ; but I really do not know three people in Europe now living who study things in this way."

The following extracts from letters to Mr G. I. F. Tupper, written in November, 1863, illustrate the imaginative sympathy which placed him so readily in touch with the men whose works he studied. "I have just found," he writes, "an 'Image of Pity'*. . . . It is very curious altogether, because it is not a separate quarto leaf, but on the blank page at the end of a little book printed at Antwerp by Matthias van der Goes about 1487. It is

---

* *i.e.* an Indulgence with a woodcut on it called by that name : see his paper on it in the Communications of the Cambr. Ant. Society, vol. iii. p. 181.

University Library, Cambridge
6th May 1870

Dear Mr Tupper,

I am sorry to hear you
have been unwell. I see
it is quite useless to attempt
to explain by letter what
is passing through my
mind, so I shall look
forward with pleasure
to your being able to run
down here some day.

The whole thing to me is
a contribution to the history
of art. You know the
painters occur in the old
inventories generally as

goldsmiths, and the period
during which there was so
much individuality—about
the types, is certainly the most
interesting. It is a branch of an

I am far from confining
my attention to English
work. Only starting from
that which one has the
best & fullest means of
studying, I then go to
Holland & Belgium the
adjoining countries from
which our art proceeded,
& I there find the cuts
from which ours were
with greater or less skill &

variation copied. Take the
delicate cuts in the Haarlem
Bartholomeus of 1485 &
compare them with the copies
executed for W de Werde's
edition of (1496). So with
the different towns in
Holland — You see where
the schools of original
engraving were instantly,
& where the mere copies
were produced, & where
thirdly, from there being no
school of engraving at all,
borrowed cuts only were
made use of An hour or
two here among my Dutch &

Flemish XV century books,
would do your heart good.
If I live, I can diverge to
Germany (which I have studied
a little) France & Italy — But
as with painting, these schools
are very different. & I am
confident that a gradual
mastery is the one, method
which is likely to lead to
any satisfactory result.

Don't trouble yourself to
acknowledge this. I shall
not tax you with want of
interest, & I know how
valuable your time is.
Yours most truly,
Henry Bradshaw

upside down, and not taken off in printing ink, but in a
pale brown sloppy stuff, which has not taken at all well,
and it is consequently not very pretty to look at. I have
no doubt the Antwerp book was lying in Caxton's shop,
and one of his men took a sort of proof impression in this
way. At least, some such explanation seems possible."
The explanation was not clear enough for Mr Tupper,
so two days later he writes again. "I don't wonder at
your not understanding my description of the 'Image of
Pity.'. . . . Imagine a quarto pamphlet. . . . Fancy then the
book coming into your possession, and your having in your
room a wood-cut block with some type in the sill ; and
then fancy your running the block and type over, not
with lithographic ink, but with some extremely dirty water
or other pale brown thin liquid, and then pressing down
upon it the above-described blank page of the Antwerp
book, and your not caring enough about the matter to
notice that you were taking off the impression upside down
when compared with the printed matter on the other side
or *recto* of the same leaf. Fancy this, if you can, and you
have what we have here."

A letter written to M. Vanderhaeghen, of Ghent, in
April, 1870, gives an example both of his quickness of
observation and the retentiveness of his memory. "Yesterday morning," he writes, "I received a book which I once
saw for a few minutes five years ago. . . . It is a fine
copy of the Ghent edition of Boethius. . . . But the
interest to me lay in the fact that I had noticed, the
moment I first saw the book, that it must have been bound
by Ar. de Keysere himself, because every quire was guarded
down the centre by little slips of parchment which showed
traces of Ar. de Keysere's familiar type. You can imagine
my satisfaction yesterday, when, after waiting in suspense
for five years, I found," etc., etc. ; and then follows an account of what the slips turned out to be—fragments of an

indulgence, a hitherto unknown piece of de Keysere's work, throwing light on several points in the history of Flemish printing.

Of the importance of fragments of this kind preserved in bindings, he writes in another place,* " Many specimens of early printing have been recovered from the bindings of other books ; and these sometimes afford very valuable evidence as to their history.† Such fragments in the binder's hands are either sheets of books which have been used up and thrown away, and may be called *binder's waste*, or else they are spoilt sheets or unused proofs from a printer's office, and may be called *printer's waste*. In early times the printers were frequently their own binders. . . . It becomes, therefore, a matter of considerable importance to use all endeavours to ascertain where the volume was bound which contains any such fragments. If a fragment is found printed only on one side it has hitherto been described as 'a remarkable specimen of anopisthographic typography,‡ probably executed in the infancy of the art, etc., etc.,' instead of which it is simply a proof-sheet of the commonest description ; and in no case does it seem to have inspired the discoverer to follow up the scent, or to inform the world of the one single fact which might give his discovery any real value."

In connection with the minuteness of the observations which often started him on a train of discovery, it is related of him that he was one day observed by Mr Coxe in the Bodleian Library, his attention riveted by a scrap of early printing which he held in his hand. He stood stock-still, gazing at the page, until at last Mr Coxe's

---

* " Memorandum," No. 3, p. 7.

† As an illustration of this, it may be mentioned that the discovery of a leaf of the Bamberg Bible (36-line) in the binding of a Bamberg account-book, which begins on March 21, 1460, tends to fix the date of this, the second printed Bible, as about 1460 (Catalogue of Caxton Celebration, p. 54).

‡ Printing on one side of a sheet only.

curiosity could hold out no longer. Coming up to Brad-shaw, he interrupted his meditations with a hearty slap on the back, and the inquiry, "What on earth have you got there?" "Well, it's *very* odd," was the answer; "I never in my life saw a W like that before!"

The Rev. S. M. Lakin records a little incident illustrative of what M. Jusserand called his "pouvoir divinatoire" which is really the rapid and unerring application of knowledge. "There is," he says, "in the cathedral library at Salisbury, a Dutch Psalter, containing the date, printer's name (Eckert), and place of printing (Delft). The date is, apparently, MCCCCXXVIII. Mr Botfield, in his 'Notes on Cathedral Libraries,' supposes the numeral 'L' to have dropped out, so that the date should be 1478. When I called Mr Bradshaw's attention to this explanation, he immediately said that in 1478 there was no printer of the name of Eckert at Delft, and he suggested that the true date was probably 1498 (MCCCCXCVIII). Since then the application of a magnifying glass has revealed that the second 'X' was originally a 'C,' the paler colour of the ink used revealing the alteration that had been made."

Mr Blades, the author of the "Life of Caxton," says of him*—and I can quote no better authority—"From an early period he perceived that to understand and master the internal evidences contained in every old book, the special peculiarities of their workmanship must be studied and classified, much in the same way as a botanist treats plants, or an entomologist insects. This he called 'the natural-history system.' . . . To make his work more effectual and scientific, he did that which many a bibliographer has to his great loss omitted to do—he made acquaintance with the technicalities of book-making. He knew how punches were cut, how matrices were struck, and how types were cast. . . . To this he added a know-

---

* In the *Printer's Register* for March 6, 1886.

ledge of how paper-moulds were used and water-marks made. Such learning gave him exceptional advantages in the study of old books, and enabled him to settle with certainty many questions in palæotypography which had till then been a puzzle to bibliographers. I remember a curious instance of this. About twelve years ago, a well-known bookseller of London found two printed slips of paper in the binding of an old book. Each slip measured three inches by nine inches, and had been cut down from the fore-edge of some waste sheets, the ends only of the printed lines being preserved all the way down the page. The type was of a peculiar bold Gothic character, and the bookseller, who had never seen its like before, having to visit Cambridge, took it with him and showed it to Mr Bradshaw. After a few minutes' examination, our book-oracle said, ' Yes, these slips are part of signatures *b* i and *b* ii of a most rare book, called " L'Estrif de Fortune," printed at Bruges about 1480 by Colard Mansion.' He had never seen a copy of the book,* but this identification of fragments through his knowledge of types was everyday work with him. . . . He would show you when the various founts of Caxton, Machlinia, and others were first used, when they got old, and to whom they were sold when a new fount replaced them ; and the simple delight which beamed over his face if he found that you understood his evidences and were interested in his proofs is a thing to remember."

Mr Blades alludes to what Bradshaw called his natural-history method in bibliography. It was a phrase which he was never tired of using. He appears to have meant by it a careful and exhaustive ascertainment of facts, minute observation of characteristics, thoughtful co-ordination of the . results, and deductions made *without prejudice* and untrammelled by preconceived ideas. With regard to

---

* This is not quite correct. He had once seen a copy of the book, eight years before : see above, p. 133.

early printed books, in particular, it meant the arrangement
and classification of them, as natural objects are classified,
under families, genera, and species. His published lists
are illustrations of this system. I cannot do better than
quote his own words * respecting the principles on which
these lists are based.

"The method of arranging these early books under the
countries, towns, and presses at which they were produced
is the only one which can really advance our knowledge
of the subject. This is comparatively easy with dated
books, though there is no safeguard against the misleading
nature of an erroneous date. But the study is of little use
unless the bibliographer will be content to make such an
accurate and methodical study of the types used and habits
of printing observable at different presses, as to enable him
to observe and be guided by these characteristics in settling
the date of a book which bears no date on the surface.
We do not want the *opinion* or *dictum* of any bibliographer,
however experienced ; we desire that the types and habits
of each printer should be made a special subject of study,
and those points brought forward which show changes or
advance from year to year, or, where practicable, from
month to month. When this is done, we have to say of
any dateless or falsely dated book that it contains such
and such characteristics, and we therefore place it at such
a point of time, the time we name being merely another
expression for the characteristics we notice in the book.
In fact, each press must be looked upon as a *genus*, and
each book as a *species*, and our business is to trace the
more or less close connection of the different members
of the family according to the characters which they present to our observation. The study of palæotypography
has been hitherto mainly · such a *dilettante* matter, that
people have shrunk from going into such details, though,

* "Memorandum," No. 2, p. 15.

when once studied as a branch of natural history, it is as fruitful in interesting results as most subjects."

The following letter, addressed to Mr J. J. Green (August 18, 1882), is a good illustration of his bibliographical method, and I am the more ready to quote it, long as it is, because it is the only *explanatory* letter I have come across in the whole series of his correspondence.

"Dear Mr Green,

"The precious parcel was delivered last night, and I was extremely glad to find that they were four consecutive leaves, the inner two sheets of a four-sheet quire. . . . The book itself is easy to identify. . . .

"Let me show you how I reached my result, and you will see how such studies are pursued.

"At first opening, it was clearly a fragment of a copy of some sixteenth-century edition of 'Caxton's Chronicle,' in the form it assumed when W. de Worde published it in 1497, that is to say, practically, the 'St. Alban's Chronicle,' with the 'Fructus temporum,' or 'Fruit of times.'

"The type was clearly and undoubtedly Wynkyn de Worde's. Every now and then, instead of the regular J of this fount of type, a J of his earlier type (used 1493–1502) appears instead, and this alone would prove the work to be de Worde's. The initials are familiar as being found in so many of W. de Worde's books.

"Any common book told me that, besides two editions by Notary (1504, I think, and 1515), there are the following editions by de Worde :—1502, 1515, 1520, 1528.

"Books apart, I knew that the little line-end ornaments were very popular from 1510 to 1515, and I was quite prepared to find it a fragment of the 1515 edition.

"We have in college a 1528. I went to the library to get it, and I saw at once that yours was older—cuts much less broken than in 1528, no line-end ornaments in 1528, a much later device at the end of the volume. Besides this a different number of lines on the page, though the quires all begin and end alike.

"I then looked into Herbert's 'Ames,' p. 153, and I found his description of Gough's copy of 1515, showing that Caxton's large device was at the end.

"This was all I could do last night. This morning I have looked at a few folios by de Worde to see his habits of printing at different times, and I give you here a few of the results that you may just see how, without any particular trouble, such things are worked out. They are all books in folio, printed in double columns, and looking, to an ordinary person examining them, very much the same.

"1. 'Flower of Commandments.' 1510. 43-line page, with abundance of line-end ornaments.

"2. 'Golden Legend.' 1512. 44-line page, with a fair number of line-end ornaments.

"3. 'Nova Legenda Angliæ.' 1516. 44-line page, with line-end ornaments but rarely used.

"4. 'Golden Legend.' 1527. 46-line page, with no line-end ornaments.

"Your fragment of the 'Chronicle of England,' with the 'Fruit of Times,' has a 44-line page, with a fair number of line-end ornaments, used not rarely and yet not abundantly.

"Until I am able to find a copy of W. de Worde's 1515 edition, I should have no hesitation in describing your fragment as *probably belonging to that edition*, and I think you will see that such a 'probably' is not a matter of random speculation, as such things so frequently are.

"The whole matter has taken me less than half an hour to investigate, and I certainly do not grudge it, since but for your kindness in sending me the thing for examination, I should not have worked up these test-characteristics of W. de Worde's printing, which will now be of service to me in all future researches of the kind."

Of the actual discoveries which Bradshaw made in the department of palæotypography I cannot venture to give an account. Some few have been alluded to in the foregoing pages, but they are necessarily for the most part too intricate and detailed in their nature to be mentioned in a memoir of this kind. I may, however, give one or two extracts from letters bearing on the date and the printer of the earliest specimens of typography. Writing to Mr Conway in September, 1880, Bradshaw says, " There are two wholly separate Indulgences printed in different types, and therefore at different presses, both in 1454. Of one of them, the 31-line Indulgence, the copy now at the Hague was *sold* November 15, 1454, so that I always consider this the birthday of *typo*graphy. Of the other edition (in different types), thirty lines to a page, the earliest copy known was not sold till February 27, 1455 * (the date printed 1454 being altered with a pen to 1455). . . . So the earliest date of typography, or printing with movable types, is November 15, 1454. Curiously enough, an Indulgence of the same nature sold in *October*, 1454, is all manuscript. So I have no doubt that printing with types came out, so to say, in the autumn of 1454."

In April, 1882, he writes to Mr Tupper, " Now that two distinct presses stand out clearly as existing side by side in 1454, 1455, and 1456—one of which is now beyond all question, I think, identified with Schoiffher working alone on the 30-line Indulgences of 1454 and 1455, and the Mazarine Bible (42-line) of 1456,† and the ' Donatus' with

---

* This copy, belonging to Lord Spencer, was exhibited at the Caxton Celebration, 1877.

† The copy of this Bible, exhibited at the Caxton Celebration (1877), is described by Mr Bullen in his catalogue as "supposed to have been printed by Gutenberg, assisted by Fust, at Mentz, 1450-55." The "Donatus" is undated, but is supposed to have been printed in or before 1456. The earliest

Schoiffher's name and the Psalter initials ; and the other with an unnamed printer (who may be Gutenberg) working alone in the 31-line Indulgences of 1454 and 1455, the 'Appeal against the Turks' of January 1, 1455, and the 'Conjunctiones et Oppositiones Solis et Lunæ' of January 1, 1457 (to which the 'Cisianus'* corresponds)—it ought to be more straightforward work, investigating all these questions."

In May, 1885, he read before a meeting of the Library Association a paper on early Bibles.† Some time before this he had made up his mind on the subject of the first printers. "I am happy to say," he writes to Mr Blades in June, 1881, "I am now quite clear in my own mind about Gutenberg and the rest. It all came suddenly upon me on Monday last. After putting all speculation apart for so many years, and trying to watch the compositors in the different printing offices at work, it all comes out quite comfortably. I honestly think I deserve to find some conclusion worth having." The upshot of his remarks on early Bibles was that Schöffer, and not Gutenberg, was the printer of the famous Mazarine Bible, the earliest book printed from movable types. It may be mentioned in this connection that a personal examination of a copy of the Mentelin Bible at Freiburg-im-Breisgau, which he made in 1875, enabled him to fix the date of this, the third printed Bible, as 1460–61.‡ His conclusions on the origin of printing are confirmed by the recent investigations of

---

dated book is the Psalter, printed "per Johannem Fust civem moguntinum et Petrum Schoffer de Gernszheim anno domini MCCCCLVII."

* An early German rhyming almanack.

† Reported in *The Printing Times and Lithographer*, May 15, 1885. "Unfortunately," says the report, "the written portion of Mr Bradshaw's remarks formed only a small proportion of those to which he gave utterance." I have been unable to find the notes from which he spoke.

‡ He had called attention to this fact as early as 1871 : see Mr Hessels' translation of Van der Linde's "Haarlem Legend," preface ; and Mr Bullen's "Catalogue of the Caxton Exhibition," pp. 55, 92.

2 B

Mr Hessels,* his most distinguished pupil in the science of palæotypography.

To the works of Caxton he paid, as his whole correspondence with Mr Blades shows, especial attention. His knowledge of Caxton formed, as he said himself, the starting-point whence he proceeded to study the typography of the Netherlands and Germany. He was anxious to do all he could to facilitate the study of the subject, but when Mr H. B. Wheatley started the idea of a society to publish facsimiles of Caxton's work, he condemned the project as impracticable. "Of course," he writes to Mr Wheatley, in October, 1860, "I think the Caxton Facsimile Society the most rampant piece of absurdity which has yet been devised. This you can understand my saying ; but having said this I have said all, and in spite of this, I shall be heartily glad to give you any help in my power."

I have already had occasion to mention the keen interest which Bradshaw took in the production of local presses ; for instance, in those of Oxford and Cambridge, of Belfast and Aberdeen. In connection with the former, Mr F. Madan, of the Bodleian Library, relates a pleasing incident. In November, 1884, he was passing through Cambridge, on his way to Oxford, and had intended to take the opportunity of consulting Bradshaw on some points connected with the history of printing at Oxford. He found, however, that he would have only forty minutes to wait between his trains, and wrote to say he could not come. The sequel may be guessed. When his train arrived, there was Bradshaw on the platform. It was a bitterly cold day, but he had walked to the station, bringing with him a manuscript which was to go back to the Bodleian, on purpose to talk to Mr Madan about his favourite subject. The time flew by in unbroken talk, and Bradshaw concluded by writing out for his friend,

* In his article on Typography, Encyclopædia Britannica, 1887.

then and there, from memory, a complete descriptive list of all the fifteenth-century books produced at Oxford —a list which, Mr Madan tells me, was to be found nowhere else, and is, he believes, exhaustive and correct.

The last piece of work which he was able to complete was his " Half-Century of Notes on John Dorne ; " his last serious correspondence was that with Mr Anderson, on the Belfast press. There was a touching fitness in the fact that he died with one of his Irish books before him, his father's favourite study and his own.

HERALDRY.

Since writing the above, I have received a letter from Mr W. St. John Hope,* in which he calls attention to Bradshaw's knowledge of heraldry. He says, "Although he professed not to be versed in the subject, a brief conversation sufficed to show that, if he was not familiar with the jargon of modern works on heraldry, he was completely at home with the mediæval armorists. He spoke in the highest terms of the great interest and beautiful simplicity of the early armory, which the modern text-books studiously avoid reference to. One of his theories, which he again and again reiterated, was that the science of armory died with the conclusion of the Wars of the Roses and the foundation of the College of Arms. He always spoke of the claim of the college to regulate and grant armorial bearings as a direct contravention of the true principles of ancient armory. Another of his maxims was, that we ought to have a 'Grammar of Heraldry,' in which should be set forth the laws and usages of mediæval armory, as exemplified by original authorities . . . such as monuments, seals, rolls of arms, etc., beginning with the earliest period when heraldry proper existed as a science. . . . As a case in point, Bradshaw raised the question, 'When were the arms of man and wife first impaled ?' Adding, 'I don't suppose you will find that stated in any of the printed works on heraldry.' To test the point, we proceeded to the University Library, and consulted every available work, with the result that in one book only, so far as I recollect, we found the general statement that 'impaling' commenced in the reign of Edward I. This did not satisfy Bradshaw, who maintained that such a statement ought to rest on the earliest known example, and it was on these lines that the proposed ' Grammar ' was to be written."

---

* Secretary to the Society of Antiquaries.

CHAPTER XII.

THIS memoir would not be complete without some review of Henry Bradshaw's work in the library which was his chief care for so many years, or without an attempt to place on record a few of the impressions left by his remarkable personality.

His management of the library was not, it may at once be allowed, in every respect quite satisfactory. The condition of that institution at one period during his term of office caused, as I have already said, some discontent. But, in the first place, the difficulties with which he had to contend were very great. The staff under his direction was numerically inadequate, the want of space was an ever-present cause of confusion, and the publicity of the library was an impediment with which no other guardian of a similar institution has to contend. In the second place, if he did not succeed in entirely removing all causes of dissatisfaction, no one who compares the present condition of the library with its condition twenty years ago can fail to recognise the vast improvement in every respect which was accomplished by Bradshaw's unremitting zeal.

When he became librarian in 1867, great confusion had lately been caused by the attempt to substitute a uniform numerical notation for the various marks—letters of the alphabet, Roman and Arabic numerals, etc.—by which the various classes of books had been indicated. The reform, however advantageous it might have been if it could have been carried through, was far too large a one for the limited staff to accomplish, and the attempt was abandoned after a considerable part of the work had been done. The simultaneous existence of two entirely different systems of notation, and the consequent confusion that ensued, may more easily be imagined than described. The first thing that Bradshaw had to do was to execute a retrograde movement towards the old system, and this was necessarily a work of time. He did not altogether give up the hope of eventually simplifying the system of notation, but he saw that it must be deferred.

There was, however, an immediate necessity for devising a plan for denoting the contents of the new building which was completed soon after he took office, and those of other rooms to be added subsequently. The plan which he adopted was simple and effective. He denoted each of the existing rooms by a single letter of the alphabet, and, having regard to the historical growth of the building, he named them in chronological order, beginning with the catalogue-room as at once the centre and, probably, the oldest part of the library. This exhausted the letters from A to K. Then, following up this system, he denoted the new rooms by the remaining letters, from L onwards. The system was not actually applied to the old rooms, nor has it been yet applied, for its substitution for the present jumble of titles would be a long and costly task. But it has been applied to all the rooms added since 1867, and could at any time be introduced throughout, without altering the additions made since that date.

The completion of the new building involved extensive changes in the arrangement of the books. Several classes, including the manuscripts and early printed books, were moved into the new rooms, and Bradshaw seems to have contemplated a complete rearrangement of the library, with a view to a classification according to subjects. But this task was too great to be accomplished by the existing staff. For some time considerable confusion was caused, and it was eventually resolved to discontinue the attempt.

To give an account of all the changes which were introduced into the library during Bradshaw's tenure of office would lead me too much into detail. Some of the most important were the introduction of printed instead of written slips into the catalogue, the formation of a code of rules for cataloguing, the issue of a weekly bulletin giving a list of all books added to the library, and the gradual elaboration of the various stages through which the books have to pass before they can be placed upon the shelves. The rules for cataloguing are called by Mr Tedder* "probably the most practically useful set of working rules yet issued." Mr Wheatley,† in his report for 1880, says, "The rapid and efficient system by which books are catalogued and shelved and the title-slips pasted in the catalogue is very praiseworthy. This is a feature in which I do not think the library is surpassed by any with which I am acquainted." The printing of the slips was introduced several years before the British Museum had adopted the plan. It is unnecessary to suppose that the whole credit for these and other improvements was due to Bradshaw; it is enough to say that they were carried out under his direction and during his librarianship. His prevailing aim was probably rather to make existing arrangements work smoothly than to alter the machinery which he found to hand. His idea of a great library was hardly that of most modern librarians. He regarded it in the light of a museum of literary and typographical records quite as much as, perhaps even more than, that of a collection of practically useful books.

The daily routine of management occupied far the greater part of his time—probably a larger share than was

* Librarian of the Athenæum, in his report to the Syndicate, 1879.
† Librarian of the Society of Arts.   •

necessary, for the capacity of working through subordinates was not one of his strong points. "He could not," says one of the assistants, "bring himself to allow any one to answer letters for him." His habit of not answering letters has been described by one of his friends as "the only failing he had." It was not his only failing, but it was certainly one of the most prominent. He wrote an enormous number of letters, but if he did not answer an inquiry at once, it often had to wait for months. He used to carry masses of unanswered letters about with him in his coat-pocket, and would take them out and show them sometimes, not without a certain mischievous glee, saying in his droll way, "I am *too* wicked; what *shall* I do?" He was well aware of his failing, and one day said to Mr T. B. Reed, who wanted some information from him, "You had better come and get what you can by word of mouth. I offend lots of my friends by not answering their letters, or losing them like yours." On one occasion Mr Edwin Freshfield, to whom he had long promised a visit, and who could not get an answer to his invitations, sent him two post-cards, on one of which was written "Yes," on the other "No," and asked him to post one or the other. Bradshaw promptly posted both. It is fair to say that by the next post he wrote to say he would come, and did so.

It was the same with books. To get a book back from him was like getting butter out of the black dog's mouth. Mr Horner, of Mells, tells a story of how he once lent him a little early service-book, one of a number of valuable books which Bradshaw went over from Longleat on purpose to see. When he had had it rather over a twelve-month, Mr Horner wrote to ask him if he had done with it. No answer was returned. He waited a month, and wrote again; again no answer. Then he presented his compliments to Mr Bradshaw's executors, and asked them to recover the lost property out of his residuary estate.

This was too much. The book came back most carefully packed, with a courteous letter, in which Bradshaw said that he was extremely sorry, but that whenever he was asked to send back an interesting book he "suffered from a chronic paralysis of the will, and could not return it till the fit had passed away."

Mr Charles Hargrove tells another anecdote illustrative of what he calls his "truly phenomenal procrastination." A senior fellow of his college possessed a copy of the Greek Anthology, with the translation of Grotius, in four volumes, excellent in all respects, except that it wanted the last leaf. Bradshaw offered to make a copy of the leaf and put it in, if the owner would send him the book. He did so, and never saw it again. He inquired after it from time to time, and was always told it should be restored at once. In course of time he died, and left the book in his will to Bradshaw. One day Mr Hargrove saw it in his rooms, and asked for the loan of it. Bradshaw told him the story, with many expressions of repentance, and offered to give him the book. Mr Hargrove accepted the gift, and, knowing his habits, wanted to take it away at once. No ; he would send it shortly, along with some other books which Mr Hargrove had lent him. Of course the books never came. The years went on, and allusion was occasionally made to the subject, with no result. Bradshaw went so far as to do the books up in a parcel, which he one day showed to Mr Hargrove, saying he would send it by his gyp next day. But the books never found their way to their owner, and when Bradshaw died they were still unrestored.

This was, no doubt, downright inexcusable procrastination, altogether a vice ; and yet it was impossible to be annoyed with him for it, or annoyed for long. His very faults had something lovable in them. And, after all, in matters of duty, in business which had to be transacted by a certain date, he was seldom behindhand. The library accounts, for instance, as more than one vice-chancellor has assured me, were always ready at the right time, and absolutely clear and correct. That he did not complete more of what he undertook—for instance, the catalogue of his beloved early printed books in the library—was principally due to the fact that he was so constantly occupied in helping students who came to him for aid. "Often at four o'clock," says one of his library assistants, "after a day spent in this manner, has he sat down, dead-beat, and said to me, ' I've done absolutely nothing to-day. It's perfectly fearful to think of;' and it was difficult to make him feel that in reality he had done a great deal."

His relations with the library assistants were of the friendliest. "To one and all of us," says the same assistant from whom I have already quoted, "he was extremely kind. He took a personal interest in us, and looked upon us as his children. He commanded the confidence of the staff, and was willing to be the sharer of their joys and troubles. Nothing escaped his eye, and if he thought something was wrong, he could not be easy till he knew what was the matter. There were times, however, when he could be very severe, and say the most crushing things. He would never listen to excuses, and would say that if a man *wanted* to do a thing he would always find time to do it. Whatever he did in the library he did thoroughly, and tried to make others do the same ; he could not endure seeing things half done. There was nothing he hated more than hearing any one say, on being shown the way to do a thing, ' What does it matter?' He would say it 'shut him up.' He was very strict about rules, and would very rarely relax a fine, whatever defence a man might make. He was very particular, too, about his young friends wearing their caps and gowns when they came to see him in the library. If he saw an undergraduate walking about with his gown on his arm, he always told him to put it on. He never permitted any reader in the library to put one book open upon another, and, if he saw it, would say to him, ' Oh, *please* let me take that book off!' Nor could he bear to see a pen lodged in an ink-pot, on account of the danger lest the ink should be spilt on the book."

Dr Zupitza, a great friend and admirer of Bradshaw, tells me that he was one day making notes in ink from the famous manuscript of Bede's " Ecclesiastical History" in the University Library. Bradshaw happened to espy him, and with the exclamation, "You Germans have no reverence," rushed at the ink-pot and carried it away. So precious a manuscript should not be approached, he thought, with anything more dangerous than a pencil.

As an illustration of his kindness to the library assistants, I may mention an incident for which Mr Hargrove is my authority. One of them was observed by Bradshaw to be in low spirits. He won his confidence, and found the cause to be a debt of some £30, a large sum for a married man with a salary of £150 a year. He took it on himself; but, not content with this, and thinking there might be more behind, he continued to press him till he knew all his circumstances, and found that his debts amounted to about £80. "So I paid them all," said Bradshaw to Mr Hargrove, "and set him on his legs again." This was not, perhaps, in accordance with the principles of the Charity Organisation Society, but if it was wrong, it was surely a fault over which "the recording angel would drop a tear."

It was in the library, naturally, that his unselfish helpfulness, his entire freedom from egotism, made itself most apparent. "A librarian," he said in his address to the Library Conference, "is one who earns his living by attending to the wants of those for whose use the library under his charge exists, his primary duty being, in the widest possible sense of the phrase, to save the time of those who seek his services." Every day that he spent in the library bore testimony to the manner in which he obeyed this principle. It will be hardly possible for any one else to obey it quite in the same way. He was fortunate in his opportunity, coming to the library, as he did, just at the time when the work of cataloguing and rearranging the manuscripts and early books was in progress. He held a post for the continuance of which, after he had done his work, there was no further need, and he thus gained a first-hand acquaintance with the contents of the library which it is hardly likely that any successor will acquire. This unique knowledge—a knowledge depending on a long and laborious apprenticeship, and the possession of uncommon mental gifts—was combined with a self-forgetfulness and a disregard for fame rarely compatible with great intellectual power. He was thus enabled "to save the time of those who sought his services" to an extent which few who did not seek them could appreciate. The list of scholars, English and foreign, who received from him help and information, is long and distinguished. To mention a tithe of these would be impossible, but I cannot help quoting a few extracts from among a large number of letters which I have received on the subject.

Mr T. W. Jackson, for instance, writes as follows:— "I had no introduction to him when I first went to the University Library to ask for his help. Two or three questions, most gently but most skilfully put, showed him that I had done some little work on the subject in hand, and from that moment he not only gave me facilities, but gave trouble and time of his own, with a kindness which nothing could exceed. . . . It is difficult to say why he, in a sense, fascinated people, myself included. It seemed to come, if one may say it, from a courtesy of thought, quite beyond and surpassing that of manner." Mr G. H. Moberly, after describing the help which he received in his edition of Bede, says, " I cannot exaggerate the kindness and courtesy with which it was done."

Mr J. B. Mullinger * says, " I shall never forget the tact and geniality with which, when I first made his acquaintance, myself a mere neophyte in literary research, he sought to put me at my ease, in asking him questions and giving him trouble, by endeavouring to make out that he would himself be a gainer by the process. ' If, when *you* have a little leisure,' or, ' That is just one of the points I should like to go into with *your* assistance,' and so forth, always managing, though without any appearance of doing it, to give me at the same time an amount of guidance and criticism such as I could scarcely have found anywhere else. And all this was enlivened by a quiet humour and occasional anecdote, in a manner which made him, I think, the most delightful counsellor in literary matters of whom I ever took advice." Dr Murray † says, " I constantly applied to him in difficulties, and never in vain. The disinterestedness of his help was something wonderful and touching."

" He was bewilderingly enthusiastic," writes Mr T. B. Reed.‡ " Having grasped what I wanted, he gave me no time to interpose new questions or dwell on old ones, but passed from topic to topic, and book to book. He told me more than once that it was the duty of a librarian to help others rather than to appear in print himself, but he added that he received sometimes with impatience the compliments of those who first praised his perspicacity, and then calmly appropriated, without verifying or working them out for themselves, his own investigations. ' You are heartily

---

* Author of a " History of the University of Cambridge," " The Schools of Charles the Great," etc.

† Editor of the new English Dictionary, now in course of publication at the Clarendon Press.

‡ Author of " A History of the Old English Letter Foundries, etc.," 1887.

welcome,' he said, 'to anything I can tell you. But don't publish *my* work ; publish *your own.*'"

The following typical anecdote was communicated to me by Mr S. S. Lewis.* " He once showed me a letter from some wholly unknown correspondent, asking him to verify a quotation from one of the Parker manuscripts in my charge. When I offered to do it for him, he replied, ' I mustn't lose the pleasure of having another look at your books. When may I come ?' ' To-morrow, as early as you please,' I answered ; and on the morrow, and each succeeding week-day for a fortnight, he came about 7.45 a.m., took a cup of cocoa from my breakfast-table, and worked on happily far beyond the original object for which he had come." " The most delightful thing in the world," he said one day to a very young scholar, " is to have people coming to you for help."

To foreigners who demanded his assistance, whether in person or by letter, he was particularly helpful. He was frequently engaged in collating transcripts, verifying quotations, copying manuscripts for them, or giving them aid in other ways. One day, an American professor, quite unknown to him, came to the University Library to see if he could find out anything about the " Family of Love," in which he was interested. It happened to be one of Bradshaw's favourite subjects. He at once introduced the stranger to the valuable collection of books bearing on the subject which exists in the University Library,† and spent over two hours in explaining their connection and discussing the whole topic. Many other American students have had a similar experience. To Dr Zarncke, who was engaged in 1875 in working out the history of Prester John, he sent transcripts and descriptions of two manuscripts at Corpus, and two others elsewhere, with

---

* Librarian of Corpus Christi College, Cambridge.
† Presented by the late Dr Corrie, Master of Jesus.

seven or eight letters, all in the space of a couple of months. And this is only one instance out of dozens which might be quoted to illustrate the manner in which he "saved the time of others" at the expense of his own time and fame.

The following is from a letter to the distinguished French scholar, M. Paul Meyer, to whom he had made some promise which he had not performed :—

"University Library, November 2, 1871.

" My dear Sir,

"Your letter just received humbles me to the dust. I cannot say more than that I am extremely sorry for all the trouble and annoyance that my negligence has caused you, and that I sincerely hope others beside yourself may be gainers by the result. . . . About the Vaudois manuscripts—I cannot undertake to do anything at all for print. I will give any one who comes here and wants to use them, any help or any information which I have it in my power to give ; but I am not a literary man, though my friends are fond of assuming that I am, and I am wholly destitute of the gift of writing. Anybody who is worth giving it to, is at any time welcome to use freely all I have to give, and I cannot say more. . . .

"Yours most truly,

"Henry Bradshaw."

From among many letters from scholars to whom Bradshaw rendered assistance, I choose the two following as of some general interest :—

"Eversley Rectory, Winchfield, November 21, 1867.

" My dear Bradshaw,

"I find I must ask you to send me the volume of Theodoret which contains the Greek of the 'Philotheus' or 'Theophilus,' as I have only the Latin translation.

Also I much want the little 'Life of St Guthlac in Anglo-Saxon,' with the translation by I forget who. . . . You are a shabby fellow, I tell you in all love. I wrote to you this summer, asking you when you were coming to see the Dogmersfield treasures, which are awaiting you, and you never answered. But that will stand over till I come to Cambridge in December.

" Yours ever sincerely,
" CHARLES KINGSLEY."

" Public Record Office, November 5, 1862.

" MY DEAR MR BRADSHAW,

"I cannot sufficiently thank you for your very kind letter and valuable list of corrections. If two or three such kind and competent critics would do the like for the portions with which they are acquainted, we should soon have a perfect catalogue of our historical manuscripts. . . .

" Believe me to be most sincerely yours,
"T. DUFFUS HARDY." *

As a final illustration of this side of Bradshaw's character, I quote a few lines from the preface to Mr J. W. Clark's "Architectural History of the University of Cambridge."

" No language that I can think of can adequately express what I owe to our late librarian, Henry Bradshaw. From the outset of my work, he took it, so to speak, into his hands, and treated it as if it had been his own. Notwithstanding the incessant demands upon his time, he always found leisure to help me, to teach me to read difficult mediæval handwriting, or to dictate to me some document which I had reason to copy. On one occasion, I remember, he took the trouble to travel from Cambridge

---

* Late Deputy-Keeper of the Public Records, and author of the " Descriptive Catalogue of the Materials relating to the History of Great Britain and Ireland " (Rolls Series), etc.

to Eton in order to settle the signification of a single contraction in one of the building-rolls, on which a good deal depended, and about which I could not feel quite sure. Not content with giving me advice on all questions of arrangement of materials—about which his singularly lucid and orderly mind rendered him an invaluable counsellor—he insisted on reading all the proof-sheets, not merely for the purpose of detecting clerical errors, but that he might copiously annotate them, and show me how difficult points in history and archæology might be set in the best light. Had it not been for his encouragement, my labours would never have been brought to a conclusion. My greatest pleasure would have been to show him the completed work ; my greatest grief is that he can never see it."

Of Bradshaw's influence in university politics there is not much to say, for it was not till late in life that he became prominent in this respect. He always felt strongly and spoke strongly to his friends on university subjects, but he avoided putting himself forward in public. Towards the end of his life the value of his judgment began to be more widely recognised, and his election to the Council and the General Board was at once a sign of general respect and an encouragement to him to use the influence which was naturally his. The late Mr Coutts Trotter informed me that his opinions on university matters carried great weight on the Council, and that his knowledge of university history was especially useful whenever a constitutional question or the adaptation of old institutions to modern requirements was under discussion. While a member of the Council he employed his peculiar skill in tabulation to draw up a sort of calendar of the business that came before that body,.by which means much time was saved and many omissions avoided.

Professor Sidgwick says, " He was a most valuable

member of the General Board. His judgments, when he gave them, were always well considered and carried weight, but he did not usually take a leading part in the proceedings. I recollect one important crisis—perhaps the most important that we have had—at which he did take the lead with great effect. There was a fundamental question relating to the distribution of the first instalment of the Common University Fund, on which the Board was divided. Influential persons held that a large part of the fund should be spent in raising the salaries of existing professors; another section thought that, in view of the urgent demands for money to provide new teaching and equipments, we should be fairly chargeable with being unduly influenced by personal considerations, if we recommended the former course. The question was one calculated to lead to disagreeable and embarrassing discussions; but, under Bradshaw's management, this danger was felicitously avoided. The matter would in any case, I think, have been settled in favour of the latter alternative, but I always attributed to Bradshaw's peculiar qualities—his perfect disinterestedness, his simple intensity of conviction, together with his geniality and *bonhomie*, and his entire freedom from dry doctrinairism—that it was settled with so little friction." Another member of the Council "well remembers his determination that all should be frank and clear as the daylight. 'No half confidences,' he would say. And for any phrase suggested by grounds of policy, he would substitute the simple words, and would remark—as if after that no answer was possible—'You mean it; you had better say it.'"

In illustration of this last characteristic, I may quote a story told me by a well-known clergyman, a writer both learned and brilliant. He was one day with Bradshaw, when the latter introduced him to another visitor—much to his dismay and confusion—as "one of the most learned men in England." "I was put out by the exaggeration. 'Bradshaw,' I said, 'how can you talk in that way?' Then, turning to the stranger, I said, 'You see, the great librarian has not given up the arts of adulation.' Bradshaw, to my surprise, fired up, and was for a moment really angry. 'I am not in the habit of saying what I do not mean, and I shouldn't have said it if it wasn't true.'"

In spite of—perhaps I ought to say, in great measure owing to—this unspoken honesty and frankness, few men have had more friends, real warmly attached friends, than Bradshaw. The friends whom he made at school, unlike many boy-friends, remained attached to him through life. As an undergraduate he speedily made himself remarkable, among those who knew him well, for the number and warmth of his friendships. From that time onward he never ceased to add to the number. The capacity for friendship is generally limited, like other gifts, but Bradshaw's capacity in this direction was infinite.

His manner of keeping hold of his friends was his own. He never lost touch with a friend once made; he never forgot old associations. However long an interval had elapsed since the last meeting, he could always take up the intimacy where it had been dropped, and make an old acquaintance at once at home. With many men such revivals of intimacy are impossible; the attempt only reveals the severance that has insensibly taken place. Other friends, other interests, other conditions of life, alter and estrange those who once protested that nothing should diminish their affection. When they meet, it is with a sense of strain; when they part, it is with a sense of relief. With Bradshaw it was otherwise. Time and distance seemed to have no effect. He wasted no regrets over inevitable separations; he never attempted to maintain that laborious but fictitious intimacy which rests on occasional correspondence, but he kept his eye on friends, however far away. He contrived always to find out where they were and what they were doing; and when they gravitated again to the old rooms in King's, as sooner or later they were sure to do, they found no broken links to knit again, no cold embers of ancient friendship to blow into a lukewarm flame. He would let fall a word or two which showed that he knew of their affairs, which proved that his interest in them was not merely revived by the meeting, that it had been continuous.

"I only know," says one of his earliest friends, who saw him again after many years, "that he was a very Jonathan in his affection. There was something so inexpressibly gentle and soothing in his lazy but earnest welcome, in his beaming smile coming back and back at the pleasure of looking again in an old friend's face, in his very touch so quaintly caressing." And another, much younger, writes, "I always felt sure, on coming back to Cambridge, that my knock at his door (an imitation of his peculiar knock *) would be welcome, even though he might happen to be at work. Then he would perhaps only point with his pen to a chair, and work on, till at last he would shut his book with a bang and come to you with both hands stretched out, to say, 'How d'you do?' properly. Then I felt as if I had never been away."

Changes of scene and occupation could not produce the same result with him as with most men, for his friendships did not depend on community of interests. It is true that there was nothing he enjoyed more than discussing with another scholar some subject which both loved; and common pursuits won him many fast friends. But after all, even in cases of this kind, his friendships were at

---

* One of his quaint habits was that he used to beat a tattoo with the tips of his fingers on a friend's door, instead of knocking in the ordinary way with his knuckles.

bottom friendships of the heart. Those who began by coming to him for help, who were first moved by admiration for his learning or gratitude for his generosity, ended by loving him for himself. But the number of such friends was necessarily limited. He would sometimes deplore, in a half-humorous, half-pathetic way, his intellectual solitude. "No one cares about what I care about," he would say. Sympathy and encouragement were very necessary to him, the sympathy of those who understood, if it could be had—which was rarely the case ; if not, even unintelligent sympathy was welcome. He delighted in finding a sympathetic listener, and would read Chaucer to such a one by the hour together, or would explain to some undergraduate ignoramus all the details of an intricate bibliographical problem. He liked to hold some one by the hand, so to speak, while his mind was at work.

But it was by no means in intellectual matters only, or chiefly, that he felt this need. He hated solitude, and craved for human companionship in his daily life. People used to wonder why he did not marry. He had a consummate belief in the advantages of matrimony ; the one thing he really cared about in the university reforms of 1882 was to abolish the enforced celibacy of older days.* He rejoiced when his friends got married, acted as best man at their weddings, stood godfather to their children, knowing all the time that he did not lose them as friends. In earlier days one can hardly suppose that thoughts of marriage did not sometimes cross his mind, so full he was of the love of home, of domestic tastes and associations, and endowed with such an ever-flowing well of warm affections. But he was not rich, and he was immersed in study. Some time after he became librarian, when he was already past forty, he fell in love, and made a serious attempt to alter his condition ; that failing, he resigned himself

* See above, p. 242.

to what he thought his fate. One day, in 1884, Mr
Tuckwell was paying him a visit. "We compared," says
Mr Tuckwell, "our lots in life—mine full of care and tur-
moil, his calm and free from anxiety. 'But,' he said, 'you
have had domestic happiness, and I have missed it.' I
laughed out a 'Qui fit, Mæcenas?' but he would not smile."

Of older friends, contemporaries of his own or slightly
differing in age, and resident at Cambridge, he had no
lack. He might have had more, but for many years
he went rarely into society, and had a reputation for
refusing invitations to dinner. Towards the end of his
life he relaxed in this respect, and in many houses in
Cambridge he was often a welcome guest. Still, these
older men, members of other colleges or living in their
own homes, could not give him the companionship which
he required. For this purpose younger men were better
adapted, and he had a strange power of attracting younger
men. Generation after generation of undergraduates passed
by, and hardly any without rendering him his toll, one,
two, or more devotees, who were perpetually in his rooms,
having tea with him or breakfast with him, reading or
talking or sitting with him while he did his work. "It
was characteristic of university life," he said, "that friends
must go, but others come," and the sequence was hardly
ever broken.

All sorts of men used to meet in his rooms. He never
seemed to select his friends; they were drawn to him
by some mysterious affinity, having often nothing in common but their liking for him. Athletes and students,
senior classics and pollmen, young dandies with faultless
collars and sizars whose outward man told only too plainly
of the *res angusta domi*, distinguished persons whose name
was in every one's mouth, together with the retiring and
unknown, sat on the same sofa and forgot their differences in the halo of his presence.

One class of men he was shy of—"intellects," he used
to call them ; the men who dwell habitually on "higher
ground," and deal only with the loftiest topics of conversation. With such superior persons he was seldom himself ; he became reserved, ungenial, sometimes even waspish,
or took refuge in a chilling silence. And another class he
could not abide—the genus "prig." If an incipient member of this order entered his rooms, his tendency was at
once detected, and a vein of irony or sarcasm, gentle or
severe, as suited the occasion, was brought into play,
which either cured the malady or drove the sufferer to
more congenial climes. Nor was any humbug tolerated
in that society, for Bradshaw's insight was far too keen.
The one thing he demanded of his friends was that they
should be themselves ; it was of no use, indeed, to attempt
to be anything else in his presence—he found it out at
once.

With these limitations, his society was open to all.
Prejudices and partialities he doubtless had. It was sometimes hard to say why he liked particular persons. He
would say himself, "I know all my geese are swans."
Not that all who came liked him. " Bradshaw doesn't seem
to care to see one," some would say,—"is so often out,
says such queer things," and so on. An undergraduate
once described him as a "prickly person," and so he
seemed to many. His quick observation of peculiarities,
his irony, his sharp sayings, puzzled and frightened not
a few. Others whom he did not take to at first came
again and again in spite of rebuffs, and won him at last.

Why men were attracted to him it is not very easy to
explain. Nothing is more difficult than to analyse the
causes of friendship. To begin with, there was a sense
of domesticity about him. He easily dropped into a sort
of paternal relation. He was fond of using pet names,
and doing little kindly actions, such as only near relatives

as a rule do for each other. He was a strange mixture of masculine vigour and almost feminine sweetness. " His way of saying ' child ' to me always touched me," writes one ; "it had such a sound of home." And this feeling was strengthened by his material surroundings. They were the reflex of himself.

He inhabited one of the best sets of rooms in college. One room looked southward over the picturesque red roofs and walls of St. Catherine's and Queen's ; two others looked northward over the court toward the chapel, with the tower of St. Mary's to the right, beyond the college-screen. They were lofty, spacious, airy rooms : one could not imagine him living in small rooms, with little air or light. There was a feeling of comfort about them, a sense of homeliness and domesticity. The furniture was not very elegant, certainly not what used to be called "æsthetic ;" it was not new and smart, nor was it, on the other hand, old or dowdy. It did not look, somehow, like university furniture ; nor was it, in fact, for it came mostly from his old home. It was solid, good furniture, the sort of furniture that carried you back in imagination to a comfortable, well-cared-for house of forty years ago. One felt it had associations ; so had the old blue-and-white cut glasses on the chimney-piece, and the vases on the table that in summer-time were seldom without flowers, and the samplers worked by his great-aunts that hung on the walls of his inner room.

To the associations of home and boyhood were added those of later days. The rooms were full of little nick-nacks left behind by friends who had gone down, or brought home by others from their travels : a couple of Tyrolese beer-mugs, a china *sabot* from Nevers, a Thun jar with withered rose-leaves in it, the original of Thackeray's famous drawing of Louis Quatorze. One of his fire-screens had belonged to G. R. Crotch, another to a departed Kingsman. The tea-pot which he habitually used was brought from Dresden by a friend, who break-fasted with him on Sundays year after year; the china stand on which it stood was given him by another. One friend, on going down, had bequeathed to him a vast sofa, another an easy-chair; the curtains in his front room were the gift of a third. One of his toys had been a little wooden model of a Long-Chamber bed. It met with a disastrous fate. One day, an old colleger, a man whose life had been made a burden to him at Eton, espying it on the chimney-piece, and overcome by angry recollections, seized it and threw it into the fire. All Bradshaw said was, " Did you think that was necessary ? "

Over the chimney-piece in the south room hung a life-size portrait of Mr Joseph Allen, the Quaker philanthro-pist, in his knee-breeches and grey stockings. He had owned a little property at Lindfield, in Sussex, and estab-lished there a model school, where boys were taught the elements of industrial arts, trade, and agriculture. When he died, he left the property to Miss Susan Bradshaw, Brad-shaw's aunt, and there, among the red-brick cottages and thatched roofs of the quaint Sussex village, Bradshaw had passed many happy boyish days. When Miss Bradshaw died, she left Lindfield to her nephew. On another wall in the same room hung some oil-paintings from his old home ; on a third, an empty frame. This had once con-tained a picture painted by his friend Ernest Muggeridge. The artist had taken it back to finish, but had died before his task was completed, and Bradshaw would never touch the empty frame.

One side of this room, in which Bradshaw slept during the latter part of his life—he rather liked moving about from one room to another—was almost entirely occupied by a gigantic chest of drawers, in plain unvarnished deal, with about fifty drawers in it, which he had had made to hold his papers. In the other large room was a grand piano, with a heap of music near it, mostly old music, songs and duets that he had sung with his sisters as a boy. On the walls of this room hung several pictures by artist friends: a water-colour of the head of Windermere, one of his favourite haunts in the Lake district; a clever pen-and-ink drawing of the view from his old rooms up-stairs; three little pen-and-ink sketches of Killarney, done on the backs of postcards and sent him from thence. Others, too, there were, all possessing some association or other. In the window-boxes of one room he kept small ever-green shrubs; in the other there were always red gera-niums, and nothing else—they were his mother's favourite flowers. The very book-shelves had a character of their own—shallower at the bottom than the top; the small books below, the large ones above; and so fixed that the lowest shelf could be reached without stooping, the highest without standing on a chair.

But the shelves did not hold all the books and papers. They overflowed everywhere; the wide window-seats were smothered with them, and many of the chairs, and they were often piled in heaps on the floor. Now and then he would make a desperate effort to clean his Augean stable, as he called it. He would transport a batch of books to the library, tie up and put away magazines and pamphlets, and get rid of heaps of old letters and papers. On these occasions he would destroy, rapidly, the accu-mulations of years; but his tendency was never to tear up anything, so the clearance was only temporary. He re-joiced in any event—a visit from a sister or his nieces, for instance,—which forced him to tidy up; but these events were rare, and he would deplore his inability to put or keep things in order without such incentive.

In spite of this, the litter was never such as to give any sense of discomfort. There was plenty of room for

all his friends, even for the gatherings on Sunday evenings, which were comparatively numerous. Not that he
encouraged anything in the nature of a crush; it was
seldom, if ever, that more than a dozen would be found
in his rooms at once. He never sought to bring crowds
together; those who came, came to see *him*. There was
no other attraction, no lions to be listened to, no music
as a rule—nothing but quiet talk. It was the charm and
originality of the man himself that attracted one. He was
not a great preacher or teacher, nor a man of ideas, nor a
brilliant talker; his influence depended on personal contact,
and more even on what he *was* than on what he did or
said. "We did not love him for this or that quality," says
one, "but because he was more lovable than any one else."
But it was in small meetings of two or three, still more
in quiet conversations, *tête-à-tête*, prolonged often far into
the night, that the full attraction of his character was felt.
He was a busy man, it must be remembered, occupied
every day and all day long, and there could not be very
many at one time who enjoyed this intimacy. The wonder
was that he found time to see as much of his friends as
he did.

Over those with whom he came much into contact
his influence was very strong. The primary cause of this
was that his interest in his friends was deep and continuous. It was in the main a friendly, but it was also
a scientific, interest. He made a point of ascertaining all
about his friends, their home-surroundings, their relations,
their circumstances, all that made them what they were;
he observed them under all conditions; he made them
tell him what was in their mind. His kindly persistence
broke down the barriers of the most obstinate reserve.
To find one's self interesting—to be treated by an older
man not as one of a multitude, but as an individual—is
a delicate flattery that opens the heart. And Bradshaw

had a way of treating you as if you were the one person in the world whom he cared about. Not a few of his friends still claim to have been his only intimate at some particular period, quite unaware that they shared this intimacy with others.

Thus, though he seldom made confidences, he never failed to win them. And, the confidence once won, he never lost it again. He never forgot what had been told him; he added to his knowledge from sources of which one knew nothing. You had been to Newmarket, perhaps, or had lost money at loo, and were ashamed to tell him, but somehow he knew all about it, and would casually say, as if continuing a conversation on the subject, "Was it pleasant on the heath?" or, "Silly boy! I wonder who were there last night?" Nothing seemed to escape him. It was almost impossible to tell him any Cambridge news; he always knew it first. As an instance of the unexpectedness of his knowledge, a friend (a Trinity man) says, "I once mentioned the name of my bed-maker as Mrs Dawkins. He inquired closely where my rooms were, and then pronounced with some decision, 'Darkins, you mean; not Dawkins.' He would not say how he came to know this, but it turned out afterwards that his 'boy,' as he called him (*alias* his gyp), was the good lady's son-in-law." It was just one of those coincidences that somehow were always happening with Bradshaw.

His observation of external peculiarities was as keen and humorous as his insight into character, and he was not sparing of criticism. Little faults of manner, unpleasant habits, he would cure in some quaint way peculiarly his own. One friend used to keep his mouth habitually open; Bradshaw, when he saw him, would drop his lower jaw with an irresistibly comic expression. Another was very particular about his company; Bradshaw would put his finger to his nose in such a way as to suggest the *nasus aduncus*, or whisper " w. p." (worthless person) under his breath when some one was mentioned who had been tried and found wanting. He was quick to detect and censure faults in dress or manners. " I remember," says one of his younger friends, " he would always send us back to our rooms if we came to see him in slippers."

But he could, on occasion, be much more severe, and never minced matters when serious faults were to be reproved. And no one could take offence, however severe he was ; the reproof was given with such humanity, such genuine interest, that it was easy to kiss the rod. · No one could be more sensitive, not from vanity, but from tenderness, than he was himself. The slightest resemblance of a snub shut him up at once. The perversities which he sometimes had to meet with in the library caused him pain of which few have any idea. Much of his kindness to undergraduates was due to gratitude for their kindness to him, as he put it, in coming to see him. Nevertheless he could blurt out to his friends home-truths the reverse of flattering. One day the talk turned on fitness for various professions. " What am I fit for ? " said one of the party. " To be a rich man," was the somewhat crushing reply. On another occasion, when some one tried to explain his motives, he said : " I hope to judge you always by what you *do*, not by what you say : I leave motives to take care of themselves."

As he felt strongly in all things, his dislikes were as strong as his attachments, and he took little pains to conceal them. When he first became a member of the high table at King's, he absented himself from hall for nearly a year, because he could not put up with one of the seniors. If he disliked a man he could show it in his manner, which was at times so brusque as almost to be rude, but he was incapable of a sneer. " That is a *viper*," he would say, if some malicious remark had crept into a

college fly-sheet submitted for his criticism, and the passage
stood condemned. Magnanimity was written clearly on
the fine-cut, severe features of his face—a face, says Dr
Benson, " less changed from its boy-look than that of any
friend I know, only grown firmer and stronger." "Don't
be afraid," he said once, "of giving any one, however mean,
an advantage by confessing yourself in the wrong. A
triumph is so helpful to such a man when it is won by his
being in the right. And if you put yourself in the right in
this point at such a cost, he must feel how likely you are
to be right in the rest."

Strict and spotless as he was in his own moral discipline, he was largely tolerant of much at which the
mere moralist holds up his hands in horror—tolerant, that
is, not in acquiescence, but in the hope of amendment,
which he would seek to bring about by gentle means. On
the other hand, an ungenerous thought or action, a paltry
excuse, anything in the nature of humbug or pretence,
never failed to fire his indignation, and his disapproval
was formidable. No one who knew him is likely to forget
the energy with which he stigmatised as "*poison*" some
demoralising argument, some ungenerous attribution of
motives, or some instance of the carping spirit, which he
detested almost more than anything else.

As an illustration of the outspokenness with which he
could sometimes administer reproof, I may quote the
following letter *:—

"DEAR MR ——,

"I have waited for a new *Athenæum*, on the
chance of there being some word from you, but as there is
not, I must give up altogether. I was very sorry to see
your suicide on the preceding Saturday, and was in hopes

---

* This letter is copied from a draft found among his papers. I have no
proof that it was actually sent.

that my letters would do something to prevent such a catastrophe. I did not expect, of course, that you would write with such needless humility as you expressed in your letter to me, but I confess I was amazed at your power of *statement.*

"Apart from the fact that in your postscript you make me say the very opposite of what I did say, your own account of the manuscript is as destructive of all you had said previously, that it is difficult to conceive how any one trained in the school of such a man as Mr —— can have committed such a series of blunders in his own department. That, after this, you have gone astray when dealing with printed books is very little to be wondered at. I am only thankful that it has rendered it quite unnecessary for me to write to the *Athenæum.* Knowing your high position, I could not help writing an earnest expostulation to you on the subject, of which you clearly knew less than nothing, and in which, after more than twenty years' hard work, I am keenly interested. It would have been easy to write a slashing letter to the *Athenæum* or elsewhere, but there are few things more offensive to me than the *Saturday Review* style of criticism, where a man is really working honestly on a subject and unhappily makes a few blunders, which the best are liable to make.

"Your printed letters only make me feel that I took too great a liberty in writing to you at all, because the only thing that could possibly justify me in writing as I did was the conviction that you were really willing to learn. I must now be content to leave you to continue your researches after more valuable *theories,* instead of the still more valuable *facts* which I should prefer to see hunted up.

"Yours most truly,
"HENRY BRADSHAW."

The frankness which marked his conversation, is equally noticeable in his letters. One of his friends, in a letter to him, says : "Among the many things you have taught me, one was to put away over-politeness." He never feared to lose a friend by saying what he felt when occasion required, as the following extracts will show.

" MY DEAR ——,

"... 'Mock' is your own word, not mine. It is the furthest possible from expressing my feeling about your tirades, which simply make me very unhappy. . . . When a man, who might by his own deeper knowledge help to make such an exhibition very much more interesting and instructive, wastes his energies in writing as you do, it naturally produces the impression that his main object is to let the world see how much more he knows of the subject than the idiots to whose care he says these treasures are submitted. Those who know you know also that that is not the object you have in view, but it is a pardonable inference for ordinary people to draw.

" Everything you write about this shows such an extraordinary absence of wisdom (by which I don't mean knowledge or cleverness, both of which are abundantly shown) ; but what pains me is, that it is all so diametrically opposed to the whole spirit of yours on ——, which you sent me—a paper which, as you know, delighted me more than any words of mine can express. You have such a fund of strong gentleness in you, that it is most cruel to see the immense power that this gentleness possesses simply wasted by a perversity as noxious as anything to be found even in ——. I hope you will come on Tuesday, and you can sit on me to your heart's content. Give my love to P.

" Yours always,

" HENRY BRADSHAW."

" DEAR MR. ——,

"... As for your second letter, you write frankly, so you must expect me to do the same. Your letter shows me that you are blind to two things, which, if you wish to get on and live happily, you must not only see clearly, but keep constantly before you. If I don't make myself clear, pray tell me, and I will try to do so. . . . About influence and influential people—what you call influence, I call jobbery. I wish I could get you to see that no testimonial is worth anything compared with the testimonial afforded by your own witnessed work. If you will keep in the wise course you seem to have begun, you may before long get precisely what you want, while *no* outside influence could possibly give it you. . . . Can you see this? It is what I have always held and preached to you, but you would not listen. I am quite aware that this must take some little time, and that time is money. But here I would gladly help if you would only be content to learn and act methodically. I will gladly pay you for work if you will do it in my way.

"Yours very truly,

"HENRY BRADSHAW."

He says in another letter: "There is nothing so unpleasant as to ask a favour." Again:

" DEAR MR ——,

"... When you touch the question of money, I feel at every line how much it were to be wished that you had some plain-spoken friend at hand who could command both your confidence and respect. I have not the least wish to offend you in the matter, or in any way, but I must tell you plainly, that if any Englishman of my acquaintance expressed himself as you always do on this subject, I should tell him that it was simply *humbug*. There is no other word in the language which expresses the state of mind where the speaker is, as you unquestionably are, perfectly sincere, and says all he says in perfect good faith, while yet the whole thing is unsound. You write this morning as follows :—' I undertook the work solely for the purpose of making the subject known ; the pecuniary question is entirely secondary. In fact, I should not have thought about remuneration at all, if Dr —— had not suggested it to me. The non-publication of the book as a book would certainly prevent me from accepting any money. . . .'

" The impression that you have always left on me is that of a person who was somehow ashamed of being thought to earn his daily bread by literary work. The English are said to be a commercial nation, a nation of shopkeepers, etc., and it may possibly be this which makes it so repugnant to me to have it constantly brought before one that in work of this kind money is a secondary object. My view rather is, ' bread and butter first ; ' man must live, and if he takes to literature, he must earn his bread by literary work. The difference between one man and another is then shown by the stamp of work done ; and in this the good man comes out. In no case, unless you are a millionaire, can you afford to do much work of this kind as the employment of mere hours of idleness. In no case can the expression of such sentiments produce anything but repugnance in any one to whom they are addressed. I must trust to you not to be vexed with me for writing to you in this way. I am not in a position which gives me any right to speak to you thus ; but at the same time I can see no one who is, and if we are to have any dealings together, these things must be made plain. . . .

" Yours very truly,
" HENRY BRADSHAW."

Such letters, if taken alone, would give an impression of a sort of sledge-hammer style, almost cruel in its frankness. This was, however, by no means habitual to him. As an antidote, I may quote the following extract from a letter to an intimate friend, young enough to have been his son. It displays the deep-set humility which was not incompatible with the utmost boldness in speaking where he thought it needful to speak out.

"MY DEAR ——,

". . . You would not believe me if I wrote what I feel about you and your work, so I will not put it on paper here. You make me feel very small, always, but in doing so there is no sting, because you always make me feel the power of rising to a higher and better level, and I try to do so accordingly. So you are helpful to others, even perhaps when you least think it. I only wish I could sometimes *see* you more.

"Ever yours affectionately,
"HENRY BRADSHAW."

Of the two following letters, the one, a letter of con-gratulation on his appointment to the librarianship in 1867, illustrates the regard felt for him by his younger friends; the other, written by him nearly twenty years later to a young scholar who had just carried off the "blue ribbon" of the Cambridge schools, testifies to the warmth of his sympathy and his affection for the college to which he belonged.

"MY DEAR BRADSHAW,

"Accept the sincere congratulations of a mouldy usher who has just exchanged 'Arnold's Exer-cises' for the *University Intelligence*. The friend of the scholar, the patron of the bachelor, the mediating buffer

between all the discordant elements of the college, you
have left very pleasant impressions on my mind, chastened,
it may be, by the socratic ἐιρωνἐια which was always
piquant, and not never intelligible. The chapel bells have
rung the old flat out and the new flat in, at your ' hebdo-
madal board ' on Sunday mornings ; and we are all ushers,
civil servants, or sucking clerks in the House of Lords,
except you alone, the unchanged. I am very proud, as a
member of the flat, that it has now got an ἀρχή upon it.
But I must drop this, and go into school.

" Yours ever,

" X. Y. Z."

" MY DEAR BERRY,

"As I don't know where or when I may be
able to see you in the next day or two, I must write you
a line of heartiest and warmest congratulation, not only on
your place and on the ease with which you have got it,
but perhaps above all for the sake of the college. The
provost ought indeed to be pleased, to have lived to see
the full fruit of his resolute move which he made the
moment·he was elected.* . . . It was long before we saw
a pure unbracketed senior classic in the college, though
classics had been for centuries the staple of our education.
. . . It has, of course, taken far longer for the college to
climb the hill of what still remains and must long remain
the chief Tripos in Cambridge. . . . There will be many, of
course, who will be delighted to see you in your place for
your own sake. There are others, who perhaps don't know
you personally, whose chief pleasure will perhaps lie in the
earnest that your work and your place give that the college
is quietly and steadily making its way to the front—who
look to you and such as you, to make the college really
deserve the precedence which it happens to hold in the

---

* See above, p. 21.

university on the purely accidental ground of its origin
Forgive me for writing at such length, but my heart is full
of many things, and I cannot help expressing myself.

"Ever yours most sincerely,

"HENRY BRADSHAW."

Now and then, though rarely, his temper would betray
him into saying things which he afterwards regretted ; but
in such cases he never failed to make his peace and that
speedily, with the person whom he had offended. It will
be allowed that an apology like the following must have
made amends for the bitterest words :—

"MY DEAR ——,

"I have to thank you for your letter just
received. . . . There is one point for which I have to thank
you most sincerely, and that is for drawing attention to my
language in hall. I feel that nothing whatever can excuse
me for having spoken as I did, and I only wish I could
say so more publicly. I met to-day two or three who
were there last night, and I did then express my regret
for having spoken as I did ; for, though put out at the
moment, I cannot for a moment excuse myself for using
strong language. My tongue gets the better of me sometimes, but, happily for me, I always pay the penalty for it.
I hope you will forgive me.

"Yours very sincerely,

"HENRY BRADSHAW."

I take the following from another letter :—

"The greater the wrong, the greater the need to acknowledge it, if one has any wish to live peaceably and
happily. The greatest humiliation would, to my mind, be
better than the misery and discomfort of an unacknow-
ledged injury, for the very simple reason that the result is

far worse to the person who does the wrong than to him
who sustains it."

In talking *about* people whom he disliked or disap-
proved, he could be sarcastic ; in talking or writing *to*
them, he was not unfrequently ironical. " Mr ――――," he
said one day, " is one of those people who never by any
means discover they can be unpleasing to any one."
But such disapproval as he felt or uttered was confined
to the sphere of morals or conduct. In the matter of
opinion he was largely and genuinely tolerant.

One who has passed through several phases, and has
good cause to know, writes of him, "The more I think of
Bradshaw, the more I am struck by his perfect tolerance
of all religions and all opinions—perfect in that it was
without a taint of indifference or contempt. He was
sincerely interested in the mental changes of all his friends,
and watched one going towards atheism and another
towards Romanism with equal respect, so long as he
believed both to be sincere. He seemed to regard opinions
without either sympathy or aversion, as phenomena of the
inner man." He displayed a " scrupulous reverence for
individuality, which he never interfered with except to
correct misstatements of fact. I think he would as soon
have tried to persuade a man to dye his hair as to alter or
not to alter his religious views."

It was, therefore, not in the region of opinion, but in
that of conduct that his influence was felt. He shrank
from dogmatic statement, except where facts capable of
scientific proof were concerned ; but in a question of right
or wrong, or in more delicate questions of taste and feeling,
there his instinct was unerring, and he never hesitated to
give it utterance. Still, his influence was due far more to
the subtle force of example than to outspoken precept. It
was the natural effect of contact with a character at once
independent and sympathetic, strong and gentle, unworldly

and yet human to the core. " He carried his atmosphere
with him," says one who knew him well. " He coloured
the talk and the looks and the habits of those who were
much with him, without forcibly impressing himself on
them." And another remarks, " It is only what every one
has said, that one felt larger and better in his company,
for no pettiness could live in his presence." One might
well apply to him the lines of " In Memoriam * "—

> !" The stern were mild when thou wert by,
> The flippant put himself to school
> And heard thee, and the brazen fool
> Was soften'd, and he knew not why."

Towards those who came to him for aid or counsel,
none could be more helpful, more wise, more sympathetic,
more considerate. In such cases, time seemed of no
account. He would spend hours in giving the help required, whether it were some old friend who came to talk
over a grave crisis in his life, some undergraduate in
trouble with the deans, or some college secretary unable
to draft without assistance the rules of an atheletic club.
A friend slightly younger than himself says, "I talked
with him with less reserve than with any other friend I
ever had. I have never known any one for whose judgment on matters of feeling I cared so much ; one *felt* he
was always right." And many others might be quoted to
the same effect. One confided in him naturally both joys
and sorrows. But he never gushed. Perhaps he said
nothing at all, but as you passed him in the street he
would put out his hand—a silent pressure and a look, that
said, " I know," and that was enough. He was the reverse
of demonstrative, but sometimes the warmth of his affectionate nature would break out in spite of himself. Archdeacon Norris remembers how " his eyes filled with tears
and his heart came into look and voice " when he spoke to
him of his friend Wickenden,† then lately dead.

* " In Memoriam," ed. 1866, cix. 3.   † See above, p. 203, note.

If he was so generous of his time, than which he could give nothing more valuable, it is not surprising that he was generous in other ways. I have given several illustrations already; many more might be given. His unselfishness was the more striking because he always made it out, if he could, to be mere selfishness. If he aided any beginner with money to work—and there were many cases in which he practised this endowment of research—he would always justify it by insisting that he wanted the work done for himself. So in small things too. If he gave up his bedroom to a friend, and slept on the sofa, he vowed he liked it best; the sofa was so comfortable. Help in money he was always ready to give. On one occasion he paid all the expenses of an undergraduate's residence during the Long Vacation. To one student he paid £35 for doing a task which was the best possible training for his life's work, and he contributed towards the expenses of a book which he was desirous of publishing. Another he sent abroad to study. For a third, who was anxious to edit a certain manuscript, he obtained the admission of her work among the publications of the Early French Text Society, and the aid of the most accomplished scholars in the subject. He did not approve of lending money, but he would sometimes lend. " I was in considerable difficulty," writes a friend, "on leaving Cambridge, about my debts, which were large for a man who had nothing. He happened to hear of it, and immediately begged me to send all my bills to him, and let him settle them at once and be my only creditor. I have known similar and even more generous deeds of unsolicited kindness towards others, friends and servants."

First introductions to Bradshaw were often the occasion for the display of some interesting bit of character. One friend writes, " The first time I saw Bradshaw, my friend Conway took me to see him. I well remember the second time I went. He was engaged in his outer room, and motioned me to go into the inner room. Presently he came in, and began poking the fire very deliberately without saying a word. This was too much for the nerves of a humble freshman. I remarked, with some precipitation, 'Conway told me to call on you, sir.' A pause followed ; after which he said, 'You mean to say, that nothing would have induced you to call on me except extreme compulsion.' From that moment I felt I had a friend."

Another typical case is that of a friend who, having been fascinated by him at their first meeting on the banks of the river, found him, when he visited him in his rooms, somewhat chilling, and did not go again for some time. When, eventually, he plucked up courage to go again, it was with others. "One by one the company dropped away, and we were left alone. I rose to go, but he detained me with some trivial question, and I saw that I was meant to stay. Presently our conversation turned on Ireland. He seemed to know Ireland well, and was acquainted with many of my friends. He led me to speak of my home and family ; and before long I had told him all about my previous life and education, the history of my family, the occupations and pursuits of my brothers, and a thousand other details, which he listened to with the greatest attention. The kindly interest which he showed, untinged with any suspicion of curiosity, led me unconsciously to speak to him as an old friend. The small hours of the morning had gone by before we had finished our conversation. From that time hardly a day passed without my visiting his rooms."

Another remembers how, on his first visit, he was questioned about his school, his home, and all the history of his life. "Very soon I found he knew all about my family —much more than I knew myself. He told me we had a common ancestor a century ago, and he brought out of his store old memoranda, pedigrees, and notes of family history to show me."

Mr Arthur Sidgwick remembers how he first met Bradshaw when, as a Rugby boy of thirteen, he was invited to Cambridge for a week by one of the senior Fellows of Trinity. " He asked several of the younger men to meet me ; but I remember distinguishing Bradshaw amongst them, as the one who took trouble to be kind to me. I was a good deal out of my element, and probably rather bored, and Bradshaw was the only one of the seniors (as they seemed) who knew how to talk to a boy. This was in 1853."

Another says, "I got to know him very early in my career. At that time I am afraid I was rather *outré* in my costume ; and one of his first remarks was, ' Ah! I've long wanted to know who the man was that I saw going about in a *trouser-hat* ' * —a remark which I do not think now quite so complimentary as I did then." Mr. W. C. Streatfield relates how he first met him in the University Library when he was looking out a bit of genealogy. " I was told he would help me. So he did ; not as I expected, but with that droll, half-asleep knowledge of everything which took away one's breath. The first thing he said was, ' Oh yes, you are Streatfield ; your mother was a daughter of Mrs. Fry ; ' and then came other details brought out of an apparently boundless store of information about all one's family concerns."

But these first meetings were not always so favourable. Bradshaw was sometimes cross. One who afterwards came to know him well, relates that on his first entering the room Bradshaw was very civil, but that after a few remarks had passed the conversation suddenly came to a standstill. " There were five or six men in the room, but

---

* This was his regular name for a soft hat made out of the same sort of cloth as trousers are made of.

for some time nothing was to be heard but the tapping of Bradshaw's fingers—you know how many curious tricks he had. With us had entered X., who had just become a Fellow. There was about him a touch of self-importance, and he took upon himself to relieve the oppressive silence by making some remark, which drew Bradshaw. The scene that followed was terrible. Bradshaw was a master in the art of taking down, and poor X. had to submit to be the victim of his skill. When he was in certain moods, not even a wise man would have felt sure of his wisdom. In a few minutes X. left the room in a towering rage, and we soon followed him. During our stay there was some tea, and somebody incurred Bradshaw's wrath for cutting the bread as if it had been a cake."

He did not often lose his temper, but he did now and then ; and when he was cross he was dangerous. I once knew him give an undergraduate, who was teasing him, a vigorous box on the ear ; but he apologised humbly for it afterwards. Nothing annoyed him more than a practical joke. No one would have dreamt of playing one on him ; but the mere mention of such a thing (with approval) made him very angry. On the other hand, he did not the least mind being misunderstood. He not unfrequently suffered from misconstructions ; but if they hurt him he kept it to himself, and was apparently only amused. He hated explanations, and there was a vein of perversity in him which, so long as no one was injured but himself, rather took pleasure in mystifying those whom prejudice or stupidity led astray in their estimate of him. On one occasion he wrote, "Newspaper controversy is at all times such an unmixed evil in my mind, that I would always rather even suffer in people's estimation than give way to it." And again, "When charges are so absolutely without foundation, I always find them easy to bear."

The coincidences that happened to him were often astonishing. Dr Benson notices it as a peculiarity of his younger days. " He always, whatever you asked him, just happened to have been looking it up. ' How odd that you should ask me that ! ' he would say. ' I stumbled on the explanation last week.' " It was the same in latter years. Every friend of his was struck by these accidents, which hardly seemed as if they could be accidental. " It was very much through Bradshaw's influence," says Mr Yeld, " that I was appointed, in 1865, to a mastership in Lincoln Grammar School. By one of the curious coincidences which constantly happened to him, he was staying at the deanery when I wrote about the post, and met there at dinner John Fowler, the head-master. One can imagine Bradshaw's delighted exclamation when, in the middle of dinner, he was casually asked across the table, ' Do you know a man named Yeld, of St John's ? ' What he said I do not know, but I got the post." Dr Benson tells me that a curious oriental manuscript was once sent to him by a friend who could make out nothing about it. It turned out to be Tibetan. Of course, Bradshaw had just been learning Tibetan in order to decipher his own manuscripts, and was able to tell his friend all he wanted to know. Professor Sidgwick has noticed the same peculiarity. In applying to Bradshaw, he says, for help about books, " I became continually more and more impressed, not only by his ever-ready helpfulness, but by the remarkable series of coincidences—as he represented them—by which he always happened to know what I happened to ask him. My inquiries related to very various topics, but none seemed to come amiss. Arabic manuscripts, mediæval politics, modern miracles—whatever it was, he always knew just what I wanted to know."

He delighted in giving, and in his gifts "he was," says Dr Benson, " of all men the most *à propos*. An undergraduate friend had to recite a college oration in which the strongly contrasted countenances of Bunyan and Herbert were described. Two or three days later, Bradshaw dropped in to breakfast, having in his hand two exquisite etchings of the very heads, procured by some special pains. 'I thought you might like to have these two faces to hang by your fire,' he said, as he laid them quietly on a side-table." "It was dangerous," says Mr Tuckwell, "to express a wish or to sound a note of admiration in his presence. He was told I was collecting Simonides literature, and I forthwith received the Mayer facsimile. One day I searched the Dublin bookstalls in his company for an original 'Anti-Jacobin.' He said nothing, but wrote off to Cambridge for his own copy, and placed it in my hands." Mr A. J. Butler tells how one day, when as yet unacquainted with Bradshaw, he "happened to go into Fred Pollock's rooms. I saw a bunch of roses on the table, and sang out to Pollock, 'Who gave you these roses?' 'Bradshaw,' he replied. 'Well, then, I wish Bradshaw would give *me* some,' said I ; and then I heard an inarticulate sound, and perceived that Bradshaw was in the room. I suppose we were both rather shy. However, a few days after, I was walking in King's garden with some one, and met Bradshaw. He had a bunch of roses in his hand, and as we passed he just slipped them into mine without saying a word."

It will, perhaps, have surprised some readers of this memoir that so little has been said of Bradshaw's conversation ; but nothing is so evanescent when not recorded on the spot. In Bradshaw's case it was peculiarly difficult to recall, for he did not utter epigrams, or say the witty things which are treasured up for their felicity or compression. In ordinary talk he was direct and vigorous, going straight to the heart of the question ; but it was rather the .matter of his speech than the mould in which it was cast, that impressed itself upon his hearers. It was distinguished for sound judgment, for practical wisdom, for insight and observation, but not for brilliancy. It was always his own, at all events. He was sometimes paradoxical ; as, for instance, when, on a friend remarking of some old book that he supposed it was very rare, he replied, "Oh no ; if it were, it would be very common." But this was generally when he was in the mood for puzzling people, not when he was serious. "A paradox," he once remarked, is not *always* true."

In exposition he was generally somewhat involved and hard to follow. The frequency with which he would help himself out by using the phrase "I mean," showed how difficult it was for him to hit readily on the right way of putting things. It was not that he thought obscurely, but he did not think rapidly, and he was not very apt at discussion. "His smiling silences," says Dr Benson, "argued with you almost as much as his reasonable proofs." He had no taste for dialectics or word-play of any kind. But his talk was nervous and pregnant, never vapid or feeble. It was, as was said of Burke's conversation, the natural overflowing of a full mind. He observed the golden rule, to talk of things rather than persons, and he was not by any means ready to give an opinion on every subject that might turn up. With young folks he generally kept his learning in the background ; and some of those he liked best went through Cambridge without ever having a notion how learned he was.

Whatever he may have been in his earlier days, he was averse latterly from discussing religious topics, but he was by no means disinclined to discuss the problems of sociology and philosophy with one or two intimate friends. What his religious views were, it is difficult to say with certainty or exactitude. His wide intellectual sympathies made him much more than merely tolerant: he was deeply interested in various creeds. As he grew older his mind did not stiffen ; on the contrary, it seemed, with a perpetual youth, to become more open to new ideas. His interest in natural science was always strong. He grasped and accepted the doctrine of evolution in its main outlines, though his innate modesty and diffidence prevented him from uttering positive opinions about a subject so intricate as the ideas particularly associated with the name of Darwin. Though by no means all things to all men, he was remarkably capable of regarding a question from the same point of view as his interlocutor, so much so that he sometimes conveyed the impression of an agreement which did not really exist. Thus it came about that different persons formed different conceptions of his views ; and I have been assured, on the one hand, that he was a High Churchman, on the other, that he was an Agnostic. Those who knew him best will probably agree that, while not caring to formulate his belief too closely, he died, as he had lived, a devout Christian, and a member of the Church of England.

In politics he was a decided Liberal ; that is, he believed in the constant possibility of amelioration, and in the potency of combined human effort to this end. He voted for the Duke of Devonshire as chancellor, and for Professor Stuart in the contested university election of 1882. But his Liberalism was that of a student of history, coloured by a reverence for the great things of the past, restrained by a conviction of the continuity of development. He had much sympathy with the movement for women's education, helped the members of Newnham College to arrange their library, and did all he could to further their cause. He sympathised neither with repression nor with crude rebellion against authority. In the microcosm of university life, he set his face equally against donnishness and against the view cherished by some undergraduates—fewer, probably, now than formerly—that a don is their natural enemy. Thus to the end of his life he remained, what he had been as a young Master of Arts, a link between the two great classes of university society.

As an illustration of his Liberal-Conservative tendencies, I may quote the following from a letter to Mr Coxe, of the Bodleian, written in 1876, when the restoration, or destruction, of Duke Humphry's Library was under discussion :—

"I am really distressed to hear what you say about your dear old reading-room. . . . I could not have believed such a thing was possible as that Oxford, however 'young,' would want to destroy such a noble specimen of work which brings back so vividly the history of the past. I am not one of those antiquaries who like to preserve everything old *because* it is old ; the old must give way to the new, or the world would never get on at all. If the places had been clumsy or useless (only kept to be looked at as curiosities, I mean), or still more, if they had been decaying, let them go by all means, however keen a pang it might cost ; but here there could be absolutely no reason of the kind. I have tested by hours and hours of work there the practical use of these old arrangements. . . . I do trust you will be able to avert a decision which would be a real shame to Oxford.*

"Ever yours,
"HENRY BRADSHAW."

His æsthetic faculties were active and discriminating. Though not pretending to be a connoisseur, he keenly enjoyed works of art. Great pictures, like the "Last Supper" at Milan, or the "Adoration of the Lamb" at Ghent, filled him with simple delight. It need hardly be said that of some branches of mediæval art, of early woodcuts and

* Fortunately, Duke Humphry's Library is still intact.

engravings, his knowledge was wide and intimate. Of architecture he knew much. I can well recollect how, on one of our earliest walks, as we rested at Madingley, he gave me a clear view of the various styles, with the dates at which they began and ended, illustrating the divisions by references to buildings at Cambridge and elsewhere, the respective ages of which he had, like all his other knowledge, at his fingers' ends. But music was the art which gave him the keenest pleasure. He seldom went to concerts, never, probably, unless he were "taken" by somebody, but he would sit and listen by the hour while one of his nieces or some musical friend played sonatas of Beethoven or fugues of Bach. Of Bach he was specially fond, preferring him to Handel, and this at a time when Bach was less often heard than he is now.

His knowledge of music, the theory of it, and the development from early church music, was considerable. He had a good ear, and could put in a correct second. He would sometimes get his friends to play the old music he had brought from home, and would hum over the tunes he knew. Among them was some Spanish music, and he was especially fond of a piece, something like a Gregorian chant, with the refrain, " No tocaran campañas quand' io muerar " (" ring not the bells when I am dead "). The quietism of it seemed to appeal to him. References in letters already quoted show how fond he was of the curfew, which rings every night at nine o'clock from St Mary's tower. " That blessed bell," he used to call it. He was, I think, the only person I ever knew who could write out from memory the well-known Cambridge chimes. When Dr Stanford was composing his opera of " Savonarola," he asked Bradshaw if he knew of any old church tune which could be made use of. Bradshaw said nothing at the time, but some time afterwards he brought him the music of the mediæval hymn, " Angelus ad virginem," which he had found in an ancient service-book in the University Library. It was very difficult to put the music into modern notation, but he had done it, says Dr Stanford, quite correctly.

Of modern literature he was not a universal reader : he used to say he read nothing. Nevertheless he read more than most men. It was poetry, chiefly, and novels and biographies, that he liked ; he hardly ever read travels, so far as I am aware, or books on political economy, philosophy, and the like. When he was travelling in France, he read a great many novels, buying them at the railway stations as he went. On one such occasion, when he was in Brittany with Mr and Mrs Cornish, he bought all Mde. Charles Reybaud's novels ; on another, he read five or six Balzacs, and an equal number of George Sand, Daudet, etc. He remembered them well, and took a Macaulay-like delight in the details. When a book was given him, he read it straight through at once, and when it was given him by the author, he always bought another copy to give away. He never bought a book which he did not read.

Among modern poets his favourites were, latterly, Tennyson, Browning, and Matthew Arnold ; among the novelists, Thackeray, Kingsley, and George Eliot. A friend remembers his reading aloud to him and another the whole of " Pendennis " in the evenings of one long Vacation. " Peg Woffington," " Christie Johnstone," " The Heir of Redclyffe," " Cranford," were also favourite books. He was fond, too, of humorous works, both English and American. I do not think he cared much for Dickens. But his taste was catholic, and his reading was to a certain extent determined by chance and the recommendations of friends. He greatly admired the writings of Mark Pattison. In his " Life of Casaubon," he had marked many passages especially appealing to him ; for instance, the following :—" Exhaustive research is . . . a process which, while it has much fatiguing exertion of eye and memory, derives its whole value from the intelligence which directs it and is engaged in sifting the material " (p. 387) ; and again, " Love of truth is the foundation of all research and all learning, and is, indeed, only the desire of knowledge under another name " (p. 519). Such passages might have been taken as the mottoes of his life.

He delighted in reading his favourite books aloud, and he often found willing listeners. He used to read at home to his sisters or his nieces, and he read at Cambridge to his friends. No one who ever heard him read " The Forsaken Merman," or any other of his favourite poems, is likely to forget the impressive tones of his sympathetic voice, or the pathos of his delivery. He was equally infectious, in another way, in his evident enjoyment as he read aloud such books as " The Rose and the Ring," or " Alice in Wonderland," or " The Water Babies."

It is not to be supposed, however, that he was always in the humour for society. He suffered occasionally from fits of depression—" the dumps," he used to call them—in which he felt good for nothing, unable to do good work, or to enjoy his accustomed pleasures. When he was in this state he liked to have a friend with him, not necessarily to talk to, but in order not to be alone, and this silent company was his best medicine. Physical causes were generally at the root of these temporary ailments. He suffered from severe headaches and violent colds, things to which a man of his sedentary life and full physique is often liable, and which the irregularity of his habits did not tend to diminish. For his habits were very irregular. His hours of rising were never fixed. Sometimes he would get up early, and do a couple of hours' work in the library before breakfast ; but occasionally he would lie in bed till nearly the middle of the day. Once long ago he was remonstrated with by the dean about his irregular attendance at chapel. " I am never

irregular," he replied ; " I always go, or I always don't go."
Perhaps he would promise to go for a Sunday walk at
eleven o'clock. His friend would come in, expecting to
find him dressed. Not a bit of it; he was still in bed.
"Get up, Bradshaw; it's time to be off." No answer, but
a groan from under the bedclothes. A second remonstrance perhaps produced the plaintive reply of, "Oh, I
can't get up ; I *wish* I could. Do stay a minute." Had
he been left alone at this point he would not have moved,
but a few minutes' talk brought him round, and his visitor
had hardly left the room before he was out of bed.

On his visits to the Lakes, he would take long walks,
and towards the end of his life he took to tricycling, which
he continued vigorously for about a year, and then left off
entirely. Generally speaking, he took very little exercise,
and was loth to take it alone. He was grateful to any
friend who came to the library at four o'clock, when the
doors were closed, and forced him to come out. If no one
came, he probably went home. His diet was equally irregular. He would often eat heartily, and then for days
he would take next to nothing. It was an even chance
whether he drank wine or not at dinner—he seldom touched
it in the middle of the day—but I have known him drink
a whole bottle of port at a sitting, in order to cure a cold,
without the slightest visible effect. There was no saying
when he would go to bed ; he would sometimes turn in at
nine o'clock, or, if he was in the humour or had any special
work to do, would sit up several nights running till three
or four in the morning. He smoked occasionally, but seldom
more than a cigarette. In one point he was regular—in
his attendance at the library. There he hardly ever failed.
It is easy to recall his portly figure as he paced along his
accustomed path, his head thrown back, his shoulders
slightly swinging as he walked, his books in his hand. He
never seemed to be in a hurry. I have seen him walking

home without an umbrella in a pelting rain, but he never quickened his pace.

In summer-time he would often go down after hall to the fellows' garden, to stroll round and watch the Evening Primrose open its saffron petals, or pluck a bit of his favourite Carolina All-spice, or listen to the chorus of song gradually dying away in that "bird-haunted English lawn." Then, as night fell, he would go back to his own rooms, where a kettle was always ready, and tea could be drunk as one sat at the window, and the curfew came pealing in across the open spaces of the court. After tea he would set to work at his table, with his books and large sheets of foolscap before him ; or, if he was in the mood for talk, would sit in his big chair, his legs crossed, his hands lying folded, one in the other, in his lap, his spectacles pushed back on his forehead, and talk on as if time and work had no existence.

"On one such evening," writes a friend, "I came to his rooms, and was surprised to find him sitting with his windows wide open. One or two other men were in the room. They were not talking, and seemed to have the air of waiting for something to happen, so I likewise sat down in silence. In a few minutes the quiet evening air was gently stirred, and the room was filled with a mysterious mellow sound, soft yet strong. 'Ah, there it is!' said Bradshaw. No one else spoke, and we all gave ourselves up to listening. It was the muffled peal from St Mary's tower, ringing for poor old Dr Bushby, who had been buried that day. I have heard the same thing elsewhere, but the bells of St Mary's seem to lend to the requiem an especial charm. It was characteristic of Bradshaw to take great delight in so beautiful a sound."

For him too the bells have now rung their muffled peal. The crowd that accompanied him to the grave was not an assemblage of the curious, nor a gathering whose object it was to do formal honour to a distinguished man. In that

crowd there were few who were not mourners indeed, for
there were few who did not feel that they had lost a friend,
few who had not received at his hands kindness or help, or
some of those nameless services which are the best record
of a good man's life. It was rightly spoken from the
pulpit of St Mary's on the Sunday after he died, that he
was "a man whom to have known and loved is a lifelong
possession ; to have lost, a lifelong regret."

> " That low man seeks a little thing to do,
> Sees it and does it :
> This high man, with a great thing to pursue,
> Dies ere he knows it."

APPENDIX I.

Reprinted from " The Chronicles of the Collegiate Church or Free Chapel of All Saints, Derby," by J. Charles Cox and W. H. St John Hope.

NOTE ON MEDIÆVAL SERVICE-BOOKS.

In the old Church of England, the services were either—

1. For the different hours (Mattins, Lauds, Prime, Terce, Sext, None, Vespers, and Compline), said in the choir,

2. For processions, in the church or churchyard,

3. For the Mass, said at the Altar, or

4. For occasions, such as Marriage, Visitation of the Sick, Burial, etc., said as occasion required.

Of these four all have their counterparts, more or less, in the English Service of modern times, as follows :—

1. The Hour-Services, of which the principal were Mattins and Vespers, correspond to our Morning and Evening Prayer.

2. The Procession Services correspond to our hymns or anthems sung before the Litany which precedes the Communion Service in the morning, and after the third Collect in the evening, only no longer sung in the course of procession to the churchyard cross or a subordinate Altar in the church ; the only relic (in common use) of the actual procession being that used on such occasions as the consecration of a church, etc.

3. The Mass answers to our Communion Service.

4. The Occasional Services are either those used by a priest, such as Baptism, Marriage, Visitation and Communion of the Sick, Burial of the Dead, etc., or those reserved for a bishop, as Confirmation, Ordination, Consecration of Churches, etc.

All these services but the last mentioned are contained in our " Prayer-Book " with all their details, except the lessons at Mattins and Evensong, which are read from the Bible, and the hymns and anthems, which are, since the sixteenth century, at the discretion of the authorities. This concentration or compression of the services into one book is the natural result of time, and the further we go back the more numerous are the books which our old inventories show. To take the four classes of Services and Service-books mentioned above :

1. The Hour-Services were latterly contained, so far as the text was concerned, in the *Breviarium*, or *Portiforium*, as it was called by preference in England. The musical portions of this book were contained in the *Antiphonarium*. But the Breviary itself was the result of a gradual amalgamation of many different books :

(*a*) The *Antiphonarium*, properly so called, containing the Anthems (*Antiphonæ*) to the Psalms, the Responds (*Responsoria*) to the Lessons (*Lectiones*), and the other odds and ends of Verses and Responds (*Versiculi et Responsoria*) throughout the service ;

(*b*) The *Psalterium*, containing the Psalms arranged as used at the different Hours, together with the Litany as used on occasions ;

(*c*) The *Hymnarium*, or collection of Hymns used in the different Hour-services ;

(*d*) The *Legenda*, containing the long Lessons used at Mattins, as well from the Bible, from the *Sermologus*, and from the *Homiliarius*, used respectively at the first, second, and third Nocturns at Mattins on Sundays and some other days, as also from the *Passionale*, containing the acts of Saints read on their festivals ; and

(*e*) The *Collectarium*, containing the *Capitula*, or short Lessons used at all the Hour-services except Mattins, and the *Collectæ* or *Orationes* used at the same.

2. The Procession Services were contained in the *Processionale* or *Processionarium*. It will be remembered that the rubric in our "Prayer-Book" concerning the Anthem ("In Quires and places where they sing, here followeth the Anthem") is *indicative* rather than *imperative*, and that it was first added in 1662. It states a fact; and, no doubt, when processions were abolished, with the altars to which they were made, cathedral choirs would have found themselves in considerable danger of being swept away also, had they not made a stand, and been content to sing the Processional Anthem without moving from their position in the choir. This alone sufficed to carry on the tradition ; and looked upon in this way the modern Anthem Book of our Cathedral and Collegiate Churches, and the Hymn-Book of our parish churches, are the only legitimate successors of the old *Processionale*. It must be borne in mind, also, that the Morning and Evening Anthems in our "Prayer-Book" do not correspond to one another so closely as might at first sight appear to be the case. The Morning Anthem comes immediately before the Litany which precedes the Communion Service, and corresponds to the Processional Anthem or Respond sung at the churchyard procession before Mass. The Evening Anthem, on the other hand, follows the third Collect, and corresponds to the Processional Anthem or Respond sung "*eundo et redeundo*," in going to, and returning from, some subordinate altar in the church at the close of Vespers.

3. The Mass, which we call the Communion Service, was contained in the *Missale*, so far as the text was concerned. The Epistles and Gospels, being read at separate lecterns, would often be written

in separate books, called *Epistolaria* and *Evangeliaria.* The musical portions of the Altar Service were latterly all contained in the *Graduale* or Grayle, so called from one of the principal elements being the *Responsorium Graduale* or Respond to the *Lectio Epistolæ.* In earlier times these musical portions of the Missal Service were commonly contained in two separate books, the *Graduale* and the *Troparium.* The *Graduale*, being in fact the *Antiphonarium* of the Altar Service (as indeed it was called in the earliest times), contained all the passages of Scripture, varying according to the season and day, which served as Introits (*Antiphonæ et Psalmi ad Introitum*) before the Collects, as Gradual Responds or Graduals to the Epistle, as *Alleluia* versicles before the Gospel, as *Offertoria* at the time of the first oblation, and as *Communiones* at the time of the reception of the consecrated elements. The *Troparium* contained the *Tropi*, or preliminary tags to the Introits ; the Kyries ; the *Gloria in excelsis ;* the Sequences or *Prosæ ad Sequentiam* before the Gospel ; the *Credo in unum ;* the *Sanctus* and *Benedictus ;* and the *Agnus Dei ;* all, in early times, liable to have insertions or *farsuræ* of their own, according to the season or day, which, however, were almost wholly swept away (except those of the *Kyrie*) by the beginning of the thirteenth century Even in Lyndewode's time (A.D. 1433), the *Troparium* was explained to be a book containing merely the Sequences before the Gospel at Mass, so completely had the other elements then disappeared or become incorporated in the *Graduale.* This definition of the *Troparium* is the more necessary, because so many *old* church inventories yet remain, which contain books, even at the time of writing the inventory long since disused, so that the lists would be unintelligible without some such explanation.

4. The Occasional Services, so far as they concerned a priest, were of course more numerous in old days than now, and included the ceremonies for *Candle*mas, *Ash* Wednesday, *Palm* Sunday, etc., besides what were formerly known as the Sacramental Services. The book which contained these was in England called the *Manuale*, while on the Continent the name *Rituale* is more common. No church could well be without one of these. The purely episcopal offices were contained in the *Liber pontificalis* or Pontifical, for which an ordinary church would have no need.

5. Besides these books of actual Services there was another, absolutely necessary for the right understanding and definite use of those already mentioned. This was the *Ordinale*, or book containing the general rules relating to the *Ordo divini servitii.* It is the *Ordinarius* or *Breviarius* of many Continental churches. Its method was to go through the year and show what was to be done ; what days were to take precedence of others ; and how, under such circumstances, the details of the conflicting Services were to be dealt with. The basis of such a book would be either the well-known Sarum *Consuetudinarium*, called after St Osmund, but really drawn up in the first

quarter of the thirteenth century, the Lincoln *Consuetudinarium* belonging to the middle of the same century, or other such book. By the end of the fifteenth century Clement Maydeston's *Directorium Sacerdotum,* or Priests' Guide, had superseded all such books, and came itself to be called the Sarum *Ordinale,* until, about 1508, the shorter Ordinal, under the name of *Pica Sarum,* "the rules called the Pie," having been cut up and re-distributed according to the seasons, came to be incorporated in the text of all the editions of the Sarum Breviary.

From the Inventory of 1466, given above in the text, we learn that the Church of All Saints, Derby, possessed at that time the following books :—

1. For the Hour Services, eight *Antiphonaria* and one *Collectarium.* The absence of all trace of a *Legenda* might seem to imply that one or more of the *Antiphonaria* were really what are sometimes called noted Breviaries, containing the whole Breviary Service, only with musical notation to the choral parts.

2. For the Procession Services, four Processionars.

3. For the Altar Service, two Missals, a Gospelar, and three Grayles or *Gradualia.*

4. For the Occasional Services, two Manuals.

5. Two *Ordinalia,* one good and one not worth much.

The Inventory of 1527 shows us, beyond these, one great Portos, among the chained books, possibly a copy of the "Great Breviary" printed in 1516 ; and three printed Missals, two of which were reserved for the Altar of Our Lady, and one for that of St Nicholas.

H. B.

Cambridge,
 March 17, 1881.

APPENDIX II.

LETTER ON CATHEDRAL ORGANISATION.

University Library, Cambridge, May 19, 1881.

DEAR MR NORRIS,

It is not a grateful task to criticise such a document as the Report * of which you sent me a copy a few weeks ago ; but I should nevertheless like to send you a few remarks on it, which you must take for what they are worth.

Every one who wishes to see the Cathedral system extended, and the Cathedral staff made the nucleus of a diocesan working body, must sympathise fully with the endeavour to obtain what the Committee of Convocation proposes to call a "Diocesan Chapter." But when the formation of this Diocesan Chapter is advocated as being a revival of an organisation which existed some centuries ago, there is surely a fundamental misconception as to the real nature of the old state of things.

There are three passages in the Report on which I must say something :

1. "Living under some sort of Rule, these Cathedral clergy came to be called Canons" (page 2).

---

* This was the draft of a Report "on Cathedrals and their Reform," drawn up by a committee of the Lower House of Convocation early in 1881. The committee, desiring to see cathedral churches restored to their position as "strong centres in our ecclesiastical organisation," recommended (1) the formation of Larger or Diocesan Chapters, "consisting of Canons Non-Residentiary as well as Residentiary, to deliberate on such matters as the Bishop may wish to bring before them, and to take part in the election of Bishop or Capitular Proctor;" (2) the assignment of "such definite duties to the Smaller Cathedral Chapter as shall oblige the Canons Residentiary to reside during the greater part of the year." These recommendations were supported by an historical retrospect, tending to show that they involve "only the restoration and extension to all our cathedral churches of what anciently belonged to those of the Old Foundation." Archdeacon Norris sent Mr Bradshaw a copy of the Report, and asked him "to obelise any historical blunders" in the draft. Mr Bradshaw's letter is an answer to this request.

G. W. P.

2. " . . . Estates called Prebends came to be attached to particular stalls of the Church; and thus some Canons became corporations sole, in legal language. Canons, whose stalls were so endowed, were thence called Prebendaries " (page 3).

3. "The Canons Residentiary shared . . . The non-residentiaries had no share in the common fund. But all alike were summoned by the Bishop to the Chapter meetings; all alike, when so summoned, had *voice* as well as *seat* in the Chapter Room" (page 3).

Any one reading these passages would, I think, naturally infer (1) that the Rule under which the Canons lived was somewhat vague ; and (2) that some Canons only were endowed with Prebends; but (3) that all Canons, whether *Præbendati* or not, had the full privilege of a voice at meetings of the Chapter.

Now, in all I have read of the English Cathedral statutes and *consuetudines*, and of the Scotch ones derived from them—and these last illustrate most strikingly the working of the system in the early part of the thirteenth century—the thing which forces itself most prominently upon my notice is the extreme sacredness alike of the *Canonicatus* and the *Præbenda*. Whether Bishop, Dignitary, or ordinary member of the Chapter, the man must be a " *Frater et Canonicus* " and live under the Canonical Rule, before he could be in any way admissible to the Chapter House. Further, the *Præbenda* was so far of the essence of the institution, that until a Canon became possessed of his *Præbenda* he was nowhere ; he had to take no oath of obedience or fidelity even; he simply had his stall assigned to him in the choir ; and it is laid down with special emphasis that he could have no voice in the *negotia Ecclesiæ* or *secreta Capituli*.

In plain words, to be a full member of the Chapter he must be possessed of a Canonry and a *Præbenda* and have gone through a full course of residence, so as to have mastered the whole business of the position. He is a man living under the Canonical Rule, having the serious responsibility of actual ownership of property in the country (much more serious than we are now apt to think), who has, further, mastered his business as a Residentiary. Otherwise he has only certain Cathedral duties to perform, which he can perform from his first appointment, and he cannot attend the Chapter meetings, unless on some particular occasion his particular opinion may be desired *pro hac vice*, but not so as to serve in any way as a precedent for his further attendance.

I will copy out the passages relating to these points, which are to be found in the *Registrum Ecclesiæ Londoniensis*, or Statutes of St Paul's, sanctioned about the year 1300, together with the parallel passages of Bishop Alnwick's draft *Novum Registrum Ecclesiæ Lincolniensis*, prepared in 1440. Alnwick's book is now known to be *nil* as a body of statutes, having never been in any way sanctioned, having never in fact reached any stage beyond that of an incomplete draft. But, for the purpose in hand, this incompleteness and want of

sanction are of no consequence, as all the passages in it referring to
this question existed long before Alnwick's time, almost *totidem verbis,*
in the St Paul's *Registrum Ecclesiæ Londoniensis,* of which, indeed,
Alnwick's book is little more than a simple transcript, with certain
large modifications to suit the requirements of the Church of Lincoln.
Indeed, I give the passages from Alnwick's book chiefly because,
from the Bishop of Truro having taken it as his text, it is liable to be
more familiarly known than other less accessible statutes.

The first passage is the one which states broadly the nature of the
Chapter, showing its normal state apart from any of those qualifications which so materially affected its outward condition and appearance. It forms in both Registers the concluding section of the
Particula Prima, which deals with the constitution of the Chapter.

REGISTRUM ECCLESIÆ LONDO-
NIENSIS
Sanctioned about 1300.
" *De numero Canonicorum.*

" Triginta Canonici ecclesie
sancti Pauli cum capite suo episcopo corpus et Capitulum constituunt, et ecclesie negocia et
secreta tractant. Hii soli triginta Canonici Episcopum et
Decanum eligunt ; set ab Episcopo canonicatus et prebendas
assequitur. . . ."
Printed edition, page 23.

NOVUM REGISTRUM ECCLESIÆ
LINCOLNIENSIS
Prepared in 1440.
" *De numero Canonicorum.*

" Quinquaginta et sex Canonici
ecclesie beate Marie Lincolniensis
cum capite suo corpus et Capitulum constituunt ; Ecclesie negotia
et secreta tractant. Hij soli Canonici cum ceteris in Ecclesia ipsa
[altered from *nͬa*], dignitates
obtinentibus, Episcopum et Decanum eligunt, sed ab Episcopo
Canonicatus [altered from -*nias*]
et præbendas assecuntur. . . ."
Printed edition, page 28 (corrected by original draft).

This is the passage which is so commonly quoted in reference
to what the Committee of Convocation propose to call the " Diocesan
Chapter." This is the statement which has been supposed by some to
warrant the distinction between a Greater or Grand Chapter consisting of the whole number of Canons, and a Lesser Chapter consisting only of the Residentiaries. This, however, is quite untenable
ground. It will be seen directly that two further points, (1) the possession of a Prebend (and that through personal installation, not
merely by proxy), and (2) a course of Residence, were absolutely necessary to any Canon before he could take his place in Chapter under the
above statute.

As regards the *Prœbenda* take the following two chapters :—

REGISTRUM ECCLESIÆ LONDO-
NIENSIS
Sanctioned about 1300.

"*Incipit secunda Particula de Canonicorum ingressu et installatione.* . . .

"*Quod installatus in dignitate sine prebenda non promittit obedientiam vel fidelitatem nec communicat de secretis Capituli.*

"Et si prebendam non habeat, Decanus vel Canonicus ad hoc deputatus ei ostendit stallum assignatum in choro; nichil amplius obedientie vel fidelitatis requirens ab ipso donec prebendam assequatur; quia nullis tractatibus secretis Capituli vel eleccionibus intererit, donec fuerit in prebenda sollempniter, ut premittitur, investitus.

"*De absentibus per procuratorem installandis.*

"Et si Episcopus conferat prebendam alicui qui personaliter ad ecclesiam non accedit, set mittit procuratorem, illi procuratori ostenditur stallus illius prebende et psalmi dicendi, et ei traditur administratio illius prebende exterioris. · Set nunquam per procuratorem admittitur aliquis in Fratrem et Canonicum, nec installatur iuxta modum supra dictum, nec eciam in tractatibus secretis vel eleccionibus faciendis admittetur, quantumcumque prebendam tenuerit, nisi ad Ecclesiam personaliter veniat, et, sicut moris est, in fratrem et Canonicum fuerit in Capitulo admissus et installatus in Choro."

Printed edition, page 37.

NOVUM REGISTRUM ECCLESIÆ
LINCOLNIENSIS
Prepared in 1440.

"*Incipit secunda Particula de Canonicorum ingressu et installatione.* . . .

"Et si præbendam non habeat, Decanus vel Presidens ei ostendat stallum assignatum in Choro; nihil amplius obedientie vel fidelitatis requirens ab ipso donec præbendam assequatur, pro quovis statu tamen [printed edition, tituli] quem habuerit in Ecclesia; nec aliquid de communa percipiet ut Canonicus prebendatus; sicut nisi fuerit per Decanum et Capitulum ex mandato nostro, vel alicujus successorum nostrorum, aut per ipsos Decanum et Capitulum, ad aliqua Ecclesie pertractanda negotia convocatus.

"*De absente per procuratorem installando.*

"Quod si forte investiendus hujusmodi procuratorem ad hoc duxerit destinandum, illi procuratori ostendatur stallus illius prebende, et psalmi dicendi, et ei tradatur administratio illius prebende exterioris: sed nunquam per procuratorem admittitur aliquis in fratrem et canonicum, nec installatur iuxta modum supradictum, nec etiam in tractatibus secretis vel electionibus faciendis admittetur, quantumcunque prebendam tenuerit, nisi ad ecclesiam personaliter veniat, et sic ut moris est in fratrem et Canonicum fuerit in Capitulo admissus et installatus in Choro."

Printed edition, page 33.

As regards the necessity of residence, compare the following :—

From the Statutes of St Paul's, made under Radulphus de Diceto, when Dean, about the year 1200.*	From Bishop Alnwick's Draft *Novum Registrum Ecclesiæ Lincolniensis*, prepared in 1440.

From the Statutes of St Paul's, made under Radulphus de Diceto, when Dean, about the year 1200.*

"*Non debent intrare consiliis.*

"Nec debent novi Canonici Residenciarii vel alii de negociis vel consiliis Ecclesie vel tractatibus intromittere, vel eis interesse, nisi ad hoc specialiter per Decanum et Capitulum sint vocati."

Printed edition, page 129.

From Bishop Alnwick's Draft *Novum Registrum Ecclesiæ Lincolniensis*, prepared in 1440.

"Nec debet novus ille [canonicus,†] sic residens ante completam suam residentiam de negotiis vel consiliis Ecclesiæ vel tractatibus capitularibus, se intromittere vel eis interesse ;‡ nisi ad hoc specialiter per Decanum et Capitulum sit vocatus."

Printed edition, page 40.

These three things then stand out :

1. Admission as *Frater et Canonicus* into a body living under Rule and having inviolable *secreta* of its own ;

2. Possession of a *Præbenda*, or estate in land with spiritual duties as well as large civil privileges attached to it ; and

3. Residence at the Cathedral Church of such extent and duration as to qualify a man for a thorough knowledge of his duties as a Canon, however much he might be absent in after years.

It is clear that these three are the absolutely necessary qualifications for full membership of the Chapter. There is no trace of any such distinction as a Greater or a Lesser Chapter. The whole number of Canons certainly formed the Chapter ; but only those of their number had any voice in the affairs of the body, who had qualified themselves in the prescribed manner. At the same time, any one or more, even though not thus duly qualified, might be called in to take part in a particular affair, if it were thought desirable that he or they should do so ; while this special invitation by no means placed such Canon or Canons in the position of full members.

From reading the Report, it seems to me that the Committee have assumed, at the outset, the existence in former times of a Greater and Lesser Chapter ; and, acting on this assumption, have proposed to revive this imaginary Greater Chapter as a definite organisation in each Diocese. It is distressing to me to see a really admirable proposal brought forward and made to rest upon a thoroughly unsound and unhistoric basis. Would it not be wiser to devise, for essentially diocesan work, some new body (call the members what you will), some

---

* This passage does not occur at all in the later St Paul's code followed by Bishop Alnwick.

† Added by the Bishop.

‡ Amendment in margin, "Non requiritur licentia intrandi quia licite intrare potest." This is drawn through, and ·the text is drawn through, and the Bishop has written " vacat" against the whole clause in the margin.

new organisation, which should have the use of the Cathedral Church, and of which the Dignitaries or Residentiaries should be *ex officio* members? They could meet in the Chapter House, they could have stalls assigned to them in the Choir, they could be called (as now proposed) the " Diocesan Chapter," as distinguished from the Cathedral Chapter. But living under no *Regula Canonicorum*, they would not, properly speaking, be Canons ; being possessed of no *Prœbenda*, they would not in any sense be Prebendaries ; and, finally, having no intention of keeping Residence, they would entirely contradict the old idea of active members of a Cathedral Chapter, in which Residence always formed a primary feature of active membership.

It would be wholly impracticable (even if in any way desirable) to revert, in the present day, to the freedom of the old system of *Vicarii* and recognised fluctuating non-residence, which was prevalent in the thirteenth but had become practically extinct before the close of the fourteenth century. The " governing body " of the Chapter necessarily dwindled in number, as time went on, from the very severity of the qualification for full membership. Altered circumstances, therefore, call for a distinctly new organisation. The one point in common between the old state of things and that which is now proposed, is the existence of clergy scattered throughout the diocese, and yet in some way having personal connection with the Cathedral Church. If the English Church has life, and the need of such an organisation is felt in it, surely the need can be met without the discredit of what is neither more nor less than a display of unreal antiquarianism. If antiquities are worth studying at all, they must be studied intelligently, and, above all, they must be allowed to tell their own story. Those who look upon them as dead heaps from which to pick and choose just what suits their purpose, while they ignore the surroundings, will surely find the Nemesis for which they ought to be prepared. The " intelligent study of antiquities " is one of the most serious duties of my calling in life. If you ask me what I have to say on this matter, I am bound to speak out, and to give you in reply what I honestly believe to be the truth.

Yours very sincerely,

HENRY BRADSHAW.

The Rev. J. P. Norris.

APPENDIX III.

—— •◦•——

PUBLISHED WORK OF HENRY BRADSHAW.

I. MEMORANDA.

1. Memorandum No. 1, February 1868. The Printer of the Historia S. Albani. 1*s.*

2. A Classified Index of the Fifteenth Century Books in the collection of M. J. de Meyer, which were sold at Ghent in November, 1869. (Memorandum No. 2, April, 1870.) 1*s.*

3. List of the Founts of Type and Woodcut Devices used by Printers in Holland in the Fifteenth Century. (Memorandum No. 3, June, 1871.) 1*s.*

4. The Skeleton of Chaucer's Canterbury Tales : an attempt to distinguish the several fragments of the work as left by the author. Printed 1868. (Memorandum No. 4, issued November, 1871.) 1*s.*

5. Notice of a Fragment of the Fifteen Oes and other prayers printed at Westminster by W. Caxton about 1490–91, preserved in the Library of the Baptist College, Bristol. (Memorandum No. 5, November, 1877.) 1*s.*

6. The University Library. Papers contributed to the *Cambridge University Gazette*, 1869. (Memorandum No. 6, November, 1881.) 1*s.*

7. Address at the Opening of the Fifth Annual Meeting of the Library Association of the United Kingdom, Cambridge, September 5, 1882. With an Appendix.* (Memorandum No. 7, October, 1882.) 1*s.*

8. The Early Collection of Canons, commonly known as the *Hibernensis*. A Letter addressed to Dr F. W. H. Wasserschleben, Privy Councillor, Professor of Law in the University of Giessen.† (Memorandum No. 8, June, 1885.) 1*s.*

---

* This address is also printed in the "Transactions and Proceedings of the Library Association at the Fourth and Fifth Annual Meetings," pp. 107–115.

† This letter is also printed by Dr Wasserschleben in his "Irische Kanonensammlung" (2nd edition, 1885), Introduction, pp. lxiii–lxxvi.

II. PAPERS COMMUNICATED TO THE CAMBRIDGE ANTIQUARIAN SOCIETY.

1. On the Recovery of the Long-lost Waldensian Manuscripts. Read March 10, 1862. (C. A. S. Communications, ii, 203-218.)
2. Two Lists of Books in the University Library. Read November 17, 1862. (C. A. S. Communications, ii, 239-278.)
3. On an Early University Statute concerning Hostels. Read May 11, 1863. (C. A. S. Communications, ii, 279-281.)
4. On two Hitherto Unknown Poems of John Barbour, author of "The Brus." Read September 30, 1866. (C. A. S. Communications, iii, 111-117.
5. A View of the State of the University in Queen Anne's Reign. With a Facsimile. Read December 3, 1866. (C. A. S. Communications, iii, 119-134.
6. On the Earliest English Engravings of the Indulgence known as the "Image of Pity." With a Facsimile. Read February 25, 1867. (C. A. S. Communications, iii, 135-152.)
7. An Inventory of the Stuff in the College Chambers (King's College), 1598. Read May 9, 1868. (C. A. S. Communications, iii, 181-198.)
8. On the Engraved Device used by Nicholas Gotz of Sletzstat, the Cologne printer, in 1474. Read November 21, 1870. (C. A. S. Communications, iii, 237-246.)
   Note on a Book printed at Cologne by Gotz in 1477, with two illustrations engraved on copper. (*Ibid.*)
9. On two Engravings on Copper by G. M., a wandering Flemish artist of the fifteenth and sixteenth centuries, with two Notes. Read November 21, 1870. (C. A. S. Communications, iii, 247-258).
   Note A.—On three Engravings on Copper, fastened into the Cambridge copy of the Utrecht Breviary of 1574. (*Ibid.*)
   Note B.—On the Engravings fastened into the Lambeth copy of the Salisbury Primer, or "Horæ," printed by Wynkyn de Worde about 1494. (*Ibid.*)
10. On the Oldest Written Remains of the Welsh Language. Read November 20, 1871. (C. A. S. Communications, iii, 263-267.)
11. On the Collection of Portraits belonging to the University before the Civil War. Read June 3, 1873. (C. A. S. Communications, iii, 275-286).
12. Notes of an Episcopal Visitation of the Archdeaconry of Ely in 1685. Read May 24, 1875. (C. A. S. Communications, iii, 323-361).
13. On the A B C as an Authorized School-book in the Sixteenth Century. Read May 24, 1875. (C. A. S. Communications, iii, 363-370.)

14. Note on the Light of St Erasmus, and on the Various Spellings of his Name in the Trinity Parish Accounts. Read November 17, 1879. (C. A. S. Communications, iv, 327–331.)

III. Various Papers, Articles, etc.

1. Letter on Dr Simonides and the Codex Sinaiticus, January 26, 1863. (*Guardian,* January 28, 1863, p. 85.)
2. Catalogue of Books printed entirely or partially on vellum, in the University Library, Cambridge.* (*Le Bibliophile Illustré,* Septembre, 1863, p. 105 ; and Novembre, 1863, p. 123.)
3. On a Fragment of a Block-book in the possession of M. Weigel of Leipsic. (*Le Bibliophile Illustré,* Decembre 1863, p. 141).
4. On the Possible Connection between Bunyan's "Pilgrim's Progress" and the "Pélerinage" of Guillaume de Deguilleville. (*Le Bibliophile Illustré,* Janvier, 1865, p. 11.)
5. On a Copy of the work entitled "Fr. Antonii Andreæ Scriptum super Logica," printed at St Albans in the fifteenth century, now in the Library of Jesus College, Cambridge. (*Annales du Bibliophile Belge et Hollandais,* No. 10, Août, 1865, p. 2).
6. Description of a Manuscript of Wyclif (B. 16. 2) in the Library of Trinity College, Cambridge. (Shirley's "Catalogue of the Original Works of John Wyclif," 1865, p. xiv.)
7. Letter on the Oriental Manuscripts at King's College, Cambridge, and Eton College, November 12, 1866. (Catalogue of the Oriental Manuscripts in the Library of King's College, Cambridge, by E. H. Palmer ; Royal Asiatic Society's Publications, June 1867, pp. 1–3.)
8. Letter on the Archiepiscopal Library at Lambeth, October 5, 1867. (*Times,* October 7, 1867.)
9. Letters on two Manuscript εὐαγγέλια (Gospel-books of the Greek Church) in the University Library, Cambridge. MSS. Dd. 8. 23, Dd. 8. 49. (*Notes and Queries,* August 15, 1868, pp. 162, 163.)
10. Scheme of Mediæval Latin Graces before and after meat. ("Early English Meals and Manners," E. E. T. S. Publications, 1868, pp. 386–396.)
11. Letter to the Senate of the University of Cambridge on Mr Kerrich's Bequest, June 4, 1872.
12. List of the Editions of Chaucer's Works. (Chaucer's "Astrolabe," E. E. T. S. Publications, 1872, preface, p. xxvi. Also printed in Professor Skeat's preface to Bell's edition of Chaucer, Bohn Series, p. 3.)

---

* These papers are not signed, but are shown to be Bradshaw's, by letters to him from the editor, M. Berjeau, who writes (December 22, 1863) : "J'ai reçu avec votre lettre du 17ᵐᵒ le supplément à Van Praet que j'ai immédiatement traduit en français," and (February 1, 1864), "Je vous envoie par la poste les épreuves de votre second catalogue."

13. Letter on Thynne's Edition of Chaucer (1532). (Thynne's "Animadversions," Chaucer Society Publications, 1875, preface, p. xxvi.)
14. Lives of St Abbanus, St Abel, St Abranus, St Achea. ("Dictionary of Christian Biography," vol. i, 1877.)
15. Letter on an Irish Monastic Missal in the Library of Corpus Christi College, Oxford, January 5, 1878. (*Academy*, January 12, 1878.)
16. List of Editions of the York Breviary. ("Breviarium ad usum insignis ecclesie Eboracensis," edited by Mr Lawley, Surtees Society Publications, lxxi, p. xiii, 1880.)
17. Letter on the Bodleian Manuscript, Auct. F. iv, 32. ("Hermes," 1880, pp. 425–427.)
18. Notes on Service-books. (*a*) On various Books "tyed with chenes that were gyffen to Alhaloes Church in Derby." ("The Chronicles of the Collegiate Church of All Saints, Derby," edited by Cox and Hope, 1881, pp. 175–177); (*b*) "On the Service-books used in the Church of England in the Middle Ages," dated March 17, 1881. (*Ibid.*, pp. 229–231.) Printed above, Appendix I.
19. Note on the Binding of the Mazarine Bible, preserved in the Library of Eton College. (*Notes and Queries*, May 14, 1881, p. 384.)
20. Godfried van der Haghen (G. H.), the publisher of Tindale's own last edition of the New Testament in 1534–35. (*Bibliographer*, No. 1, January 1882, pp. 3–11). Privately reprinted by Mr Blades, 1886.
21. (*a*) Some Account of the Organisation of the Cambridge University Library. ("Transactions, etc., of the Library Association," 1882, appendix, pp. 229–237.)
    (*b*) On Local Libraries considered as Museums of Local Authorship and Printing. (*Ibid.*, pp. 237–238.)
    (*c*) On Size-Notation as distinguished from Form-Notation. (*Ibid.*, pp. 238–240.)
22. Descriptions (*a*) of the Cambridge Manuscript of the "Historia Ecclesiastica" of Bede, Camb. Univ. Libr. Kk. v. 16; (*b*) of the "Book of Deer," Camb. Univ. Libr. Ii. 6. 32. (Publications of the Palæographical Society, 1873–1883, vol. ii, plates 139, 140; 210, 211.)
23. Statutes for the University of Cambridge and for the Colleges within it, made, etc., under the Universities of Oxford and Cambridge Act," 1877. Edited by Henry Bradshaw. Cambridge, 1883, 8vo, pp. lviii, 763.
24. On "Toyes of an Idle Head." (*Notes and Queries*, September 6, 1884, p. 187.)
25. Letter on a Copy of the Work entitled "Fr. Antonii Andreæ scriptum super Logica," in the Library of Wadham College, Oxford, January 8, 1885. (*Academy*, January 17, 1885.)
26. On the Wants of the University Library, May 6, 1885. (*University Reporter*, 1884–85, pp. 679–682.)

27. Letter to the Senate of the University of Cambridge on the University Registry, June 10, 1885.
28. John Siberch. (*a*) On the Books printed by John Siberch at Cambridge in 1521 and 1522. (Introduction to reprint of Bullock's "Oration," Macmillan and Bowes, 1886.) (*b*) Note on the Variations in the first sheet of Siberch's edition of the "Hermathena" of Papyrius Geminus. (Reprint, Macmillan and Bowes, 1886, appendix.)
29. List of Editions of the Sarum Breviary, Diurnale, Legenda, Antiphoner, Ordinale, etc., Expositio Hymnorum, Expositio Sequentiarum. Breviarium secundum usum Sarum, ed. Procter and Wordsworth. Fasc. iii, pref. pp. xli-cxxx, 1886.)

INDEX.

PRINTED BY WILLIAM CLOWES AND SONS, LIMITED, LONDON AND BECCLES.